GW00792719

THE WABENO FEAST

THE WABENO FEAST Wayland Drew

A Novel

Copyright © 1973 Wayland Drew

All rights reserved. No part of this publication may be reproduced
or transmitted in any form or by any means, electronic or mechanical, including
photocopying, recording, or any information storage and retrieval system,
without permission in writing from the publisher.

This edition published in 2001 by
House of Anansi Press Limited
895 Don Mills Rd., 400-2 Park Centre
Toronto, ON, M3C 1W3
Tel. (416) 445-3333
Fax (416) 445-5967
www.anansi.ca

Distributed in Canada by
General Distribution Services Ltd.
325 Humber College Blvd.
Etobicoke, ON, M9W 7C3
Tel. (416) 213-1919
Fax (416) 213-1917
E-mail cservice@genpub.com

Distributed in the United States by
General Distribution Services Inc.
PMB 128, 4500 Witmer Industrial Estates
Niagara Falls, NY 14035-1386
Toll Free Tel. 1-800-805-1083
Toll Free Fax 1-800-481-6207
E-mail gdsinc@genpub.com

First published in 1973 in hardcover by House of Anansi Press.
Published in 1984 in paperback by General Publishing.

Excerpt from the poem "Interval" on page 181 reprinted by kind permission
of Miriam Waddington (from *The Second Silence*, Ryerson Press).

The author gratefully acknowledges the assistance of the Canada Council
and the Province of Ontario Council of the Arts.

05 04 03 02 01   1 2 3 4 5

Canadian Cataloguing in Publication Data

Drew, Wayland, 1932–1998
The Wabeno feast

ISBN 0-88784-425-1 (bound)   ISBN 0-88784-663-7 (pbk.)

I. Title

PS8557.R3W3 20001   C813'.54   C73-002834-8
PR9199.3.D63W3 2001

Cover design: Angel Guerra

THE CANADA COUNCIL   LE CONSEIL DES ARTS
FOR THE ARTS   DU CANADA
SINCE 1957   DEPUIS 1957

*We acknowledge for their financial support of our publishing
program the Canada Council for the Arts, the Ontario Arts
Council, and the Government of Canada through the Book
Publishing Industry Development Program (BPIDP).*

Printed and bound in Canada

to GWEN

And to these *hommes du nord*,
CHARLIE ERICKSEN and BILL SMITH

And to the memory of
CHARLIE SUPINGER,
who chose to leave only footprints

"Think of yourself as already dead ... and live your remaining days in harmony with Nature, as though they were but a sequel to your life."

Marcus Aurelius Antoninus,
Emperor of Rome

CHARLIE REDBIRD'S shack squatted among weeds and alders beside a river that in the hot months became a stream, and then a creek, and then at last a rivulet so small that the old man would sometimes pass out before he had scooped a basin in the stones, or before the water which collected there had cleared enough for him to slake his thirst. Then he would lie in the sun on rocks covered by baked slime, and if his ear were close to the water he would dream of a river and tall grass bending and the laughter of swimming youngsters in the pools. Sometimes the laughter would continue after he had wakened, and he would watch the playing young and try to match his trembling mouth to the pool he had made, and so drink and cleanse himself of vomit.

The smell of him drew insects from the bottoms of damp stones. It was miraculous that in Spring as he lay foul and open on the riverbank he was not destroyed by mosquitoes and black-flies, as old drunks often were. And it was miraculous too that he had not drowned long since, or suffocated in vomit, or staggered at a locomotive's light as at the sun, or sucked some rusty muzzle and blown his diseased brains across an acre of November leaves. For he did not, as the scoffing white men said, lack the courage for self-destruction, and he should have known that he spread stench and squalor like a mist.

But he did not know, for the years of shoepolish, perfume, and Sterno had eaten his brain like cheese and left him beguiled by visions. And it was this world of which he was god and sole perceptor, where friends forgotten and unknown dipped to pay him homage with their brief dance and tale, that sustained him in what seemed a travesty of life, that urged him sometimes to break the necessary sticks, to warm spaghetti in the shack and to eat it staring through the plastic window at a world that was other than the sere bracken and reach of mudbank which he saw. There, what was done was not done. What was lost was found, and lost, and found again a thousand times among the filaments of wonder. Women who had loved him loved him yet; and one, a golden creature enticing the sorry raddled mind upon the stones, showed him again that what had once lived remained forever, transmuted by sheerest chance, and that he had been right, so right, to abdicate the forms of memory and of hereditary grief.

Wet, wavering, as a man walks who has received a heavy blow and who struggles to keep his dignity, he wound through the grey-yellow sapling trunks, following the stream bank among aspen which had passed from green, to gold, to brown, and which now scattered upon him in the gathering wind leaves the colour of old pennies. They stuck to the shoulders of the thin plaid jacket, and to the toe-caps of his torn boots. The forest moaned and closed behind his passage as if it sought to mould to significance the broken singing in his head, or to find the melody upon which his descant memory played, or simply as if to ingest and resolve to wholeness this broken, human part which followed the autumn trickle of the creek down to the lake, alone.

Emptiness hummed in all the white buildings — the white store, the white cabins, the white boathouse with docks in its teeth. To this emptiness he had not yet become accustomed, although he thought many weeks had passed since the last knot of men had searched the radio dial for signals which never came, and gathered their belongings, and swept away from the dock in a flourish of outboard spray, not looking back, and leaving Charlie Redbird squatting alone on the steps because he was rotten, and dying, and too stupid to know that they were leaving that place for good.

Automatically he sat for a time in his place in the long grass beside the blue and gold government plaque which said:

FROG LAKE POST

This site, an ancient meeting place of the Ojibwa and the Cree, was used as a trading ground by coureurs de bois *as early as 1700.*

The first fort was constructed here in 1785, and trade was conducted under the factorship of Drummond MacKay, a native of Perth. In 1825 the post was acquired by the Hudson's Bay Company.

In 1887 the post was abandoned, but was re-opened in 1921 as a general store to supply the growing needs of summer visitors.

Sometimes men and women in shorts would come there to read the sign and to eat candy, and if he moved in the grass and held out his hand they would give him money. But now there were no people. There was cold; there was the rolling sky and wind under it; there were two ravens croaking in the balsam.

Soon he rose and followed the path farther, to a place where the rock was so flat and smooth that even small waves swept like giant tongues across it. Here he sat again and drew his knees up to his chest and wrapped his arms around them against the cold. And here beside the water he began to wait for the visions of his world to reassert themselves.

chapter one

If you drive northward from Lake Ontario, you will ride a hundred miles on an antiseptic highway. Green signs suggest green diversions. Occasional factories and yards of machinery loom disturbingly and pass, fenced back from the highway and its grassy flanks on which yellow tractors tow clusters of mowers. For this hundred miles nothing is likely to impede your flight northward, but eventually you will enter resort country. The highway curves, the signs indicating sad, trampled little beaches become more numerous. Ranks of gas stations anxiously upstage each other with flags and pendant signs. The protective fence vanishes, together with the swaths of mown grass, to be replaced by gravel sidings, raw gouges in the earth, derelict lunch-spots, and clouds of dust from the sideroads announcing cars full of men in peaked caps, and dogs, and ice-creamed children.

No doubt you will slow here. You will want to see the sights. For forty miles it will be so, and then imperceptibly the restaurants and service stations stretch apart, and the highway, beginning to roll again, narrows to two lanes. All through Muskoka you will catch glimpses of the lakes. Each will be lined with cottages and cut by outboards trailing grim waterskiers. At any point you may stop and hire a boat in order to digress an hour or two, staring at other boaters who will return your stare indifferently. If you wish you can buy a substance which will tan you deep brown within hours, despite the sun.

North of Parry Sound the road changes again. Relics nudge against it. Decayed log cabins suggest a rawer time, and the inhabited buildings turn in on themselves with little care for ostentation. It is as if the bite of winter and the wild is remembered all summer, a thing to be prepared for. The buildings hunker down; nature moves back against them, sending skirmishers of blueberry, hazel, hemlock and jackpine in through unkempt fences. They surround broken hulls and discarded machines; they push up through forgotten auto rims; they skirt the fringes of last year's brave garden. This autumn the milkweed will sift its seeds against the insulbrick walls of the house itself.

Soon you will cross the French River. If you wish, you may stretch your legs before a plaque which commemorates the passage of explorers, traders, and missionaries through three hundred years. The plaque stands in a gravel space with its back to the fence which protects you from the river. Motorboats full of fishermen rush up and down. A few ragged gulls hop close, eager for cracker-jack.

After this, the highway curves like a stringy arm around Lake Huron, entangling itself briefly in the blight of Sudbury. Then, freed, it leaps westward in flat strides, piercing atrophied communities and shuttered dreams, skirting Indian reserves which seem forever in cloud, sweeping past beaten resorts beside muddy streams. Here people have died on the land, bound to it by memory and heritage and hope, becoming part of it in a silt of poverty. Here you may find yourself driving faster than usual.

But the Soo, with its oasis atmosphere, will be a surprise. Here you can watch great ships slide up and down through the locks. Here you can buy good liquor in American hotels and walk barefoot on the rug in your room. The streets are wide. Rich houses gaze across the rapids.

Drive north. For a hundred miles you will brush Superior.

It lies like the sea, full of undulant menace. If the day is wild you will be washed by spray as you drive and you will struggle to hold your car on curves; but if it is calm you will stop in the hills and look out over Agawa Bay and Old Woman Bay and over the promontories pointing west.

You will not see Sable Creek, not even the smoke from its mills, for it is several hours' drive away, along the North Shore; but you might plan to stay there overnight, in one of the motels which announce its outskirts. If you do so, the town will seem no different to you from any of the others which you have passed that day — Wawa, White River, Marathon, Schreiber, Terrace Bay —all mill towns stinking yellowly of pulp. It is no more memorable than the others, and when your slides come back from processing you might snap your fingers, searching for the name of the place where you photographed the log booms floating like giant lily pads in the bay.

Originally, however, Sable Creek was different. Unlike the others it sprang to life as an idea in the mind of a single man, and for its first years it grew according to plan. Bob Mansfield chose the site for his town carefully and well. Winding through great hills, the river disgorged thousands of tons of logs every Spring, and they were gathered by the booms in the harbour. Bob Mansfield saw it happening before it happened, for the supply of pulpwood seemed inexhaustible. To the north and west, miles of spruce and jackpine stretched away. Little white pine remained, for that had been taken years earlier by lumbermen who had passed to other limits, but pulpwood was plentiful, and Bob Mansfield bought licenses to cut it all.

He had built his mill and run a branch line from the CPR main line. He built ample houses on broad streets and leased them to employees. He built stores and leased them to merchants. He built three hotels, six saloons, two churches, and two whorehouses. His bush camps gained a reputation for space and cleanliness. He paid good wages and gave good holidays. His food was unsurpassed. Men stayed with him for years, and inveterate wanderers lingered on and settled, running the logs down in the Spring to spend their pay along the boardwalks of Sable Creek.

As more families leased and built, borrowing from Mansfield's bank, the town spread westward along the shore, fulfilling a plan laid out years before. Schools were built. More churches raised their spires. By 1929 the population had reached eight thousand, and during the Depression old Mansfield drew on his own reserves to keep the town intact. He knew the slump would not last long, and that when it was over the land, the men, and the logs would repay him well. He held tight, and kept his town together. By 1933 he was expanding his mill on the land reserved for that purpose, and his bush camps were again cutting at full capacity.

In 1935 he had made a second million dollars, although he did not know it. He was then seventy-eight. To the consternation of his son, he paid less attention to his accountants than to the men in the camps, and for weeks at a time would be away from his office, living in some distant bunkhouse and exchanging yarns with other old men. He had planned a town of ten thousand souls, and an industry to support them. He had seen all his plans fulfilled, and it was as if in the instant of consummation he had lost interest. His shrewdness diffused, his intent softened. At night in the bunkhouses, with a soft hat on his knee and a handrolled smoke between his fingers, he dreamed back to a time young Robert had not known and for which he had no patience. He spoke of his wife, and of the day they had first come to the bay that was now Sable Creek, driven to the beach by a great storm. He spoke whimsically, in the way of regretful old men, and not like Bob Mansfield. Not like Big Bob Mansfield.

The next year he was dead.

Young Robert, wearing his father's watch chain across his vest, took over his mill with new plans, new methods, new men, and the old shrewdness. The town thrived and continued to expand. It had, in fact, grown beyond Mansfield control and now sprawled audaciously westward along the bay, urged on by speculators from the city. When, in 1940, under the pressure of government contracts, young Mansfield embarked on further expansion of the mill, he found that an entirely new plant would be most economic; so he built it a mile beyond the town limits, to the west. During the war a new village of Sable Creek sprang up there, and to the residents of Old Town it had all the rawness of a camp or a transient trailer park. In fact, New Town contained a large trailer park, and women in slacks washed babies there beside the cars.

Old Town too had changed much in a generation. The merchants had flourished. They had acquired title to their lands and built stolid brick and stone homes. The saloons had become drugstores and the whorehouses refurbished residences — one of them a manse, much to the delight of the old timers, who for awhile pestered the pastor's wife. The war brought easy women and easy morals to the mills, and the lines would never again be so clear as old Bob Mansfield and the honest whores had drawn them. Like the socialism Old Bob had feared, a haze of ambivalence settled on Sable Creek and thickened in the affluence following the war. Life was comfortable, to be sure. Life had never been so comfortable. But where, then, was the enemy? How was one to know him? Perhaps he was coming. Perhaps he was next door. Perhaps he was already here, inside.

chapter two

A black curtain of cloud rose from the southeast, covering the stars and all traces of dawn. Deep inland, thunder rolled. Racing down from the hills, the first breezes of the storm plucked feathers and scraps of bark from the beaches and carried them over the lake, swirling them into the ripples which spread like dark hands across the water. Offshore, a group of islands broke the wind, and for a time before the storm descended calm waters stretched to their lee side, like a soft wake.

On one of these islands a grey canoe lay overturned, protected by underbrush. Nearby was a tent, grey-brown and rounded, the colour and shape of the surrounding boulders. The walls of the tent moved restlessly. Small bushes began to scratch against it. Inside, a man and woman slept among four large packs. From the top of one of these the butt of an axe protruded; from another, a sheathed rifle pointed like a raised finger. Near the man's head lay a hunting knife and a vial of matches. He slept soundly.

The woman, however, grew restive as the storm approached. At times she embraced the man only to turn away again almost at once. She frowned and murmured in her sleep. Her hair spread on the bundle of clothes which served her as a pillow. In her dream a telephone was ringing, and when she answered it, moving like a woman under water, the headmaster's voice played tricks with possibility. Laughter came first, laughter poorly controlled and bursting out around the shrill inquiry whether she was indeed Mrs. Paul Henry. The laughter rose swiftly to a desperate pitch, like the ringing of phone lines along deserted winter roads. "Michael, your son ... your son is dead ..." *What? No! Call again! The number's wrong! You want a different Liv Henry! Call again!* She dreamed the waiting. She dreamed that her hands were cold with sweat. Again the flat ringing came, and with it this time an assassin's hiss. "We done what you wanted ... send the fee ... we educated him real good ..." *No!* But again, again, now in the unctuous tones unfashionable even in rural parishes. "Ah, Mrs. Henry, I have terrible news ... terrible ... please prepare yourself for the worst ..." *Mike.* "Yes, for the worst in the worst of possible worlds ..." *Mike.* "Yes ... but as consolation ... loss ... remember Saviour's words ..." Then, unmistakable, merely a balding and bifocaled voice full of shadow courage and hoarse from the calls, "You are

11

the twenty-seventh ... Michael is dead ... a poisonous exhalation ... the plant nearby ... pushing production ... excessive
... above tolerable levels ... fault? Fault? Why, no one's fault,
of course ... deplorable ... a local accident ..."
The storm descended on the islands and the tent. Beneath
the thunder, rain and wind lashed the thin walls. Screaming and
awake, the woman sat upright in the pale light of morning. *"And
so what did he die of? An excess of tolerance?"*

chapter three

Early in the war an army doctor had laid his stethescope against
Fred Hale's chest and heard there the murmurs of rheumatic
fever, like whispers from a childhood game. He shook his head
and scowled at Fred Hale as if he were spoiled merchandise.
"No. No good. Might just as well go on home, young fella.
Next!" And Fred's relief had engulfed him. Shuffling up in the
naked line of draftees, clutching his file, the wafer-thin ring
of a peppermint lifesaver suspended on his tongue, he had
approached the doctor terrified. He was not a coward; the prospects
of Hun jackboots and hissing Jap steel were too remote to terrify
him. But this shrivelled medic and his stethescope held the power
to separate him from Narah, for months and years, and that
was unthinkable.
Fred Hale was hopelessly uxorious. He knew it. He loved
his Narah with a happy blend of lust and simple adoration. She
was part of his biology, and he could no more have stopped
the film of sweat which covered his palms at the thought of
her undressing than he could have stopped breathing, or ended
overnight his addiction to peppermint lifesavers. Never had he
ceased to be amazed at her consenting to marry him, for he

was convinced he did not deserve her.

The townsfolk shared his wonder. It was not that Fred was incompetent, exactly. He was a dedicated teacher and he found endless time and energy for community projects. But he was lacking in, well, style, flair, panache, and given to plodding, chronological recitations of trivial events. Men tended to look over his shoulder when he spoke.

By contrast, Narah was anything but dull. In a town like Sable Creek she was a continuing event. Large, boned, tanned, her blonde hair flowing, she crossed and re-crossed the town as if it were the domain of a Saxon queen. And she drew no jealousy, no resentment. Fretting crones mused when she passed, as if she had restored them at a glance to better times. And the men? Like young Bob Mansfield's, their eyes narrowed when they saw her, and they would draw hands across their mouths and turn back into the barbershop with looks that caused laughter to swell under the smoke and bayrum.

Delighted at his rejection by the army, like a boy on an April Saturday, Fred Hale hurried into his trousers, pried a lifesaver from his pack, and strode grinning home down the main street of Sable Creek, home to Narah.

Of course, he had done his bit for Democracy in other ways. He urged Narah to knit socks and balaclavas, and she actually tried to please him, although the balaclavas which she produced and modelled all had the slant eyes and scowling mouths of Noh masks. He bought bonds. His class led the school in the purchase of war stamps, and each child pasted the red and blue squares into his own little war book every Friday. He collected paper, and grease, and milkweed pods for ersatz kapok jackets. He taught the geography of battle, the history of idealism, and the cadences of Churchillian rhetoric. He raised his strong voice whenever possible. There would always be an England.

And he became a scoutmaster. His troop was drilled to perfection. Pre-adolescents clicked their heels, marched behind fluttering pennants, and tied brisk knots. Their semaphore was immaculate, their Morse impeccable. They won prizes, trophies, and adulation. Fred glowed, and shared their triumphs with Narah in a pleasure not at all vicarious. They were part of him, and he of them, and none of the dankness of caricature scoutmasters ever attached itself to him. He was decent and honest, straight-arrow Fred Hale. His energy was boundless, and he was in every way a good citizen, a good scoutmaster, and an adoring husband.

"Pity," said the townswomen, pondering Fred's drive and Narah's easy laugh. "Pity there's no children." And this was, in fact, the single conscious regret of Fred's life. As for Narah, who could tell?

She kept a scrapbook of the war. Indolently, browsing the papers after Fred had rifled them for headlines and maps, bulletin board fodder, she clipped only the photographs of blasted earth. Often she mused many minutes over a picture. She seemed compelled by ruin and by the landscapes of disaster, and since these were only of peripheral concern to the photographers she often clipped only portions of pictures, backdrops worthy of a Goya or a Bosch, against which the human madness had been played. Here, the remnants of a forest fuzzy in drifting smoke, consisting only of shattered stumps and grotesque arms pleading to a black sky; here a vineyard uprooted and strewn with rubble; and there the earth itself, the raw earth churned seedless by treads, by wheels and engines, by the scurrying boots of infantry. Such pictures she clipped and preserved with a lick of mucilage, tossing her hair away from them. They formed her private war, along with the ludicrous knitting, the victory garden to which their backyard had been converted, and the ranks of cans, full of grease drippings, which passed across her kitchen window ledge.

Fred had once flipped through her scrapbook and been perplexed at its randomness. Nothing was captioned, nothing identified. His own scrapbook at school was precisely chronological and geographical. "Hey," he asked. "Why'd you keep this one? Where's this one taken?"

She leaned over him with her chin on his crewcut and her

hair falling about his ears, squinting defensively at the yellowed scraps of newsprint. "Oh," she said, "I don't know. They do all look the same, don't they? I think that one was in Italy someplace."

"But what's the point in keeping them if you don't know what they're *of*? I mean, from these you can't even tell who's winning."

She laughed. "Oh," she said, "but I know *we're* winning."

Her laughter disturbed him. It came from deep in her throat and flowed like black water. He was swept up and borne along by it; and perhaps because he had lost control, and perhaps because he heard a scratch of ridicule in the depths of her laughter, he had never been at ease with it. He liked to know where he was. "You bet we are! You bet we're winning!" He punched his palm and rolled a fresh lifesaver around his tongue. "It won't be long now. You'll see. Two, three months at most."

He was right. In May 1945 they celebrated equivocally, like chessplayers who know they see the end but must be careful still. Then in September, at the beginning of the Canadian year, the game was over for good, and some of the men with whom Fred had once stood in naked line were coming home. Watching, listening, Narah found no one who was not sad. Under the jubilance it was as if the very reason for action itself had been withdrawn, and Fred's question, "Well, what shall we do now?" meant to be jocularly rhetorical as they left the last party, revealed the same gulf she had seen in other eyes, drunk and sober.

When the paper boy next came to collect his pay, she leaned on the door frame and asked him, "Miro, what do you think the news will be about now?"

"I duh duh duh nuhnuhnuh know, Miz Hale. Muh muh maybe there'll be nuh no nuhnuh newspapers."

But she knew there would be newspapers. And she knew the game would curve insidiously, and adapt itself, and continue under a different name, perhaps, but with the same players. With exactly the same players.

That winter was the coldest and most tenacious in many years. To Fred Hale it seemed that victory had brought only emptiness, and that life itself had paused like a man lost in the forest, listening, wondering whether he should continue, and if so, in what direction.

"A trip!" he decided. "That's it! That's what the boys need."

"What kind of a trip?" she asked him.

"Well ... something more than just a hike. Something longer. A canoe trip." He paced the bedroom, swatted his hands fore and aft, happily shuttled a fresh lifesaver across his teeth. What an inspiration! And on a night with a gale that whipped the snow in clouds across the window.

"Why?" she watched him with interest.

"Why? Well, teach them woodcraft, you know. Teach them endurance, orienteering. Self-reliance. Good idea, eh?"

"I suppose so," she said doubtfully. "How many will you take at once?"

"Five, six. The older ones. The ones who'll get the most out of it. Why?"

She shrugged. "But if you want to give them self-reliance, why don't you let them go in one at a time? Alone. As long as you're all together, isn't it just the same?"

"The same as what?"

"Well, the same as being together anyplace else." Her smile was defensive, as it had been when he criticized her scrapbook, and yet Fred feared that her laughter would begin.

"No, no," he said hurriedly. "That's important too, co-operation. Teamwork. No better place to learn that than in the bush. Right? Yessir, that's how boys grow up. How men are made."

In fact, the boys themselves had been urging just such a trip. They had grown jaded with the day-hikes which never left the sulphurous odour of the mill, or the dreary residue of picnickers, or the raw hillsides cleared for pulp. It seemed pointless that the hours of drill, semaphore, knot-tying, first aid, and club house woodcraft did not prepare them *for* something, just as school prepared them for life. Surely scouting should train them to seize leisure manfully, to subdue the unknown and wrestle into submission whatever threatened them. Their parents concurred, and a subtle pressure had begun to build on Fred.

He consulted maps. Glistening, imaginary lakes opened to the thrust of his canoe. He questioned fellow Kinsmen, suppliers, foremen from the camps. He heard old timers speak softly and elliptically about the land that lay beyond the roads. Fish? If he had a minute they would tell him about one fish .... And of course he had the time. He had all the time. He thumbed lifesavers out to the storytellers for as long as they would talk. "Lakes that have never been fished," that was the magic phrase. That was the phrase that struck the chords of wildness, and conjured back the boyhood tales of vastness, mystery, treasure to be won. For it was more than the lure of fish which drew him. Far more. It was something he had never before struggled to define, so much had the war and his incessant busy-nesses preoccupied him, but something he knew to be at the core of his being and manhood. Like adrenalin it surged in him, this traitorous desire which led him off from Narah.

Finally, in the first spring rains he announced to the troop that if they could raise the money, if the apple day, the magazine campaign, and the paper drive were all successful, then they would leave in mid-August. For the first time they would go on a real canoe trip, into the wilderness. As he spoke, he was surprised at the intensity of the anticipation which had caused sweat to film his torso under the green scout shirt.

chapter four

The storm passed quickly, leaving the lake calm in its wake.
All that day the man and woman in the grey canoe paddled
hard, and by late afternoon when the wind rose from the northwest,
they had come to a section of the shore where a brooding line
of cliffs offered no hope of shelter. They knew that to swamp
would be death, either from the shock of the water, cold as
the sea, or from battering against the rocks, and they struggled
to round the last headland before the waves engulfed them. The
lower shore on its far side promised a beach behind, but at first
they were disappointed; there seemed to be none. Then, as they
drew closer, the man saw a passage through the line of islands
which he had thought to be the shore, and he guided the canoe
through it and into a calm and shallow lagoon behind. The beach
waited, its sand warm despite the wind. The canoe's flank scuffed
against it.

"For a little while," the woman said, "I thought it might
end out there." She sat unmoving, leaning forward on the gunwales.

"So did I," he said.

They camped. He overturned the canoe, and while the woman
gathered wood he pitched their tent on the grass behind the beach,
in the shelter of young spruce. They spread their clothes on
driftwood logs to dry. Later, when they had warmed food and
eaten, they took tin mugs of tea onto the rocks, rounded by
storms into the shape of pregnant bellies; and there the man
drew a manuscript from a small packsack and, while the woman
drank and watched the last of the sun, he began to read. At
first his voice was uncertain; but soon it strengthened, countering
the wind and matching itself to the cadence of the waves.

April 30, 1785. This morning we raised Cape Race, after such
a crossing as our captain swore he had never experienced in his
thirty years as master. The pious men gave thanks to God for

their deliverance, for we had all in our various ways resigned ourselves to Death four days ago when our compasses were both destroyed in a single foreboding blow of fate, and we found ourselves lost and running in a howling gloom. To the spiritually inclined it must have seemed indeed providential to emerge under clearing skies exactly off Newfoundland, and on a fair course for the Gulf of St. Lawrence.

As for myself, I confess that the prospect of death, so much in my thoughts throughout my misfortunes of the past year, had no further terrors for me, but that on the contrary I felt invigorated by its proximity. In the storm I oftentimes wandered on foaming decks where no mortal should have ventured, challenging the gale and exhilarated even to laughter. On one occasion I heard the voice of Elborn, faint and crying like a gull, "Come back, MacKay! Have you gone mad?" And I nodded my head and waved to him even before I had properly understood his words.

However, even I have not been unaffected by the fairness of this new morning, and by the fortune, good or bad, which has brought me safe to Canada; and I have resolved to put behind me all dwelling on past events and to welcome this new land and my employment in it as a man chastened, purged, and refreshed. Antoninus has said, "Wake up! Shake off your stupour and come to yourself. You have only been dreaming, and if you have been able to gaze steadily on the monsters of your nightmare, think how eagerly you should welcome the events which lie before you in real life."

So it should be, and so I am resolved to make it. But as for falling upon my knees this morning and giving thanks to Almighty God for the sight of land, that I could not do. I turned away my head so that the others should not see my derision; for I have little stomach for hypocrisy, and my separation from the Church is as final as it is from her whom I have left behind forever . . .

May 5. In Mr. Elborn's view, navigating this river resembles nothing so much as the hapless progress into the vortex of a funnel, and our diminishing tackings across the Gulf so many spirals on the downward voyage. I can scarcely conceal my dislike for this small man and his endless dark imageries, all of which he delivers with a bright countenance and a sidelong, shrewd glance, as if to guage their effect upon me. I remarked that he could think in such terms if he desired, but that I for my part would content myself with noting our *upward* progress, against both current and wind.

Throughout our crossing, Elborn has clung like an appendage on my spirits, and shown both a most unseemly interest in my affairs and an unwelcome solicitude for my health. My fervent hope regarding him is that the plans of the Company call for our posting at some considerable distance from each other, for I would not care to endure his presence through an isolated winter.

The weather has been clear, and we have for several days been hailing vessels of many types, mainly shallops and doggers on their fishing grounds, but yesterday a small barque coasting north, and this morning the *Maxine,* a splendid frigate under full sail and in the Company's charter, deep with furs for England.

Our approaches to the shore have thrice brought us in view of Indian encampments, and I have used a glass to observe the savages in their flitting canoes, having heard that they are an inferior breed and corrupt beyond redemption. I could tell little from the distance. They appeared uninterested in our passage and drawn in upon their own activities which consisted often in my observation of sitting in large groups lethargically regarding their smoking fires. The effect, to an observer upon a solid British vessel brisk with the activities of coming about, was, to use Mr. Elborn's phrase, "as if even their children were old."

I was informed by the captain that his ship's masts and spars had been cut from these very shores, and I thought I spied still much fine timber on the cliffs.

We have left the mouth of the Saguenay and are approaching the sparse cultivations surrounding La Malbaie. The settlements are rude indeed and their grasp on the landscape tenuous, although the inhabitants make a brave front with white-wash and announce thereby that their dwellings are separate from the surrounding wilderness, and that they intend to keep them so. Such fortitude is heartening, and a contrast to the anonymity of the savages.

May 8. In Quebec I made contact with Mr. Harmsworth, the Company's representative, who expressed some concern at my youth; for he expected, as he said, clerks to be men of twenty-seven or eight, and not boys escaping adolescence. I assured him that I, for my part, would acquit myself to his satisfaction and to the Company's, and that youth was no impediment in the face of my desire to succeed. At this he laughed shortly, for he appeared a disgruntled man preoccupied with notices and bills, and chafing under his years of deprivation from culture. "We shall see what your impediments are," he said. "And as for your resolve to succeed, I wonder how long that will last, my lad, west of the Grand Portage. There is a fine boneyard there of such resolves!"

He was a pale and phlegmatic personage to whom I paid scant regard — a gatekeeper only, fit for passing messages, — and he was more agitated by our delayed arrival, by the amenities of my dress, by my stubborn refusal to be over-awed by his authority, and by a dozen similar affronts both real and imagined, than he was interested in my welfare and in answering my queries. "You will find all that out soon enough," he replied. "You must now get on to Montreal with all haste, for they will be awaiting you; and I suppose I must hire a boat to put you there within two weeks, for the road is a perfect mire."

I said, "We appear to be a great inconvenience to you, through no fault of our own."

"Oh yes," he sneered, "it is never anyone's fault! Never. It is the weather and the contingencies of travel that are alone responsible for delaying the Company's affairs, and for the losses to its accounts. I have never yet, in all my years, met a single gentleman who would accept the blame for a particular misadventure without he would add some proviso, some *explanation*" — he said this with a mincing emphasis — "some qualification on his own incompetence. Before God, I hope ere I die to hear one man who will say candidly, when brought to task for the state of things, 'Yes, *I* am to blame!'" And here he flung his arms with a deranged and agitated expression as if he himself, in that instant, were the man.

We took our leave of him. From his office, which had a pleasing enough prospect, down over the peaks, porches, steep roofs, and jumble of narrow passages above the port of Quebec, we descended the precipitous incline of Breackneck Stairs, bearing our introductions to superiors in Montreal and our specific instructions to the owner of the boat which would take us there. Mr. Elborn allowed as it was hardly an auspicious start to our endeavours; but I cautioned him to ignore such unhinged assaults wherever they occurred, as if one stood on the bank of a racing stream and observed, too distant for any aid, the last struggles of a drowning man. In my opinion, nothing is to be gained under such circumstances by losing one's own composure.

As we returned to our lodgings I read him aloud this passage from Antoninus: "A disturbed expression is utterly unnatural. Let it be frequently assumed and the charm of the fairest face will begin to fade, never to be rekindled. Therefore be vigilant in the detection of anything contrary to reason; for if you should lose all perception of error, what would be left to make life worth living?"

May 18. Our journey to Montreal, which should have occupied the space of one week, was stretched considerably by the dilatory captain of our schooner, who had no appreciation of our need for haste, but must stop at least at every town and hamlet, each three leagues distant from the last (and often as well at the cottages, homesteads, and seigneuries between) to relay messages, drop and pick up goods, and relish the latest gossip. All of this he did with such consummate and impenetrable good humour that no sense of urgency could pierce to him, and we at last resigned ourselves to such a tedious repetition of bonhommie at each obscure landing place that I prefer not to recollect it.

The shamelessness of the riverside women disgusted me beyond measure, for it appears that our fellow is something of a favourite here-abouts, and not having seen him since the previous autumn, their joy in him and in the unbuttoned spring expressed itself in such kisses, caresses, and laughter that, had I been their various husbands, I would not have gazed on with such great good humour. They were for the most part inclined to a certain stoutness, although I spied some who were young and comely bent on the same activities. After each stop, our fellow would return to his schooner with innumerable waves, winks, and adjustments of his red nightcap, as if to impress on us and on the world the portentous nature and unlimited prospect of his conquest.

For my part, I took the advice of Antoninus and thought what revolting creatures men are in eating, sleeping, sexual intercourse, and all the other operations of nature, and I expressed disdain by paying his cavortings no attention whatever.

On arrival at the Company's offices in Montreal we were peremptorily received and hurried most unceremoniously to the wharves at Lachine, where we would embark for the interior having had no opportunity properly to present our credentials. Mr. Nute, a junior bourgeois of the Company, accompanied us, regretting as he said such haste and apologizing gracefully when I reported the reception accorded us in Quebec; however, it appeared that no further delay could be contemplated if I was to reach my post before the Autumn ice. Nor had I any satisfactory discussion with Nute as our cariole lurched the eight miles to Lachine, for when I hinted at the matter of separate assignments for Elborn and myself he assured me that he was in no way responsible for the disposition of clerks. Again I regretted the haste which had so far prevented my conferring with a high official, and was not reassured by Nute's observation that this was frequently the case, that most of the Company's business was executed through correspondence, and that upon my arrival at Grand Portage such questions would be answered and full instructions given. But that arrival is six weeks distant at least, and it appears that meantime we must travel in a limbo, as it were, wrapped in ignorance.

Elborn cared nothing for my discussion with Nute, but contented himself the while by watching intently the formation of a thunderstorm to the West, a massive and black protruberance which rose to block the sun itself, and which spread hulking shoulders and gnarled arms as far as one could see on either side. Elborn thought it ominous, although he continued to smile; but I assured him that, judging from my reading, such storms were not uncommon in Canada.

The storm fell upon us at Lachine, together with sudden and furious winds, and forced us to shelter in one of the Company's sheds near the docks. Here, in the half-dark, with the rain drumming the cedar roof and thunder rolling over us, I made my first acquaintance with the voyageurs who would take me north. They are rough fellows, smelling of onions and smoke; and for all I had heard of their colourful garb, these were plainly dressed in woolens and buck-skin, with arrow sashes draped loosely around their waists. They gave curt nods and went about their business, which at that moment seemed to be a boisterous gambling with cards. The tallest is not more than my own height. They are uncommonly thick about the chest and arms, and bandy in the legs.

Nute shouted above the wind to tell me that these ten were men selected for their strength in paddling, and that our lateness had necessitated holding back a light canoe from the brigade which had gone ahead, and that for the task of catching up these men would receive extra wages. I had passed their over-turned canoe on entering, a bark construction some thirty-six feet in length, called by them a *canot du maître,* and painted beneath the gunwales with a trim of green, red, and white. Upon its prow it bore a strange configuration in alizaron red, like the impress of a frog's foot, about which I inquired. They answered with subtle, laughing glances at each other that this sign had a certain religious significance among certain savages in the *pays d'en haut.* They struck me, in all, as good mannered (a characteristic unlikely enough, considering the scars some bore), but cultish and superstitious. These would not, for example, begin their voyage without the blessing of a priest descended from his manse for the ceremony, and the scattering of tobacco grains upon the water.

Then, the storm having abated and with the first streaks of blood-red sunset appearing in the West, our canoe was lifted by four of these fellows, and launched, their personal effects (packed in satchels weighing thirty or forty pounds apiece) stowed with great care so as not to upset the craft, which despite its weight was very delicate, and finally ourselves, Elborn and I cheek by jowl in the waist of the canoe, settled into a crude board seat and warned against kicking, lest we chip the brittle caulking of the seams. Thus immobilized, we faced West, while our paddlers entered like lithe cats and took their places. At a signal from the steersman we drifted out, nodding our farewells to Nute. Then, at a second signal, the vermillion paddles dipped together and we rapidly gained momentum, the prow lifting with each fresh impetus, speeding towards the Ottawa River and the lands beyond.

"Well," said Elborn with his ingratiating smile, "we are now truly on our way."

"Yes," I said. "We are finally going in."

I write now by the glow of a fire, before retiring to sleep within a tent for the first time in my life. Elborn has been eager to encourage these voyageurs in spinning their tales of death and terror, which they now do readily enough before an attentive listener, their faces ruddy in the fire's glow. I am surrounded by the tattered shadows of their gesticulations. They tell of the wendigo, a mythical creature of Indian lore, and each elaborates on the other's imagining until in his fantasy Elborn beholds a creature thirty feet in height, a naked, hissing demon whose frog-like eyes search out unwary travellers and roll in blood with craving to consume them! Another whispers that the creature lacks lips to cover its shattered teeth, and a third describes its feet like

24

scabrous canoes on which it rocks howling through the swamps
at evening
They are children who listen to such stuff!
For my part, I have read my instructions again, as well as
a passage from Antoninus counselling the suppression of fancy,
and I have determined to meet with a level mind whatever vicis-
situdes await me.

The wind had dropped with the sun. By the time the man had
finished reading, loons circled close in the dusk, loosing their
haunting cries among the waves. The man and woman stood,
stretched. He embraced her shoulders as they crossed the beach
to their fire, which had burned to embers. Adeptly he built it
again with fresh sticks until it flamed and crackled, sending sparks
aloft. For several moments he squatted beside it; then, one by
one, he fed into it the pages which he had just read, picked
up his knapsack, and followed the woman into the tent.

chapter five

The basement of the United Church was a dismal place even
on winter evenings when it was full of light and heat. But on
a June Saturday the dank flags on the platform drooped even
more disconsolately, the Jesus poster seemed more wrinkled and
woebegone, and the walls opposite the stairway dripped with
the day's hot breath.

Miro Balch knelt among hillocks of discarded newsprint, much
of which he had delivered pristine, with a snap of his paper-boy's
wrist, against the front doors of his customers. Miro was fourteen.
He was a master of Morse and a smooth semaphorist, skills
which had helped to make him the only King's Scout in Sable
Creek. He wore thick glasses and tattered running shoes. His

slight body coiled tensely, like the pig's-tail fuse on a cartoon time bomb. Even when he was relaxed he walked with an elastic stoop, as if he might explode suddenly erect and raging. Now, crouched among the newsprint mounds and stricken momentarily dumb by an excess of lust, he held up to the dim light a *Police Gazette,* spread at a clutch of aggressively mammalian molls, their eyes blanked.

"Guh guh gosh," he said. "Luh look at THAT!" To whisper, for any stutterer, is an exquisite ordeal, rather like pressing a healing wound, and Miro's attempts were never successful. The first syllables would burst from him in a sibilant pack, followed, as his taxed vocal chords gave up, by a shout.

"Shh! Shut up, Miro. For godssake!" Gerry Rattray leaned close, his broad forehead wrinkled and his lips appreciatively compressed. Miro had found one of the three prizes of paper drives. A nudist flimsy called *Sunbathing* was another. In *Sunbathing* everything was brown — nudes, rocks, trees, and sky — as if the editors had sought in this way to give it a patina of age and respectability. Sometimes *National Geographic* explored lands free of the mu-mu, but *National Geographics* rarely appeared on paper drives. *The Police Gazette,* bluntly full of boxers and breasts, was the rawest of the three.

Paul Henry turned away first, back to the sorting of the papers. The illustrations at once titillated and revolted him. "Ah, you guys," he said. "You guys. Listen. Those women are cows. Cows in a barn."

"Yeah? Well, I'd sure luh luh like to be in there wuh WITH them!"

"And what would you do, Miro?"

"I'd grab thu thu THOSE, for a start!"

"Me too," said Gerry Rattray, brooding darkly. "Me too."

Paul held the cord with his knee and knotted a loose bundle. Black hair fell across his eyes and he shook it away, scowling in mingled embarrassment and frustration. He hated being used. He hated reacting predictably, like a zoo animal. Yet he was as fascinated as the others. He nudged Miro's porno-hoard with his sneaker and the titles splayed out — *Sunbathing, Savage, Men Only, Assault.* "What're you going to do with that stuff, Miro? Where're you going to keep it? Your dad finds it, he'll beat hell out of you."

"Yeah, I knu knu knu . . . yeah." Miro flipped ruefully through the pack.

"Well?"

"Bet you'd like to keep them, eh Paul?" Lounging back on the papers, Gerry watched them narrowly. Often he protected Miro. He was quick to catch the moment when games turned subtly against him, and quick to react. "Eh Paul? Just think about that." His face, malleable as plasticene, contorted, and his body bent. Shuffling, groping, leering, whining, he pawed at the magazines, conjuring a succession of belles with whom he cavorted ape-like across the mounds of newsprint.

Paul laughed, watching his own phantasies purged and ridiculed. And Miro laughed too. Miro laughed in a high-pitched monotone like the wail of a ruptured insect, or like a safety valve blowing steam. He looked surprised when he laughed, as if he had never expected to learn how. Soon they filled the basement with echoing, mad sounds, clutching their sides, legs buckling, crumpling into the newsprint as Gerry's pantomime mounted in frenzy, so that Fred Hale, jumping from the cab of Ben Osaduyk's borrowed half-ton, had to call three times down the stairwell before they heard him. "Hey, what've you guys got down there, a pack of monsters?" Happy, sweating, pounding his palms together, Fred was engulfed in juvenile exuberance. Already the paper drive was a huge success. "Let's go," he shouted to the boys on the truck. "Let's go," he shouted down the stairs. "Let's get this stuff unloaded!"

When it was over, Paul Henry wheeled his bike from the alley behind the church. A muggy dusk rolled across the town. He waved to the rest, envying them their boisterous ride in the truck back to New Town. At times he wished he lived there too, for his friends' lives seemed colorful and brisk beside his own. They gulped experience like hot food, unthinkingly, and they seemed more at ease in Sable Creek than he whose family had lived there three generations. Pawns of the war, they adapted quicker to novel events, and seemed to think no more of the brash, transient, often brutal tempo of New Town than he thought of the gentler rhythms of his own life. Miro, he knew, would get his own supper tonight, from a can, for he had only a sometime father who blundered in and out, kicking hell out of everything, and his mother worked four to twelve at the mill. So did Franklin Hook's. Sometimes it seemed to Paul that his generation's mothers were women without roots, some of them restless and defensively cruel, some of them furtively resigned to widowhood, actual or anticipated. In some cases a motley parade of fathers had passed during the war, and his friends adapted to them as easily as they did to changes in food or habitation. Considerately, in the way of children, they attempted to support one another's fictions when required. Miro, for example, sometimes liked to think that he had a real father, and then they all tried hard to believe that it was true. Franklin's father had been reported missing in action, and the boy had constructed a little scenario concerning him: could be he only had amnesia. Could be that someday he would stumble and knock his head and remember in a flash who he was and where he belonged. Then he would come home, with medals.

Paul knew that his own father would not be coming back.

Gliding downhill towards the shopping district, Paul thought about his father. Evening was a bad time; tired and hungry and cold, you were most vulnerable at evening. A year earlier he could cry at will just by recreating the keen hurt that some evenings had brought him. It was like a cavity, that hurt — a cavity in the center of his chest, with a rough paw stroking the walls, wanting out. Now, as he rounded the drugstore corner with his sneaker scuffing the pavement, it came again.

His father was a moustache and a column of vest buttons.

That was all he could remember distinctly — the moustache because it prickled his neck and the vest buttons because they would rub his back when his father read him the comics. The rest was hearsay, and the memories of memories. There were photographs, of course, showing a trim man with a quizzical smile, first in a business suit and then in uniform with an air force wedge cap; but except for the greatcoat and knapsack he could not recall these clothes distinctly. Neither could he recall the day of the telegram, although it was not so long past. As in a dream, he imagined the maid weeping at the head of the stairs and preventing him from seeing his mother. Indistinctly he imagined Bob Mansfield advancing somberly from his car and silently laying a hand on his shoulder when Paul opened the door. But he remembered that a procession of people had come through several days, and that his mother had taken him for a walk in wet November woods, holding his hand. He had marched along. Her tears were part of the drizzle darkening the trunks, and when she spoke of the man she loved her voice rose and blended with the passage of wind in naked branches. "Your father was a gentleman," she had said. "And a poet. You must never forget those two things about him."

A gentleman's death he had died, one of the last of the duellists. And a poet's? Who could tell. Somewhere over France, the Hurricane had paused in its climb and shuddered beneath a lash of steel. In a stolen dusk, Paul had read this:

> Dear Helene, you must not think he died painfully for it was over in a moment. On my word, he had no time to suffer. I saw the German on his tail and called a warning to him, but he was himself attacking and did not change course until it was too late. I shouted again for him to get out of it, and his voice came back, very calm, "It's all right. I'm going up now." But he had no time left.
>
> It was very strange and easy to be mistaken with

the air so full of voices, but when he saw how good
the German pilot was, clinging on his tail, I thought
I heard him laugh.

I gathered his effects myself and sent them on.
I know there was a pocket-notebook full of poems,
but I haven't found it and I guess he had it with him.

Had his father laughed in the sockets of death? Is that what
poets did? It seemed a strange way to die. He had understood
that other people prayed.

Maybeetles hurled themselves against the store fronts and fell
thrashing on the street. Paul noted their agonies. Soon the street
would be sprinkled with their corpses, but by morning, when
the night-hawks and the birds of dawn had finished feeding,
the pavement would be clear. Things got used up.

The street narrowed as it rose, and acquired shade trees which
now spread shadowy hulks over and around the lamps. At the
steepest point Paul dismounted and bounced his bike over the
curb. A low retaining wall fringed the sidewalk and followed
the curve around. Looking back from this point he could see
the shopping district spread beneath him, with lights oozing out
here and there like lava in the crust of earth. Frail car sounds
and laughter reached him. Beyond, in the silver bay, the massive
circling booms squeezed their contents inexorably through the
mills; and the mills churned, and smoked, and rattled with metallic
dyspepsia.

Paul leaned on his bike, swinging it across the sidewalk as
he climbed. He could see home. Like others on the hill in Old
Town, the Henry house was set at arm's length from the street
which led directly to the main mill of Mansfield Pulp and Paper.
The low walls which the executives and merchants had built,
the ambling lawns, the formidable porches, all took on at this
hour of mid-evening the appearance of so many breastworks
and buttresses, as if the houses sought to protect themselves
from the straight road to success.

Paul's grandfather, Michael Henry, had built their house a year before he died. Indulging himself, he imported a bargeload of good limestone, along with two Scots masons who worked half a year to mould it properly. The result was a forbidding edifice in three stories with several rose-blown entrances, something between a cottage and a keep. He had hoped to fill it with the anarchistic laughter of children, for its planning and construction had drawn out in him an Indian Summer of virility. When it was finished he would marry Rose Stacey, his mistress of fifteen years. She was still young, scarcely thirty-four, and there was time, he told Bob Mansfield and himself. There was still time.

But there was not time.

Rather to his dismay, Paul's father inherited the house in 1938, and had not decided what to do with it before he vanished among French clouds. So the house was much as Michael Henry had left it, with only the ground floor and part of the second storey decorated, and with five bedrooms unconsecrated by the dreams of children. Helene and her son lived in two bedrooms on the south side, and in the kitchen and living room, which she had reduced to human scale by deft touches of drapery and furnishing. They rarely visited the dining room. In fact, Paul could remember eating there only once, when his father had been alive, and it was as if he had peered over the edge of a glittering plateau.

He swung up the drive, leaned his bike against the garage wall, and pulled down the hanging door. The kitchen was alight. His mother waved through the window and met him.

"Hi," he said.

"Hello. Good paper drive?" Helene Henry was thirty-two. She wore her hair drawn back and tied in a bun, so that her face seemed always framed by brown hands. She wore lace sometimes, and cameos, which made her seem older than she was. A reflective and good-humoured woman, she had been refined by grief and wistfully disoriented. She may, in fact, have been slightly deranged, like a powdered moth by a burst of sun, but although she wept at improbable associations, and although for three years she had discouraged as suitors several attractive men, choosing aloneness in the great house, her friends recognized in her a stratum of sanity like bedrock.

She watched her son closely, sensing in him with a maternal seismograph the tremors and changes of the day.

"Fine," he replied, embarrassed, building himself with scraps of privacy. "Great. Great paper drive."

"Good. Will you get enough money for the trip, do you think?"

"Sure. Fred says we will, anyway. Oh, hey, I brought you this." He laughed apologetically. "It's sort of beat up, but I thought you'd like it." *Hemlock,* said the cover. *A Review of Poetry.* Scuffed, it was nonetheless unread, with a few uncut pages, and had probably been sent as a hopeful sample to some Old Town matron.

"Thank you," she said, kissing him. "I'll enjoy that." And indeed, already she leafed through it, holding it like an expensive gift. "Get washed for dinner now. It's almost ready."

The next morning he found the magazine on the living room table. It had been read. It lay pressed open at a back section where advertisements of a literary nature were to be found. Here, secretaries offered to type manuscripts at seven cents a page, a fledgling writers' school promised sudden greatness, and travelling professors sought quiet couples to rent their cottages on Georgian Bay. Yawning, Paul read the ad circled with his mother's neat penstroke:

> WANTED: Any writing by, or information on, Drummond MacKay. PhD. thesis in preparation. Please contact Kenneth Malcolmson, 345 A King Street W., Toronto.

Such a tiny inquiry, Paul thought. Like a feather in the wind. Did the advertiser really expect anyone to notice it, and to respond? But then, his mother had seen it and circled it. Yawning again, he wondered why.

Then she called him, and there was a smell of toast and bacon.

chapter six

At dawn they came to the painted rocks.

Far above, on the edge of the cliff, the brush was filled with sun, but at lake level the shadows were deep and cold. Water dripped from the overhangs. A long ledge sloped like the back of an enormous fish, and the swells spread across it like webbed and transparent hands. Warily, the man let the canoe drift close.

"There," she said, pointing. "A canoe. A deer. A pair of snakes. And a ... a ...."

"And a monster."

"What is it?"

"The water lynx. Missephesshu. He would churn lakes with his tail. He would steal children and eat them. If one were going on a journey it would be well to pay homage to him."

"But they're beautiful! I want to see them closer." She climbed out onto the ledge and stretched to touch the paintings. The swell frothed across her bare feet. "Look. Some are very, very old, so faded that they're almost gone." Slowly she moved up the ledge, touching the paintings as she found them. "More canoes," she called. "And a horseman."

Holding the canoe, watching the mist race westward across the lake, the man waited.

When she returned she asked, "Don't you want to see them?"

"I have seen them. When I was very small I was brought here. They frightened me."

"I believe they still do," she smiled. "Even now."

"I have respect for them."

She gazed at the Missephesshu. "Was it an act of respect, do you think, to paint that?"

"Yes."

She brushed the smooth rock, down the spines of the creature's back. "And pride," she said. "And love of life."

chapter seven

August equivocates. Some of its days are warm as June, timeless, breezeless, muffling all point and purpose. On such days even heron cries are blunted and diffused, as. if in the instant of birth they had been resolved to their elements. These are the gravid days. But at other times August rips at the lakes with iron talons, and flings shreds of sky, like sodden blotters, against a cold horizon. Then, if he is alone in the wilderness, a man may contemplate his frailty and feel himself the victim of a ghastly accident.

Northwest of Lake Superior, August 15, 1946, was one of the hot days. Braced on the dock, Fred Hale took charge of his breathing and sucked the air of challenge through hairy nostrils. "Smell that!" he ordered. "Smell that air!" Already his war surplus khakis were stained with sweat. At his haunch dangled an enormous hunting knife, embedded in a scabbard tooled with tepees and smoking fires. On the crown of his scout hat, the crest of leadership rode precariously in its BE PREPARED motto, like an overloaded canoe. "All right, men. Let's go! Let's get organized here!"

Actually, they had been organized for weeks. Strewn about them were all the accoutrements of a military campaign — sleeping bags, mess kits, canteens, axes, shovels, and bulging packs of rations, — everything but weapons and transport. And the transport was on its way. "Should be here," Fred Hale muttered, tapping his watch, scanning the still lake as if he expected to conjure canoes with the force of his displeasure. "Should be more punctual than that." He turned to see Franklin Hook squatted behind his Brownie, intent on a black speck skimming the water. "Look!" he shouted. "See that duck?"

"Where? Oh yeah. Yeah."

"See that duck, Miro?"

"Yeah!"

"That's a merganser."

"Merh merh . . ."

"Merganser. That's a good survival duck. Nests in tree cavities. Easily trapped."

"Yeah?"

"Good eggs, too," said Fred, relaxing. "You won't find them now, of course. Breeding's all over."

"When do they bruh bruh breed?"

"Spring."

"Gosh, what a dummy!" Gerry rose from the packs where he had been lounging, peaked cap low over his eyes. "Listen, Miro . . ."

"Early Spring," said Fred.

" . . . everything breeds in Spring. Didn't you know that?" Miro inspected his compass.

"Everything. Ducks, snakes, frogs, geese — everything."

"What about muh muh man?" Miro's glasses glittered sunlight from Fred to Gerry.

"Yeah, well, man . . ." Gerry began, smirking, but Fred shouted, "Here he comes!" They heard an engine whining behind the point, and the next moment an amber runabout appeared trailing two canoes like sausages. OTTERSLIDE OUTFITTERS, said the sign on its prow. A massive black dog strained over its stem like a figurehead.

"Transport!" said Fred. "Get the gear together."

They shuttled the packs close to the edge of the dock, and when the canoes had been secured, began to load them. They were old canoes, toughened by repairs, and heavy. Their ribs were cracked, their canvas bottoms scabrous with patches. Fred had misgivings. He ate a lifesaver. He sweated lightly, jovially. "These the best you got?" he asked the Outfitter.

"Yup." The Outfitter had a paunch, a monkish fringe of hair, and narrow eyes. He was lying. He had six new Chestnuts sitting on his racks, but he was goddamned if he'd give them to any goddam pack of boy scouts. "Solid," he called to Fred as the boat drifted out. "Stable." He wrenched at the outboard starter, watched the motor kick and die, and began to rewind the cord. "They ain't likely to dump those uns," he said. This time the motor caught, roared, and swept the boat's prow in a neat arc. The Outfitter squatted. "See yuh here week Sunday," he shouted.

They watched him loop round the point. It suddenly seemed a long way to paddle, to that point; and when they reached it they would not have even begun their journey, for all the shores of this lake, which was merely a widening in the river, were dotted with camps and cottages. They would not reach the wilderness until after the first portage.

Fred clapped his hands and they made an empty sound, like a boot on a hollow log. "Well, men," he said, "we're going in, eh? Finally." He fumbled for a lifesaver and dropped a bright point of tinfoil. It spiralled past his open shirt, past the calisthenic flattened belly, past the pressed pants, past the parachutist's boots. Waiting in the bow of his canoe, Paul Henry watched it fall bright against the black pilings, bright against the water on which it settled buoyantly, like a dry leaf.

"The bearing," called Fred, pointing with his compass, "is 309 degrees." There was a flurry of compass adjustment in the two canoes. "That's the portage. Right over there. Easy paddle, men. Easy paddle. Ready? Gerry? Franklin? o.k." He extended his paddle and drew it back in a long, slow-motion gesture. "Strr-ro-ke!"

Paul stroked. He watched the false leaf of tinfoil sucked down into the vortex he created, and in the same instant his paddle clattered against Miro's.

"Gees," said Gerry Rattray from the stern. "We haven't even left the dock and already you guys are out of time."

"Sorry," said Paul.

"S-sorry," said Miro Balch.

"Stroke!" said Fred Hale, happily, from his canoe. "Strrr-OKE! Strrr-OKE!"

By four o'clock on the following Sunday the Outfitter had heard nothing of Fred Hale and his group. But his telephone had been busy most of the day, and he concluded that Fred had tried to reach him from the landing and had been unable to do so before the bus left. Probably he could go and pick up his canoes. He wasn't worried about being paid his balance. He knew boy scouts. And he knew a couple of the school board members in Sable Creek. More than once he had helped them into sleeping bags, dead drunk and raucous. He wouldn't even have to raise hell; the blackmail of his friendship would be enough to put pressure on Hale, if need be.

Humming "Mareseatoats and Doeseatoats", he swung round the point and buzzed for the landing. It had been a good season, and it wasn't over yet. He had four parties lined up for moose hunting and good guides to take them, and he had more overnight duck hunters than he cared to think about. He'd clear five thousand before the snow. An easy five thousand. "Little lambs eat ivy ..." He sang in a blunt baritone that pushed back and forth through the engine's roar. "A kid'lleativytoo, wouldn't you?"

The landing lay sombre and deserted. Black clouds massed above it. No canoes.

"Christ!" That would mean at least another trip, and maybe putting all those kids up in the guides' bunkhouse until the morning bus and God knew what else. And time was money. Besides, what if one of those old dogs of canoes had sprung out on them on a rock? Maybe he should have given them new Chestnuts. Maybe he should have given them canvas and Ambroid anyway, just in case.

Anxious under the stormclouds which were beginning to send ragged squalls racing on the lake, he turned for the portage. If they were over he might at least get them in before the storm hit, and keep them dry. Wet kids around a place were worse than wet dogs. He wished he hadn't drunk so much last night with the boys from Fort Frances. He couldn't take it anymore. His kidneys hurt.

By the time he reached the portage the beach was a chaos of waves and wind. It held no canoes, no packs, nothing to indicate that a party was working its way across from Anna Lake on the other side. The Outfitter stopped the motor and rocked heavily toward the beach. He knew that nothing, absolutely nothing, was to be gained from going ashore and walking the portage. He'd get soaked, that was all. And yet, cursing softly, he hauled the boat stern first as high as he could up the beach, raised his shirt collar against the pelting rain, and lumbered onto the path under a lashing forest. "Jesus H. Christ," he observed, travelling at surprising speed for the bear of a man he was, "goddam fuckin boyscouts got no more fuckin place in this goddam bush than Millie's tit!" The storm churned around him. The four hundred yards of gray-green tunnel became a fluid slide down which he stumbled and slipped, like a large, awkward child.

In a few moments he stood in the mud that was the shore of Anna Lake and peered northwest. The lake writhed. Thunder rolled like the moans of giants. No one, he knew, would be paddling across the lake into *this,* for on the open water the waves would be three feet high. He laughed abruptly. Flung from the trees behind, sheets of rain washed over him. "Goddam boyscouts won't get far in this," he said.

An hour later, fed and dried, he looked out on a steady downpour which gave no hint of easing, and called the police.

"Reg? Ben."

"Yeah Ben."

"Reg, gotta problem here. Bit of a wrinkle."

"Yeah Ben."

"Party of boyscouts. Went in two weeks ago and didn't come out."

"Jesus Christ! That's all we need. When due?"

"Today."

"Well, give me a call this time tomorrow."

"Sure."

"Where're they from?"

"Sable Creek. Fella name of Hale."

"Well, nothing we can do tonight. Listen, you look after the mothers, eh?"

"Goddam!"

"Sure. Suuu-re. You think they won't be calling? Matter of fact, maybe you better drive down to Sable Creek and comfort them yourself. How many kids?"

"Five. No, four and Hale."

"Ben m'boy, that's just a good night's work for you, all those waiting ladies."

Later, the Outfitter said: "No, there's nothing to worry about, Mrs. Henry. It's not unusual for a group to be a day or two overdue. Anything could cause it — headwinds, or a little sidetrip, or . . . Pardon? Yes, the police are looking after it. Sure. Sure I will, and, oh, Mrs. Henry? There's something you could do for me. Call the other mothers? Let them know everything's o.k. and that they shouldn't worry."

Later still he said: "Mirror who? Balch? No, I don't know the kid's got a paper route. Don't even know the kid. Yeah, well that's tough, you gotta deliver them yourself. Listen. Listen, friend. You want this kid outta the bush, you just come on up here and bring him out yourself, o.k.? Sure, and the same to you, buddy!"

chapter eight

They laughed loading their canoe in a new morning. The sun rose with a vigour which promised a hot day.

"But I must have told you that story," he said. "It was then I found the pistol."

"No. No, I'm sure you haven't. Poor Fred."

He nodded, hitching a pack closed. "Like bats. I remember looking back down that point from the edge of the forest, and they all looked like damaged bats in those ponchos. Fred was trying to start a fire and had sent me for birchbark. I was crying. I was wet, and cold, and hungry. There were big red pines on the point and on the shoreline behind the forest was all spruce. He'd seen a clump of lighter leaves farther back and above the rest, and he thought these were birch, so he sent me for bark. 'Burn wet or dry, boys,' he kept saying. 'Wet or dry. Just find a little birchbark and we'll get a fire in no time.' "

"So I went. I kept tripping and falling down in the moss, and when I came to the grove I saw that they weren't birch at all, but aspen. Their trunks were shining, black and green, and their leaves shook so that there was a fine spray under them. For an instant I thought I had been there before."

"Déjà vu."

"Something." He folded their tent carefully, and packed it. "The moss was thick. It looked as if an undertaker had laid out artificial grass all around. I remember thinking that. There was a depression where several of the trees clustered, and I slipped there and some of the moss peeled back. Underneath were the ends of timbers, locked into a corner post, red and grey and shredding with decay. I pulled more moss away and saw that they were part of the corner of a building. They were soft as sponge. When I pressed them bits clung to my hand and pulled away. I remember standing up and rolling the rotten shreds of wood between my fingers, looking into the darkness among the trunks for some hint of the building's size. But the moss had hidden everything. A few yards from where I stood, the hump that was one wall smoothed out and disappeared entirely under the moss. The other wall went only a few feet, and ended at a grove of aspen. It had crumpled there, and the trees had seeded in the rotting wood."

The woman had stopped smiling. She stood with her hands in the straps of the pack she had been about to pick up, watching him. Below, near the water, the canoe waited.

"I knelt down and dug at the corner. I found the pistol in loose humus. At first I thought it was just a stone, but then the earth fell away from it and I saw the trigger. I remember raising it and swinging it in an arc at the forest. I remember the rain wetting it and trickling a line of rust across my wrist. It was just old, flaking iron."

He shrugged and lifted the two packs, and she walked beside him toward the canoe. "You didn't dig farther?"

"No. Fred called me then. Somehow they had started a fire. I smelled smoke. I knew that if I stayed there all the rest of them might come swarming up to see what I'd found, scratching and tearing away the moss. I kicked the earth back and covered the place with moss again. Then I gathered some sticks to hide the gun, and I took it back with me."

Enough swell lingered from the winds of the previous day to make loading the canoe tricky. They managed by wading into the water on either side of it, keeping the bow out. They worked quickly together, and soon they had pushed out beyond the lines of surf and were paddling steadily through the shoals and islands which enclosed the bay, towards the northwest.

chapter nine

"If lost in lake country," said the scouting manual, "stay where you are, keep calm, and burn an island. Fire watchers will find you."

Twice they had done just that. Twice they had watched the pall from an incinerated island blend with the clouds which had covered them for two weeks. The clouds were very thick, dark, and about three hundred feet above the ground. No fire watchers had come. On the islands, pine cadavers smoked.

They had kept moving and arguing. "Right," Fred would say, too decisively. "Now, according to my calculations, the portage should be just ... about ... *there*!"

"Naaw."

"I say it's there, Fred. 207 degrees."

"Hell no. Look. You guys are both wrong. Supposing we're in *this* lake, and that last portage is *this* one on the map. Then the portage should be down here someplace."

"Yeah, but what if that last portage wasn't *on* the map? What if it was all new beaverwork, like we thought it was? That means that we're in *this* lake someplace and the portage is way over there."

"O.K. men. All right. Now here's what we'll do ..."

"Hey Fred, why'd you teach us all this orienteering stuff if you don't want us to use it?"

"Got a lifesaver for us, Fred?"

"It was the fog that fouled us up, boys."

"Sure it was, Fred."

"The fog and the wind. No sun. But my compass says we go ... there!"

"*If* we're in the lake you think we're in, right Fred?"

"Well, Gerry, we just have to assume that, I think. We just have to take a bit of a chance on that."

They wandered through sprawling lakes full of deceptive bays and promontories, paddling for hours down cul-de-sacs where at last the deer flies rose in swarms and deadheads snagged the bottoms of the old canoes.

The days rolled softly in Fred Hale's mind like rotting mushrooms torn from their mycelium. He clutched the scraps of his authority. He had thought only to keep them moving, to keep them preoccupied, to keep alive the illusion of control. He had lost his knife. The sheath with the teepees scored in it jounced fussily against his hip. His hatbrim drooped in a scalloped ringlet. His eyes had softened into small bogs of puzzlement. "If we knew *how* we got lost," he kept saying, slapping the taunting map and flinging out his arms on the word *how*, "we'd know how to get back there!"

The boys no longer listened or cared. For Miro especially the trip had been a horror, a monochromatic nightmare of mud, rock, endless waves, and cloud. He was surrounded by such terrors and grotesques, that sheer survival would be triumph. His soul shrivelled in greyness. Shuddering, feverish and exhausted, he spent hours watching insects in dead stumps, and envying the crispness and precision of their world. Often he had fallen on the portages and been unable to free himself of the pack which suddenly grappled him with leather tentacles. Then he would lie like a helpless beetle with the rain on his chest, waiting for help. At such moments his meagre adrenalin simply drained away.

To their initial delight he and Gerry had drawn the right to use two war surplus jungle hammocks, plastic and rubber constructions of an evil green which, when suspended in the dusk, resembled the cocoons of monstrous moths. In theory they were rainproof, but in fact they collected gallons of water on their roofs and trickled it inside through a complexity of folds and wrinkles. To make matters worse, their ropes had rotted in tropical storage; they would support the sleeper a night or two before snapping suddenly and sending him tangled into puddles and soggy moss.

In the night, Gerry Rattray would hear Miro whimpering in

his jungle hammock, a small center of misery. "Hey Miro," he called once, through the rain. "Wake up!"

"I'm nuh nuh nuh ... I'm aw-w-wake."

"Whatsamatter? Well, whatsamatter?"

"I'm guh guh gonna luh luh lose my p-paper route!"

"Ahhhh shit. No yuh won't. Ah jeez, Miro, listen, don't be a suck. Listen, Miro, we'll go see the guy, o.k.? We'll tell him what happened. He can't fire yuh for something you couldn't help."

"Can so."

"No he can't. It's not fair. It'd be like punishing somebody because he's sick. See?"

"Well ..."

"Well o.k. So we'll go see him, then. I'll vouch for yuh."

"o.k.... Gerry?"

"Yeah."

"You know what?"

"What?"

"My old muh muh man's gonna beat HELL outta me!"

"Jeez, sorry Miro. Can't help you there. You're on your own there, Miro."

And he was. He knew his present father would be furious if in any way the fact of Miro's existence were drawn to his attention. And if the police had been around ... Miro shuddered.

At last they came to a promontory fringed by beach, a promontory which probed three hundred yards into the lake. "All right, men," Fred said. "This is the one. This'll do it! But this time, *this time* ..." he raised a finger and waited until he held the lethargic attention of all, " ... we wait for a plane."

Opposite the promontory were two small islands. Around the shore of one of these they heaped great brushpiles. They gathered sheets of birch bark and split logs for tinder. Then they camped, and they began to wait. They huddled near their campfire, or in the dank tent, and they waited.

The plane came at last, first as a mere tonal shift in the sound of drizzle on the leaves and tent and lake's face, but sufficient to snap Fred Hale awake and upright, saying, "Listen, men! Listen!" And then it came small and distinct, complete in its way as the night humming of a mosquito in the ear, and unmistakably an aircraft.

"Out! Outoutout!" They tore the tent flaps. They tore the mosquito screen. They tumbled like maddened bearcubs towards the lake. They wrenched the canoes upright, flung in their torches, and raced for the island. The plane had materialized, a distant, droning dot, on a course almost at right angles to them. "Quick," said Fred Hale, gasping. "Quick! Quick quick!" His body contorted crazily. "Light the fires! The fires!"

The first fire raised a smudge like a rotting mushroom. In the aircraft, the ranger pointed wordlessly and the pilot, nodding, began an easy bank to the left. The second fire was lit, and the third and fourth. In moments, flames were licking up neat trails of tinder and into the island, drying as they went and gaining strength, merging and spreading in decades of bracken until the great pines themselves began to smoke and crack and launch soaring embers in the heat.

"Gee zos!" said the ranger, droning in. And the pilot, banking off and away from the pyre, squinted at two canoes standing off in the lake and at the small figure of Miro Balch snapping out a happy semaphore. "What's he saying," he grinned. "Help?"

The ranger levelled his glasses. "No," he said. "No-o-o. He's saying, 'Magnificent Miro, master of monsters!'"

"Code!" snorted the pilot. "Damn boy scouts! Always playin games!"

Later, when the canoes had been lashed to the pontoons, and the Beaver had gathered them all into its warmth and lifted them above the clouds where the sun shone and the engine purred like a mother's heartbeat, the ranger leaned back and shouted this story at Fred Hale: "Seems there was a man with diarrhoea in an elevator. Ran outta the elevator and down the hall, spraying everything with shit. Little cleanup man comes along, mop and pail, scrubs the elevator, scrubs a hundred yards of hall and comes to this fella's door. When he's finished he knocks on the door and says, 'Mister, we all got problems sometimes. I don't mind cleanin up. That's my job. But there's just one thing, one thing I wanna tell yuh: Next time, *stand still!*' "

No one laughed. The ranger nodded slowly, and Fred Hale nodded too. He got the point. There was no excuse for wandering aimlessly, thirty miles off course. There was no excuse for not staying on one campsite as soon as he realized he was lost. He had simply compounded his blunder, hoping miraculously to make it right.

For a while he stared through the plexiglass at yellow clouds, dreading the meetings and explanations to come, dreading the laughter, dreading Narah. Then, shaking himself and smiling a little, he leaned across the aisle. "Well boys," he shouted, "this is certainly the way to go, isn't it?"

Gerry Rattray regarded him wearily. "Fred," he said, so softly that his words were lost in the roar of the engine, "why don't you just stick those goddam lifesavers up your ass?"

Franklin Hook sneezed carefully away from the camera in his lap, drew an encrusted plaid sleeve across his nose, and starcd unsccing through the window. "Yeah," he said, "it's a good way to go. Anything but a canoe's a good way to go. I never want to paddle another fuckin canoe as long as I live." He had been thinking of the trick door or wall section then popular in movie matinees. The wall, part of an ordinary room, would spin when leaned upon, scooping some thug or gorilla or clown out of chaos to replace whoever had triggered it. Without reason it happened, and just when you thought you knew who was who and what they all stood for, the wall would spin and the situation would change in the flash of an eye. The device had fascinated Franklin; he looked now at Fred Hale as if he were a trick, a pretender, someone else in Fred's clothes and body.

Miro slept.

At the rear of the plane, Paul Henry unstrapped his haversack and carefully drew out the scrap of iron which, for him, had justified the trip. Exposure had raised gills of rust along the barrel. The hammer with its flaring thumbpiece was welded forever against the powder pan, still clenching a scrap of flint. A stiff iron leg, once the core of the butt, ended with a corroded copper plate; the wood had rotted completely.

The pilot feathered his engine and began his slide into the bay below. Paul saw the ranger station nestled into the forest like a set of wooden play blocks he had once been given in a string bag, long ago. He rewrapped the pistol and stuffed it into his knapsack, watching the Beaver's reflection rise to meet them. The floats bumped, bumped again, hissed across the surface, and flashed by the waiting crowd on the dock.

There followed reunions full of joyful cries, and embraces, and tears in mothers' eyes. Flashbulbs sizzled. The atmosphere was one of relief, and there was even some laughter. For Fred Hale the confrontations were not nearly so disagreeable as he had feared. Steve Hook, Franklin's uncle, slapped him on the shoulder and said, "Hey Fred, couldn't yuh find moss on the north side uh the trees? Eh?" And Fred, grateful, the foolish compass still dangling round his neck, knew that one of the terms Sable Creek was offering was that he should never make excuses. Never. Not even explanations, for the thing was inexcusable. He had gotten lost in the bush, and he had done it with maps, and compasses, and four boys. And he was a scoutmaster, and a teacher, and from now on nobody would take seriously anything he told them about orienteering. Worse, he knew that never again without terrible risk could he discourse in class on his beloved explorers. Radisson, Noyon, La Verendrye, Hearne, Fraser, MacKenzie — all the magic names of the company to which he had aspired were lost to him forever. He grinned. He shrugged. He kicked a sheepish ropeend on the dock. David Thompson slogged alone into the mists of Athabaska.

"Hey Fred. Why didn't yuh saw down a tree, see, and take

a good look at the stump, see, to find out where the rings were thickest? Eh?"

"I don't know, Steve."

"Eh?"

"I don't know."

"Isn't that inna book anymore?"

"Yeah, but it's just one of the things we didn't do."

"Rings're thickest to the south. You'd uh done that, you'd know where south was. Big help, eh Fred?"

"Sure."

"Eh?"

"Big help."

It was not nearly so bad as he had feared. He had imagined a gantlet of righteous motherhood, but nothing like it materialized. Slowly the cars were loaded and driven off one after the other, until he was alone with Miro Balch and with the current father of Miro, a pockmarked, strawhaired mechanic of twenty-four or five, who flicked his Sweet Cap, brushed ashes from a stained Hawaiian sport shirt, and sidled as if expecting a kick.

"Hey, you the guy took these kids onna trip?"

Fred nodded.

"Well this kid's gotta paper route, y'know. Gotta job."

"I know."

"Been deliverin goddam papers myself four days."

"Sorry."

"Well why the hell d'juh take em way off in uh goddam bush? Why didn't juh bring em back on time?"

Fred bent for his knapsack. "Well," he said. "I tried." He looked over the bay down which the Outfitter was coming to collect his canoes, his dog like a sentinel in the bow, and over the shore which was again breathing fog into low clouds. "I tried," he said, laughing at the absurdity which had suddenly revealed itself as through an opening in cloud, "but it's one of the hardest things in the world to bring kids back on time. Don't you think it is?"

"Yeah," said the mechanic warily, "well ..."

Later, Fred watched the birthmark on his wife's throat. Narah leaned back with one hand behind her head on the pillow and the other circling on Fred's back, between the shoulder blades. The pulse in her throat moved the strange birthmark there, which was the shape of a small frog's foot and the colour of shore mud and humus. "If only I knew *how* it happened," he said.

"Why does it matter?"

"Because ..." he faltered, knowing that he was giving up easily, even here, even with her, "because ... well, so it won't happen again. So I won't make the same mistake twice."

"Maybe you had too many compasses."

But he went on as if she had not spoken. "It was in a big lake," he said. "I know that much. A lake so big that even when the sky cleared you couldn't see the other shore. And there were islands. And a wind ..."

She drew him to her, and although he longed to lose himself in her his mind prowled, searching back through scraps of recollection shuffled like cards of time. His mind raced to luring promontories and to clearings where the portage out was sure to be, but which drew back, and changed, and enticed him until they vanished in the rain. "If only I knew *how*," he said again, and the answer seemed so close, seemed a presence almost palpable, seemed to hover just beyond this drifting fog.

"Will they go again," she asked thoughtfully, after a while. "Will they ever go back in again?"

"Who? The boys? Sure they will."

"Little Miro?"

"Sure. If he gets a chance."

"Franklin?"

"Oh yeah ..."

"Gerry?"

"Yeah. Listen. It wasn't that bad, you know. Not for them."

"And Paul?" she asked. "What about Paul?"

"Sure. Honest, it wasn't that bad for them. It was an adventure. You know. It was the sort of thing kids remember."

"But if they fear the wildness . . ." she began, and left the thought unfinished for he was not listening. He had got up and was crossing to the bureau for his peppermints, ignoring her, his feet making small, wet sounds on the varnished floor.

chapter ten

The day stayed hot and calm. Piece by piece as the sun rose they discarded their clothing until at last they paddled naked. Eyes half-closed, he watched the arms and shoulders of his woman, and the way her body swept the horizon as the canoe rose and fell. Her paddle glinted silver, threading droplets across the surface with each fresh stroke. Around her the water glowed and darkened, umber, silver, grey like a wrapping pain, and ultramarine, undulant, curving into black. With evening, the flourishes of red shifted and darkened also. Crimson, orange, some scarlet, and a deep yellow like molten gold, all traced through the shadows of the clouds.

Several times during the day they had passed deserted buildings. In the broken windows of some, scraps of curtain fluttered. Twice they saw places where settlements had been burned, and the ruins still smoldered, and sent smoke spiralling inland through the trees. Once they saw dark figures surrounding a building that might have been a lodge, and heard a popping like tiny fireworks in the distance.

They kept a mile offshore, and swung even farther out as they approached settlements of any kind. They saw no other canoes and no boats but one — a small trawler without lights, heading out off Michipicoten.

They camped in a cove secluded from the lake, and he pitched their tent in thick underbrush while she made supper. Afterward, he again brought out the knapsack containing the manuscript, and again, unbidden, began to read aloud.

May 25, 1785. Caught as I am among these voyageurs whose company I must yet share several weeks, I have amused myself with speculation on the nature of their private lives and personal endeavours. Antoninus has said, "The way to gain contempt for the charms of song, for dancing, or athletics, is to take the voice singing in tune, resolve it into its component sounds, and ask thyself of each, 'Is this too much for me?' Assent would be shameful. Then treat the dance in a similar manner, breaking it into its several motions and attitudes; and so too with athletic exhibitions. In short, with the single exception of virtue and all her works, remember always to consider every object through its parts, and by this analytic process learn to despise them all. Nay, more, transfer the habit to life itself in its totality."

They are dull fellows, of course, bred to a grunting life of paddle and portage like beasts to burden, and, from all appearances, sustained by an endless round of ritualistic trivia. No portage is crossed, no rapids poled, no campfire set ablaze, without that the stories of the place are told, as if they lurked like spirits and emerged through the vehicles of men. Here was such-and-such a great storm; there, such-a-one lost his life, and they will doff their caps and pray at a glimpse of any cross along the shore, for they mark the graves of others of their kind, most of whom have perished in the frenzied rapids (of which we have passed a great many), or by over-exertion and rupture at the carrying places. They strive like children to race each other and to surpass in weight the burdens of their friends when they are transporting trade goods or furs. Like children too they lack the true sense of continuity and sequential time, and often fall to arguing the date of a particular event, which they do energetically, embellishing the event itself in the process, confusing it with similar occurrences, and in general so obscuring the facts of the matter that their older tales have acquired the amorphous qualities of myths and legends, quite detached from truth and floating free at the mercy of any charlatan. Most are illiterate. Written records and true accountings mean nothing to them. They sign their indenture licences with blunt marks.

On the second night these fellows, under the guise of conviviality and insisting that such threats were tradition, offered to hurl me from the rocks and into the water. In this way they quickly extorted a cask of rum from Elborn, who laughed heartily and joined them in their revels. I made clear to him that I would take no part in such squandering of Company supplies, and pointed out that this rum was intended for use in the Indian trade; but he replied that it paid the Company well to be generous with its spirits. He spoke this with the sly smile and glance so typical of him. So I was threatened with much jostling and bantering of the kind which passes between haughty children and temperate adults on All Hallow's Eve; so I was over-ruled.

The camp was soon transformed to a Bedlam, as I had foreseen, with these banty fellows strutting and howling their filthy songs. Your voyageur, drunk or sober, is a bladder of venery, and more salacious, more promiscuous, more indiscriminate, licentious and wanton than the basest lout in all of London, and I have heard such tales since I began with them as to lead me to believe that they are exempt from all but the lewdest motives. I hung in the cool shadows where I could observe their revel and record their boasts of an amorous nature, for they are shameless braggarts. In the firelight they cavorted like demons, roaring their drunken laughter and befouling themselves.

It is possible that my detachment troubled what conscience remained to some, for shortly our old gouvernail, or sternsman, named Gustave, peered through the lunging flames, signalling with his cup, and called to me to join them, for the love of God and life. I called back that I had forgone the love of God and that I was not equal to their life of love. I said this with as much pretense of good fellowship as I could muster, for the Company's sake, and it satisfied all but Gustave, for they were far advanced in drink and applauded merrily. For his part, the old man left the circle, which had meantime launched on some new bawdy song, and approached me where I stood among the trees. He scrutinized me closely and I pride myself that I did not flinch from the smell of him. He was shorter than I, and it appeared to me that I gazed upon him from a height, as one might upon a frog in the water of a well. Indeed, with his pinched face and crooked limbs he was closer in form to a frog than to a man, and yet at the moment I perceived this similarity he said, as if to deny my thought, "Moi, je suis un homme!"

I replied that I did not doubt it.

Nothing would suffice, however, but I must hear the drunken recitation of feats of strength, love, endurance, and extravagance by which each of these fellows defines himself, and which he will present as his credentials at every opportunity. I confess that even when done by the most brutish it is often carried off with panache. So with Gustave. I heard of his wives and running dogs, his encounters with bears, great pike, moose, murderous Indians, and a baker's dozen sinister beasts never seen by other human eyes. Finally, when by these tales he had sufficiently identified himself and established in my sight (as he thought) a respectable stature, he made bold to advise me in my conduct, as if he spoke to a pubescent lad and not to a clerk of the Company and his superior. The men, he said, were humble in calling but proud in deed. It may be that they were mere servants of the Company, but who was not? And did they not transcend their servitude through good humour and simple *joie de vivre*? As for myself, he predicted that I would not long survive in the *pays d'en haut* unless I made comrades of all who faced the wilderness with me, regardless of birth, of calling, or of office, for a man alone had little hope against the elements. We were, he said, each of us as frail as a butterfly in the wind above Superior, or as a naked child upon the steppes of winter. It behooved us to be tolerant, to bend like lithe young birches before the gale, for inasmuch as we stiffened did we invite our own destruction; and a warm fire and a warming drink were little enough for a man to share in the darkness which stretched forever. As for women, what were they but the repositories of forgetfulness, wherein a man died and was reborn, wherein a man exchanged his tears for laughter, wherein death, at last, was of little consequence? Was not laughter their fit tribute? He bade me listen: Did I not hear the boiling of La Chaudière, where thirty-one crosses told us that life was of the moment, that the past was past and the future a lone mound of rocks and the wolf's howl on a moonless night? Life was a story beside the fire. Life was a laugh, a dance, a cup of rum. And the man alone in the darkness was a man who was not alive.

I thanked him for his solicitude. "You will observe," I said, "that my eye is clear and my mind unclouded. Tomorrow I shall journey on in this same condition, and not in memories of shame, and blear-eyed."

"Then you will travel alone," he replied, "apart from all the rest of us, although you sit in the same canoe. And may God help you at the end, my young bourgeois." He turned and began to stagger back toward the fire and the revels.

"We shall see tomorrow who requires the ministrations of God," I called after him, for he had annoyed me, and I did not wish to allow him last word. My laugh was harsher than I had intended.

He halted and hunched around to face me. In silhouette against the fire his bent frame and dangling arms were even more monstrous and frog-like. He called soothingly, as if to a troubled child, making a swimming movement in the air the while. *"C'est égal.* It's all one." Yet his voice mocked me, and the firelight which trembled in luminous flesh about his neck and head, between his legs and fingers, thickened him into the merest caricature of a man, so that whatever small understanding might have grown between us shrivelled away, and in disgust I retired to my tent.

May 27. We travelled yesterday in a steady rain which I felt as a further depression on the spirits, for it remains cold, and in such a rain all colour is drained from the landscape as from a corpse. It is in any case tedious enough, this brute countryside, with its never-ending rocks and brooding meadows. The portages, furthermore, are quickly transformed into so many morasses in which even I, lightly laden as I am, sink to my knees. I am amazed at the brute strength of these Canadians who bully their way through the muck like percherons. This they manage even when debilitated from their carouse, for they are bred to it and it is their nature. I am told their usual loads commonly exceed one hundred and eighty pounds, which loads they transport in the same manner as their lighter packs, suspended upon the back from carrying straps across the forehead. The canoe is carried by four of them upon their shoulders.

Once I advised against travelling in such rains as we have had, for it is more than unpleasant; but again I was over-ruled. I was told that their orders are to come up with the main brigade with all speed, and that this they mean to do at the rapids of Ste. Marie. And so I must endure, although I little comprehend the frenzy of these people, to hasten on as if pursued by the very demons which they themselves create. So I have no choice but to bundle myself as tightly as possible against the rain and to contemplate the correcting of my own actions and intentions;

for as Antoninus has said, "It is an absurdity not to flee from our own vice, which is possible; yet strive to flee from the vice of others, which is impossible."

We have begun to pass Indian habitations in the meadows — birchbark hovels already rotting back to earth. The people rise listlessly from smoking fires, and stare at us. Even the dogs lack energy to bark. I deduce from the jests of the men that these tribes (or remnants thereof) have been in no way elevated from prolonged contact with Europeans, for they are by nature lazy, depraved, and so thoroughly addicted to alcoholic liquors that all men of good intentions sent among them by both Government and Church have despaired. One must needs conclude that if the "noble savage" is not mere phantasy he does not exist on *this* continent, and it is small wonder that these have so easily been overwhelmed by our superior planning, determination, and execution whenever it has been necessary to take arms against them.

One of our paddlers calls a mock plea to the steersman, urging him to take them near the shore so that he may leap out, have his pleasure of all the Indian women in the camp, and catch the canoe again before it passes the bend; and this suggestion causes much hilarity. The squaws seem docile creatures in their skins and poor tents. I am told they are thick with vermin and loathsome scabs. Indeed, seeing me intent upon them, Annable, the milieu at my back who has lost both nose and voice to syphilis, couples his hands with such grins and gestures as to indicate that if I would be like him I need only put ashore for a moment's dalliance. I told him that such women had no attraction for me, and that the Company was now my sole enterprise. At this his mirth engulfed me, together with the stench from his raddled throat.

Elborn also laughed, pretending to be moved by his book. I turned to him and asked, "What are you reading that so amuses you?"

"Why," he replied, "it is a very ancient book of meditations, given me by my uncle on my departure. The writer was a Faust *manqué,* a man who had no chance to make his pact, although he would dearly have loved to do so."

"A most fortunate man," I observed.

"Yes," said Elborn. "Except that he missed his tour of Heaven also."

"And how could that be?"

"A small error. A matter of map-reading. He kept mistaking the location."

"Of Heaven?" I wished eagerly to deride him.

"Oh yes," Elborn laughed. "Certainly he mistook the location of Heaven; but of the pact also, for he kept searching through the world for his own terms to be met."

The man is a sink of equivocation! I trust our ways shall diverge at last beyond the Grand Portage.

The rain persists, but there is no wind upon the lakes and for several days I have not urged that we lay over in our tents, for each day's travel sweeps me closer to congenial company, and to some alleviation from the presence of this Elborn, who is an oppression upon my spirits.

June 1. Evidently I shall not be so easily rid of him.

The Company has assigned him as my assistant.

His revelation of this fact appalled me, for there had been no mention of it in my orders, an omission which I thought more than passing strange. But in the ruin of an old building on Grand Calumet Portage, where we sheltered alone from a vicious squall, he asked between puffs of his pipe if I knew the location of this Nibbeke Omuhkukke Lake, to which we had been assigned. I replied that I knew the location neither of his post nor of my own, having had, in the haste of our journey, no access to maps of the high country, but that I was confident that the Company's administrators at Grand Portage would send us accurately on our separate ways. He removed his pipe and repeated my last three words with an insidious accent on the word "separate", so that it was no true question, as he pretneded, but rather a wicked probing at my fears. "But surely we have been appointed to the same post," he said, and began to unfold his orders, smiling all the while.

"Oh, not so," I answered him, feigning indifference, "for my orders refer to a Lake Omuhkukke, where I am to establish a new post, now being constructed under the aegis of a Mr. Henderson, and they make no mention of you."

"A clerical oversight, clearly," he said, pointing with the wet stem of his pipe, "for see here in my document, ' . . . thence to proceed by Company transport to Lake Nibbeke Omuhkukke as assistant to Mr. MacKay, and there to trade with the Indian at all times in the Company's best interest, and at all times to keep a true accounting of his transactions.' ''

"But it is on *your* document that the omission has been made," I laughed, "for see, the Christian name of this MacKay under whom you are to serve has been left off, and it is your own conjecture, merely, which supplies the name of Drummond."

Glancing at me, he replied that this could very likely be the case, and that we would no doubt be further enlightened upon our arrival at Grand Portage. He added that, in any case, it was all one to him. Then, the storm having abated, we knocked out our pipes and departed that gloomy place. I am not so sanguine as I pretended, however, and place little hope in the ambivalencies offered by some bungling clerk. I have in the ensuing days resigned myself to his presence in the *pays d'en haut,* and resolved to bear this unhappy development with fortitude and grace, as befits a man who would control his fate. If this be indeed the will of the Company, then it shall be borne with equanimity, as one accepts disease. I intend therefore to speak of it no further at this time; but shall make most pertinent inquiries into the matter at Grand Portage, for although I am resigned if need be, yet I do not intend to bear with him as the result of a mistake.

I have taken comfort (and refuge from Elborn) in the observation by Antoninus that in the mind of a man who has been chastened and purified, no festering wounds and no uncleanness will be found. Nor, in the conduct of such a man is there anything that need fear scrutiny or hide itself from the light of day.

We passed two days ago, near to a place called the Portage des Paresseux, a marvellous cave set in a hillside, the mouth of which, overgrown with shrubs and dangling vines, had a peculiar fascination for me as the most welcoming place in all this inimical route which we have travelled; and although I am of no fanciful temperament, yet I would scarce have been surprised had a Siren's song issued forth from it, or had a luring creature beckoned us. It appeared a very place of solace and repose. Yet our men hurried past with murmurs and swift glances, as if they cared not to look at it, or to remain long in its sphere of influence. As I have noted, they are of a superstitious bent, and I afterwards learned that the place is frequently inhabited by one shaman or another from the tribes, and that these men garner a baleful power from such spots, and would not be loathe to use it against any voyageurs interrupting their reveries. I learned further that the walls of this cave are painted with weird devices which have come to those shamans in dreams, and that even if the cave were empty the spirits whose likenesses had been captured would congregate there, ravenous to be whole. Such fearful images did the men conjure in their descriptions to me that they afrighted each other and concluded by telling this nonsense in hushed tones and in the cadences of childhood.

We are camped tonight in a region called La Cloche, a place taking its name from a wondrous rock which rings hollowly like a bass church bell when struck smartly. At evening we passed cautiously through a narrow gut of river where, I am told, renegade savages sometimes leap upon small companies and slaughter them. But we ran through without impediment, although I looked to the priming of my pistol, taking small comfort from Elborn's presence on my left. The rocks were clean of Indians, however, and shone pink and white in a low sun.

We are now in Lake Huron, not far from St. Joseph's Island, and little more than three days' travel to Sault Ste. Maries. I have for some days past been feverish and troubled by severe headaches, an affliction common in these parts and due to the noxious effluence from Indian encampments on the river. I am told that the usual reason for their moving is that the land has become so sotted with their filth that they cannot live upon it, for they are in the habit of letting their droppings fall where they might.

So I have made my first contact with the savages, and much merriment has been made at Gustave's comment on my dysentery

    that if I allow the savages to make me such generous gifts while expecting nothing in return, then I shall be no small success as a trader in the *pays d'en haut*.''

Liv Henry, gazing into the fire and thinking about her son, was only half aware that Paul had stopped reading and was burning the yellowed pages. A chill had settled. Nearby the loons cried. She shivered. ''When he was small,'' she said, ''we read a lot of Indian legends. They enthralled him. He was drawn by the very qualities that made them seem dull to me — the shallow characters, and the stock repetitions, and the rather bloodless monsters. The disinfected atmospheres and plots didn't bother him at all, because it was just raw material to him. He devoured it. He liked the wendigo especially, because it was so plastic and became whatever the story teller wanted it to become. He drew endless pictures of it.''

''I don't remember them.''

''You were away, I guess. Probably he destroyed them a day or two later. He would do that, you know. He would make marvellous creatures with his watercolours and he had a way of letting the colours blend so that the monsters were never distinct from their backgrounds, or their characteristics distinct from each other; and yet they were vivid and gorgeous shimmering things. Then suddenly, for no reason, he would destroy them. I always knew when it was about to happen. I would see him regarding one of those pictures solemnly, his arms across his chest and his head cocked, like this, and then he would crumple it up and begin another. It didn't seem enough for him just to forget. It was as if he were cleaning up. The wendigo was his great favourite. It had a thousand shapes.''

Paul said, ''I never saw him do that.''

She sat silent.

He said, ''Why did I never see him do that? Such an important thing?''

After a moment, when it was clear that he wanted an answer, she shrugged. ''There were so many other things,'' she said. ''There wasn't time,'' she said. ''How is one to know,'' she asked, feeling after the moment's groping that this was the right response. ''How is one to know what is important, except in retrospect?'' She rose, stretched, bundled her coat against the cold. She turned to face the night, and when her eyes had adjusted to the darkness, she saw the borealis glint like a folded veil. ''Some people said the northern lights were the souls of departed warriors dancing. But when Michael saw them he said they looked like a berserk TV. Do you remember that about him? The way he had of diminishing things of great beauty?''

''He deflated adoration,'' Paul said. ''He thought it useless.''

''Yes. That was it. He told me once that he thought we should look down more and up less. He must have been about eight. He spent half his time on his hands and knees, searching for whatever was to be found. He said he felt comfortable that way, when he couldn't look up at the sky. He said he thought light was something to see by, and not look at. He would say these things casually, in his child's voice, mixed in with the usual comments and requests. Why do I remember them, especially? But I do.

"Once I asked the doctor about the business of running around on all fours, and he laughed and told me not to worry unless a tail began to grow. He said it was probably healthier for Mike than marching with his shoulders back and his spine straight so that all his little discs gradually got squashed down to nothing. In fact, I got a lecture on schools and their medical undesirability. In the doctor's opinion they were all still winning the Scopes monkey trial, and they would crush anything which suggested the animal nature of man. He said he couldn't prevent my sending the boy to school, and that once there he couldn't prevent his being made to pretend that he was a figure in Pythagorean geometry instead of a man, but that he *could* tell me to leave the boy alone when he was at home, and if he wanted to walk around, relaxed, on all fours, to let him. Do you remember that?"

Laughing, Paul nodded. "Fortunately," he said, "it didn't last long."

"Oh no. Of course he grew out of it, like the measles or whooping cough, and I suppose that at the end he was as brave and stiff-backed as anyone else." When she turned back to the fire her eyes were wet. "Oh Paul, I know regrets are useless but I have them all the same. And I wish we had never sent him. I wish we had kept him home with us. Right from the very first, from the first day of kindergarten, I wish we had said no to them, and kept him. Why ..." She covered her face and turned back towards the night. "I'm sorry. It's the little things that do this to me, that make me good for nothing.

It's the little things I remember.''

chapter eleven

The summer he began work at the mill Paul Henry was seventeen and going into his last year of high school. He ran a machine that stripped the bark from logs, and it was his job to keep the drums turning properly, and to keep the water flowing. Each day his machine barked scores of logs, and his days were full of its throbbing and of the smell of torn spruce.

Every morning at seven thirty he coasted down through Sable Creek on his bicycle, and out to where the new mill lay at the edge of town. Many of the men rode bicycles, and the Company provided bleached green racks that held the front wheels upright. Often he met Gerry Rattray there, or Miro, and they would go in to work together, already looking forward to the lunch break when they could come out again and walk beside the lake.

At five, sweaty and tired, Paul would pump home through the back streets of the town, hunched over the dropped bars of his bike. While he showered, his mother would make supper and they would eat together in the vast, dark dining room, Paul at the head of the table and his mother beside him.

"Mansfield offered me a job," he said one night. "After university."

She sipped her tea, looking away from him. "He must like your work," she said.

"I had an idea that would save him money. He liked *that*. But I think he really did it for my father — and my grandfather."

"Don't be silly. Bob Mansfield knows character and ability when he sees it. He wants *you*, my dear."

He shrugged and ran a hand over his brushcut. "Maybe.

They're expanding, he said. If business keeps growing they'll be opening a Toronto office soon. He said they need good men. He said that if I'm interested I should study commerce and finance at university." He glanced at her, and away.

"Oh. I see. And did you tell him that you planned to study humanities?"

"Yes."

"And?"

"He laughed. He said that was fine — for a hobby, but that a man should keep his work and hobbies separate."

"Your father used to say that too."

"Well," he stood up, "I'll have to think about it. It's a pretty good offer, I guess."

"And Bob Mansfield is nice, isn't he. He's such a kind man."

Paul grinned. "Around the mill," he said, "there are different ideas about that."

"Workers are never satisfied. The unions stir them up, you know. Bob has always been a gentleman to me, and he was very kind after your father died. Very considerate." She sighed. "Of course, I know that he's interested in profits. And he didn't go with your father and the others .... He made a lot of money during the war."

"That doesn't matter now, Mother. That's just history now."

"I suppose you're right," she said. "I suppose we should try to forget those things."

Sometimes in the evenings he took his mother's car; sometimes he went with Gerry. In New Town there were always girls who would go to the movies or to a restaurant with them, and afterwards to the hills that looked down over Sable Creek and the lake. But none really interested him; he could never content himself with their bodies only.

Gerry had no such problems. "What the hell's the matter with you?" he would shout, driving up in the empty streets. His fist would pound the seat between them. "She was *ready*, for crissake. A beautiful, lovely girl all ready for you, and what the hell do you do? *Kiss her goodnight*! Jesus Christ, that's not even *polite*!''

''Too ready.''

''Oh too ready my ass! What the hell do you want?''

''More than that.''

''Listen, don't be too choosy. Okay, so maybe she didn't have the greatest personality in the world, and maybe she was no Jane Russell, but you don't look at the mantle when you're poking the fireplace, for crissake!''

''Knock it off, Gerry.''

''Yeah. Okay. All right. Goddam monk! Listen, tell me you're keeping it for your wife. Go ahead and tell me.''

''I'm keeping it for my wife.''

''Attaboy. You'll die a virgin. Snow white.''

Usually his mother would be awake, reading, and would call from her bedroom as he passed.

''Great,'' he would answer. ''Thanks. A really good evening.'' He would stand at his darkened window and stare out over the lights of the town, and the mocking echo which rose to him at those times would be not only Gerry's voice, not only the screaming of the machine with which he spent his days, but the deep and resonant emptiness that had been his summer.

One evening in mid-August he was bicycling home later and slower than usual. He went very carefully, keeping a sedate distance from the curb. For the first time in his life he was a little drunk. Until then he had declined invitations to go to the hotel with the others after work, but that day had been one of the hottest of the summer. It was a Friday, his mother was away, and he had just been paid. Hell, he thought when they asked him, why not? He went, and in an hour he had drunk three beers in the dingy parlour with the MEN'S ENTRANCE sign above its door. There was a lazy fan turning near the ceiling, and pickled eggs in a bowl on the table. ''You twenty-one?''

the waiter had asked, and he had said he was, sure. It was his birthday, he said, and the waiter had shrugged and served him.

He felt nauseous and dirty, and his first impulse when he saw Narah Hale on the sidewalk was to turn up a side street and go home another way. She was walking away from him carrying a bag of groceries, her long hair moving across the back left bare by her summer dress. Smoothly she passed through the shadows of the trees, and her woman's calves and the arch of her back suddenly made the girls he had been dating uncertain and pallid creatures. He did not turn off; he overtook her and scuffed his foot on the curb beside her. "Mrs. Hale."

"Hello, Paul." She smiled. She turned towards him and shifted the bag of groceries across her breast. "How are you?"

"Good. You?"

"I'm fine."

"Fred?"

She shrugged. "He's all right, I guess. I don't know, really. He's away at summer school." She came close across the grass of the boulevard, and he knew she could tell he was drunk. "You're working at the mill, I hear."

He nodded.

"Do you like it?"

"Sure. I mean, well, it's a job, you know." He forced himself to meet her eyes and saw that she was laughing, not at him alone, but at them both, as if they were trapped in the same joke. "I mean, I wouldn't like to spend my life at it," he said.

"But I hear you might. I hear Bob Mansfield offered you a job."

"You know that?"

"It's a small town."

"But I haven't told any ..."

"A small, small town," she said, laughing. "Are you going to join the Company, Paul? Hm?"

"I don't know. I haven't decided."

She came closer. He watched the pulsing of the birthmark on her throat. "Don't decide when you're drunk," she said.

"I'm not really drunk."

"Just a bit."

He nodded.

"Shall I tell you the best thing to do, Paul?"

"Yes."

"The best thing is to go home and sleep for a while."

"Yes."

"And then, later on, come and see me."

He stared.

"Wouldn't you like to?"

"Yes."

"But you need a pretext. Oh dear," she sighed, "pretexts are such a waste, but never mind. Let's see ... Well, I have something of yours, will that do?"

"What?"

"A pistol. A piece of iron, really. You gave it to Fred, remember? He's finished with it now, and if you'd like to I think you should come and get it. All right?"

"What time?"

"When you're ready," she said. She turned away, crossed the boulevard, and continued up the sidewalk. She looked back once, and when she did, what began as a wave to him went past him, out towards the street; for at that moment Bob Mansfield had passed slowly, sunk deep in his black Buick. The teeth of the car's grill leered beyond its bumper.

He did not sleep. He bathed and ate, and by the time he finished he was sober. He rode down to Fred's house through a warm night full of traffic sounds and cicadas. He was trembling.

"Let's walk," she said.

They did. The house was on the outskirts and they had soon left the town behind and entered the region of meadows and pine thickets which spread eastward overlooking the lake. She took his arm. Her breast lay soft and heavy against it.

"Will you make love to me?"

He nodded.

"Right here," she said. "Now."

They were under pines, near the edge of the bluff. In a moment she had removed her skirt and sweater and spread them on the cushion of needles and lain down on them. She reached for him, one knee lifted. She was wet; her mouth enclosed his and her arms encircled him and drew him into her, and his desire burst at the first touch of her. "I'm sorry," he said, his eyes tight shut and his mouth rocking against her throat. "I'm sorry, I'm sorry . . ."

"Shh," she said. "Oh no." And what he thought had finished too soon only began with her fingers on her lips, and with her mouth circling on his lips, matching the slow rotation of her hips, and with the laugh of pleasure in her throat which continued indifferent to his apology. And his surprise at finding that she would take her own time absolutely, for both of them, for as long as necessary, that surprise kept him erect, and soon her laughter became more rhythmic, and then a continuous moan, and then at last a long soft cry in which he joined.

He watched her eyes. They never closed entirely.

When he stood up he looked back over the lights of the town. Hamburgs were being cooked there, and pinball machines thudded under fly-blown neons, and girls in pink underwear drank rye in back seats. He laughed. "It's so easy."

"Too easy?"

"No," he said. "Right, that's all."

She put on her skirt but her sweater she left off, and it trailed through the weeds as she walked. "Let's go down this way. Along the bluffs." Below, the lake gleamed under a new moon. "I think it was a coincidence," she said. "Our meeting today."

"Why?"

"Because I've been thinking about you. I've thought that I might even call you."

"But why?"

"Because I have a weakness for young men going wrong. Losing themselves."

"And that's what's happening to me."

"Um hum."

"Look, Mrs. Hale . . . Narah, all right, when I met you today I was a bit drunk. I got paid and I had three beers. Hardly the high road to hell."

Her lips pursed. She shrugged. "No. I don't mean that, you know."

He waited, watching her pull the sweater on and free her hair, but she said nothing more. "What then?" Anger touched him. "Men, you said. Plural. So you make a habit of doing this."

"No."

"But there *have* been others."

"Yes."

"Well then, okay, maybe you're not the lady who should talk about other people going wrong." He had wanted to hurt her, but there was no sign in her face that he had done so.

"Please," she said, "don't be moral in small ways. It's worse than nothing. Isn't it enough to be content with moments? To expand them? Hm?" She kissed him. "Come, let's go farther." And as they walked she said, "Would you go away with me, Paul?"

"Away?"

"Yes. Oh, I don't mean for good. That would be a great mistake, wouldn't it. No, just for a few days. Could we take a canoe, do you think?"

"I'd like that."

"Let's do it then."

"Fred?"

"He has another week of summer school. And exams."

"And my mother will be in Vancouver until September."

"Settled then."

"Hey, wait a minute. I also have a job, you know."

"Oh, that." She wrinkled her nose. "Just quit it. Tell Bob Mansfield you need a holiday before school. Tell him you need time to think about his offer. She gathered the seeds from a small dried weed pod and scattered them in a broad arc. "Tell him anything. Believe me, it's very easy to say no to Bob Mansfield. I do it almost once a week."

"Sure," Bob Mansfield said, shouting above the tumult of the mill. "Draw your pay Friday." He sat with his fingers drumming the walnut desk which he kept absolutely clean. He was a short man, but less stocky than the peculiar squatness of his neck suggested. He was only forty, but already his close-cropped sandy hair was greying at the temples. Smiling, he watched Paul closely. "Going far?"

"No, just a little trip." He waved toward the country to the northwest. "Back a ways."

"Uh huh. Be anywhere near the river mill?"

"Probably not. We intend to stay away from people pretty much." Paul dug his thumbnail hard into his palm.

"I see." Bob Mansfield's smile was humorless, like something he had fitted his mouth around. "Going with anyone I know?"

"Oh, a friend."

"Uh huh. Well," the fingers ceased their tapping and the hands, clamping the desk edge, beat out a flat tattoo-shave-and-a-haircut-two-bits. "That's fine, then. Fine. Matter of fact, why don't you pick up your pay Thursday night. Take Friday off."

"Thanks, Mr. Mansfield."

"And have a good trip. Thought about my offer, by the way?"

"A little."

"Well, you've got time, haven't you. All the time in the world. Remember this, though," for an instant the smile shifted, hardened, became even more a mere showing of teeth, "I want a businessman and not a bloody poet!"

"I'll keep that in mind," Paul said.

chapter twelve

For many days they had seen no other people nor sign of other
people, except for the deserted highway and its white posts where
it swept close to the shore. Now, here was the town. She would
have preferred to have passed it, as they had passed others lying
stunned and silent, like flotsam on the shore.

"Are you afraid?" Under the brim of the old army cap his
eyes searched the recesses of the town and found them empty;
he moved his head to the breeze, listening, but there was no
sound except the water.

"Yes," she said.

"Don't be. It's already dead, you know. Dead and beginning
to crumble."

"But with people."

"Yes. Maybe some." He picked up his paddle and trailed
it, ready to turn either in towards the town or out towards the
dropping sun and the headland far across the bay. "Well?"

"All right," she said. "One last time. In case there's someone
to say goodbye to."

She began to paddle, and he matched his stroke to hers, guiding
them close to the shore and around the first of the log booms
which floated like giant lily pads in the bay. Already one had
broken in the swell, and spilled its contents in a brown hem-
morhage.

No one greeted them.

Nothing moved in Sable Creek except smoke, trembling in
a haze above the town.

They tied the canoe in the shelter of booms and pilings, and
found their way into the mill up one of the ramps. Except for
the moaning of the wind under the eaves and for their own foot-
falls, it was utterly silent. Hulking machines frowned as if maddened by the inactivity. Their bared thighs and sinews gleamed
in readiness, and the switches which had once activated them
held a crisp, clench-fist salute in ranks along the walls. A nest

of cables sprouted from the head of each and twined lasciviously into the upper shadows. But all was halted, hushed, the monstrous revels frozen. Gross teeth, upraised paws, curled fins, tissues of web and meshing, winding ligaments, all the stark and skinless shapes of a diseased imagining hung listening in the grey light, listening, as if that moment they had caught a rusty laughter fading with the dying surge of life, as if that moment the lights had flickered off, the dynamos hummed down, the first damp stains of their mortality darkened an inner wall.

"Shh. Listen . . ." She touched his arm, for the cadence of their footsteps had been joined by another sound, at first distant and faltering but soon distinct, a spidery voice singing, spinning its careful way among the echoes.

"I love you tru-u-u-ly,
Tru-u-u-ly dear . . ."

And the singer himself materialized fleetingly among the tricks of light and distance like a shadow thrown by a billowing curtain, at first like a flickering mirage of the polished floor; and then, as he emerged definitely from the recesses and into the corridor, clearly a small and intent old man, a cripple, flinging a stiff leg with each slow pace. At his waist they saw a grotesque swelling, a tumour which seemed at first to be enclosed by the grey shirt and trousers, but which, as he approached, took the shape of a timeclock of the sort carried by watchmen on their rounds.

"What?" he said, "what?" stopping and then coming on faster, gesticulating like an angered crab. "What're yuh *doin* here? Hey? Hey?"

"Hi, Andy."

"Hey? Who's that?"

"Paul Henry."

"Henry? Henry? You're dead aintcha? You was killed in France."

"My father was."

"Oh, *young* Paul! The boy." He came to them, an old pensioner in his Legion beret. Besides his stiff leg he bore the deep scar of a wound above his eye. His smile was conciliatory yet defensive, watchful, and he carried his head crouched upon his shoulders and chest as if he would be sure never again to raise it above the lip of any turret. "Just lookin around, are yuh? Eh? Just showin the little lady something of the old spot?"

"That's right, Andy. We're just passing through."

"Well Miss, it's not like it was, right now. I can tell yuh that! You have to imagine it like it was. But you come back. You come back, and next time you'll see her workin at full speed. You'll see those logs comin down again and that white paper rollin out the other end. White as you please, and miles of it! Yessir!" He grinned confidentially. He tapped Paul's arm. "They say we're shut down, now. Say there ain't no more call for paper. Now I'll tell yuh, that ain't true. You know why? Because I see em! I see em workin just like always, and most times this place is goin just like it always was! Ah, you hit a bad time, that's all. Just a bad time ..."

They walked with him through the mill. Whatever phantasies assaulted him in the recesses of the place, whatever cronies laughed again amid the dragon teeth, to the clock he was devoted. It was his duty to insert keys located at points throughout the building, and to turn them at appointed times, thus registering on the passing tape inside the clock that he had not slept and dreamed his watch away, but had met his obligations. And to this task he was faithful. Near the door, they watched him insert the dangling key and wait to turn it until the very second dictated by years of habits that meshed like blue glaciers in his mind. Then, holding his breath, he turned it, exhaled completely after the prompt clockwork registration deep in the leather case, and said like a smiling addict satisfied, "Perfect record! That's what I've got. A perfect record!"

Because no cars moved in Sable Creek it seemed at first deserted, as if the lawful inhabitants had fled a diseased encampment. But as they neared the center of town they began to glimpse automobiles parked and drowsing — here and there behind half-closed garage doors, fringing a curb in the silent shopping centre, abandoned beside expired meters. At every station the makeshift signs announced "No Gas," and at a few the ancient handpumps resurrected to draw the last gasoline from underground tanks now lay dry and discarded.

Fires burned in New Town. Most were small, set in backyard barbecues or in firepits ringed with stones, and they were tended by squatting men who rose and stared suspiciously. Meat hung on spits, and sometimes they saw what appeared to be the corpses of small birds. Furtive children lurked among the bushes; once, they saw a band of several dart in eerie silence along the street ahead and vanish through a broken storefront.

Paul stopped and spoke to a man he recognized. The man looked grubby and trapped. "We're not leaving, and that's all there is to it," he said. "It's the same all over, isn't it? Worse, farther south. You're crazy to go! All those people are crazy to go, but they've been pulling out every day, God knows where." He waved an arm at the ranks of dead windows down his street. Asters and marigolds shone in the long grass. "And besides, this is my place, isn't it? I've worked hard here, haven't I? Built a good place? It's almost paid for. Another ten years and it'll be paid for." His eyes narrowed shrewdly. "And who's goin to collect mortgage payments, eh? Tell me that. Won't they have to just tear up those records when this is over?"

"Where's your wife?" Paul asked.

"Aw, she's out somewhere. The women are talking about some plan to get together, to pool everything and work together. But I don't see it. Um *mmm*! Listen, see that garden down there at the end of the lot? That's mine! This lot is mine! Why, I can grow all the food I need right here. I gotta fireplace in the house. Enough wood to last two years. We have to pull the water from the creek, but what the hell, one thing we learned real quick was that we could get along on damn little water. No sir, the way I see it, we sit tight and see this thing through.

We stay where we belong. We keep what we got!''

"How about the kids?''

The man scoffed. "Never see them, unless by accident. They're gone night and day. Back in the hills, mostly. Ah, they stayed around for a while, but then they just sort of drifted off with the others. And just when I needed them. Isn't that the way? Huh? Always? Somebody's gotta hunt. Somebody's gotta fish, and pull water, and dig that garden. Somebody's gotta keep this family together. Do they think I can do it all?''

"It looks to me," said Paul, "as if they don't give a damn for your family.''

"Yeah ..." The man spat. "Yeah, that's the way it looks to me too. Well, the hell with them! If that's the way they want it, every man for himself, then I can sure as hell look after *me*!''

"What will you do when you run out of shotgun shells?''

The man laughed with a kindly derisiveness, as at an outsmarted competitor. "You moving on?" he asked, watching narrowly.

"Yes.''

"Then I'll tell you something. Listen, do you think we couldn't see this coming? *I* saw it coming! And I got me a little stock of things all ready and all stashed away in a spot nobody knows about, not even Margaret. One of the things I got is a lot of cans, a whole lot of cans with chickens and hams and beef stew inside, enough to last a *long* time. And another thing I got is *shot* ... *gun* ... *shells*. Three gross." He held up fingers. "Three. What do you think of that? Eh?''

"What will you shoot with them all?''

"Oh come *on*! Game! Game! Whatever's around. And that number of shells'll put a lotta meat over this fire, let me tell you! Now wouldn't you say they were pretty dumb kids, not to trust their old man better?''

They shrugged and began to move on, but he called after them down the street, "Wouldn't you say they were *stupid*, those kids? Eh? Wouldn't you say that?''

Between the towns they saw more bands of children. They seemed compact and earnest, more watchful than threatening, passing with the grace of a single body through tall brown grass. They moved under signs that said, "5000′ THIS VALUABLE COMMERCIAL PROPERTY FOR SALE", and "ANOTHER ESSO STATION", and "DUMP CLEAN FILL HERE". Some of them were eating and laughing, and they waved brown arms as they passed, calling unintelligible greetings in the distance.

Most of the shops in Old Town were carefully boarded, as if their owners intended to return. But in some cases there were no delusions. Gillespie's Drugstore had been left with its shelves full and its doors open, as had most of the smaller groceterias. Tacked on the open door of Saul Levinson's Men's and Children's Clothes, a typewritten note said, "God helps those who help themselves!"

They walked in the middle of the street. The town hall was closed and locked, and no one had broken in. The police station was locked, and no one had broken in.

The library was open. A sign on the door said, "WELCOME. HOURS: 10 a.m. to 10 p.m."

Inside, alone, Rose Stacey read by the slanting grey light of the afternoon. She was a trim woman in her seventies, and she was enjoying what she read, for as they approached they heard her laughing. Her desk was clear, except for the book, and a stamp pad, and an old-fashioned librarian's pencil with the rubber date attached, ready to do business. She peered over her glasses as they entered. "Good afternoon," she said.

"Hello, Rose."

"Paul!" She stood up and took his shoulders in her old veined hands. "Paul." Her voice was thin but tough, like a good leather binding.

He held her waist. "This is my wife," he said. "Liv."

"How do you do."

"He's told me a lot about you."

"About his *grandfather* and me, I hope," Rose Stacey said.

Liv nodded.

"Yes, that was the important thing." For a moment, despite her smile, her brow furrowed. "Well! We must have some tea. Do you know, you're the first people to come in here for days? And the last was a skulking no-good wanting fuel! Imagine! He wanted to take my books and cook his rabbits!"

Paul laughed. "What ones did you give him, Rose? Let me guess."

"Oh yes," she said. "I know. There was a time when I would gladly have burned some of them. But not now. Not today. There isn't a single word in this building to be burned while I live! Not a syllable! And I told him so. I drove him out with my umbrella! But sit down. Sit down and I'll heat the kettle. I have a little stove, with *gas*. I don't use it often, but this is a special occasion, and I might as well use it up before it's stolen, or seeps away. Sit down.

"Yes," she said later, when she had poured the tea and spread wafers on a plate, "That was the important thing, you know. To have been loved by a man like that." She tilted her china cup so that the light filled it, dropping through the tall, leaded windows behind her. Thin cords looped down from the ventilators.

"You've never told me how you met him," Paul said.

"Why, I met him here. Right at this desk, in June, 1922. It was a very hot day. He came in very gruff and dark, and he leaned his fists on my desk, leaving smudges of sweat, and he said, like this, 'Miss, I must have books on proper excavation. Archaeological excavation.' I remember the silver in his black hair and moustache.

"I was new, you understand. I was frightened about losing my poor scraps of authority. I pointed to the card index and to the sign that said SILENCE, and I tried to look at his wet hands on my desk as if they were something left by a nasty dog. I was also very angry. Trembling. I wanted to shrink him. But he brushed all that away. He said, 'Hell, woman, I don't have time for nonsense. *You* get them!' And I did. I told myself it was to avoid a scene, but I was afraid, too. Oh yes, I was very much afraid, not only of losing my job, but of *him*, and of the way it seemed he *would be* obeyed. I mistook that for mere brutishness.

"When he had gone I whispered to the other girl, 'Who is that *thug*?' And she said that he was Mr. Henry, manager at the mill, and that last year he had given the library a thousand dollars for books, and that this was the first time he had ever come in the door!''

"Why did he want archaeological texts?''

"He had found something. The books came back next day, of course. They were quite useless to him. He didn't return them himself, but sent your father to do it. We had no technical books on archaeology, but we did have the first volume of Arthur Evans's *The Palace of Minos,* and Flinders Petrie's *Ten Years' Digging in Egypt,* and Joyce's *Mexican Archaeology.* I had given him all of these, as well as something called *Excavating for Your House,* which I had thrown in out of pure spite.

"Well, your *father* returned these. He couldn't have been more than ten or eleven. He stood back, obviously with something to tell me, but waiting for me to speak first. I stamped the books in, and while I was doing that I asked him if they had been helpful to his father. He said that they hadn't, but that he had told him to tell me that when he found a pyramid in the bush he'd borrow them again.

"I asked him to take a note to his father, and I wrote: 'Dear Mr. Henry: I am sorry to learn that we did not provide you with the information you required. If you would take the trouble to give me more complete particulars, I shall try to acquire the books you need.'

"That was a Thursday evening. Friday noon he came himself. A man from the mill drove him in an open buggy. It had yellow wheels. He wore a grey suit and hat, and he came up the steps two at a time, and when he talked to me he tapped the hat brim against his knee. He said, 'Well, Miss Stacey. So you'll order the books for me?'

"I said yes, I would. He seemed amused. He asked me how I would know what books to order. I began to tell him that he would have to describe exactly what kind of excavation he intended to do, but he cut me off. He asked if I could paddle a canoe. I said I could. I was blushing. He was so inexorable. Everyone in the library was listening, pretending to read.

" 'Well then,' he said, 'I'll do better than tell you. I'll show you. Will you come with me?'

"He said it like a challenge, and I answered in the same tone, as defiantly as I could. Yes, I said, of course I would go!

" 'Tonight at five-thirty, then,' he said. 'It will take the weekend.'

" 'Tonight,' I told him. 'Five-thirty!' "

Rose Stacey laughed. She took off her glasses and pressed a hankie to her wrinkled eyes. "Oh," she said, "if I were nineteen again I would do exactly that." Her brow wrinkled in determination. "I would stand behind this desk, angry, and frightened, and proud, and I would say yes to Michael Henry. Yes. Yes, I would say. Five-thirty.

"I remember exactly where we went. I can see the route as on a map. But I promised him then that I would tell no one, and I never shall. I hadn't seen the country, except in sepia post cards, and a bit from the train window, coming north along Superior. It had frightened me then, and fascinated me. It seemed so full of menace. But he was at home there. He liked to pass close to shore. He taught me to paddle quietly, and in the shade we saw such life as I never knew existed. He knew the name of everything. Even when we walked the portages he noticed things from under the canoe that I had missed, and he would stop and show me, pointing with his foot.

"On Saturday morning we came to a lake that was larger than the others we had crossed, although the portage into it was overgrown and little used. In the distance a promontory thrust out into the lake, down to the west. Reaching it was a two-hour paddle. As we approached I realized that the entire shore was a beach, a magnificent beach, shaded by the pine groves behind it.

"When we had landed he took my hand and we walked up among the trees and back into the deeper forest. The mosquitoes were furious, but he turned up the collar of his jacket and paid them no further attention. We came to a kind of clearing — not exactly a clearing, but only a place where the trees were different somehow — more open, smaller, all yellow and orange. And here he pointed through the underbrush and traced the outline of a building which lay covered in moss.

"It was bigger than the trapper's cabin we had passed that morning, but it was impossible to tell exactly how large it had been, for the walls had tumbled down in all directions. He told me that he wouldn't know what it was until he began to dig, and that he wouldn't dig until he knew how to do so properly. And that was why I must get him the right books. But he said it wasn't a trapper's cabin. He knew that for certain. For one thing, it was too large. He drew me to the corner of the building, dropped to his knees and lifted the moss to reveal part of the actual structure. It was much decayed, but I could see clearly that the corner had been made by slotting an upright log on two sides, at right angles, and then dropping into those grooves the tongues of the horizontal logs. He said that no trapper would have taken the time to do that.

"I asked him why, if he thought it might be important, he didn't write to the museum. He laughed and said museums were tombs. I told him that I thought museums kept history alive, and culture, and curiosity. But he shook his head. 'They keep alive the terror of dying and decay,' he said.

"If that was the case, I asked him what he intended to do with any objects he found there, and he said he didn't know, but that he certainly didn't want it all exposed again, measured, dated, catalogued, bathed, mounted with neat labels in glass cases saying look! Look! We didn't really die at all! Look how we live on, safe from nature!

" 'But *you're* the one who would open it up,' I said. 'You're the one who already sees those things restored in their clean cases. And the cases are in your mind!' I had said it without thinking. He looked at me as if I were a saboteur. 'Yes,' he said. 'That's true. You're right. What should be done, then?'

" 'Leave it alone,' I said. 'Just let it be.' "

"And that," Rose Stacey said, "is what he did."

"He never dug there?"

She shook her head. "Oh, we went back sometimes, but he never disturbed the moss. He was content with his restraint. Does that surprise you? When I knew him better I saw that the busy man of action was just a mask he wore, a camouflage, although in that role he was certainly efficient, and he made the mill roll out more paper than it had ever produced before. But that seemed something he did because he was trapped, somehow, and had to protect himself. Do you know, this may be silly, but I think that if he had had the time he would have preferred to go among the trees as we did that first time, and been satisfied to *imagine* their being cut, and barked, and pulverized, and ground to paper. I think he might have seen that process as just one of a myriad possibilities."

The old woman gazed into her cup. From outside came a sound of running, and of a stick ringing on aluminum lamp posts, fading down the empty street. It was growing dark.

"We must go, Rose."

"Yes, I know you must."

"And what will happen to you? What will you do?"

"Do? Why, I shall just stay, of course. What else would I do? I shall stay, and read, and keep my books together, and drive out vandals for a while longer. Oh, I know that old people grow afraid sometimes, just when it seems they have so little to lose. But I'm not afraid at all. I shall go on giving books to anyone who asks."

Liv took her hand. "Good-bye," she said.

"Good-bye, my dear. I can't ask you to come back. But I envy you. How good to be in love, and to be going on. It is all that you could wish."

They pushed away from the pilings.

Although the sun had set, the evening was still clear and red-hued, and it seemed that they could paddle for at least an hour before the light died.

Behind them, the town lay in the shadow of hills, covered in light smoke, ash-grey like the campfire of a hiding monster, or the char of a failed experiment. Small dark figures sprang, and danced, and gestured along the piers and platforms of the mill as if seized by a sudden, desperate need to summon them back, now that they had gone. Their cries, sharp but inchoate, grew ever less distinct until they fluttered out like broken mayflies on the lake.

June 7, 1785: At Sault Ste. Maries we met with our brigade and changed canoes, and for four days since we have passed in low and uncertain weather, frequently swept by showers which drain like trailing ghosts upon the forest. Today we have had only fog for our companion. Far into the morning each canoe carried its pitch torch, and it was unsettling beyond my expectation to be suspended in that shroud, and to peer through an oily smoke, and to hear the phantom voices call their signals. Often I was overcome by so severe a vertigo that I was certain we remained fixed like the revellers of the Beaver Club in their inebriate and stationary voyages, and at those moments I grasped the canoe's edge and looked close into the water for the paddle bites swirling their vortices towards the stern. Once when I had done so I turned back into the canoe to find Elborn regarding me across his book. "Oh yes," he said, nodding in his sprightly way, "yes, we are progressing, MacKay. We are progressing as fast as you would wish. You need have no fear."

I replied that fear I had none, but that my dysentery had left me feverish still, with some slight dizziness. For the most part he has stayed aloof, and we have passed these days in silence.

Fog has subdued the men, and frequently they glance about them as if monstrous beings lurked unseen near at hand; but they are glad enough of the calm, through which we have passed unhampered.

This afternoon the fog rose, blown off by the quickening west wind, which increased the turbulence of the lake, and its passage left us amidst swells twelve feet in height, exposed in the mouth of a great bay. The canoes were quickly scattered, the most fortunate holding farthest upwind close to a patch of islands which promised a fair harbour and protection from the storm. Towards them our steersman turned us, and our fellows laboured hard before the full fury of the storm should fall upon us. The suddenness of the change dismayed me, for one moment we were proceeding in the fog to which we had almost grown accustomed, and the next we pitched in a wild sea, the bowmen's paddles flailing the air above me before we plunged headlong down in such a rush I feared we must be torn to pieces by our momentum and the tumbling weight of water. Indeed, before we found shelter among the islands one of our seams had opened sufficiently to set Elborn and I bailing with kettles, our haunches awash and cold as ice.

On shore our men unloaded, agile as monkeys, and took up our canoe upon the beach. Others had arrived before us and were similarly engaged, while others were still far down in the open water and naked to the storm. Out half a league, a single canoe lay broadside to the wind and in distress. I found my glass where it had been placed with the rest of my belongings, and followed the others up onto a height of rock which gave a clear view of its plight. Elborn smiled and filled his pipe. "My dear MacKay," he whispered as I focussed my glass, "let us remember that there is nothing to be gained from the loss of one's composure."

A great rent had opened in the canoe's flank and grew larger with every wave. Each time it rose the craft was laid further open to the thrust of the water. As I watched, the storm increased in fury and surged upon them, and in the crumpling of their craft the men were thrown one by one into the water, some clinging to the remnants of the canoe, some seizing upon bales of goods, some vanishing at once in the tortured water. Soon only one remained. He had contrived to brace himself high on the stern of the craft, and from this vantage point he had endeavoured to save those of his companions who had grasped the gunwales, only to see them torn away one by one, and parts of the canoe with them. When the last had gone he rose erect in what had become a mere sinking piece of flotsam, raised both his fists and head to the howling sky, and suspended in that attitude, sank from sight. Who he had been I knew well from his contorted posture, for in all our brigade there had been no *gouvernail* more like a frog in shape than was Gustave, and at the moment of his death I recalled well his approaching me where I had stood sober beside the fire, and his urging me to join them, for the sake of love, and life.

I watched the woeful drama out. Packets sank beneath their human cargoes, or the grip of those who clung to them was loosened by the cold and the packets drifted free. At no small peril to themselves, for the turmoil of the storm had again increased, two canoes fell back and searched among the wreckage, but survivors there were none. "As easily us as them," said Elborn as I lowered my glass. "A hazard of the course, so to speak, and I daresay the Company will make some recompense to the families concerned."

Little was said when all had landed. Without ceremony the canoes were emptied and overturned, and kettles of pitch hung above the fire. Those who have had experience of this lake say we shall remain in this place at least three days, for although the wind might abate, the swell will continue hazardous long after. Of the drowned men, beyond the prayers and crossings, and a depressed atmosphere among all excepting Elborn, no further acknowledgement has been made.

June 11, 1785: The wind has continued ferocious these three days, to the point of riving ancient pines whose warped postures, twisted trunks, and great roots clenched like serpentine fingers in the rock crevasses testified to their endurance. Spray from windward sifted incessantly through the foliage and, together with the driving rain, has added much to our discomfort. The men idle away their time in cards and dice beneath their oil cloths; Elborn hovers at the edges of their groups, ever ready to ingratiate himself among them. As for myself, when the rain abated somewhat I commenced an exploration of this island, which took me less than an hour. Small though it might be, yet it is the largest of its group, the others mere rocks sparsely covered, close to the northwest.

For a time, exposed and exhilarated by the spray, I watched these smaller islands and the churning of the lake upon them. With some surprise I saw that other travellers had taken refuge here, for on the nearest, a few rods distant, the slim flanks of Indian canoes gleamed dully, overturned on a beach which was a small replica of our own, and scarcely distinguishable from the rocks near which they lay. I used my glass to search the island, but could discern no sign of human life, and I concluded therefore that the savages were hunkering in their tents among the boulders, waiting for the storm to pass. This first viewing aroused my curiosity, for there was a tautness and precision in the alignment of those canoes which I had not seen hitherto among the savages; I have found them for the most part content to leave their canoes like their persons, all unkempt and disarrayed.

During this afternoon the wind abated, and by evening it had dropped almost entirely. The lake calmed to a degree, and the black clouds lifted and broke slowly into wads of copper bunting, giving the promise of a fair sunset, a still night, and a calm surface for our journey on the morrow.

I had finished my evening meal, and had drawn from my supplies some mild tea, of which I had had the foresight to bring a small quantity, for I could not stomach the raw and noxious stuff which passes for tea among these people, when I heard above the breaking of the waves and above the talk and rollicking of the men, a sound such as I had never heard, except in my darkest dreams. Like the moan of an animal it started low, undistinguished from the water coughing along the shores, and I could not have foretold whether it was a cry of pleasure or of agony, or, as so it proved to be, both and neither. It rose, and with it rose the hair on my neck and arms, while all conversation ceased about our fire and men hung suspended in attitudes of spooning food to their mouths or touching a coal to their tobacco. It rose, and spiralled in intensity and pitch, strengthening and quickening with every undulation and full of rage, or terror, but of submission also — a horrible submission — which above all chilled my blood. I thought of Gustave in that moment, erect on his bit of sinking bark and cursing heaven with both fists; so it was that a man should die, cursing death with all the last of his life, and not in this long pallid and futile howl from which all life had been sucked like substance from a cowl of fungus. Yet it rose quavering to a continuing shriek beyond the lungs of man or woman to support; and when I believed that I must shriek myself to blot it out, it ceased. In the silence it echoed in my mind, and it was some moments before I let go my pent-up breath, and moved my tongue in a dry mouth.

"There are Indians," I said, "on the island next to this."

A canoe was quickly launched. In the twilight we rounded the end of our island and approached the next, drawing close to the beach where their canoes lay, and from this vantage point I saw the tents which had previously been hidden. They also were arranged with a symmetry uncommon in Indian encampments — a precision, indeed, almost military. We did not touch, but swung broadside off the beach, and one of our men who spoke Ojibbeway hailed the tents asking what was amiss and if we could assist them, for we had heard a screaming. At this three men emerged from the central and largest lodge, and two from another. I had seen no savages their equal. Not only were they statuesque in bearing and haughty in demeanour, but although featured like Indians their skin bore an ambivalent pallor, neither white nor dusky. Their dress and decoration also distinguished them from others of their tribe. These wore buck-skins bleached until they rivalled in brilliance the sheerest linen, and all their hands and arms up to their elbows were dyed by what appeared in that distance and falling darkness to be greased ochre. They moved warily towards us, and from them came one of remarkable height and slenderness of frame. He it was who answered our spokesman, telling him (so our man reported) that they needed no assistance, and that if we had heard a crying it must have been the wind, or the circling gulls. His voice was high, and he spoke both slyly and arrogantly, as if he did not expect to be believed and cared little if he was not.

We turned away with the merest of civilities. When I looked back I saw that the five had been joined by some six or eight others, all men, and all clothed in the same uncommon manner. They stood indolently, laughing among themselves.

"Wabeno!" said our translator, and spat into the lake. He showed a great reluctance to speak further, grimacing and waving his hand toward the Indians' tents; yet I saw fear in his expression also, and a mingling of respect.

"There is a wabeno encamped next door with all his party," he told the others when we had again reached the fire, "and I daresay from the screaming that you will see a *wabeno wekoon-*

dewin if you care to watch, at the time of the morning star.''
I pressed him further. He had lived long among the Indians in
the *pays d' en haut* and knew much of their customs; and reluctantly
he told me that this wabeno is the most powerful of their shamans,
but whether his influence be curative or pernicious he knew not,
although he thought the latter. The wabeno, he said, would use
any means to cure disease or to quench an unrequited love, and
those who placed themselves in his influence and used his potions
on themselves or on others must submit entirely their will to
his, for the remedies might grow extreme. When he had spoken
my informant spat several times into the fire as if to rid himself
of a sour taste. It was good, he added, that the power of the
wabeno had declined, and that such sorceries as he practised so
as to conjure an overturn of nature grew less common as the
Company's influence spread.

By evening the lake had calmed and the night spread high
and cool. Before it was fully dark most men retired, anticipating
an early start. At last only Elborn and I remained beside the
fire. ''Now, MacKay,'' he said, shifting closer in the smoke,
''these mummeries our friend has spoken of . . . I confess I
am not adverse to seeing something of them for myself. Judging
from his remarks, the opportunity will not soon present itself
again.''

I remarked as dryly as possible that his interest did not surprise
me.

''Oh indeed yes, I admit it freely, and note that you also have
not retired. I therefore presume some little curiosity on your part?
I propose, MacKay, that we cross the island and see what entertainment the savages have planned.'' So saying, he rose, extinguished
his pipe, and set off down the beach. I followed, assuring myself
that as an officer of the Company I could do worse than to learn
the customs of the natives, for even the most outlandish ceremonies
might find their place in the uses of our trade.

Throughout the night Elborn and I shivered on wet rocks opposite
the Indian encampment, and were rewarded with neither light,
nor sound, nor movement. The island was clearly visible and
distinct from the others in the light of stars, for the night was
clear. Had I not brought my glass and been able with it to descry
their canoes still where I had seen them, I would have thought
the Indians had quitted that place at dusk, so profound was the
silence. At times loons called; once there was a crackling on

the far shore, as of some large animal. At three, Elborn touched my arm and pointed to the east. Whether the sky had lightened there, presaging dawn, I cannot say; but there hung a multitude of stars above that eastern shore, and one far brighter than the rest, like a miniscule sun. "Venus," Elborn whispered. "The morning star."

As if his voice had been a signal, figures appeared on the island opposite, but so silent still and so obscured by shadow and murky background that I scarcely distinguished them until they reached the heights and stood outlined against the sky. There they remained in what appeared an irregular ring — perhaps a dozen or fourteen in all. At first they made no sound; but then began a faint and slow drumming which increased in volume and tempo until it reached its climax. At that instant a fire sprang to life and quickly spread. It revealed on the one side a half-circle of men with folded arms, facing eastward, and on the other the wabeno himself, rising with his arms outspread as if for warmth. Light from the dancing flames glowed on his bared chest and face. These were of the hue I have described, more grey than brown, and in the firelight a most lurid and unhealthy tone, not unlike the skin of a drowned man. Despite the chill he wore a breech-clout only, secured about his loins. Strips of ochre radiated from the centres of his face and chest. About him there hung a most baleful and malevolent intensity which caused me to catch my breath and start up from where I had been lounging.

He rose to his full height and strained backwards towards the cast with upraised arms until the light of Venus struck his face, and in that arch he remained while the drumming commenced again; whereupon his body shuddered to the new rhythm. For several moments he writhed in this position, uttering cries to match the wilder gesticulations of his arms and torso, which with the increasing tempos of the drums fast became a desolate and demonic wail sent heavenward through upraised fists. At its conclusion his hands opened and he again sank to his knees before the fire which he had called into being.

The other Indians now relaxed the crescent line they had kept throughout this brief performance, and moved forward — some to heap dry wood upon the fire, some to fix for the cooking stakes on which dripping chunks of meat had been impaled. What we witnessed now could have been the scene in any encampment we have passed since leaving Montreal, except that there were neither women, nor dogs, nor children to give it a domesticity. My glass showed the wabeno crouched alone beside the fire. Even in the most convivial of his followers' exchanges I detected an alertness and anticipation altogether foreign to other Indians. It was like a knife edge in their voices which probed across the water; it glittered in their eyes which roved over the company, and the roasting meat, and into the darkness beyond the island. But the foremost difference between this scene and others similar lay not in the participants but in the fire. Never have I seen such a blaze among the Indians, who for the most part liked small and smoldering cookfires dwindling towards extinction. This, by contrast, was already a conflagration. Flames leapt from it to scorch boughs twenty feet above, and sparks and embers soared as high again, lighting such an area that Elborn and I, fearing we might be seen, crouched behind the boulders. The spitted meat was drawn back as the fire grew, and already some had been wrenched from its stakes and eaten with much gusto and laughter, although to my glass the center was raw and stringy, and the blanched skin repugnant.

"Bear, no doubt," said Elborn, watching with narrowed eyes and his ever-present, intolerable smile. "A bear eager for death, which has swum to their island through a day of storms. Ah, think how in their extremity they must have welcomed that bear, MacKay!"

My stomach revolted at his insinuation. "I presume," I replied, "they have carried their own food here, for who would venture upon Superior improperly victualled?"

"Who indeed?" smiled Elborn. "Ah, you are right, of course; I daresay they have brought their food with them, as you suggest."

Even through this exchange the fire had grown larger and now commanded half the plateau where it was built. On its fringes the Indians ate, and brought forth fresh meat from a carcass beyond the firelight, and burst into rapid, impromptu dances towards the fire and back, as if they would soon embrace it. Most had now shed their clothes except for mocassins and loincloths, and their bodies gleamed with sweat and with the grease they rubbed on their chests and shoulders. The shaman had now commenced a clockwise movement around the fire, a dance slow and ragged at first as some joined, some bent to feed the fire or tend the meat, and others fell away like men drunk on heat; but relentlessly this circling grew and so contained them all at last in a round itself composed of turnings and smaller circles as men sought to escape the fearsome heat by exposing another side of their bodies, turning as if they themselves had been spitted into place for roasting. Throughout, the master of the dance remained impassive, closer to the flames than all the rest, and when at last several at once reached the limit of their endurance and spun away whooping with pain and nursing scorched flesh, the drumbeats throbbed to a crescendo and the wabeno continued and quickened his contortions almost onto the fire itself, writhing like a lean snake the while, and for a time this lone dancing continued amidst the very flames until I swore the man must be consumed. Yet he emerged, his loin cloth in smoking ribbons and his face flickering with mingled pain and pleasure which was horrible to look upon.

The flames grew; the meat sputtered and dripped, was consumed and instantly replaced, and the drumming again increased its tempo, urging another man to follow the wabeno's example, and another, and yet another until the fire appeared to vomit bodies; and although none moved with the litheness of the tall man, yet some displayed a readiness to expose themselves equal to his, and a fortitude among the flames which I would not have credited. The cause of their colour thus became apparent — ash-white from the scars of burns, and as one by one the loincloths were burned off or dispensed with I saw that in some cases their very manhoods had been seared away.

This revelation, more than any other, touched me to the roots of my being. Singly, through my glass, I searched the faces of these revellers and found there neither explanation nor hint, and was left to conclude that the intensity of this playful competition led some to that ultimate test, whereby manhood itself was sacrificed; but to what end, or to what god or goddess, that I could not tell. The inferno, the drumbeats which still increased, the wanton swaying of these dancers, all acted upon my senses until I supposed I beheld a dream, a nightmare wherein fiends of neither sex made their mockery of both.

At the height of the dance, the fire suddenly spread swiftly through the island in undulating runnels and rivulets, seizing its own liquid life, and for some moments I watched uncomprehending, bedevilled by what I had seen and what I saw. Their bodies gleaming red with grease and burns, the revellers had seized great brands and, holding them aloft, moved outward through the forest to the fringes of the island, keeping the rhythm of the drums and punctuating the night with such cries and wailings as the damned in torment might have uttered. The island's shape was soon pricked out by these flailing torches. Only the wabeno himself kept beside the fire, rigid as if entranced, his head thrown back, his teeth exposed, his fists clenched at his groin. For some moments he remained thus, and then the drumming ceased, the cries from the island's fringe diminished. In a silence broken only by the surging of the blaze he spun snakelike towards the largest of the nearby pines and flung his hands out and up in a gesture which included it entirely. What trickery he employed I cannot say, but the tree shimmered in malefic radiance, contracted as if swept by giant hands, and burst with flame. Its boughs thrashed, its trunk cracked, spewing resin. Smoke and embers rolled upward in a wanton cataract. Howls from all the island greeted this new pyre, and in an instant a dozen other fires from torches thrust like cartridges into bark and bracken swarmed lasciviously towards it and joined with it in a general consummation.

The island blazed. So intense was the heat that we were forced to leave our vantage point for the protection of the forest, encountering others from our brigade who had been roused from sleep. Ash and embers fell everywhere on us and around us, and fearing fire on our island also, we retired with dispatch to load our canoes. Within the half-hour this was done. Behind the trees to the west the conflagration had meantime reached the peak of its ferocity and, by the time we embarked, had begun to decline.

Our file of canoes passed silent in the half-light, all eyes on that smoldering island which lifted its charred trunks and branches, horribly bejewelled, in futile supplication.

Of the Indians nothing visible remained, but there floated across the water, far to the southwest, such a cry and laughter that our men crossed themselves on hearing it, and some few spat towards it. Elborn maintained that they had fled, and that they would spread their dementia like a plague until the last had been run to earth; but for my own part I believe that we had heard the dawn crying of the loons, and that the shaman and his band had found that morning the death which they had sought so eagerly.

Our canoes drew close, and in fan shape passed northward until those islands had been put astern. The brooding silence of the men deepened my fatigue and weighed heavily on my spirits. I was not unpleased when, with the breaking of the sun, the lead canoe struck up one of their chanting songs in which all soon joined, increasing the regularity of their paddling. Rocked by this now-accustomed rhythm, certain in the knowledge that we proceeded in a fine day towards Michipicoten and the West, I lowered my hat upon my eyes and slept.

chapter thirteen

Miro had no blue suit. In fact, he had no suit of any colour, and so what he wore to the Commencement was what he had worn for one half of the school year — black gabardene trousers with a high gloss on the seat and a maroon cardigan over a white shirt. The white shirt he had bought that morning in Saul Levinson's Men's and Children's Clothes, thinking as he did so, *Beware of all endeavours which require new clothes.* The sleeves were too long and the cellulose collar hurt his neck. He felt ridiculous in it and smiled bitterly at his own pretension. *Four bucks up the slot,* he thought. *Half a day's pay!*

By craning his neck to the right he could see through a thicket of heads to the front row where the teachers sat, and past them to the tables half-emptied of their trophies and diplomas. Franklin Hook hovered at the edge of the stage, his camera flashing. Beyond, the audience sat in two massive dark blocks, filling the gym. Miro had not yet taken the effort required to focus through his inadequate glasses and find his mother and latest step-father. They would be sitting somewhere near the back, he knew, his mother bright and defiant, her lover's indifferent belly bulging on his thighs. A brief fury shook Miro at the thought of them, and he raised his fist to hide his grimace. He coughed. Later he would look for them. Later. For his mother, anyway. As for the man ... Miro entertained a brief fantasy in which he drew a neat scalpel down that gross belly from sternum to pubis, spilling out yards of guts and purple organs on the gym floor. He smiled.

The valedictorian whined towards her conclusion. Miro yawned audibly and snickered when heads in front twitched with disapproval. Fuck them. They knew and he knew that he should have been giving the address, not her, and he would have done it, despite his stutter, despite the maroon cardigan, despite of and because of everything if they had not fiddled the marks just enough to edge him out. His marks were best. He knew that. Baker had told him. And if he and not that tight-assed broad whom he despised had written the valedictory he would have told them precisely what a farce and torment their sweet five years of education had been to him, and what they could do with their school brick by brick, and with each separate piece of equipment that lined the gym walls. Except for Baker, of course. Old Baker was all right. He was a keen old guy, very straight and moral, in Miro's estimation. Baker kept himself together, and for that Miro admired him greatly.

Idly Miro looked right and left at his colleagues, the girls in crisp pink and organdy, the boys crew-cut and impassive, beginning to applaud dutifully as the speaker finished. Yes-men, Miro thought, shrugging. Brown-nosers. Ass-lickers, the bunch of them. Even Gerry.

Abruptly, Gerry Rattray turned and their eyes met. Under his folded arm he raised a middle finger at Miro in an obscene suggestion, and in spite of himself Miro began to laugh. Goddam him, he thought. Bastard! He bit his lips.

" . . . call on Mr. Baker," the principal was saying, his amplified voice bounding like basketballs from the speakers, "to present the Ferguson Prize in Upper School Biology to Miro Balch." And in a polite flurry of applause old Baker was stooping at the microphone like a grey heron, talking about Ferguson and the history of the Prize, and about how in his predjusht opinion no winner had been more worthy than this year's reshipyant.

Miro was galvanized. *He's drunk,* he thought. Baker!

He was not sure of the point the old teacher was trying to make. In slurred syllables he spoke of biology, and of respect and responsibility, but Miro scarcely listened. Smiling cynically, Miro had retreated behind his defences. He sat stiff and invulnerable, waiting to go forward. At last, the old man reached out carefully and seized the microphone by its scrawny neck. Until then there had been neither laughter nor any other sound, but the last words in his little speech, emphasized for effect, were spoken too close into the microphone head, and feedback sent the amplifier shrieking. The laughter came then, together with applause, and Baker turned saying, "C'mon, Miro," and groped on the table for the nearest article — two books which were the Cadwalder Prize for English.

"Might have known," said Gerry as Miro passed, "myass Baker. Everything he touches turns to shit!"

The old man leaned forward to greet him. "Hope doanmine," he said, grinning crookedly and pumping Miro's hand, "drunks skunk."

"I don't m-mind, sir," Miro lied. "Honestly. I think it's a f-fine guh-gesture."

Near the edge of the stage Franklin Hook focussed his camera and squatted for the proper angle. "This way, Miro, Mr. Baker." And the flashbulb popped with Miro laughing into the camera and Baker squinting up into the rafters above the crowd. When he turned back his eyes were watering. "For godsake," he said, "make room for morn gessures!"

Smiling thinly, the principal came forward to stitch up the rent in the evening, and Miro returned to his seat amidst applause which he knew was fuller than he deserved. On the empty chair beside him he placed the Cadwalder Prize for English beside the scholarship which was his passport to university. His grin was sour. Never mind, he told himself. You won that scholarship and you won that prize, and those bastards can't take that away now, no matter what. They can laugh at you. And they can fuck up everything important, but they can't keep you from university now. No matter what.

Carefully he adjusted his imperfect glasses on the bridge of
his nose where they functioned best for viewing distances, and
as the presentations continued (decorously now with Baker
slouched in the second row), he began to search the rows of
parents, friends, and other students. Quickly he found his mother
and her man, and his gaze rested on them only a moment before
it passed on, sliding like a shuttle back and forth through the
auditorium. At last, near the front, he found Fred Hale. Fred
was unmistakable. His bullet head and ruddy, vacuous face shone
out from the rest as if lit by a tiny spotlight. His brow was
creased, his jaw worked thoughtfully. With rising excitement
Miro forced himself to watch him until disdain and anticipation
erased any pity he might have felt, and then he allowed his
gaze to shift to Narah. He exhaled in a long, low sigh as he
did so.

She was beautiful. She was so beautiful that Miro's eyes closed
at the sight of her. She wore a black sweater and a grey skirt,
and her hair was drawn back with a nunnish severity that left
her face and throat exposed, but to Miro she was naked. Folded
across her stomach her arms offered breasts whose nipples begged
for his lips and teeth. "For you," said Miro softly. "You."

Had the commencement ended then and the audience risen
for the anthem, Miro would have stayed seated and oblivious;
for he had reentered another evening and was already deep in
its horror and ecstasy. He was in the Altona Grill, puddling
his glass in the spillage of his second milkshake, and listening
to Gerry Rattray's wide-eyed recitation of his, Miro's, many
faults and shortcomings. Solemn Franklin was there beside him
hunching his big shoulders, and two or three others who called
themselves his friends. Thick frost glazed the windows, radiating
out from the cracked corners.

Gerry flipped up his fingers as he spoke. "Chemistry, math,
history, English. You failed every one of them, right? Christ,
Miro, you even failed health! You know what's gonna happen?

You're gonna fail your year, that's what.''

"M-maybe.''

"Maybe shit. You're gonna fail your goddam year!''

"Well okay, so I'm gonna fail m-muh-my year. So why should you cuh-care?''

"I dunno. Believe me, Miro, I don't know why I care. I just hate to see a guy screw himself up that way.''

"You're always p-p-pushing me. All the time nagging. You're worse'n my muh-muh ...''

"Yeah, well it's a good thing, isn't it? You wouldn't be managing the hockey team if I hadn't said you were the guy to do it. That's been fun, eh? Had some good trips?''

"Yeah.''

"Sure. You wouldn't have got your job last summer if I hadn't talked to guys at the mill. Christ, Miro, you wouldn't even be in *Grade Twelve* if I hadn't helped you cheat in physics. Is that right?''

"Yeah.''

Gerry pushed back an imaginary bad smell. "So don't come down on me, buddy. Jeez, I don't know why I bother!''

There was silence except for the steam and the frying behind the counter. Miro circled his glass in the brown pool of milkshake.

"You know,'' said Franklin, "maybe what we have to do is figure out why your marks are down this year, eh Miro? I mean, they were low last year, too, but not this bad.'' Miro shrugged. "So what I'm thinking is that something must've changed. Gotten worse.''

"Aw, school.''

"Okay,'' Gerry said. "We all know it's the shits but we're in it, right? What you've gotta do is get out as soon as possible. God, do yuh want to clean out septic tanks like your old man?''

Miro flushed. "He's a truck driver.''

"Truck driver, then. What difference.''

"Thing is,'' Franklin continued, frowning, "you can do the stuff when you want to. Grade Ten, you got a first in science.''

Miro shrugged.

"So you can do it. If you were stupid there'd be no point, but you aren't. Of course, Grade Twelve, it's not so easy any more. Not for me, anyway. I find I've gotta study two, three hours a night."

"Anyway," said one of the others.

"Miro?"

"Yeah. I kn-know that. Around our place it's not so easy. Noise and stuff."

"Sure."

"Yeah. And then ..." Miro glanced furtively around the circle, a smile beginning.

"Then what?" Gerry leaned forward.

"Nuh-nothing. Skip it."

"No, come on, Miro. What?"

"Well, you know. It's hard to cuh-cuh-concentrate."

"At home, you mean."

"Yeah, but not just there."

"In class? In the library?"

"Yeah. Anyplace where ..." he spread his hands.

"Anyplace where there are girls," said Gerry Rattray. "Right?"

"Yeah."

"That's it!" Gerry slapped the table. "Goddam, I should've known." He looked at Franklin. "Well, he's gotta get screwed, that's all there is to it. The question is who. What about Annie?"

Franklin frowned and shook his head.

"Wuh-wuh-wait a m-minute! I c-c-can't ..."

"Joan? Susie? Kate?"

"Umm. Unh-unh."

"Okay. Let's see. Molly! What about Molly?"

Franklin considered. "Maybe," he said. "Yes, I would say that Molly is a definite possibility."

"Right." Gerry rummaged in the pocket of his coat. "We need five bucks."

"Four," said one of the others, "if she doesn't get undressed."

"Four bucks. And there's two of them."

"One for me," said Franklin.

"There y'go, Miro m'boy. One dollah!"

"Hey! You guh-guh-guys d-d-on't ..."

Gerry gathered the crumpled bills. "Okay. So all he needs is a safe."

"Here's one."

Gerry examined the package.

"What're you doin, for crissake? Think it's been used?"

"Anyway, who's M-M-Molly?"

"They get old," Gerry said. "Carry them around in your wallet, they get holes worn in them."

"Yeah, well I've had it three days. Three days. And if you don't like it give it back. Let him get a dose, for crissake."

Gerry stood up and pulled on his coat. "Right! Let's go, Miro. Into Molly, and on to better things." He pulled down his toque low over his eyes.

"Jeez, I duh-duh-dunno, Gerry ..."

"Trust me, Miro."

"Yeah, but a *whore*! God, what'f she's got s-syph or s-something?"

"She hasn't. Clean girl, Molly. Choosy."

"So what'f s-she's ..."

"Look," Gerry reached out, grasped Miro's neck and shook him gently, "you wanna masturbate the rest of your life?"

"I don't muh-muh ..."

Gerry was pulling him along. "Know what happens to guys who beat their meat too much, dontcha? They grow hair on the palms of their hands."

Miro looked, and the other hooted in laughter. Their laughter burst with their bodies out of the steam and warmth and into the frosty street. In spite of himself, Miro laughed too.

"Yeah," Gerry grinned, his arm slipping around Miro's shoulders, "I can see it now. Miro, thirty-three years old with beards on both hands, still trying to cuh-cuntcentrate."

"F-fuck you," said Miro, but again his laughter joined the others' in a high, whining monotone.

They reached Gerry's car and climbed in, two in the front, three in the back, Miro in the middle. "Maybe he should have a drink, first," someone suggested. "Loosen him up." And at the same instant as Gerry said, "Nope. Not necessary," Miro saw with a hellish clarity the half-empty bottle, the spilled liquor and broken glass on the kitchen floor, and, on the livingroom floor beyond, his mother's bare heels pressing a new rump between her thighs. He saw the dropped trousers and the flung-open blue kimono, and he heard sounds which he would rather not remember. And he would have protested in earnest, then, perhaps even insisted that they stop the car and let him out, had not he already begun to laugh once again, hopelessly caught by the neat darts of Gerry's monologue.

"Who's M-M-Molly," he asked Franklin when they had left the main part of town and were travelling out to the northeast.

Franklin scratched his head. "Well, Miro, I think you'll like her or I wouldn't have said so. You know that. Molly is a very calm person. Very placid. She was a very good-looking woman, I think."

"Was," Miro said. "Oh b-boy!"

"Is. I should have said is. In her own way, a very good-looking woman."

"In her own way."

"Well, she's cross-eyed, for one thing, but as you'll see that's no real disadvantage. In fact, it was once considered a mark of great beauty among her people."

"Her people."

"Indian. Klootch."

"Lovely," Miro said. "Just great!"

Franklin melted a fist-sized hole in the frost and peered out into the night. Again he scratched his head. "And probably I should mention that in her trade there are certain, well, occupational hazards.''

Miro waited.

"A scar," Franklin explained, drawing his finger from scalp to jaw. "Right here."

"Oh b-boy. Oh boyohboyohboy."

The cabin stood alone, although the lights of others shone on the hillside and in the woods behind. From what Miro could see it was neat enough. Snowshoes hung near the door, beside a child's sleigh and a galvanized washtub. The downstairs windows were covered with heavy curtains around which only a little light escaped onto the snow. The upstairs window, in what appeared to be a loft, was dark. Woodsmoke curled from the chimney and spiced the air.

Gerry shifted to neutral and pulled on the parking brake. "You guys stay," he said. "Miro, let's go."

The door window also had curtains, but they were not pulled back before the door itself opened to their knock. She was twenty-five, perhaps, or thirty. She was smallish and not bulky. Her hair had been braided and hung over her shoulder to her breast, tied with a white ribbon. She wore a grey sweater, jeans, and moccasins. The sleeves of the sweater were bunched above her elbows. She was fair, for an Indian. The scar was less obtrusive than Miro expected, and she did not try to hide it. In fact, it seemed to Miro that she turned it slightly towards him. "Hello, Gerry," she said.

"Hi, Molly. Well, can we come in?"

"One at a time. No pairs. No gangs. You know that."

"Yeah, I know. It's just Miro, here. C'mon, Molly, let us in. It's bloody cold."

She turned away from the door. Stamping, they entered. Gerry took off his hat and nudged Miro to do the same, and in the moment before his glasses fogged over Miro saw a clean room sparsely furnished. The chairs had cane seats. Rag rugs lay under the table and in front of the stove. He took off his glasses and thrust them in his armpit. The woman became a comfortable blur in the larger haze which was the room.

"Five," she said, holding her hand up.

"Yeah, well the problem is, Molly, that he just hasn't got it, you know. Couldn't scrape it up. So he thought . . ."

"You thought."

"We thought that maybe under the circumstances . . ."

"White boys," she said, but there was no malice in her laughter, but only a large pity and a larger resignation. "So how much has he got?"

"Four."

Miro felt her eyes on him. "First time?"

Gerry nodded.

"All right," she said. "Okay. Leave it there."

Miro fumbled his glasses on in time to see Gerry departing, his face in the closing doorway a satyric mask of lust, two fingers raised — V for victory. Then he was gone, and the woman stood watching him with her gaze awry and unsettling. "For four dollars," she said, "I usually just lift my skirt. Oh well . . ." She shrugged, pulled off the sweater and unzipped the jeans. By the time his glasses had cleared completely she was naked except for her moccasins and a string of white beads which had been hidden by the sweater. She came slowly around the table, rubbing her hands on her hips. When she had almost reached him the front door banged open and Gerry re-appeared. Wide-eyed he looked from Miro to the woman and back again. "Take this," he said, thrust the small packet into Miro's hand, and vanished.

Molly locked the door behind him. "It's private now," she said. "You can take your coat off."

"Oh. Sorry."

"Don't be sorry. Your shirt too, if you like."

He unbuttoned it, watching her. Indolent, she came closer. "There's no hurry," she said. Her moccasins were soundless. Her breath smelt like sage and chicory and some wild spice he had never smelt before, and her body gave off a tang of sweat, smoked sweat, fresh and not sour. "You're pretty thin," she said. "Dry, too. White men are so dry. It's not good for love. Come. Close to the stove. Don't be afraid to sweat."

"I'm nuh-nuh-not afraid."

"Ahh," she said, looking long at him through her crooked eyes. "I see."

She brought him close to the stove and took his shirt off. She undid his trousers and slid them off. She unknotted his shoes. She rose so that her breasts brushed over his thighs and his belly and his breast. She kissed his mouth, drew back, and then kissed him again with her head tilted the other way. She reached up to embrace his neck and she rubbed the back of his head. She moved her groin against him. She leaned away a little so that her nipples trailed on his ribs. She stood pressed against him without moving. After awhile she stepped away and circled in a little slow dance, displaying her body and watching his eyes. Then again she came close with her hands low and caressed him with cunning and tenderness. She brushed him against her. With her eyes closed she kissed his throat and face. They were both sweating. She took his hands and pressed them on her breasts. She slid his hand over her body. She spread her legs and rubbed his palm and wrist between them so he could feel the moistness there. She said his name. She squeezed him hard in a convincing show of urgency. She lifted her leg until her heel pressed the back of his thigh. She held him motionless for a long, silent time.

At last she stood back and, sighing, put her hands on her hips. "I said there was no hurry. I didn't say we had a week."

"I'm sorry."

"Don't be sorry. But you can't, eh?"

He shook his head.

"Okay. Maybe another time. Come without your friends." She dressed, opened the door, and beckoned Gerry in. Miro pulled his clothes on.

"Okay, Miro? Ready to go? She's great, eh? Isn't Molly

great?''

"I d-dunno.''

"Whadyuh mean you don't know? What's he mean? You're not gonna tell me ... Oh no. Oh for goshsake! Four bucks.''

"Take it,'' Molly said.

"Nope. It's yours. Not your fault. C'mon, Miro. Don't forget your hat.''   ·

"No good,'' he said in the car. "We should've tried Annie after all.''

They drove two miles in silence. Miro sat with his fists clenched and his legs stiff, pushed into the back of the seat. When they reached the main road he sobbed once, and then said quickly, "It was all the other m-men!''

"Sure,'' said Gerry.

"It *was,* goddam it. I could suh-*see* them!''

"Yeah,'' said someone else, "well if you're that interested in other men we can't do much to help you, Miro.''

Suddenly Miro's body coiled and lunged. He kicked the back of the seat so hard the fabric gave way and his heels snagged in exposed rods and springs. The packaged condom hit the windshield, a squashed lump of foil, and as it did so a torrent of obscenities burst out of him in a high and desolate wail. He lashed out furiously, smashing his arms against heads and windows.

Gerry swerved onto the shoulder. "Grab him, for crissake! Hold him down!''

Protecting his face, Franklin leaned over and pinned the flailing body. "Easy, Miro,'' he said. "You're among friends.''

"Fuck you bastards! You're not my friends. Lemme out!''

"You can't go out,'' Franklin said. "It's too cold.''

"Shithead! Cocksucker! Goddam whoremongers! Lemme out of this fuckin car!''

"Easy, now,'' said Franklin, calmly. "Get ahold of yourself.''

Miro's voice broke into a pure scream of rage which was almost instantly smothered by Franklin's shoulder, and his body lunged convulsively, sinking lower under Franklin's weight until his head was crushed into the seat and the spasm ended in short, stifled twitches. Gerry climbed on the front seat and grabbed Miro's knees. "Knock it off! You hear me? You wanna walk you can bloody well walk. I don't give a shit!"

"Hear him, Miro?"

"Umph."

"Okay. All right, then." Cautiously Franklin sat up.

"My fuh-feet are caught."

"Of course your feet are caught! You damn near kicked my bloody car apart! Hold still!"

"Now lemme out."

Franklin scrubbed at the window. "Honestly, Miro, I think you'd be very unwise. It's zero, at least, and four miles home."

"Let him out."

"Hey, Gerry, he'll freeze his balls off."

"Let him, for crissake. What difference?"

On the road, Miro watched the car spin wildly for a hundred feet and skid to a stop in a cloud of snow and exhaust. Gerry's fist shook through the opened window and Gerry's voice jabbed thinly back at him. "You stupid little prick! It'll be a long time before I help *you* again!" Then the car roared, the wheels screeched on patches of bare pavement, and swiftly the tail-lights grew small and vanished.

The night was very, very cold, but windless. There were no house lights to be seen, only the glow of Sable Creek beyond the distant hills. The sky was brilliant with stars. The phone lines whined; a tree cracked in the forest. Miro felt the cold instantly pressing like big steel needles through his pants and jacket. In the scuffle he had lost his cap, and already his ears ached and the sweat had turned icy on his forehead. His worn shoes slipped when he tried to walk on the snow-packed shoulder and he moved out into the center of the road, now thrusting his hands into his pockets, now covering his ears. No cars passed. Cursing and weeping, he broke into a little trot but after a few moments the air hurt his throat and lungs and he stopped. He walked fast, breathing shallowly through his nose. He'd walk all the way. He was damned if he'd ask for a ride, even if a car approached. He'd freeze first. He wanted no more favours.

After half an hour fear crept into his belly. His right ear had stopped hurting and a deep, ominous aching had begun in both thighs. His toes had lost all feeling. Again he tried running, but after a hundred yards the cold filled his chest with knives. Desperately he turned around, searching the highway, but there were no cars behind, no warm lights ahead, only the ruthless stars and the wires singing.

By the time he heard the car fear had constricted his breath into little gasps. He was stamping his feet with each numb step and swatting his legs and buttocks. He had taken off his glasses and so was unable to judge both the car's closeness and his own distance from the shoulder, and was startled by the sudden blurred shape beside him, swerving across the white line. Fortunately, it was going slowly. The brake lights came on and it stopped. Miro stumbled towards it. "I didn't ask," he thought, trying to smile. "Remember, I didn't ask."

The door swung open and a wash of blessed, powdery warmth engulfed him. "Miro! Get in."

"Miz Hale?"

"Get in, Miro. What are you ... You're frozen!"

"Walking."

She reached across him, shut the door, and took his face and head in her hands, turning him towards her. She was a warm pink-grey blur of flesh and parka. Her touch was life itself. "Oh *Miro*," she said. "Miro." She drew the car off the road, pulled on the brake, and then as artlessly as if he were a child, shifted across the seat and embraced him. He was trembling so violently that he shook them both. She opened her parka and wrapped him in its folds of fur and eiderdown. His breath shuddered in and out against her shoulder. She chafed his legs through the thin trousers, pulled off his shoes and held his feet. Slowly, in little sparks of pain, the feeling began to return. "I d-d-didn't ask."

"You didn't have to ask," she said.

At last, when his shaking subsided and he began to breathe normally, she took her coat off and laid it over him. "I'm here," she said, "because I drove Fred down to the winter jamboree. What's your excuse?"

"I got left."

"Who left you here?"

"Aw, well I d-d-didn't really get left, I guess. I got out."

"Why?"

He shrugged, groping for his glasses. "Fight."

"Who with?" Her face and hair and the whole interior of the car came suddenly into marvellous focus.

"Aw, Gerry, Franklin. Those guys."

"Oh," she said. Her left arm stretched out on the steering wheel. Her right, laid on the seat back, still held his shoulder. "What about?"

"N-N-Nothing."

"Tell me."

"It's n-n-not important."

"Where were you?"

"Up the road. The r-reservation."

"Ahh," she said. Her hand dropped from his shoulder and she looked at him for a long time in silence. The concern left her face, and in its place there grew a placid, tender, but indomitable resolve which Miro did not see. He was watching Gerry's Ford approach and cruise past searching. Its lights filled Narah's car. She glanced at it, turned in her seat, and let off the parking brake. "Do you know what I think?" she asked. "I think it's a fine coincidence, our meeting tonight." She accelerated smoothly into the highway. "I think it's the best coincidence anyone could imagine. Don't you think so? Hm?" To Miro her laughter was as warming as her caress, and he had entered with her into her pure and deliciously private joke.

"For you," he said again.

Despite the fans, the gym had grown very warm, and the back of the principal's neck, as he made his farewell remarks, shone with sweat. The atmosphere was like a warm, unminding bath. Miro was only partly conscious of Franklin's slipping into the seat beside him and passing over Miro's prize and scholarship. He was only distantly aware of the tiny ratchetting of Franklin's camera as he wound the film back.

"Who're you looking at?"

"Wha?"

Franklin stretched across into Miro's line of sight. "Ah, Narah, huh?"

"Go to hell."

"Don't be like that, Miro. Seriously, it must be a strain to be so bitter all the time. Don't you find it a strain? Look at her all you want. I don't care." Franklin adeptly dismantled his flashgun.

"*You* don't care."

"No. Why should I? She's a very beautiful woman. A very beautiful fuck."

"How do you know that?"

"Well she is," said Franklin. "Narah Hale is a gorgeous fuck. Hell, Miro, we all know that!"

In front of the stage, the pianist struck the fulsome first chords of "O Canada", and the audience, teachers and students rose as one, solemnly united. But as the anthem proceeded, those on stage were disturbed by a small and keening sound. It was, as Franklin was the first to realize, the whining of Miro's laughter — that laughter with which he confronted the last, the gravest, the most piercing betrayal of the night.

chapter fourteen

The river was broad at the mouth and sluggish, so that in the rain she had no perception of leaving the lake and entering it, but only of a slow curve along the right shore, grey and indistinct. She was deep in her thoughts. A long time passed before his voice, like a slim thread, drew her back. The rolling of Superior had gone, and the shore was no longer stark black and green, but was muddier, and broken by odd buildings. It was both more intimate and more ominous than the coast itself. She shuddered.

"Pardon?"

"A penny."

"Oh," she laughed. "I don't know. Daydreaming."

"No memories?"

"Perhaps a few."

They paddled in silence. He asked, "Is it important to remember?"

"I suppose we have no choice."

"Yes, we do."

"Well, yes."

"And we persist in it, this remembering, as if we could change what has happened that way."

"Perhaps we do."

"Or as if we could prevent the same mistakes. As if events might be repeated."

"Is that possible?"

"No. Of course not. And even if it were, we could never remember enough to understand what happened. It would always be random, unrelated, like stars in the night. No matter what systems we impose to console ourselves, we'll always know them to be placeboes, finally."

She was silent.

"And so why must you and I share memories even now, and grow our little systems?"

"Perhaps it's a way of forgetting," she said, "a way of getting rid of things, of discharging what is no longer useful.''

"Time does that.''

"Time. Something in us. Something urging us back ...''

He had stopped paddling.

"What?'' she asked, twisting on the seat. "What is it?''

"There.'' He pointed with his paddle. "Something moved there.''

They waited, listening to the hiss of rain. The canoe swung sluggishly across the current. A mile ahead, the river curved out of sight behind a promontory where several cabins huddled. Indistinct and distorted in the distance, these buildings stared like damaged crustaceans through black eyes, and Paul imagined their groans, their broken shells and entrails, their webbed claws gripping the rock.

In that mile the river suddenly broadened into a small lake, across which moved another canoe, unmistakably another canoe, travelling fast and in mid-stream. It passed through curtains of mist. One man paddled it. For a moment Paul thought he heard a chant so faint, so blurred by drizzle, that he could not be sure of it. But then a quirk of breeze brought it clearly, and although he could not distinguish words he heard a vigorous, rhythmic grunting.

"He's singing,'' Liv said.

"No. It's not a song.''

She turned. "Do you think it's safe?'' For there was an audacity about this figure, and a challenge.

He did not answer immediately. He squinted intently at the lone figure, a filament of recognition settling across his mind. "What?'' he said. "Safe? Oh yes, I think it's safe.''

Still she hesitated. But then the other canoe vanished in the mist along the left shore, and she began to paddle. It seemed they would not encounter him. When they reached the center of the lake there was no sign of the other canoe, but only the tight knot of cottages on their right and the mists ahead and to the left. Then suddenly the strange, grunting chant resumed close to them in the mist, and in an instant the figure of the

paddler loomed out at them, grey as the water. "*Stroke*, uh,
uh. *Stroke*, uh, uh. *Stroke* . . . "

She cried out in fear, shielding her throat, for he passed only
inches from them, and his enormous paddle blade flashed almost
across the bow of their own craft, gliding forward. He did not
see them. His eyes were fixed on some internal calculation. Ten-
dons strained from his throat, through his arms, into his bare
chest. His muscles bulged precisely, as they do on aging athletes.
His head gleamed, close-shaven.

"Fred!"

His momentum carried him past. He faltered and then paddled
a few strokes more, as if he desired not to hear.

"Fred Hale!"

"Who's there?"

"Paul."

He turned. His eyebrows met in a hostile line. "You've interrupted my practice," he said.

"Fred . . . "

"You've interrupted it! My pulse is dropping every second.
It's going down. It was up to one thirty when you stopped me,
and now it's going down."

"Do you remember me?"

"Remember? Why did you stop me? What right do you have?
Don't you know that I'll have to start again, now? That all this
has been for nothing — right across the lake and back? It will
have to be done again, and it's cold."

"Fred, listen. Are you alone? Is Narah with you?"

"Order, that's what I remember! You've got your order and
I've got mine. Everybody's got his order. You can't interfere
like this!" He paused, and then said abruptly, "She's here."

"Where?"

"Here. Here. Part of it. Intervals of 0.8 seconds. You can't
stop it once it's begun. You know that!"

"Where is she? Can we see her?"

He sat immobile, and then suddenly tilted his head and cried,
"Naaa-rah!" in the bawling tone he would have once used to

summon a child from the school-ground borders. There came no answer, no echo, but only the flat fact of rain on the river's face. "She must be out. Gathering mushrooms," he said, staring at the shore. "The Boletaceae are blooming. The Coprinus . . ."

"Fred, can we help you? Can we do anything for you?"

"You can tell her to come home," he said. "It's cold. It's getting dark . . . " And then, savagely, "And you can not interrupt again!" He lifted the huge paddle. "I had it once. I had it. Point eight seconds. Better than they were!"

"What . . . "

"The voyageurs."

"What will you do? Stay at the cottage?"

"And keep order," he replied. The paddle bit, and the canoe, which was the slim and shallow type used by racers, sprang ahead. In a moment they heard his chant once more, gathering momentum, fading in the mist.

June 15, 1785. At noon we had our first sight of the fort of Grand Portage, which appeared momentarily through an opening in the fog that has for three days encased us. At this, our fellows set up a cheer and increased their paddling to a speed greater than one stroke per second, and the entire brigade surged forward with an alacrity and jubilance I have not seen since our approach to Sault Ste. Maries. It appears they are urged on by the prospect of native delights awaiting them, and these they anticipate so keenly and tumultuously as to render them virtually accomplished.

This eagerness I shared to some degree, for it has now been several weeks since I have enjoyed civilized companionship, and I am assured I shall have some days' respite from travel at this place, wherein I might consult with officers of the Company.

First, however, we must satisfy further the rituals of these voyageurs by approaching behind the cover of an island lying a mile from the fort and, having reached that place, restrain ourselves sufficiently to disembark on the further shore, there to get all in readiness for a proper approach and entry. For nothing is done on these occasions without the ceremonies of the land. Off come the clothes which they have worn, waking and sleeping, since departing Montreal, to the accompaniment of much merriment and shouting, so that they must be heard in the fort itself. Some appear capering and naked as white apes, flinging over each other the frigid waters of Superior, so that they suffer a wash of sorts, and boasting all the while how they will sate their passions this very night, winning over each other the favours of the most pliant and comely women of the settlement. In all of this I remain an observer merely, for I have washed assiduously throughout the journey, in spite of considerable inconvenience, and am quite presentable.

At this place, called Cap du Chapeau, their child-like love of flamboyance is fully indulged, for they garb themselves in their most cherished garments, carefully preserved through the journey; and out come the combs for their matted hair and beards, out come the fresh shirts and beaded moccasins, the red woolen caps and dangling *ceintures flèches* which they have not required since Ste. Maries. Out comes every appurtenance of their pride, and I confess that when they swagger and compete thus these voyageurs acquire a contagious glamour, so that when the canoes were reloaded and marshalled in a line abreast, I found myself wishing to contribute to the chant which would carry them through the last mile of fog, and was restrained only by a timely recollection of the dignity I must maintain as a responsible officer of the Company.

On shore, pandemonium greeted us. The fort itself lies at the foot of a considerable rise, almost a small mountain, but is itself elevated above the water so as to command a view of all approaches. Below it and around it, stretching a hundred rods from the base of the palisade, lies a motley encampment, composed mostly of the tents of Indians, but also of several log shelters wherein, I am told, some Company men, having grown too old for journeying, are allowed to live out their lives. As we swung round the point, our canoes well spaced and the paddles flying in unison, a cannon was fired from the parapet, and a ball of smoke rose heavenward. We heard a frail cry, "The canoes are coming! The canoes are coming!" And this cry was taken up and echoed in a hundred throats as the encampment sprang alive with running, gesticulating figures and scores of barking dogs. So we approached majestically, the voyageurs keeping their steady pace to the time of the leading canoe. From the fort descended a pell-mell of residents' children, followed by a more stately procession as the officers and their ladies came forth to greet us. A small ship lay in harbour, her crew lining the decks, and we passed close under the anchor chains. On the docks all was jubilation. Men and women embraced riotously, jigs were danced, dogs raced with out-stretched necks, caught in the excitement of the moment. Two pipers played "Gillie Callum" and some children, Indian and white alike, capered and parodied the Highland dances. A thousand questions were shouted and answered in the din, messages from Montreal delivered, hobbling old men thumped by the voyageurs who remembered them and their feats of former days, until it seemed they must have their heads loosened by such violent respect.

The women of the camp were greeted like comrades, embraced, swung screaming off their feet, faces flushed, eyes eager, clothes and hair in disarray. Some were acquainted with most of our brigade and worked their way from one man to the next, all anxious for the assignations of evening. Even the ladies of the fort smiled their way through this confusion and made their greetings.

Withal, almost an hour elapsed before our men hoisted their burdens and began to make their way to the fort, pipers in the lead, surrounded by the riot which clung to them inside the very gates. Our canoes were lifted and overturned on the embankment so that they might dry and be repaired for the return journey. Our personal baggage was seized by the children, and I have no doubt some pilfering ensued. I carried as much as I was able, and shook my head at all who would assist me.

The fort itself is twenty-four rods by thirty. Within the palisade are contained several dwellings and shops, as well as the main meeting hall, where the affairs of the Company for this district are conducted. Here we dined, but such was the prevailing mood of excitement that I was allowed no proper opportunity to make myself better known to any of the Company's officers, or to discuss my prospects with them.

Immediately following our meal, Elborn and I were set to work assisting in the payment of the men, for their contracts had expired with our arrival. When, at supper, I had questioned this policy of the Company, pointing out that it would be preferrable to guarantee the men by writing contracts for the full trip, to Grand Portage and return, my opinion was met by those amused glances with which the knowledgeable greet naivete, and the conversation proceeded without my receiving a courteous reply. But Mr. Duff, a long-time employee of the Company, a florid and earthy man with white side-whiskers, leaned to me and spoke in a quiet and wheezing manner: "You may suppose we are not wise in this, my young apprentice, and that we stand in danger of losing these men with their full pay, once they have acquired it. But consider two points which will serve you well as the Company's representative. First, note how all men wish to be regarded as free beings who sell only a certain portion of their lives for pay, and not themselves; and note how their indenture must seem not too long a period lest they let slip this illusion of freedom which lies too distant in the future for their comprehension and begin to consider themselves slaves and captives, thus rendering a merely perfunctory service.

"Note secondly that men may be indentured by contracts more subtle than those composed by ink or paper. Did you not see on your arrival the number of willing lasses who swarmed to the canoes and who have come, of their own accord, of course, for a share of the largesse which will flow tonight? And have you some notion of the gallonage in rum, shrub, and raw alcohol carried here today by your brigade and stored with the fort's formidable supply? To lubricate the trade, you say. Yes, but not with the Indian alone, for those same free men who transported it hither will be most anxious to buy it freely back, with their freely-gotten pay; and not for themselves alone but also for their consorts of the evening, so that the revel might be heightened." He spoke quietly to me beneath the level of the conversation continuing about us, and he tapped my wrist with a finger to emphasize his moral. "Oh yes. Measure out careful freedoms, young man, and you will serve the Company excellently well. Observe how, by morning, these same free-spending fellows will be shorn of all autonomy, except that which is sufficient to sign their contracts for the journey back to Montreal and to familiar entanglements. Nor will they sign *these* contracts merely, but they will ask to be allowed to transport packets across the portage at a paltry rate; yes, and at Fort Charlotte they will squabble with the Northmen to carry the fur packets here. And all the time they will consider themselves free men. Men who control their destinies. Men who make decisions." Again he tapped my wrist. "Encourage this, my young friend. Be generous with such freedoms. The Company has need of them." He closed a heavy eye to me. His jowls drooped down upon his-collar.

Following supper, Elborn and I were set to work assisting at their payment. One by one these men who had carried me safe from Montreal appeared at the counting window in response to their names, and made their marks on the receipt. They are like shrewd children, knowing exactly how much is owed them, and oftentimes standing in their place to recount it. Then I would pass them the pint of rum which is the Company's bonus to them, and they would touch their caps and hurry away with it. The more shameless brought the women of their selection to the counting place; in the background could be seen the husbands and owners of such women, watching attentively and awaiting the price previously agreed upon. It is certain that many have the venereal complaint, as well as afflictions of the lung.

Later, impelled by curiosity and by that same peculiarity of temperament which had drawn me as a child to waterfalls and to the lips of cliffs, and which has sent me often alone into storms where there is no little danger, I left the banquet hall and its decorous gathering, and made my way past the palisade to the environs of the fort.

Here indeed was a scene of mayhem and debauch. It was nearly the eleventh hour. The fires which earlier had blazed so zestfully now cast a lurid glow from their shimmering embers, and by this light, and the light of the rising half-moon, I made my way through the encampment. The music of fiddle and pipe which had led dancing on a grand scale through the evening had now grown halt and lugubrious with the drunkeness of the players, so that now it sank for the most part into the merest facsimilies of jigs, to which some staggered and others reeled, pretending sobriety. Throughout the camp hung a pall of lust and violence such as I have never felt in any place. Was this, then, the lot of man in this new world, to hurl upon it the vices of the capitals, by moonlight, in a raw and bestial manner? And was this the culmination and apex of human labour, these lurching seconds on some filthy pallet, wherein he empties himself, this man, this animal, of his accumulated dreams and visions, his angers and his fears, his petty longings, hopes, and disappointments? Is this the end of all his journeys, to couple in a brooding wilderness? Could I have written it, my song for this night would have been no dance, but an endless moan of anguish, or a laugh sharper in irony than any I heard here in the tents and hovels, that we should come to this each time, that all our aspirations should be twisted at the end to this, that our climax should be a whimper of despair, and that alone.

In the tents grease lamps flickered, enabling me to see upon the skin walls the gross, distorted shadows of venery in every stage of its sating. Some writhed and contorted themselves in postures the beasts of the forest would have scorned. Some had not troubled even to drop the skin curtain across the entrance, so that their antics were visible to all who passed and cared to watch. At some entrances, in fact, drunken groups had gathered to urge on those inside, and so increase their own desire. They skulked and grinned like dogs circling a fire.

Here is a woman weaving towards me, her arms extended, her clothing opened and besotted, her gestures as lascivious as the numbness of drink will allow; and here is another, spread in her blanket before the fire, with her man looking dully on, pleading to me for rum as I pass; and here yet a third, scarcely a woman, indeed a mere child, imitating the advances she observes on every side around her. A knot of our men summon her, raising an earthen flask to her, and she enters laughing among them. How should one consider a people debauched so absolutely that they might be led to pander, for trinkets and oblivion, the very chastity of their daughters?

"Savages," said Mr. Duff, for he had joined me quietly, walking in the portly manner of a man of substance, and yet not foreign entirely to the smoke and lusting of the camp. "Look at them well, young MacKay, and understand that you have no place among them." Yet his own eyes devoured the scene. "Come now, for I have been sent to draw you back to the Company's affairs." He perceived my hesitancy and implied then that it was my duty to return; so we turned our steps upward out of the camp. But before we had left it entirely we chanced at one fire on a small boy, an Indian child not more than six or seven years of age, sitting alone and weeping. Duff took short notice of him and would have passed, but I squatted by the child, and found in my pocket some bit of sugar, boiled from maple sap, which is a condiment in our provisions. He took it and kept it, watching my face the while. Upon my asking why he wept, his tears renewed themselves and I saw that he understood some English.

"Come along, MacKay," said Mr. Duff. "We have no concern here for young savages until they have grown strong, and can bring us the skins of their brother Beaver."

But I remembered my childhood. "The child is frightened and alone," I answered him.

"Indeed he is, and so are we all, each one of us. He had best learn to abide by that, and play the man."

The child had buried its face upon its arms. "In a moment, Mr. Duff," I told him, surprising even myself at this insubordination. "Let me but comfort him a little." And so he proceeded alone, and I sat by the child, knowing I had weakened myself in the Company's sight.

I built the fire. The child appeared comforted by its new warmth and by my presence. At length, I told him in such simple language as I could the tale of Theseus, and how he wound his way deep into the labyrinth at Crete, where he found and battled with the Minotaur. When I came to describe that creature, the child, who had followed closely and forgotten his tears, stopped me in puzzlement. I perceived that he had never seen a bull and had therefore no conception of the creature's enormity. Consequently I substituted 'wendigo', which he understood at once. I described the marvellous battle at the heart of this story, which I myself had not heard since childhood. I took such liberties as equipping our hero with a trade knife, and with bow and arrow, and when at last the monster lay pierced and slain, the child laughed aloud and clapped its hands together, as if the very monsters of this night which had roared and prowled around him had themselves been vanquished. I then described the return of Theseus, and the slender thread which linked him to safety and the woman who loved him, and the child repeated her name, Ariadne, with the blunt accents of its native tongue until, under my correction, he could speak it properly. I created sharp angles and protrusions which could have torn the thread in that darkness, and at last, after much suspense, I drew the hero out into the light of Greece and a view of islands and sparkling sea which must have seemed, to the child, like the dancing waters of Superior.

Before I had concluded, I grew aware that we were alone no longer and that a tall Indian stood observing us just where the firelight caught his greased hair, and the metal trinkets on his breast, and the knife at his belt. He appeared as a figure of solace to the child, who went to him immediately and gripped the seam of his legging. They exchanged some words in their language. It appeared that the man questioned the boy, after which he regarded me with several slow nods, but with no further overtures.

I took my leave of them and went on to the fort, where I found that the meeting had been of no great import, if indeed it properly occurred at all, and where dancing was in progress.

When I had retired, I chanced on this passage from Antoninus: "When one is kind to a child, one should whisper to himself, 'tomorrow, perhaps, you will die.' And if this seems a hard saying, remember that nothing can be hard if it gives expression to an act of nature; otherwise we must say that it is hard and ill-omened to speak of the garnering of ears of corn ..."

June 16. This morning, while storing supplies with Elborn and the other clerks under Mr. Duff's direction, I learned that a killing had taken place. This information was delivered by Mr. Duff, who chafed still under my refusal to accompany him at his insistence last evening, and since the incident had occurred near the place where I stopped to comfort the child, this Duff revealed a lurid imagination in his jesting, making bold to imply that, the victim being a comely native woman, I had perhaps grown over-importunate in my demands upon her. So commonplace are such crimes that implications of this sort are lightly regarded, and although I remonstrated heatedly with the man, my very outrage became a further cause for merriment.

Later, Elborn alone accompanied me to the scene. The body lay where it had fallen, watched over by black crones hunched like vultures. They muttered and grouped together at our approach. They had tried to force rum down the throat of the corpse, for what reason I know not, lest in their superstition they thought to revive her in this manner into another world. In the sunlight, after its orgy, the camp itself lay like a corpse around us, grey and white. I confess that even Elborn's company was not unwelcome in this baleful place. A few native men hung their heads beside their tents. I assumed that later, when they had roused themselves sufficiently, the corpse would be laid to rest, no doubt with scant ceremony and notice.

She had been a handsome woman, and even in death retained some attractiveness. Upon her were few of the marks of debasement and depravity I had come to associate with her kind. Instead, her features were open and spacious. Such was the capriciousness of the light that I thought she smiled. A single mark distinguished her clothing and decoration from those of the other women, this being an insignia in dark red, painted in the center of her brow and visible because her hair had fallen back. It was in size and shape similar to the impress of a small frog's foot.

She had been impaled through the breast and had no doubt died swiftly.

The man and child I had met in that place were nowhere to be found.

"What action should the Company take in this case?" I asked Elborn as we returned to the fort.

"Action!" he replied with apparent incredulity. "Why, what action is necessary in the death of a drunken woman in the course of a drunken night? I gather that such incidents are rather the rule than the exception, and if the Company were to attempt to mete out justice among the savages, who conduct their personal affairs with more forthrightness and dispatch than we are accustomed to, I daresay its time and resources would sink as surely as into a bottomless mire. Are you forgetting the purpose of your presence here? Are you forgetting that your success will be measured in furs, and in furs only?" He rubbed his nose with his clenched hand, so that I could not tell whether he smiled and mocked me, or whether he was in earnest. "Let me remind you of Antoninus, my dear MacKay: A clear mind, a clear resolve, and no watery affection to trouble either!"

When he had finished reading, Paul flipped his thumb across the edges of the manuscript pages, and the sound snapped like a beaver's tail amid the heavier, authentic slaps which had punctuated his reading.

Liv yawned, squinting into the darkness. "Why are they so active?"

"Just playing," he said, beginning to burn the pages. "Sometimes they go on like that all night."

chapter fifteen

Crewcut and blazered, Paul Henry pulled his luggage off the train and strode up into the concourse of Union Station, behind

Gerry Rattray. "That way," Gerry said. The foyer was full of sun streaming through its western windows. They crossed it, bumped past the two sets of glass doors, and emerged under the columns on Front Street. For a moment they stood uncertain which way to turn, and in that moment a watchful beggar gauged them and sidled up.

"Off to school, eh? Off to university?" His glance shifted between them. "Listen, you boys help me out? I've had real bad luck, boys. Not like you, eh? You boys seen psoriasis? Oh God, I've got a case! Look here." And glancing about as if he did not wish to be observed in an act of indecency, he raised his trouser leg to reveal a scabrous shin. White flakes spiralled to the concrete. "It itches, boys!" He watched eagerly for their revulsion. "My God, how it itches! Sometimes I get into the park and I scream with the itching of it. I stuff my shirt in my mouth, like this, and I put my head inside my coat and I scream and scream so nobody'll hear me. But I'll be honest with yuh, now. I'll be honest. There's one thing that helps me out. If I can just have a little beer every hour or so that just seems to soothe it right down. Now that's a funny thing, isn't it? You'd think a man who was like that over most of his body ..."

"Take a walk!" said Gerry Rattray.

"Yeah ..." said the beggar, hobbling back, gathering his insult like spittle, "yeah, you ..."

"Here," Paul said.

"Why, thank you, sir. Thank you." He touched a finger to a non-existent cap and shifted to face Gerry. "Think again, young fella?"

"Nope."

"Anybody can have bad luck, my boy."

"I've got better things to do with money. Besides, you should have that treated."

"Let's go," Paul said.

"Just a minute, now. Just a minute." Flickers of fear and

malice played on the beggar's face. "There's one thing I want to ask your friend here. I'm only curious, you understand. But suppose you had a disease and you lived off it. Suppose the disease kept you alive. Would you want to cure it? Answer me that, now." He regarded Gerry from under ragged brows, as if his neck were stiff.

"If I had a disease, I'd cure it. Now bug off!"

The man spat as he backed away, grinning with hatred. Before he was lost in the fluids of the city he turned and shook the fist with the coins Paul had given him, but what he shouted was lost in the clamour of traffic.

They caught a Bay streetcar and lurched down the aisle to the back. It was not crowded. The ticket collector watched them from under an oversized cap. Paul settled by the window and turned his face to the warm evening air flowing under the sash. His arm rested across his knee. "The easiest thing to do with guys like that," he said, "is to give them what they ask for."

Gerry snorted. "Buy them off? Shit! What if he'd asked for a buck?"

"If you've got it, give it. What the hell, it's only money."

"Charity!" Gerry settled himself with a leg stretched in the aisle. "Fuck that!"

But it *was* only money, and if you had it, if by chance you had more than you needed, why not give it away? Paul shrugged. The grasping, niggardly performances of the businessmen he knew when they gave their charitable mites dismayed him. Why not give whenever you were asked? Give gladly? Give always more than the request? And then, if ever you needed food yourself, or clothing, or medicine, or anything, then surely other people would be as generous with you. He knew he was right.

The old streetcar faltered on the uphill grade. "Come on! Let's go!" Gerry straight-armed the seat in front of him. "Let's get on with it!"

"Ethics!" said their instructor in business law. A flicker of disdain passed over his eyes and mouth. "Do not imagine that there is a legitimate entity called 'business ethics'. There is not. There is only, first, what you may and may not do, that is to say the Law; and second, the means you must employ within the Law to out-manoeuvre your competitor, subdue your subordinates, and pacify your associates. You are engaged in a prolonged struggle. You are here now only because others, sympathetically inclined towards you, have engaged successfully in that struggle. Your competitor is your enemy. Ideally, you would kill him, but the Law restrains you. You must therefore endeavour to operate inside the Law in such a way as to crush your antagonist and leave him impotent. It is my duty to instruct you in that process. Those of you who listen carefully will live to be glad that you did so. Those who do not, those who believe that I have over-simplified, will simply be indentured to the others. The choice is yours now. At each future moment it will become less distinct.

"The body of law to which I shall introduce you is both a mechanism for your protection and the rulebook of a game. The game is business life. Let us have no illusions and no talk of ethics. 'Ethics' are shadows in which weak men hide themselves. Play the game efficiently, use the Law effectively, and you can go where you wish. Choose not to do so, and you will be either a criminal or a fool, or both. If you wish to examine the Law with that understanding, then I shall meet with you again on Thursday at 2 P.M. If you wish to entertain the notion of business ethics, join the Rotarians. Good day to you." He shut the snaps of his briefcase with synchronized thrusts of his thumbs, so that a single, metallic sound echoed briefly in the classroom.

"Sharp," said Gerry Rattray. "Definitely a very sharp guy."

So were all their instructors, Paul thought, except for Malcolmnson. Malcolmson was hopeless. He taught English Literature to engineers, dentists, architects, business students, pharmacists, foresters, and others whose interest in the subject was assumed to be slight. If all the students registered had attended his classes, the hall to which he had been assigned would have been filled. But by mid-term it was usually three-quarters empty, and his diffident voice was grotesquely distorted by the rows of seats which spread from his lectern like a graph of broken sound waves. For the few who came, he approached the texts like a bumbling, confused, and inquisitive child, amused by his own ignorance. He asked the questions the students themselves had wanted to ask but thought ridiculous. He speculated, he hypothesized, he wondered, mused, mumbled, scattered incoherencies, and behaved in all ways like the apologetic incompetent he evidently was. After a session he would linger at the front of the room, peering over his glasses and gathering together the confusion of notes and texts from which he never managed to sift any real order. He looked as if he hoped someone would come forward and ask a question in the answer to which he would find a container for the whole sorry mess, the container he could not quite fabricate alone. He was always the last to leave. He would deposit everything in the wicker basket of his antiquated bicycle and pedal off up St. George Street like a disoriented insect among iguanas.

By October Gerry had given up Malcolmson's classes in disgust. Paul continued. "Bloody masochist," Gerry snorted.

"Optimist," Paul replied. "Maybe he'll improve. Maybe he's just nervous."

"Oh for Christ's sake! He's over fifty! He's *had* it!"

One night as Paul was leaving, Malcolmson pointed a bony finger. "I know you," he said.

Paul hesitated. They were alone in the classroom, with the December night pressing the windows. "Henry, sir," he said. "First year Commerce."

"Yes, yes. I don't mean your name. I know *you*. Know your mother. At least we've corresponded. She sent me some manuscripts I wanted, years ago. A fine lady. A gentlewoman as the early Victorians would have said. And," he leaned across the lectern, "I knew your father."

"At school?"

"Yes, at school. And in the Air Force, too."

"You were a flier?"

He laughed at Paul's surprise and moved closer. His white hair was wild on a bony skull. There were liver spots like small burns on his hands and in front of his temples. He smelled musty, like old books. "That seems strange to you, I see. Well, we were all of us caught up, even the least likely. And it had to be done, you know. Oh yes, something certainly had to be done."

Paul set his books on a desk. "Were you ..."

"With him when he died? I knew you would ask that. Yes. At least, we were in the same air. We heard the same sounds, saw the same fires." He moved still closer and looked at Paul intently. "How old were you?"

"Eleven."

"Ah well, how can I help you? No matter what I say you'll keep looking the rest of your life, won't you. Asking questions, finding worthless substitutes." He spread empty hands. "Ancestors," he said.

"But you knew him well."

"We were friends, yes. We both wrote bad verse." He paused. "I ... have some of it, you know."

"His poetry?"

"Poetry and pictures too. Photographs. Do you want to see them?"

"All right. Yes."

Malcolmson spun away, his black gown swirling. "Good. Good, good. You'll have supper with me, then."

Paul grinned. "All right," he said.

"Ah, splendid." He gathered his notes, went for his coat and hat, and soon they were striding north through the wet night. Malcolmson smoked as they walked. Snow lay on the patches of grass. Exhaust rose from a sluggish stream of traffic under the street lamps. "Half-way man, that's what I called your father. He found it amusing. He knew well what I meant, of course, only half a dreamer, reluctant to go the whole way. He had his reasons, I suppose. I daresay you were one of them. Yes. But he knew what he should have done — let go, done away with all that pretense, all that efficiency. And he might have, if he'd come out of it. Who knows? Yes. Paul Henry, half-way man. Should I tell you these things? Well, what difference can it make. You have to know. It will never be enough, of course, but you have to know."

They stopped for the lights at Bloor and University, where the Park Plaza shed its neon glow. A Salvation Army Santa Claus swung his bell and stamped.

"When I marked your term paper I thought of him. Why did you choose Thoreau? Unlikely, isn't it, for a Commerce student? 'But lo! men have become the tools of their tools. The man who independently plucked the fruits when he was hungry is become a farmer, and he who stood under a tree for shelter, a housekeeper. We now no longer camp as for a night, but have settled down on earth and forgotten heaven.' You quoted that. You were the only one. Only you picked Thoreau. Why?"

"My mother talked about him."

"I daresay. And your father, too." He touched Paul's arm. "Imagine if you will the Channel sky clear as crystal. Imagine a flight of Hurricanes suspended off the French coast, the air among them full of instruction, fear, the false courage soon to be real enough. Imagine your fresh lambskins. Imagine your father's laugh, his voice: *Beware of all enterprises that require new clothes!*" Malcolmson flung back his head so violently Paul thought his scrawny neck would crack, and whooped a laugh at heaven. "Oh yes, his sense of incongruity was keen enough, wouldn't you say? The half-way man, indeed." He drew deeply on his cigarette, suddenly solemn. "I'm chattering," he said.

"No you're not, sir. Really. I want to know."

"I see too few people, too few students." His arm lashed out to include the streets, the weary city. "Prisoners, you see. All busy in separate cubicles. Measuring. Organizing. Terrified by chaos. Pretending it doesn't exist, in them, all around them. You're the first I've talked to in a week. At least a week. But you must pay no attention to what I say. I'm as guilty as the rest. Oh yes, quite as guilty.''

They entered a dingy apartment and climbed wooden stairs. It was very warm inside and the air was thick with the smells of cooking. Malcolmson's rooms were on the third floor, down a hallway with smudged and yellowed walls. Still talking, he found the key, flung the door open and switched on the light. There were books everywhere. Ranks of books rose to the ceiling on spindly shelves. The corners bulged with stacks, some of them tumbled over into dusty heaps. Mounds of manuscripts, magazines and papers lay on the floor, on the radiators and window ledges, on the chairs and table. My God, Paul thought, it's the sort of place where old skeletons are found sometimes. In tunnels of paper, with spaghetti cans. At one end of the table, in a small cleared space under the lamp, sat a bottle of Scotch and an unwashed glass.

"Not troubled by disorder, I trust? Mind, I didn't say confusion. Oh no no. There is an important distinction, is there not? Here you may find dis-order, perhaps even disarray. But out *there* is the confusion. Yes." He pulled off his coat, gestured for Paul's, and hung them both on a hook behind the door. "And it can only get worse. It can only get worse, not better. Ah, but I forget your origins. I forget how the good grey city must appear to you fresh from such a place as — where was it? — Sable Creek." He drew close, eyes wide and guileless behind his glasses. "You *like* it!"

"Yes I do."

"Yes, yes, of course you do!" Arms high, he sped away into the kitchen, and Paul heard the clink of glasses. A refrigerator door opened and shut, and an ice tray banged in the sink. "Ever the optimist. The blind optimist like your father. No doubt you would also have enjoyed the other triumphs of progress, conveniently forgotten. Mayapan, for example. Utatlan!" The ice tray banged the sink. "Illusions from their very birth. What was Chichen Itza against the forest? A pebble! What was Tikal? Copan? Illusions! Grand illusions." The ice tray banged. "Remember Knossus and Tyre and Antioch. Think of the Sumerian cities, the lost gardens of Babylon." BANG. "Ukheidur. Firuzabad. Constantinople." BANG. "Imagine the sands sifting through Persepolis, through Nineveh, through the halls of Petra." BANG. "And the theatres, Paul my friend; remember their broken circlets emptied of comfort — Bosra, Miletus, Ephesus and Pompeii." The ice tray banged a final time and the cubes rattled in the sink. Malcolmson emerged and poured drinks, smiling genially. "Think of all of *that*, and then tell me that you have hope for ... Toronto?"

Paul drank and cleared his throat. "Well," he said. "We do have some distance to go."

"Mmmm. Yes indeed." Malcolmson traced a narrowing spiral downwards, leaving cigarette smoke hanging in the air. "This way. And do you know why? I shall tell you why. The reason is very simple. It is because we have been too afraid. We shall be undone by caution!" Again his head dropped back and he laughed uproariously. "What a fine joke! What a magnificent irony! Don't you *see* it? Ah, your father would have seen it in an instant." His laughter subsided. He pressed a knuckle against his mouth, then pointed at Paul. "Your father. Of course. Forgive me. That's what brought you here — my saying I had some poems and pictures. I shall have to find them, now." He gazed blankly at the clutter.

"If it's too much trouble ..."

"No, no. No trouble. Just a question of remembering." He pressed his fingers to his temples. "Perhaps I should think about it over supper. Yes. Yes, that's what I shall do." And again he darted into the kitchen, weaving dextrously through the litter.

Throughout supper, which was more scotch, and soup and crackers, he talked incessantly, and when Paul finally extricated himself on the excuse of having to pack for the Christmas journey

home, he jogged back to the residence without seeing either
poetry or pictures.

"Broad?" Gerry asked.

"No such luck. Malcolmson."

"Kept your back to the wall, I hope."

"No, nothing like that. He's just a lonely guy full of old
names and booze. A bit off his stick, I think."

"Of course," said Gerry, spreading his hands. "Didn't I tell
you? Crazy as a shithouse rat!"

To his surprise the blue spruce on the front lawn was full of
lights. From the bottom of the hill he saw them — red, blue,
green and white and yellow — spreading a soft glow into the
snow-filled street from their caves inside the tree. Other trees
were also lighted, but the top lights on his mother's tree shone
like a beacon above them all.

"How did you do it? You didn't climb a ladder, I hope."

"Oh no, dear. Bob Mansfield sent some men up from the
mill. Wasn't that nice of him? He's been so kind. — Oh *Paul*!"
She fluttered about him, taking his hat and coat, warming his
hands, looking hard at his face. "It's so good to have you!
Why didn't you let me know what train to meet? Why didn't
you call from the station? I would have picked you up."

"I wanted the walk. I wanted some fresh air."

Her eyes were bright with excitement, and they seemed out
of place in the rest of her face which was pale and which, it
seemed to Paul, had not smiled for a long time. "I got a turkey.
See?"

"Mother, we'll never eat it all."

"Yes we will. That is ... unless you're leaving early."

"I'm not. I'm here for two weeks. You'll have to put up
with me."

"Marvellous," she said, embracing him. There was a grey
hair on the shoulder of her sweater; otherwise she was as immaculate as ever. But she was frailer, more uncertain.

"You've lost weight," he said.

"A little. Not much. One doesn't cook for oneself, you know."

"You should."

"Oh yes, yes, I know. But I don't."

He strode through the high, dark dining room and into the living room, clapping and rubbing his hands. "It's freezing in here!"

"Is it? I'll turn up the furnace. And why don't you light the fire? Yes. Light the fire, and we'll have some sherry. Would you like that?"

"Fine, but when did you start drinking sherry?"

"I got it special," she said. "For your homecoming." But he noticed when she brought in the tray that the bottle of wine, red as blood in the firelight, was three-quarters empty. "Now then," she sighed, sitting down and drawing her feet up. "I want to hear all about university."

He talked for an hour, and they drank the sherry. He told her about his courses, his teachers, the ideas that hung in him like irritating burrs. He described his city. He told her about Malcolmson and she said, "Oh yes, those old journals I sent him years ago. Something of your grandfather's. He must be a charming, cultivated man, to judge from his letters. Did he say he knew your father?"

He nodded, and she smiled when he told her what Malcolmson had said about her. At last, when the fire had burned low and they both sat gazing at its embers in silence, they were surprised by a singing from beyond the lawn and the glowing tree, a singing made faint by the drapes and the thick old walls of the house.

> Hark! the herald angels sing,
> 'Glory to the new-born King,
> Peace on earth, and mercy mild,
> God and sinners reconciled!'

They opened the front door and stood together while the little

choir came near enough for them to recognize Fred Hale, robust
in toque and mackinac, and a dozen boy scouts trampling the
fresh snow on the lawn.

> Christ, by highest heaven adored,
> Christ, the everlasting Lord,
> Late in time behold Him come,
> Offspring of a virgin's womb.

"Come and see us when you're home," Fred called when
the carol was finished. "Anytime. We're always there." And
Paul nodded and waved, watching the little group move off.
"Merry Christmas," his mother said. "Merry Christmas."

Beside the coals, with the last of the sherry, they heard the
faint singing start again from the neighbour's lawn, "O little
town of Bethlehem, How still we see thee lie! . . ." And Paul
cradled his glass and drank, not knowing what to say.

"You used to go with Fred, remember?"

He nodded.

"You and Franklin. Miro." She gazed at the embers, remembering other Christmases and other times when she was young
and in love, and his father's greatcoat and kit bag had hung
in the hall closet, forgotten for the ten-day leave. Perhaps it
was 1941, when there had been no gasoline for the car and
she had walked down to the station in her fur coat and hat,
running the last half-mile because she had already heard the
train's whistle moaning in the hills. Or perhaps 1942, the eve
of his father's departure, when they had sat by this same fireplace
listening to the BBC news and to Vera Lynn's promise that
the lights would someday come on again, all over the world.
And suddenly, seeing his mother's tears, he was filled with a
pale anger at that necessary and futile sacrifice, that time which
had swallowed his father up while Bob Mansfield remained
behind, growing fat on his essential service.

"Madness," his mother said, and drank. "Oh Paul, I've been

so lonely!''

"Ah," Bob Mansfield smiled. "The young crusader, home for his spoils. Come in. Come in."

"I want to know if your offer still stands."

"And what offer might that be?"

"To join the Company. After university."

"Ah yes. I did say something about that, didn't I. A year ago. Haven't seen much of you since then. You were going on a little trip, as I recall. With a friend. You were going to let me know."

"I had a lot to think about."

"I'm sure you did. Well, of course, my boy, the situation's changed a good deal since then. Money's tighter, market's far more competitive. Who knows what we'll need in three years' time?"

"Does the offer stand or not?"

"Let me put it this way. Your grandfather and my father started this business. Your father and I continued it, made it grow. Now I suppose that leaves me with a certain . . . obligation, doesn't it?"

"You're dealing with me, not my father."

"All right. All right. And what do you think *you* have to offer?"

"Ability. A fair mind."

"I can buy that from any university."

"A sense of place."

"Maybe that's valuable, maybe not."

"Experience, then."

"In what, precisely?"

"Your mill."

"Then you'll be able to tell me what kind of hydraulic barkers I should buy. Barkers were your speciality, weren't they?"

"You don't need hydraulic barkers. You know that. Stay with the drum type, but get larger ones — 12 by 45, maybe."

Mansfield nodded.

"And get rid of that vertical splitter. It's hurt too many men. Also, your cylinder machines are getting old. You should think about Fourdriniers."

"Money?"

"Government loans. Forgivable."

Mansfield laughed. "Go on."

"You should investigate ammonium."

"And produce no newsprint?"

"Think about it. One issue of TIME requires more paper than you produce in two weeks. If you could sell the right people you could share that market for glossy stock. You'd need calendering machines, of course. Now with ammonium you wouldn't require any more bleach, but you'd save on cooking time, maintenance, sulphur and steam, and you'd have a fifty per cent reduction in screenings. What's more, you might soon be able to recover the chemicals. There's an experimental process, McCarthy's, that uses ion-exchange resins."

"That's years away."

"Maybe. But even if it never comes ammonium would still pay you."

"You're guessing."

"Try me. Get a cost analysis."

"A cost analysis and a good salesman in Toronto, is that it?"

"That's it. Toronto, Montreal, and New York. Someone who could get you into the tissue and paperboard markets even if you decide to stay in newsprint. Your selling has been very lax, very lazy, and you won't do much sitting on your tail in Sable Creek."

"Tell me more."

"All right. Your cellulose process. Boards are clumsy to ship and they don't bring the return you should have. Why live with a dead end? Have you read Gemmell's White Paper?"

"Not yet."

"It's very revealing. What it means is that you can expect more restrictions on your cutting on all Crown lands. So you'll have to make better use of what you can get."

"And you see that happening in cellulose."

"Partly there, partly in your woodlands operation. It's very wasteful. Why let good wood rot? In one season you leave enough birch to supply a small veneer or plywood mill. Get a loan to start one. Rehire the men your automation will make redundant and you'll be a hero."

"And then?"

"Then look at shipping. For short runs south through Fort William you should use your own transports. Amortized and tax deductible."

"American markets don't pay."

"Yours don't. Not now. But look at their supplies. You know sustained yield is a myth. Before long the Americans will be crying for the wood your father tied up in long-term leases. Then you can set your price. You'll be able to write off a pair of semis every second year, together with drivers' salaries, and still see a profit."

"Pretty optimistic, aren't you?"

"Realistic. Come on, Mr. Mansfield. You're in business. As you say, either you swim or you go belly up. Now what I want to know is whether your offer stands. If it doesn't, say so, because I'm not interested in little games."

"It stands."

"All right. Then I propose that it include a summer job for the next three years at a salary which will cover all my school expenses. This year they'll be eighteen hundred dollars. Next year, more."

"And if I say no?"

"Then I'll work for Abitibi, or Weyerhauser, or Boise Cascade."

"You've got a bloody nerve," said Bob Mansfield, smiling. "What I should do is kick your ass right out of here!"

"If I want theatre I can buy a ticket. Do we agree?"

"I'll think about it."

"I'll wait."

"We agree," Bob Mansfield said.

"Who is it?" Fred's voice rose from the cellar where he had his little den, piled high with exams, and notebooks, and student essays, and bristol boards splotched with dried leaves.

"It's Paul."

"Who?"

"Paul," she said more softly, smiling. She untied her apron and shook back the strand of hair that had fallen across her face. She kissed him on the mouth. "Hi, Paul," she said.

Fred's footsteps thumped, taking the stairs two at a time. "Who'd you say? Paul! Glad to see you." He shook hands vigorously, gripping Paul's shoulder. His balding head was close-cropped, almost shaven. Massive biceps bulged in the arms of his T-shirt. "C'mon in! We'll have some tea, eh? Narah?"

"Okay."

"Come in. What've you been up to? Tell me about school."

"There isn't much to tell, Fred. It's hard work, but I'm learning."

"Play football?"

"A bit, not much. I'll play intramural next year when things have settled down."

"How's the city? Awful?"

"It's not so bad, actually. There's always lots to do."

Fred grimaced and shook his head. "I dunno. I don't know if I could take it or not. I've been thinking about moving, you know."

"You have?"

"Oh yeah. I had a good offer from the Toronto Board. Principal."

"Congratulations."

"New school. Nice district. But I dunno." He frowned. "I

think people can get lost in the city, know what I mean?"

"No."

Fred gestured vaguely, watching his wife enter with the tea tray, her hips comfortable in slacks. "Lose touch with themselves. Lose touch with other people. Peppermint?"

"Thanks."

"Cream and sugar, Paul?"

"No, just clear, thank you. Fred, I thought you might be interested. You remember that old pistol?"

"Pistol?"

"The one I found on our trip. The scout trip."

"Which trip was that? There've been so ... Oh, sure! Sure! I remember now. You were with that group when we had the terrific storm, weren't you?"

"Storm?"

"When we got blown way off course and the rangers came out. Sure." He nodded happily. "That's right. You found an old pistol of some kind. I had it here for awhile, didn't I? As a matter of fact, I thought it was still here — in an upstairs drawer someplace." He laughed.

"I got it before I left," Paul said. "Your wife gave it to me."

"Oh good. You know, I don't like having other peoples' things around. Too much responsibility. But that was all rusty. Couldn't have been very valuable."

"Not really. I took it to the historical weapons people at the museum, and they dated it and told me something about it. I don't know why I thought you'd be interested ..."

"I am. I am. Go on."

"It was made sometime between 1770 and 1780 by a firm called Dalton, in Dublin. Pretty obviously it was carried to where I found it by some fur trader. What puzzled the archaeologists is that it wasn't a trade item — far too much silver and tooling on it. So it must have been his own personal gun, and they couldn't understand why it had been discarded, or how it could have been forgotten. They asked me where I'd found it and of course I couldn't tell them."

"No," Fred shook his head ruefully. "That was a hell of a storm, wasn't it? That storm blew people off course all over the district. Did you know that?"

"No."

"It did. When we were flying out the ranger told me that if it hadn't been for the scout training we would have been in real trouble. Said the thing that saved us was organization."

"Organization."

"That's right. And listen, it's even better now. I've got one of the best scout programs that you'll ever see. Yessir. Got trips going out and coming in almost to the minute. Timed perfectly. Perfectly." He slapped his palm with the edge of his other hand, as if chopping something very fine. "Well, that's certainly interesting about that pistol. Can't remember where you found it, eh?"

"No."

"Too bad. Probably more relics there. If you knew where it was I could take the boys back for a little digging. Good history lesson, eh Narah?"

She wrinkled her nose. "Oh I don't know, Fred. It's better to leave things alone sometimes."

"I don't see why. Learn all you can, that's my motto. That's what I teach my students, too. You know, Paul, I've been trying to think who else was with us on that trip. There was Gerry, and Miro, and ..."

"Franklin."

"Franklin! Sure. Good old Franklin. What's he doing now?"

"He's in Toronto with the CBC. In television."

"The coming thing," said Fred. "Ten years from now nobody'll even listen to the radio anymore. Bright boy, Franklin. Do you remember how he was always taking pictures? That whole trip! Every time I turned around there was Franklin pointing his camera. Great big lens. Bright boy. And old Gerry ... Listen, do you know what we should do, Narah? We should have a big party. All the boys who ever went on a trip with me.'' His eyes brightened, and Paul glimpsed his vision — the room crowded with young men, their robust laughter as they reminisced, their backslapping. Good old Fred Hale. God, what we owe you!

''I don't think there'd be room,'' she said, smiling at Paul. ''Not all at once.''

''Just the ones who've gone tripping. Know the country. The *pays d'en haut,* eh Paul? We could even make it like the old Beaver Club in Montreal, have wild game, mushrooms, sing the old paddling songs.''

''I don't like parties, Fred.''

''But you'd come, eh? Sure you would. They all would. You know, Miro was in the other night, and he was saying what he owed to scouting.''

''*Miro?*''

''Sure. Well, he didn't mention scouting in so many words, but his stuttering's not so bad, did you notice that? And he said he just wanted to thank us, that he felt it was a direct result of going into the wilderness and learning how to survive. Isn't that what he said, Narah?''

She nodded.

He stood up. ''So I guess that storm did some good after all, eh Paul? That storm, that training. Well look, if you'll excuse me, I have work to do. Exams. Marks have to be in tomorrow. But let's keep that get-together in mind, shall we? Maybe for the spring.''

''I have some parcels to deliver,'' Narah said. ''Can I drop you?''

''All right. Thanks.''

''Glad you came.'' Fred pumped his hand again. ''Keep up the good work, now. Learn all you can down there. Have you ever thought of teaching, by the way?''

''No, I haven't.''

"You should. Definitely. Things are improving every year, you know. Salaries are going up, straight up. No ceiling." He vanished into the kitchen, and they heard him whistling back downstairs and into his den.

"You drive," Narah said, when they were outside.

"Where shall we go? The lookout?"

"All right." She turned in the seat to watch him, one leg drawn under her. "Don't laugh at him, Paul. It's all chance, isn't it?"

"My being here's no chance."

"Think you know what you want?"

He reached over and drew her close.

"I think you do. I think you'll probably get whatever you want."

They drove two or three blocks in silence. He wanted to tell her about his meeting with Mansfield, not in detail, but only to let her know what he had decided, and to receive a kind of shriving in that shared knowledge. But when he began, she stopped him. "Ugh! Please, not Bob Mansfield!"

"Now *you're* being uncharitable. He's a very kind and sensitive person, and yesterday he made me a generous offer ..."

She put her hand on his mouth. Her forehead came to rest against his shoulder. "Un unh," she said. "You don't have to earn me, Paul."

chapter sixteen

Liv Henry woke cold. All night, beavers had played beside their campsite, and after the rain ceased the swatting of their tails punctuated her dream like the shattering of icicles. Someone hammered a coffin. The mirrors had been turned to the walls.

"You don't need it," she cried from her window. "He isn't dead! No one has died!" But the man refused to heed her. He fastened the tiny boards with massive nails. He was muffled against the cold, his face covered by a bright scarf, white and blue. He was a young man, susceptible but unheeding. He wielded a two-hand mallet. Skiffs of snow encircled him. She longed to run to him but could not. She was imprisoned in the window. She could no longer even call. But the nails were much too big; they would split the fresh wood! He took slow and regular strokes. Even as she watched the wood shattered and the splinters rose and fell; but he took no notice and the coffin was again intact. And yet it was not a coffin, but a huge book, a record or ledger, and he stamped upon it with a massive rubber implement beneath which the pages shuddered and heaved. She could not see what was stamped upon them ... She was on a hill. She was cold and in her nightdress. She was alone with a machine of the type used to drill wells, and its hammer rose and fell and pierced the earth with yards of steel. And yet the well was sterile ... She lay in a wood. Someone shot birds above her. Their feathers crinkled out like arrows as they fell. Snow gathered on the soles of her feet and on the fleshy portions of her arms. She ran. She floated in enormous strides, and at each contact the earth cracked beneath her. She tried desperately to stay aloft, to cease the damage, cease the pain, but relentlessly she fell. At her touch the earth exploded in chunks of rock, glinting ice slices, frost in the hearts of trees. She cried for help. Men came and looked at her. Men thumped their feet on hollow boards. They were muffled hunters searching her, but she was beneath the ice with no room to cry on the rough underside of the ice. Their shadows crossed above her. They were enemies and she was a hunted thing. They were chopping a hole to reach her ...

She cried, "Paul ... " And his arms found her. In his sleep he drew her close to the warmth of him.

When she had calmed a little she rose and began to dress.

She had thought she had mastered fear; rather, she had thought that she had simply left it behind after Michael's death, together with hope.

Bending, she unzipped the tent and entered the morning. The forest dripped with the rain of the previous days, but the sky was now clear. Behind the mist, the sun gleamed like a white plate. From under the canoe she gathered dry sticks and lit a fire. She dipped water from the river and hung a pot to heat. Then she washed. Like a squaw, she thought. Like a greased squaw hunkering to dab away some of the sweat, to smooth her hair, to fasten it with a cord. And why not. Wasn't this what she had always thought should be? Through all those hours of applied beauty, wasn't this what they all had wanted but lacked the courage to take — a simple wash, a smoothing back of the hair so that the man could see the face clearly, and an erect, open approach to him which said: Here I am. Take me as I am or not at all.

She lingered at the water, watching the ripples spread. In spite of herself she remembered her other lives, and she laughed at herself and at this process of forgetting which seemed to demand such precise recollection. One remembered meticulously at first, but then there were two images to be recalled — that of the event and that of its memory, and they fitted like frames in an imperfect stereoscope, blurred and ringed by shadows that belonged to both, yet to neither; and with each recollection one added to one's creation of the incident until it lay inert beneath accretions, static, stored, and safe, exactly as it should have been or as it needed to be at that moment. Of course, there was another way: you could simply drift on currents you refused to understand. You could watch the water. You could let images and horrors purge themselves out of you unthinkingly, like sweat from a feverish body. And after a time you might be cooled, with no further need of visions.

Images from girlhood rose to her first, like pale skirmishers, and she knew they would not trouble her. But behind them came

138

dark and heavy shapes which enclosed her suddenly and bore her roughly down. They were countless, faceless ... Paul's reflection joined her own in the water. He bent and embraced her. Behind them the fire crackled. Behind them a turbulence of herons burst from the forest, and she turned to watch the great grey birds lift above the mist and into the warm sun of morning.

chapter seventeen

Miro lived apart from the others. For three years of university he had done so not by choice but because he couldn't afford the fees of residence. His scholarships barely covered his tuition and his frugal meals, and he had taken his night job as a short order cook partly because of the food which he could eat when the manager wasn't looking. Summers he worked in laboratories, doing menial things at first but finally donning a white coat and entering the marvellous glass world where fluids hung in tubes like crinkled guts. Often he would stay there very late at night, silent and secure, forgetting the emptiness of the place where he slept, and oblivious to the needs of his stomach.

Hunched at his desk, he had spent the morning reading Delevoryas on plant diversification, and Burnett and Eisner on adaptation. About ten, he had finished making notes from those books, but he did not push them aside until he had checked some dubious points against Odum's *Fundamentals of Ecology*. Satisfied at last, he glanced at the clock, saw that he had two hours, and with a sigh of anticipation drew down his frayed copy of Kropotkin's *Mutual Aid*. The old anarchist's stately prose surrounded him like a warm bath, and he sank gratefully into it. To Miro, Kropotkin's advice was like a father's calm voice beside the fire; Kropotkin's indomitable optimism assured him that all was well, that we need only trust ourselves to find ourselves adequate to any challenge; the wealth of the old man's scholarship was like coming home to all that had never been and would never be, a gorgeous and unanswerable fantasy before which Darwin and Malthus and Thomas Huxley cringed and shuffled and hid their gloomy souls. "Don't compete!" he read. "Competition is always injurious to the species, and you have plenty of resources to avoid it ... That is the watchword that comes to us from the bush, the forest, the river, the ocean ... That is the surest means for giving to each and to all the greatest safety, the best guarantee of existence and progress, bodily, intellectual, and moral."

When the alarm went off Miro cursed and thumped the clock into silence. One P.M. Reluctantly he shut his book and replaced it where it belonged, beside *Memoirs of a Revolutionist*. He switched off the desk lamp and got up, unbuttoning his shirt. Naked, he splashed himself at his sink and rubbed cold water in his hair. He shivered, rubbed himself dry, and began to dress in a white shirt and the blue suit which he had bought three years before with part of the money which was the Ferguson Prize for Upper School Biology. He disliked the suit because he disliked the occasions which had required him to buy it and to wear it. Out of habit he stood in front of a yellowed mirror, but he did not watch himself buttoning his shirt, tying his tie, pulling his trousers on. Instead, he watched the reflection of the print which hung on the opposite wall. There were no pin-ups in Miro's room, only this brooding silkscreen of Tom Thompson's *Northern River*, which lost nothing, in Miro's opinion, in being viewed backwards. What interested him most was true whether the river wound to the right or to the left — its apparent impassability beyond the tangle of underbrush which sprawled out and covered it. What interested him most about Tom Thompson was the fact that he had travelled alone in that grey canoe. Miro believed that someone had finally brought down his paddle across

Tom Thompson's forehead for reasons which had nothing to do with money or women, but with the man's lonely pride.

He finished dressing and turned to face the picture directly. The river was not even a path, but a tangle of creepers and twining second growth where a man could be frenzied by black flies and sent howling. Was there a way through? There seemed to be none, and yet the viewer was drawn in and forced to search, and through the underbrush came the enticing flash of water vital as blood, here, there, not a single river at all, but a blending of fragments, tributaries and spongy marsh.

But how far should one go? Surely there were questions which should not be asked, trips which should not be started, tangles which should not be simplified. Surely some confusions should be left to generate, and if one were wise one would not always look for the way through. Expecting no answers, one would soon tire of asking questions . . . .

"Nope," Miro said. "You gotta keep going."

He cleaned his glasses and pulled on his coat. He felt constrained and ridiculous in the suit, and he slouched a little, hands in his pockets, striding down the dingy hallway. By the time he reached the front porch he was angry. Goddam! Why was he doing this? Why was he going out into the city, dolled up like a bloody pimp, on a perfectly good Saturday afternoon that could have been used for studying or just for reading. Jeez, if it was a choice between Kropotkin and Franklin Hook's moronic ceremony . . .

He cleared the front steps, took two strides, and neatly kicked a tricycle which was overturned in his path. It clattered against the fence, its bell jangling, and as it did so the landlady's child, who hated him deeply, set up a fierce howling from its lair under the steps. Miro spun and snarled at it. "Shut up, you little creep! And stay outta my goddam room or I'll break your fingers!" The child screamed with fury, drawing its mother out of the house. Miro had just reached the street when she appeared, an ample lady bloated further with indignation. "You hit him!"

Walking, Miro spread his arms in innocence. She descended the steps and gathered her baby to her breast, torn between comforting it and screeching imprecations at Miro. Disapproving neighbours appeared. Past the corner of her lot, Miro walked backwards, smiled, shrugged, waved. *That's right, Mrs. Fratranelli. That's exactly what I am, an ungrateful, vicious child molester. Yes I am ashamed. Yes, Mrs. Fratranelli, I am sure my mother would also be ashamed for me. Deeply chagrined. Yes, mortified.*

"Screw you, Mrs. Fratranelli," he said, walking on. And then in a sudden surge of bitterness he shouted back for all the street to hear, "And you're a rotten cook! On your lasagna, Mrs. Fratranelli, a man could die!" He chuckled, feeling better.

When he reached Huron Street he hesitated, unsure of the time and uncertain whether to walk or to blow a dime on carfare. At last he decided to be safe and turned towards Bloor and the streetcar stop. He chose a back seat and squinted out into the October afternoon. The tram clanked along, hissing at the stops and clanging monotonously at impetuous cars. Miro paid little attention to the people and their activities. Window shoppers bored him, ambling lovers made him sick. Instead, he looked for the sites of new construction and peered eagerly over the hoardings whenever they appeared, happily and deeply troubled by glimpses of the gouged earth. Nothing would grow in that earth again; not ever. At least, not until the buildings themselves came crashing down, the bent girders flaking with rust, the bricks crumbling to powder. But what caused the most baleful, most perverse excitement in Miro were the visions of destruction themselves, and there were many of these along the route. Everywhere old buildings were falling to the wreckers. In every stage of disassembly they stared at the street through shocked, dead eyes. Some had lost their roofs; some their roofs and upper walls; some had crumpled inwards under the hammers, and lay in rubble. Several times he saw cranes at work, their balls smashing the old masonry, churning it to dust. And over all the ruins men teemed like ants, crowbars prying, laughter bent crazily in the chilled air.

At Bay Street, Miro transferred. For the few blocks to City Hall the scene was less intense but similar. The buildings of human scale were toppling; skeletal, the new spires rose, dwarfing their creators. Descending into the heart of the city, he felt as he thought miners must feel, trundling down in their little trains out of the light of day.

At Queen Street he got off and crossed to City Hall. A popcorn merchant, his whistling white cart festooned with candy apples, leaned out cajolingly but Miro passed him by. The crowds were thicker here, crossing and recrossing the street while a police-woman held out white gloves for them, whistle in her teeth. Eatons was having a sale; blue banners proclaimed it, and flourescent posters in the windows. Ties! Miro snorted. Cheap little underpants and nylon socks for the old man!

He climbed the steps two at a time, entered City Hall, and asked directions from a pimply youth at the desk. "Second floor, turn right, third door past the divorce court."

Franklin rose to meet him. "I was going to phone," he said. "I thought you might have forgotten."

"Where's the can?"

Franklin stooped a little and took his arm. "Come and meet Julie first."

"I've gotta piss!" Miro protested, but Franklin drew him along. "You know Mona," he said.

"Hello, Miro."

"And this is Julie."

"Hi, Miro."

In that dim place they were like gorgeous insects. Like Luna moths or zebra butterflies. Or like arachnida. Their hair rose elaborately. The knitted skirts covering their trim thighs and their bottoms rested lightly on the wooden bench. The petals of their corsages fluttered. Miro shifted from one foot to the other. "Nice day," he said, trying to smile. "Good day for a wedding."

"Aren't we lucky?" Mona said. "Imagine what Muskoka will be like." Her laughter was not intended to be lascivious, but it was.

"Yeah," Miro said. *You'll never see it*, he thought. *You'll never see even a single goddam tree. You'll spend the whole two weeks in a hotel room fucking your ass off.*

"Excuse us," Franklin looked up and down the hall. "I wonder where ... "

"Little boys' room?" Mona pointed. "That way."

They stood side by side at the urinals.

"Isn't she lovely?"

Miro grunted. His bladder drained in a rich stream.

"She is very, very beautiful, isn't she. And so is Julie, don't you think?"

"Indian," Miro said.

"No, she's not Indian. She's half Chinese. Also a model."

Miro made a sound, shaking himself.

"Do you know what I plan to do? I'm going to make a book about Mona. Photographs. Just of Mona. I've been thinking a lot about it, and I plan to photograph her all through this trip. You know, mostly in natural settings, stressing the affinity between woman and nature, you know. The theme of allurement and regeneration. Mona's perfect for it." Franklin nodded happily. "In fact, I've already begun. I've got maybe forty, fifty contact sheets ... "

"Don't do it!"

"Watch it, Miro! Jeez, I nearly peed all over your foot!"

"Don't do it!"

"What d'you mean, don't do it. It's a very interesting project. You should *see* some of these pictures."

"Don't get married!"

"What?"

"Listen, you're so interested in nature, right? Always borrowing my books, asking me questions. Well lemme tell you, marriage is unnatural!"

"Come on, Miro."

"It is. I'm telling you. Do you know how many p-primate species mate for life?"

"What's that got to do with it?"

"Everything, g-goddam it! Marriage is unnatural. Against instinct!"

"Miro," Franklin zipped his trousers and reached down to take Miro's shoulders. "Man, Miro, has been heterosexual and homosexual. Man has been monogamous, polygamous, polyandrous, and even celibate. It depends completely on the needs of the society. There is no programming."

"There is! There's what's right! Inside!"

Franklin stared at him solemnly. "Miro, don't you think it's about time you took things a little easier? Sort of accepted things a little more? Hunh? Live and let live, Miro, for goshsake."

Miro shrugged. "Ah hell," he said. "It's your life."

"That's right. And she's beautiful, isn't she?"

"Yeah."

"Okay, then. Here's the ring." Franklin slapped his shoulder. "You look good," he smiled. "Clean shirt, nice suit. Listen, why don't you take Julie to dinner after we've gone?"

"Naw ... "

"Seriously. On me." Franklin pulled a bill from his wallet and stuffed it into Miro's pocket. "And comb your hair before we go out. You forgot. It's all standing up on end."

After the ceremony they walked together to the parking lot and Franklin pulled down the top of his MG. "It's so warm for October," Mona said, sliding in. "I can't get over it."

"Have a g-good trip."

Franklin shook hands earnestly. "Thanks, Miro. See you when we get back. You'll have to come over for dinner."

"Julie, too," said Mona, winking.

The car roared, reversed, and whined smoothly away into the traffic. Franklin waved. Mona's scarf fluttered out behind.

Julie unpinned her corsage. "Well," she said. "That was

nice.''

"Yeah."

"I like simple weddings, don't you? After all, it's what people *feel* that counts, isn't it, not all the ceremony.''

Miro looked at the sky. She *was* pretty. She moved like a small and confident animal, her skin tawny in the autumn light. She smiled at him. The trace of epicanthic fold above her eyes moved him strangely. And she was shorter than he was. And she smelled marvellous. His hand found the bill in his pocket, and his gaze came down suddenly, wide-eyed, through his thick glasses. "How about d-dinner?''

"All right, Miro.''

"Just the two of us. Alone.''

"Why sure,'' she smiled. "Where do you suggest?''

He had a momentary flash of panic. He knew none of the good restaurants, even the mediocre ones. He held his breath, desperately searching for the name of the place where Paul had once taken him after exams. "Bassel's.''

"Sure,'' She glanced at her watch. "How be I meet you there at, oh, six?''

"Meet me?''

"Is that okay? I have a job to do at four.''

She would leave him! She would move off into the currents of the city before he had even found her. He didn't know her last name, her phone number, where she lived. He foresaw her carried away in the crowd, her suit coat open and fluttering in the warm breeze, her neat bottom swaying. "Can I come?''

She frowned. "Oh, you wouldn't like it, Miro. It's just a modelling session. They're very dull.''

"No, I'd be interested. Really. And I've got the t-time.''

"I don't think so, Miro.''

"Please,'' he said.

She looked at him, then shrugged. "Okay. I guess it'll be all right.'' She took his arm. "You're a big boy now, aren't you.''

They walked down Yonge to Gerrard, then east. By the time they reached the studio Miro was close to exhilaration. She listened to whatever he said. Every poor joke he made amused her. She was free, and relaxed, and — to his amazement and delight, she seemed happy to be with him. The mere weight of her arm aroused him. He was furious with himself, but overjoyed. Afterwards, he thought, alone together in the emptiness of the city, they would have supper, and talk, and she would lean forward with her chin on her hands, smiling as he had seen other women smile behind windows at their men, and she would be totally and only his. And perhaps afterwards, after they had finished . . .

SCARFELD ASSOCIATES, the sign said. They entered a small and cluttered office where a young man bent under flourescent lights. His tie was loosened. His short sleeves revealed thick and hairy arms. His lips, Miro noted with distaste, were also thick — very thick and sensual. "You're late," he said. "Twenty minutes."

"Sorry. I'll make it up."

"Can't do it. Got another session right at five. It'll have to come off your cheque."

She shrugged. "This is Miro. He wants to sit in, okay?"

The man looked at Miro's glasses, his thin chest, his out-of-date blue suit. He showed his teeth. "Long as he stays outta my way. Let's go."

Behind the office, the building opened up into a vast cave, a sort of warehouse where boxes and crates were stacked high in the semidarkness against brick walls. The walls themselves were ridged with cables and studded with fuseboxes. Above, forming a false ceiling, hung a complex network of tracks and pulleys, and from adjustable racks huge paper backdrops dangled. Around the center of the room were batteries of lights, some high, with rotating sets of filters, some low and pointed, perched on their tripods like the beaks of herons. There were several step ladders of various sizes, and on these other men made adjustments to the lights. In the center was a large brass bed; to one side was a stack of sheets of various colors, and behind this was a storage cabinet full of what looked like theatrical props.

As they approached the young man clapped his hands and called instructions. The others moved briskly about their business. Lights came on. The bed was swivelled slightly and fixed in place. Far above, fans hummed alive, and for the first time Miro noticed how hot the room was despite its size.

Julie touched his cheek, smiling. She raised a finger. "One hour," she said, soundlessly, and then, to Miro's horror, she took off her clothes, hung them on a chair back, and walked naked into the circle of lights.

Suddenly the lights swarmed upon Miro as if they had come alive and ravenous. On their ladders the technicians swayed like demons. "Stop!" he shouted. "Stop it!"

The photographer turned slowly, his camera dangling, his smile saccharine-sweet. "Your friend," he said to Julie. He checked his watch. "Cool him, or he goes out."

She came back quickly over the swarm of cables and took his arm. "Hey, Miro."

"You said we'd be alone!"

"We *will* be. Honest. But I've got my job to do, Miro."

"To hell with that!" He seized her clothes from the chair back and thrust them at her. "P-put them on! God," he swung his arm at the bemused group of men, "they're all l-looking at you!"

"That doesn't matter. It's a *job*, Miro." She squeezed his arm. "It doesn't *mean* anything."

"Yeah?" He smiled bitterly. "Well, I'll tell you what it m-means!"

"Look, why don't you wait in the office, huh? Read a magazine. In an hour we'll go have dinner."

He shook his head.

"Well, okay." She looked dubious. "But if you stay you've got to be quiet, Miro. Honest."

The photographer came over and patted her hip, looking at Miro. "Let's go, Julie. Time's money."

"Don't t-touch her!"

"Look! Where do you think you get off, buddy? You come into my place, you interrupt my session ... "

"Just don't touch her!"

Indolently, one of the technicians moved close. He was very big. Sweat gleamed on his bald head and he looked at Miro through narrowed eyes. "Out?"

"Maybe, Arnold, maybe."

Miro glowered at them both and at the camera. "Goddam d-dildo!"

"Listen! You know what that *is*? Huh? That's a Hasselblad, my friend. That camera cost more than you'll ever make in half a year. Now if you don't like the heat get outta the kitchen, because I've got no time for your kinda *crap*!"

The technician smiled very faintly. His arms hung motionless. "Wasted a lotta time, this fella."

"Damn right he has! Let's go, Julie."

"He'll be okay now," she said, looking back. "He'll be quiet now."

"Christ, he'd better be. What're you doing anyways, bringing freaks in here? Jeez, if he flips out before we even get started ... Okay, on the bed. Let's have the magenta on numbers one and two. Right. Now up on your elbow, hand on the thigh." The camera clicked. "Smile. Now spread your legs. *Spread!* Don't you understand English, for crissake?"

Dancing reflections blurred Miro's vision. He could not remember running. He could not recall uttering the cry which warned the picture taker and gave him time to extend a foot. But he could, later, remember every detail of that face above his own — the narrowed eyes never changing, the high cheekbones, the mouth broken in the faintest of uneven smiles. He tried to scream but his face was crushed against the floor and there was a paralysing weight on his neck and between his shoulder blades.

"All right, that's it! Arnold, throw the bastard out! And you stay right there, lady! Jesus *Christ*, you've got a bloody nerve, bringing something like that in here! Lie down, goddam it! I've paid for this hour and don't you forget it!"

Pain surged in Miro's arms and shoulders. He cried out. His glasses were twisted, maybe even broken, and he could see nothing distinctly. He knew that he had been carried out of the lights and was being pushed into an alley, past a heavy door. He lifted his foot and kicked hard backwards, briefly gratified to find a shin; but the next instant a pain far more agonizing than that in his shoulders paralyzed him utterly, causing his mouth to stretch wide open. "Uh," he said. "Uh, uh, uh."

The other man's face was close to his. He felt the voice, rather than heard it. "I wouldn't come back in, if I was you," the voice said. "Being disobedient, that's how a fella really gets *hurt*!"

The fire door clanked shut and Miro sagged against it. There were no handles on the outside. He kept slipping until he hit the pavement.

At dawn Miro got up from the desk where he had read all night, and looked through his window at the stars in the eastern sky. "I am convinced," he had read, "that whatever character such a movement may take in different countries, there will be displayed everywhere a far deeper comprehension of the required changes than has ever been displayed within the last six centuries."

He felt a good deal better. He had discovered that one of the most endearing things about Kropotkin was the fact that the old revolutionary never, ever, spoke of sex.

chapter eighteen

They ate, and packed the canoe. The rising sun sent mists rolling down to the west. Opposite their campsite, on the east bank of the river, several cottages lay shadowed by the forest behind, their windows cavernous, their docks like truncated arms. No lights had glowed in them the previous evening, but they were not necessarily deserted. In fact, Paul thought he glimpsed movement near some of them, but the dawn played tricks, and the rising sun glared in his eyes. To the north, promontories lay like fingers on the river, black, black-green, grey and lighter grey, until the last one vanished in a pale fusion of sky and water. It would be a hot day.

Liv wore a sun hat he had given her years before. It was white with a blue interior and a floppy brim. She had pulled it down so that it shaded the upper part of her face and her neck. At first it had reminded him of the sad, wilted scout hat Fred Hale had worn through the rains of their trip years before, but gradually that resemblance faded and was no longer a source of amusement to him.

Paul swung the bow of the canoe clear, gripped the gunwales, and pushed off from the rocks in a motion that sent the craft in a deep glide into the river, settling toward the stern as it gathered his weight. It was a moment he loved. The substance and repose of the woman, the solid accumulation of packs in the midsection, their flanks against the thwarts, the feel of his own paddle, exactly balanced and right, all excited him; and then this moment, this magic moment of suspension between the craft that was all his world and which contained, distilled down to these few images, everything he held important from the other world and all he would now take from it.

The canoe lived. He could not have entertained any notion of life which excluded the canoe at that moment, nor the cedar which composed it — great, towering cone already hollowing at the center — nor its seed, nor its mother tree, nor the canoe-maker sounding it with his axe-butt. His skill lived in the canoe, the sharpness of his knife and the moulding breath of the steam cabinet, and his blunt half-breed's eye examining Paul and deciding he would sell. A hot day it had been, like this, with sawdust thick on the floor . . . .

Their paddles dipped. He guided the bow north, up the center of the river, and they passed silently through a thousand broken suns.

In a while they approached a landing. They saw it first as a mingled sheen and glinting, a deposit of hard and foreign things in the forest, at the end of the road. Two of the abandoned cars had been pushed or driven down the gravelled ramp where boats were once launched, and lay like turtles in the shallow water. The others had been left with doors ajar, and the sun glanced off exposed window edges and chrome handles. A few windshields had been smashed. The glass lay strewn on dusty hoods.

Neither spoke, but the bow of the canoe swung inperceptibly away from the place, and as it crossed the center of the river, tracing towards the left bank, a noise, a small but distinct scratching sound like a hunting dragonfly's droned out from the landing, or from behind it, where the shoreline crumpled into islands and deep bays.

"A motorboat," he said. It penetrated the mist like an arrow, and came at them. In the bow, teeth bared and ears flattened by the wind, the black dog seemed at first the only occupant, for his erect body, on guard over the foam beneath his forefeet, obscured the lower, bulkier, twin bodies of man and motor. But then the craft heeled and slowed, the bow settled, and the thick form in the stern rose into sight. A pith helmet sat squarely across his brow, and his eyes glittered in its shade.

The Outfitter grinned. He had lost a tooth since Paul had seen him last, and he was heavier, squatter, grosser in a hunched and neckless way. Power throbbed in him. "Hi there," he said, watching. "Where you heading?"

"Up the river," Paul said. "In." The boats drifted together, and the dog clattered drooling along his metal gunwale.

"Gee-zos," said the Outfitter, eyeing their cargo, "you sure as hell have got a load! How long you goin in for?" Then he laughed, a thin laugh for so large a man, shook his head and slapped the gunwale. "You know, I keep forgetting? I still keep thinking that people goin in now will be comin out someday. Still keep lookin at my calendar to see how many dinners we have to make at night. But it's blank." He reached over and gripped the canoe close to Liv's knee. "Listen. Why don't you come over for some lunch? Eh? I got lots of food. Enough to last a year. Hell, why should you use up that stuff you're takin in? Well, how about it?"

"We should go on," she said.

"Why? What's the rush? Hell, you got all the time in the world now, haven't yuh? Eh?" He shook their canoe playfully. In the shadow of the hat his eyes shone.

Paul glanced at the curving, rivetted prow. He tried to guage the threat but could not. He knew only that on water they were most vulnerable. "Where?" he asked.

"Just there. Behind the point. Not even half a mile outta your way." He tipped his head back, watching. "Well, what d'yuh say?"

"Paul, we should go on."

"Haaaay, now. Haay ..." The hand on the gunwale groped closer to her knee. "You're not gonna refuse a friendly little invitation are yuh? Huh? What's the rush? What's time matter now?"

Paul said, "I want to get up to the marshes by tonight."

"You'll make it. You'll make it easy. River's like a mirror. Besides, you hafto eat someplace. Huh? Huh?" He jerked the canoe with each interrogation, and he was no longer smiling.

For a moment there was silence except for the soft scraping of the boats and the dog's panting. Then Paul said, "o.k. You win." And he smiled.

"Now that's better. That's more like it. Eh? Eh, Rolf?" The dog growled and clattered in the boat, shaking its head. "We're gonna have guests again, Rolf boy! What d'yuh think of that, eh? About time, isn't it? Eh?" The dog pranced, sneezing, swatting his tail on the boat's side. "You go ahead," the Outfitter said to them, pushing their gunwale away. "Can't miss the place. I've gotta slide over for some gas." He pressed the starter. The engine roared alive and the bow rose, then planed, curving toward the landing.

"He's monstrous!" she said as the whine faded and the canoe rocked in the last of the swell. "Do we have to go?"

"I think it would be wise." He smiled. "Don't you?"

"Yes."

"Frightened?"

"Not really. More repelled. He brought back so much."

"A game."

"Yes," she said. "A game that we should play. Once more."

They arrived at the camp before him. It was a typical fishing-hunting camp, with its central lodge and a scattering of solig-numed, cedar-planked cabins. Canoes lay overturned on their racks, and a second runabout, its engine gleaming, hung in a calm at dockside. All lay in eerie readiness, as if that night the camp would fill with light, with stories, with the laughter of rough-shirted men free for a week from razors and neckties. The dock had been freshly stained and bumpered. The buildings were in good repair. On the path up they passed a maintainence shed, its door ajar, revealing ranks of tools, a clutter of equipment, and a neat row of batteries under the bench.

Liv asked, "From the cars?"

"Probably."

"Strange, the things people collect. All that stored energy. So he can pretend as long as possible, isn't that it?"

"Yes, I think so."

The boat arrived, its swell rocking their canoe against the dock. The dog clattered out, patrolled the landing with his nose low, then came sniffing towards them up the path. It circled, grinning. "Won't hurt you," the Outfitter called. "Knows you're company." He came up, threw open the door of the main lodge, and ushered them inside.

The room was dim and cool. A massive fireplace dominated it. On one side, a double woodstack rose to shoulder height, and on the other an assortment of guns gleamed on a rack studded with deer hocks. Various mounted heads hung on the walls — fox, wolf, deer, lynx, a moose, and several shellacked bass and muskellunge, glass eyes wide and mouths open to gulp forever the fluttering point of death.

But to these conventional and predictable trophies had been added others. They lined the shelves and cluttered the mantle. They hung from dozens of tacks in the walls. They covered the tables, covered parts of the floor. They rustled like hasty beetles. They clicked like the mandibles of silverfish nibbling the fabrics and hides of the room. The room was alive with clocks and watches, all running perfectly.

"Hobby," said the Outfitter. He tipped back the pith helmet. His face shone with sweat. "Pretty good, eh? Just started a year ago — hell, not even that. Just a few months, except for some of the watches. Listen, you think we couldn't see this coming? Hell, *I* saw it coming. So did a lot of other guys, but they just kept on, kept on. So what are they now, eh? No fuel, no food, no hobbies. What are they? You tell me. All those guys used to come up here, big operators, big executives." He laughed softly, savouring his prudence. "Well, I said to myself, 'Ben old boy, you've gotta stock in everything you need just like a seige was comin. Everything. You gotta keep things going.' So I started pulling it all in, little by little. Had lots of time. Losing money, but I had time. What the hell good's money anyway? Nothing to buy anymore. Just take what you want, don't you? So I figured, well, now take the clock, for instance; running fine, sure, but what if it wears out? Or what if a part breaks? I figured I'd better have another one just in case. Maybe two. So I ordered a couple new ones, and they came in on one of the last trains, and I went into The Creek and picked em up in the express office. I said to old Jimmy Dale, I said, 'Jimmy, how long you plan to keep that station clock goin, now there aren't trains no more?' And he said, 'By jees, Ben, I'll keep her goin till the trains start again!' Well, I set both of those clocks by the station clock and brought em home. Those two right there.'' He thrust his chin at them and hitched up his trousers, which had begun a slow rappelling down the underside of his belly. ''The others come from here and there. People leave em. People let em run down. I brought em back and cleaned em up. Those over there, now, all those I got outta cars. The ones that weren't smashed.'' The heavy face suddenly drooped morosely. ''You'd be amazed how many I found smashed. Why, some cabins down the shore, the only thing that's broken at all, besides the windows, sometimes, is the clock. Somebody's put a rock through it, or just picked it up and thrown it. Goddam, that's something I can't figure out at all, why anybody'd do that to a clock.''

He watched Liv. She was walking slowly through the room, her arms folded, examining the rows and clusters of white faces. She paused before a section of the wall which was covered with ranks of watches, men's and women's, each suspended by a nail tacked through the end of its strap. Expansion bracelets had been sheared and hung like the others. All were running. ''These . . .'' she began, turning.

''Found,'' he said steadily. ''Here and there. Or just left.''

''But so many?''

''Yeah, well. No need for em, you see, where the people were goin. No planes, no appointments, no need.'' He watched her closely. ''Why, you'd be surprised how many I got in the old days just from people taking em off a day or two after they got here and forgetting em when they left. I used to give em to the cooks and cleaning women for their husbands, but then I just started hangin em up there. Sometimes a guy would come

156

back in a year and say, 'Hey, that one's mine!' and take it.''

"But there are dozens!" she said.

"Yeah. Well, I've had a lotta guests. Recently. They've all been leavin their watches," he said.

"And you look after them," Paul said.

"Sure. Look after them. Keep em wound, keep em running."

"Good idea." Paul examined the mounted lynx head. "I'd leave mine with you, if I had one."

"But the little lady's got one, hasn't she." The Outfitter breathed shallowly. "She's got one. Sure she has."

Paul looked at her. She had covered her wrist, massaging it gently, as if it had been injured. He remembered his shock when they had first made love, and he had slipped his hands upward over her flanks and breasts and shoulders to discover that she had worn her watch. He had been surprised at that, surprised at her fear. Later, he had suggested that love and time were incompatible and she had agreed; but when he had given his watch away — to a beggar in Union Station, as they were waiting for the train north — she had kept hers. And even now,. even as she laughed, and pulled the thing off and gave it to the man who held it almost reverently a moment in his great paw, he knew there was a part of her which let it go reluctantly, although it was against all reason to keep it.

"Tell me," she said. "Which clock is right?"

The Outfitter was still breathing quickly. "They all are," he said. "I set them every day."

"But ... if some need setting, how do you know they all don't?"

"What? What?"

"I mean, they're only machines, after all. Aren't they? And even the most accurate ones must get dusty or worn, so that they begin to run slower than they once did, and are no longer reliable. So although you have them synchronized perfectly, how do you know that any of them tells the right time?"

The big man regarded her like an injured child. "Why do

you have to ask that? Why? Do you think I don't know that?
I don't ask you any questions about how you try to survive,
or about the things you decide are important. Goddam it, can't
you see it's the decision that counts? Listen. Someday somebody
will ask me what time it is, and I'll say, 'It's exactly one-fifteen
. . . NOW!' And it will be. *It will be because my clocks say
so!* And that's enough." He hit the table with his palm. "Goddam
it, that has to be enough!"

Later, paddling north, entering a confused section of the river
where the main channel could easily be lost among islands,
marshes, and the enticing mouths of bays, she said, "No, I
wasn't afraid. Not really. I'm even sorry now that I was unkind
to him, he seemed so familiar. But he brought back so much."

July 3, 1785: West of Fort Charlotte the country falls into a
dense assemblage of ponds, streams, small lakes, rivers and
marshes which altogether make up a maze so confusing that,
were a man to wander from his route at any point, being unused
to the country, he would very soon be lost entirely, with slight
prospects for a safe return.

We are now a company of six canoes, each with five paddlers
and one and one-half tons of burden. Such craft are used throughout
this savage country by the Company because of their lightness
and shallow draft, which enable them to pass safely in low waters.
Our paddlers now are northmen, fellows who have largely forsaken
the culture of their birth and chosen to follow the trade routes
year upon year in the Company's employ. Their emolument is
meagre — less than twenty pounds, besides clothing, tobacco,
and keep — but it appears sufficient to their needs. Several, I
am told, have descended almost to the level of the savages; indeed,
most have adopted the dress of the country and have allowed
their hair to grow long. Were it not for their beards, which the
Indians lack, they could be mistaken for Ojibbeway or Cree. They
disdain their counterparts in the Montreal brigades, whom they
call lard-eaters because of their pork fat rations, and much rivalry
occurs on the Grand Portage, where the two types insult each
other, sometimes coming to blows on the posés. These northmen
regard themselves as an elite corps, and it is true they bear privation

and risk perils the Montrealers seldom meet, except on the rapids and in the crossing of Superior. They are full of tales of ambush, of casual violence, of starvation, and of natural calamity, all of which they relate with a certain calmness and fatality. They wave away the past and shrug at the future. "We are here now," they will say, "in this little present which is gone almost before it lives. Do you see this paddle? This canoe? This lake which we are crossing? These are all of life, these things. And even these are already become as dreams . . ." Such an outlook I find prevalent among those who have lived long with the Indians, and I perceive that it is in the Company's interest to encourage such simplicity in them, since it increases their dependence. The present can be bought cheap with a pipe, or a pint of rum, or, perhaps, a woman.

Thus I am embarked for my post at Lake Nibbeke Omuhkukke, which our men call Frog Lake, and I am instructed to conduct trade from that place with the Ojibbeway, with Elborn as my assistant. He appears well pleased at this prospect, and I have resigned myself to it, since it is the Company's wish. Antoninus, also, has admonished me to "look on every man who displays pain or discontent at any development, as on a level with the pig that is led out to sacrifice kicking and squealing. So also the invalid who lies moaning on his bed, instead of considering in silence that our hands are bound, and that it is a prerogative bestowed on the rational life alone to yield voluntarily to whatever befalls us . . ."

Indeed, Elborn's presence has of late been less onerous than formerly; no doubt our mutual dedication to the Company will be the basis of our communication during the months to come.

Thirty workmen, including carpenters and hunters, have preceded us by several weeks, in order to commence the construction and provisioning of the post. Of these, eight, together with the present company, will winter there; so that in all, I shall have in charge thirty-eight Canadians, as well as the women which they have taken in the manner of the country, and the half-breed children sprung from these unions. For all, places must be found within the palisade, and provisions laid in.

July 5, 1785: I am making strides in the French language, which I see I must command more proficiently in order to deal with my men, and also in the Ojibbeway dialect in which our trade will be conducted.

We have continued to the north-west into a maze of waterways. The sun remains hot, and all is still. We have frequently spied the birch canoes of savages, and sometimes they have come forward and sometimes not. If they are encountered on the portages — which are very short here-abouts, rarely more than half a mile — it is considered etiquette to talk with them and to inquire after the success of their hunt. An opportunity is thereby gained to enlist them as customers of the post. I have instructed that trinkets such as awls, needles, and fire-steels, as well as rum, be given whenever we encounter them, even if it be on water, and I trust that the trifling expense of this inducement will be paid a thousand fold in winter furs.

They are placid creatures, drawn irresistably to our panoply and superior utensils. These, whose lodges are within a two weeks' journey of Grand Portage, have had long experience in bargaining with us and in setting traders one against the other, so that, without their predilection for rum, our rivalry would place us at a disadvantage. However, we expect no other wintering traders in the region of Frog Lake this season, the nearest Hudson's Bay post being some fifty miles distant, and I am therefore confident that we shall reap the whole benefit of the trade. I am resolved that there is no beaver in the land but shall leave his hide in my store-room! I am told they breed marvellously, their populations growing commonly as much as twenty per cent each year. This area having lain fallow two years, the small-pox preventing both trade and hunting, I forsee a rich harvest for the taking.

"Our prospects are good, MacKay," said Elborn last night, as we took our tea alone after supper.

I agreed that they were.

"Do you think our journey will end, then, at Frog Lake?" He was asking a question behind a question, as he did frequently, and without warning. He then smiled to gauge its effect on me.

"What journey?" I inquired warily.

"Why, the journey in, of course. The journey we have been on these many weeks." His smile curved round the lip of his metal cup.

"Why should it not end there?"

"Why should it? Can we not go deeper? To the center? Is it not likely that the Company will send us on?"

"Perhaps later, should the trade decline."

160

"But for now you believe we have come to the end, and shall find what we are seeking?"

I threw the remainder of my tea in an arc across the water. "Yes," I replied. "Beaver!"

So I have narrowed down my purpose, and beaver are constantly in my thoughts. How to induce the Indian to kill them in the quantities we require? How to indenture them completely? How to assemble such an assortment of fine furs that the Company will grow strong and stronger, and myself with it? How best, in short, to work to a profit the harvest in peltries of this land which is otherwise so barren and destitute of the necessities of life?

Otter, muskrat, martin, bear, fox, lynx, fisher, mink, wolf — all strange animals whose furs I had not seen in a raw state until two weeks ago, but with which I am now familiar, having been well examined by Mr. Duff on the values of each and what I must trade for them, and against what tricks and cunning in their delivery I must be on my guard. But above all I am instructed to harvest beaver, and so well have I been taught the necessity, that this curious animal has become for me a sign of how I must grasp the country and extract from it the wealth which, as Elborn would say to my annoyance, "Providence has laid at our disposal", raising his voice as if to question me. Providence or chance, no matter; but that the fur is here, and that it can be gleaned and carrotted to good felt for the *chapeaux bras* of gentlemen, and that we get our price and make our profit — for these reasons we have skewered this country like a fat ham from Quebec to Athabasca.

Antoninus has said, "What is the firmest action or statement possible with the equipment at your command? Whatever it may be, its execution or utterance rests wholly with yourself; so let us hear nothing of impediments!"

Let others talk of Providence, and see designs where none exist. I shall talk of beavers, and make the ways to get them. For *my* faith is in the Company to meet demand; and further, to maintain demand as long as the supply exists. I perceive that simplicity prevails, that crooked lines are best made straight, and intentions clarified to a single point. Therefore I am determined on beaver and success, and shall do what I must to obtain them both.

July 31, 1785: I came today to my post, and was met by the chief carpenter, Mr. Henderson, together with his Canadians who have been busy on construction these past six weeks. When the unloading had been accomplished, I ordered that a half-pint of rum be given to each man, in celebration of our arrival, and also to the few Indians who were on hand to greet us. Foremost of these is one Shongwashe, who is the local chieftain. He had been given word of our approach and arrived shortly after ourselves. He is a man of thirty-five or forty who has newly acquired his leadership and is anxious to entrench his prestige in our good relations. I perceive that he is not uncorruptible on this account, and might be persuaded to bring us the hunts of his people for personal aggrandizement. We shall see. He presented me with a gift of a fine and sprightly canoe, saying *"Kemenin maundun chemaun,* I give you this canoe, believing it will teach you to know our country."

In return I presented him with one of Mr. Bond's elegant fusils, brought for this purpose, with a barrel of 34 inches and fine scrollwork upon the breech; together with three clear black flints, and pouches of shot and powder. I told him that these were intended to help him make better *use* of his country so that we could know prosperity together, and he assented gravely while accepting them. I saw that they added much to his prestige.

I then endured an hour of his speechifying with as much grace as I could muster, and I noted that it terminated as the rum intended for himself and his followers was brought from the post.

Mr. Henderson discussed with me the matter of a stockade. He has completed the store-house, the common dwelling for the single men, several cabins for those with women and children, and most of the central hall and residence. In all, he expects three weeks' work to finish the whole. I instructed him to build a stockade as well, for I do not intend to have drunken, pilfering Indians wandering at will across the premises.

When enclosed, the post will be twelve rods square. It commands a pleasing aspect over a clearing to an extensive flat rock, which has been a meeting place of the Savages, and where the Chippewa and Cree would frequently confer and trade. Beyond, Lake Omuh-kukke reaches far to the south and east. It is the largest of all lakes in this district, and can be reached with equal ease from all points of the compass. In placing the post at such a natural juncture in the routes, the Company seems therefore to have chosen well.

The hunters have good success when they go out. I am told that these waters are rich in pickerel, trout, and sturgeon, the latter commonly exceeding two hundred pounds, and that we should on no account suffer the deprivations of the western posts. Blueberries and raspberries are to be found in profusion. I am told to expect a supply of pemmican from the West in the latter part of August.

I went alone this evening to the main hall where we shall do our trading and receive our pelts. I expected Elborn but he did not accompany me, no doubt for reasons of his own. Many of our goods have been unpacked and stand in readiness: mounds of blankets from Oxfordshire, strouds, coatings, moltons and flannel, cotton from Manchester, dimities, janes, fustians, shawls and handkershiefs, gartering and ferretting; Irish linens, Scotch sheetings, nets, twine, thread, yarn and bird lime; brass hardware, copper and tin kettles; the pistols and Indian fusils with their accoutrements and fox-head emblems; vermillion for the adornment of bodies, paddles, and canoes; beads, drugs, and trinkets. All lay spread as an irresistible enticement to the savage heart. The trading counter itself is constructed on kegs of rum and high wine. By the light of my candle I examined all, and was well pleased. In my imagination I saw them replaced by furs. I saw the new racks, gleaming white and fresh with the odour of barked spruce, heaped with furs to the ceiling. I saw the room tight with packets flattened in the press; and in their odour, in the musk of raw hides which had at first repulsed me in the sorting rooms of Grand Portage, I now found the aroma of success. Canniness, persistence, and resolution, these I have in large measure, and this room will soon show the results of their application.

There was some drunken chanting among the Indian lodges. The canoes bulged like living slugs upon the rocks. I examined the craft which Shongwashe gave me upon my arrival, and found it snugly made. Tomorrow I shall give orders for it to be stored, for I do not intend using it this season.

Liv had fallen asleep, her head on her knees. The fire of pine knots had crumbled to grey ash and to coals, stirred by a growing breeze.

He laid the pages on the log where he had been sitting, gathered up the woman like a child, and carried her to the tent. Her arms went around his neck. By the time they had undressed, the wind was strong enough to scatter the manuscript with a fluttering indistinguishable from that of the moving braken. Before morning, the leaves that remained on shore had been drenched grey by rain, and sprinkled with fallen needles. Already some had torn, and some had melted to fibrous paste. Of those that had been blown across the waves, nothing could be seen.

chapter nineteen

To the south of the apartment where Kenneth Malcolmson lived, two high-rise apartments and one office building were going up, and their girders threw nets of shadow across the lower dwellings.

"*Retiarii!*" the old man laughed, peering through his window. His wild hair was stark white, his clothes dusted with ash. In the latticed sunlight the smoke from his cigarette swirled around him. "Those naked gladiators with their nets, do you recall?" He pointed at the cranes. "Their nets and tridents. And of what use is any sword or dagger when the net has trapped you, hm? Perhaps you have a weapon which you have honed to a fine edge, a weapon over which you have laboured with love and skill, readying it for the contest, and in an instant it is useless. Oh, you have it still, of course, but it is suddenly an anachronism, and you are dead." He flung up his arms, laughing and smoking, pacing the room.

"When did they fire you?"

"Last week. 'Services will not be required for the autumn term,' the letter said. Do you want to see it? I have it here, someplace." He rifled through the mounds of paper on his table.

"No, it's all right," Paul said.

"Knew it was coming, of course. My classes have been falling off for years — were when you were there — students staying

164

away in droves. Oh yes. But that's true of all the humanities,
isn't it. Everyone going into engineering, and business, and
medicine, and ... and ... '' he gestured scornfully towards
the window, *"architecture*. So it wasn't my *teaching,* you know.''
He looked hard at Paul.

"I know."

"Oh no. What it really was is that my book has never been
published. Publish or perish, the cardinal rule, so it seems. The
Chairman admitted as much when I confronted him. 'Ken,' he
said, 'you've been working on it twenty years.' Of course he
was well aware of the problems of research, tracking the journals
down, sorting them, fixing dates, even deciphering. It takes
months. Months and years. And of course he knew all that,
but it made no difference. Faster and faster, that's the way it's
going. That's what they all want. Madness! The death of scholarship! Why, do you know that in the last few years I've seen
young men come on the staff — with just an M.A., mind you!
— publish some pamphlet it's taken them scarcely a year to
throw together, and be given tenure? You wouldn't believe it,
but it's true. Think of the duplication, the callowness! Think
of the waste! And you, my young friend, encourage it, don't
you? Paper is your business. The more we use, the happier you
are! Oh yes, I know. You're part of it, you and your offices
and mills. Do you ever stop to *think*? Fifty thousand journals
in science *alone*. Two million new articles a year! Madness!
Confusion and madness! Who can cope with that, I ask you?
Why, there are two hundred organizations which do nothing else
but make abstracts, and the abstracts are themselves the size
of dictionaries! Ach!'' He threw up his hands.

"I'm sorry," Paul said. "Business is very good."

"Ah, and you come asking me again about your father, about
the half-way man. There's nothing half-way about you, is there?
You're on the spiral staircase. Racing down." He laughed and
lit a fresh cigarette. "Are you reading? I daresay you don't have
time."

"You're right. I don't."

"Except for magazines, correct? And business reports, and abstracts, and newspapers and promotional flyers. Oh yesyesyes, I know. Well, in any case, the answer to your question is no, I've found neither the poems nor the photographs. But they are here, you know. I'll look again."

Paul stood up. "I'd appreciate that."

"Must you go? Yes, obviously you must. Time is important, isn't it. I'm sorry I can't offer you a drink, but the price ..." he spread his arms.

"That's all right. Next time I come I'll bring something with me."

"You *will* come again."

"Certainly."

"Please. And forgive me. Forgive my upset ... It's only momentary. But I don't see how ... "

"Call me if I can help. I'd be happy to."

"Ah, a business card! I can tell you I see very few of those. I shall put it in my mirror, like a barber." He laughed and punched Paul's shoulder, his fist a child's. "Tell me, how is your mother?"

"She's well. She's living in Vancouver now. With her sister."

"Ah, the flight westward, towards the sun. Yes, yes. Give her my regards. Tell her I know. Tell her I understand," said Kenneth Malcolmson, and he closed the door.

chapter twenty

All morning she had paddled strongly in a jubilant sun. All morning memories had passed through her and away like currents of air through her lungs. Paddling came automatically and left her free — unless they were struggling against a headwind; but all that morning the river had been as calm as a mirror (in fact, she could see her reflection vividly before her paddle blurred it on each stroke) and they had travelled fast and silently up its center. She was only distantly aware that Paul had spoken. It may have been seconds or minutes before she answered; she was remembering Janet, and Janet's lean beauty, and Janet's great longing for the children which had never come. She had been talking about baby-sitters for Mike, how hard the good ones were to find, and when she saw Janet's face in the powder room mirror she bit her lip. "Oh," she said, "this is a nuisance."

"What?"

"This," Liv gestured at her handbag and the mirror.

"Of course," Janet had answered. "Of course it's all a great nuisance, but did you ever see a woman who didn't want to look her best?"

"*Whose* best?"

"Why, her own best."

"But Janet," she persisted, "isn't that what she was born with? Only that?"

Janet lowered her lipstick. "What she was *born* with! Well, for starters, you weren't born in a dress, or in a brassiere and panties. Care to leave here without them?"

"No ... "

"Well, then!" She pronounced the *well* with a certain finality, half laugh, half simple exhalation. She flattened her lips against her teeth and leaned forward at her image.

"Perhaps I'm being silly ... "

"Yes. You are."

" ... but women *do* go without them."

"Oh, yes, Hottentots and aborigines, I suppose. But even they scar their faces and smear cow dung around so they'll be more beautiful. Oh, I know beauty is only skin dope, as Gerry says, but still ... "

"But the dope attracts men."

"Well, men are attracted by the familiar, you know. By what they understand. By what they've been taught to like. I suppose the purpose is to give them that any way you can. Aren't you going to put your face on?"

"Do I need it?"

"A little eyeshadow wouldn't hurt. Raise them at the corners a bit. You always look so pensive and sad, Liv. As if you're going to cry. I think you ask yourself too many silly questions."

Outside, the music began — a soft-shoe fanfare, the first gravelly currents of alto saxophone.

And if she seemed on the verge of tears, so what? "No," she said. "Un unh."

"Suit yourself, dear."

"Janet, this is wrong." She stared at the mirror as if it had spoken, and not herself.

"So my Methodist mother told me."

"Seriously, don't you think ... "

But Janet suddenly turned and took both her hands. "Oh, Liv dear, no. No I don't think. Not anymore, Liv. I'm too old to change anything or to worry about anything like that. It's too late for us, you know."

"But you're scarcely thirty! How could it be too late for anything?"

"I'm thirty-one. Thirty-one. And a realist. I know that when I go out of here I'll find Gerry waiting for me. He'll be well into his second drink, and he'll be leaning back with his jacket open over that flat belly he's so proud of, and he'll be smoking his third cigarette of the last twenty minutes. And I know that the rest of this evening, right down to the time we fall into bed, both of us almost too drunk, will be like a bad O'Hara novel. But I also know what he likes, and so I'll give him that. I'll give him that because I want to keep him. I don't want to take chances anymore. If he wants to see a face without a blotch or a pimple, then that's what he'll see. If he wants breasts against him that feel pubescent, then that's what he'll feel. And

I don't give a damn whether that's right or wrong. I don't know, Liv. I can't figure all that stuff out, and I've given up. Time is too valuable, now."

Dear Janet, Liv thought. *A salute in thought to you.*

"Pardon?"

Paul laughed. "I said that that point looks like a good place to stop for lunch."

"All right," she said. "Let's do that."

chapter twenty-one

The handball court was sweltering. By the time they finished their game Paul was drenched in sweat. The dull ache in his right ankle, forgotten during the excitement of the game, pulsed annoyingly, and in spite of himself he limped as they left the court.

"You haven't slowed down much," said Gerry Rattray. "Hurt?"

"A bit."

They emerged into the gym. Above the second balcony hung the ropes for bars, rings, and other gymnastic equipment, and around the track a dozen men walked, jogged and ran, glancing anxiously at the clock as they passed. Some laboured at push-ups and chin-ups; some twisted through complex calisthenics. On the first balcony a pair of fat men, towelled and sweat-suited, pedalled madly nowhere. On the floor a basketball game was in progress, and as the action surged back and forth, scorings were greeted with cheers and raised arms. In the second gym a volleyball looped helplessly over its net and back, over and back, its passages begun and ended with the thump of doubled fists. Through the open door of the weight room they saw the collection of black frames and monstrous dumbells, the lifters heaving in grim silence. Tilted mirrors distorted them.

"That was a bad break," Gerry said. "Remember that big bastard who hit you? Jesus, he weighed 250 if he weighed an ounce! And when he tackled, he twisted. Sonuvabitch!"

Paul laughed. "I guess it didn't heal straight."

"Lotta little bones in there. Maybe you should see about it again."

"It's not bad. It hurts a bit when I've been travelling, that's all."

They wound downstairs into the locker room, stripping off their jerseys. Under the low ceilings, the ranks of lockers stretched away towards the mirrors and showers like the vanes in a battery, and between them men dressed and undressed, scratched themselves, sprinkled powder and splashed cologne, murmured earnestly, laughed, shouted. *Hey, Gerry boy! How's your belly where the pig bit yuh!* Men packed and unpacked kit bags, worked combinations, banged locker doors. The exhaust fan hummed behind its grill. Razors whined at the sinks. *Did you see that shot? Did you SEE it? Man, was I HOT! I'll tell yuh. You wanna know the secret, I'll tell yuh. Either you're great or you're not, and if you are then you just can't do a damn thing about it!* Men towelled themselves, examined themselves, hitched buckles, knotted ties. *Did you hear that? Sonuvabitch. Somebody oughta stamp that right on his ass!* The attendant swept his mop under the fountain and around the sinks, and dragged away a sack of soggy towels. Off the shower room naked men leaned over urinals, weighed themselves, sat on zinc benches reading papers. *Yeah, well you don't have to look very far to see the reason for Hughie's success with the dames. Very simple. Hung like a moose!*

The showers coursed over them. Paul lathered himself luxuriously. He lifted his face to the water, turned so that it drummed his neck with tiny fingers, bent down while it caressed his spine. He watched the soapy water swirl away.

"Been out of town?"

"New York last week. Montreal the week before."

"Bob Mansfield keeps you moving," Gerry said.

"Bob Mansfield's not around much, that's the problem. He comes down two or three days a month. The rest of the time he sits in Sable Creek with Johnny Walker."

Gerry snorted. "My practice may have its problems, but at least I haven't got a bloody lush for a boss."

"Any great cases?"

"One or two last month. Small stuff, mostly. Incorporations, real estate, divorces, that kind of thing."

"I want to see you," Paul said. "I want you to handle our business."

"You've got my number."

Dripping, they entered the steam room and the heat enclosed them. They turned and stretched in it, feeling the pores open above sore muscles. Paul sprayed a bench and sat down. Gently he worked his ankle. Gerry sat opposite him, hands on his knees.

"Good, eh?"

"Incredible. It's up fifteen percent over last year."

"I meant the steam."

Paul grinned. "Great."

"What you need is a good 2 IC."

"Um hum. I've got one young guy who should work out pretty well, but for the moment I've got it. Right here." He cupped his hands.

"And no wife. No girls."

"Thank God."

"No diversions. How's the klootch in Montreal, for example?"

"Gerry, I haven't got time for that."

"I thought so."

"Jeez, that's all I need right now! To get strung up with some woman who'll tell me what time to be home."

"It doesn't have to be that way." Gerry smeared the sweat on his chest. "I take no orders from Janet. Believe me."

"Janet's a very understanding woman."

"Um hum. And what Janet doesn't know won't hurt her. Know what I mean?"

They showered again, and still sweating gently, went into the sunroom. "Three minutes each side, Arnold," Gerry said, and the attendant set the clock. Tiny cups on their eyes, towels covering their genitals, they lay spread under the lights. "What I'm going to do is give you a name."

"I'm not interested in pros, Gerry."

"She's not a pro. Really. It'll be up to you."

"What's the name?"

"Liv."

"Nice."

"Nice name, nice girl. A little morose at times, but a very sweet girl. When we go out I'll give the number and the address . . ."

"If you come in will your work suffer?"

"I've forgotten about work," he said. "All evening."

"It's easy to do that, isn't it?" She turned. Her hands brushed past his temples and clasped at the back of his neck. He kissed her. "So easy," she said again. Far away a bell tolled midnight. Traffic groaned on the city's hills. She moved against him, saying his name, holding his face, and her whisper grew urgent, flickering between insistence and request. He kissed the tendon in her neck and his lips traced down across the frail chain on her throat. Gently he kissed her lips, feeling the teeth behind, feeling the gathering in his loins which told him yes. When they had lain down, when he had entered her, there occurred for him the vision of a hawk in the instant before its dive, suspended, motionless, its entire world the infinitesimal shuddering of a blade of grass.

Later, in her bed, he slept a shallow sleep in which dream and reality mingled. In the shadows which moved all night across the walls her face formed and faded, calling his name, and they were together in the shadow branches, embracing, naked while the world passed far beyond the field where the tree stood splendid and alone. When they kissed they kissed in dream and reality, for he was sure at times during the night her face was on his own, above him, under him. Somewhere, someone had burned leaves in the evening. On some curb a mound of ash smouldered, glowing when the breeze touched it. And from it the smoke drifted through her window and became a part of his dream and of their meeting, so that its odour seemed at times to be the touch of her hands on him, drawing him close. They moved in the smoke and the leaves, and an old man, raking, paid them no more attention than if they were romping children, and he himself were lost in the dreams of youth and love. He turned back the leaves like a weightless comforter.

When Paul woke, the shadows had faded and the room was filling with grey light. He lay on his back. Asleep, she had flung an arm across his chest and a leg between his own. When he moved she made sounds of denial and drew him closer, but it was not long before she slept more deeply, and he was able to leave her and dress. The elevator purred up obediently at his command. He found his car safe where he had left it, and he drove home to his own apartment through the waking city.

They lay belly-down on the tables while the masseurs worked over them. Gerry was grinning broadly. "What're you doing now, Arnold? This doesn't keep you busy, does it?"

"Fella gets along, Mr. Rattray. Fella makes a dollar here and there."

"Yeah, I'll bet you do. This guy," he said to Paul, "this guy's done just about every damn thing you can imagine. Tell him, Arnold."

Big hands pressed rhythmically on Gerry's spine. "Job here and there, that's all, Mr. Rattray. Nothing special. Fella takes what he can get, that's all, same as anyone."

Over his folded arm, Paul watched the flat, impassive face through half-closed eyes. There were flecks of grey at the close-cropped temples.

Grinning, Gerry shifted his chin onto his arms. "Tell me, Arnold, how's the love life?"

"Profitable, Mr. Rattray."

"With bags on their heads they're all sisters, eh?"

"Business is business, sir," said Arnold, smiling.

"And to the victor, the spoils."

"Correct, Mr. Rattray." He covered Gerry with a sheet. "And may the best man win." He moved off to another part of the room, carrying his plastic bottle of oil. Paul's masseur finished and did the same.

"Amen," said Gerry Rattray. "The only prayer I know." Smiling, he gazed at Paul for a long moment. "See her?"

"Um hum."

"Was I right?"

"You were, my friend."

"See her again?"

"As a matter of fact, tonight."

"Watch that," Gerry said. "It could get serious."

chapter twenty-two

Paul set down his cup and spread his hands to the fire. The loons had ceased their crying, but in the far distance a single wolf howled twice and was silent. *Ethics have failed because they are merely human.* Schweitzer, he thought. He tried to recall the exact phrase but he could not do so, although he could hear Miro's voice. *Ethics have failed because ...*

"I'll be blunter," Miro had said, slouched in the front seat of Paul's car. "Ethics are the cosmetics of aberration." He had laughed. "The osprey, for instance. What do ethics say about the osprey? Nothing!"

"I used to watch them when I was small," Paul said, "working the marshes west of town. They were magnificent."

Miro waved the word away as if it brought a bad smell. "Of course they're magnificent! They're lone types, final consumers, m-masters! There are no words to describe such a creature. You can only watch them, and be envious." He stared sourly through the window. People were passing in other cars, in the rain. "I dissected one this afternoon. Somebody shot it and sent it to me. He said he had found it in agony. DDT. At first I was just angry. I thought I should write a little p-paper for one of the quarterlies, saying that the bird had died so that fat men could be fatter, so that crops could be harvested with less inconvenience to machines."

"Will you?" Paul had asked.

"And be part of it? Play their little game of time and tolerances? Hah! The fools! It was *man*'s tissues I saw in my microscope. Those residues were in *man*'s liver, *man*'s gonads, *man*'s cholesterol! Don't you see that? It's only a matter of time. Fools! they'll ban that pesticide and be proud of themselves. They'll ban others one at a time, and be proud of themselves. Can you imagine it? Cosmetics! Lipstick on a mouth ravaged by cancer! Talcum on a syphilitic groin! Sweet God in heaven, why do we not take ourselves away and be done with it!"

"Maybe we're cowards ..."

"Eager for delusions, yes, like addicts."

"Maybe there really is a way."

Miro's laughter filled the car. "There has been no way, my friend, since our great agricultural revolution, our fine technological advances, our great breakthroughs in medicine. Let me disillusion you. There is nothing we can do but speed it' all up! Open the throttle while there's still something left to survive the crash! Please, let us have no more talk of changes and solutions. It is much, much too late for that ..."

Liv knelt beside her husband at the fire. "Tell me," she said.

"I was thinking of Miro."

"Poor Miro."

"No. He had to use what he had been given. And without his passion, what would he have been? At least he acted. At least he outgrew conscience. Do you remember the tension of the man? Sometimes you feared that if you said a wrong word he would explode. Fly all to pieces. Sometimes when you talked to him you wanted to put your hands on his shoulders to prevent his doing just that. But he would always warn you back, with those eyes and their glasses."

"Yes," she said. "I remember."

chapter twenty-three

In 1961, Fred took a job in Etobicoke and they moved south, into the city. The money, he had said, was just too good to refuse. Narah took little pleasure in the move. As they drove south ahead of the moving van, she gazed for hours at the passing forests without speaking, and frequently looked back at vistas of the lake and its islands until they vanished in the mists. She heard Fred talking about the city, about the house he had bought for them, about the fresh challenge of the job, but she didn't really listen. All her thoughts were elsewhere, in other times.

To celebrate their arrival they went to dinner at the Park Plaza, and afterwards they saw *La Dolce Vita*, a film which had left her shocked and arid. "The only good man in it kills himself," she had said. "And he kills his children. Why did he do that?"

"Ah," Fred had replied, "it's only a movie. It doesn't mean anything."

They had driven home to their bungalow with the neat lawn and the stunted little mugho pines beside the porch.

The years passed softly and indistinguishably for her. Fred progressed. He became an inspector, and then an administrator whose job involved only paper and figures, and every second year they bought a more expensive car. Sometimes she saw people she had known, and twice, at parties, she saw Paul Henry. His voice still turned something deep inside her. She knew that if he had asked she would have met him again anywhere and anytime. But he did not ask; he had grown away from her, and towards his wife. She was sorrowful to see the hint of grey at his temples, and when she went home she looked closely at herself in the bathroom mirror, finding her hair even greyer than his, and her face more deeply lined.

Of all the people from Sable Creek, she heard regularly only from Bob Mansfield. Once a month he called her, importuning. "No," she would say. "Ununh. No." And as the months and years passed the tenor of his calls changed from a pleading to a perfunctory rancour, and she dreaded the bitterness in his voice at her refusals.

One evening she came home to find Fred holding a telegram. It was near Christmas and her arms were full of parcels. He met her wordlessly in the hall, dangling the telegram by its ears for her to read.

YOUR WIFE SCREWS BOYSCOUTS STOP ASK MIRO STOP ASK
GERRY STOP ASK FRANKLIN STOP ASK PAUL STOP ASK . . .

She looked up at Fred and his tears shocked her more than the telegram, for in all their years of marriage she had never seen him cry. She wanted to comfort him. She wanted to tell him that it was not like that at all, that it was not the way he thought it was, but that what she had done those years ago meant nothing to her love for him, not then, not now, but that it was something else entirely. She wanted to kiss him and hold him. She never thought of asking his forgiveness.

He hit her once, with the back of his hand, and his ring opened her cheek. The parcels fell. She remembered thinking that blood was hard to remove, and that she must sponge it off the broadloom before it dried.

After that their lives changed. They began going to parties with different people, and the parties had an edge which frightened her. Sometimes Fred would go away with another wife, leaving other men to surround her, to put their arms around her. The games grew ominous. She went along for Fred's sake, hoping that perhaps, were she to enter this new world he had discovered, then they could meet in bed again before it was too late, and she would be able to draw him into the mystery of her again and lose them both together. But it never happened; he grew ever harder and more separate, and at last there came a night when house keys were tossed on a livingroom rug, and Fred threw theirs among the rest.

After that she didn't care much for anything. Life was like painting by numbers — a morning filled in, an afternoon, an evening — and every day was a fresh canvas with its little lines and numerals. Every night was a blotting, erasing wash of turpentine. She began to use a little rinse to cover the grey. She began to use a little powder to hide the star-shaped scar on her cheek. She began to rub a little pink over the pallor of her lips. She went along.

"N-Narah Hale?" the boy asked. "Telegram. Sign here." He was very thin. His cap was too large, and it pushed out the tops of his ears.

"Thank you."

She dropped it on the hall table and looked at it a long time before she opened it. Even then she did not read it immediately. She smoothed it out with the tips of her fingers. She did not pick it up.

MUST SEE YOU STOP PLEASE STOP RM 1422
SUTTON PLACE STOP 5 PM STOP
PAUL H

Somewhere inside her something flared. It was very small, but very warm — as if someone had struck a match in a vast autumn night. She looked at her watch. She looked at herself in the mirror and was surprised that she was smiling. She smoothed her hair, she smoothed the lines in her forehead. It had been so long since he had seen her ... Like a girl she ran upstairs, undressed, washed, and began to work carefully with vials and tiny brushes.

The traffic was heavy. Twice she was stopped at intersections while police cars and ambulances flew past, their sirens screaming, and once as she neared the heart of the city a crowd of demonstrators surrounded her car, waving fierce placards. By the time she reached Wellesley and Bay fear and excitement swarmed together in her stomach and because she was a bit late she ran a changing yellow light and was nearly hit by a green Austin Healey which swerved past with its horn blaring.

She claimed the lobby when she entered it. Her figure had stayed good — the figure of a woman twenty years younger — and she smiled broadly under the bell-hops' gaze, her shoulders straight and her hair flowing. The elevator took an age to lift her up. She bit her lip at every stop, but at last she was on the fourteenth floor and going down the hall — 16, 18, 20, 22. She knocked softly and held her breath.

A paunch bulged out his shirt and trousers. His tie was undone. His face was florid and gross, and his red hair had thinned considerably. Even from where she stood she could smell the whiskey.

"Surprise," Bob Mansfield said. "Come in."

She almost cried, but she didn't. Instead, she blinked rapidly and her face hardened into a cool mask. She almost turned back down the hall, but she didn't. Instead, she stepped forward, holding her purse with both hands. "All right," she said. "You win."

"Drink?"

"Yes."

Outside the November night closed in. The city lights stretched away as far as she could see.

"This will be strictly business," she said.

"How much?"

"A hundred dollars."

"Done." As he turned to give her her drink she was shocked by a man's tears for the second time in her life. "Goddam," he said. "If only you had been reasonable. If only you had been reasonable twenty years ago!"

chapter twenty-four

Gerry loved the car, the Healey, which he had had restored at considerable expense. He loved its weight, its power, its obsolescence. He loved its contours, its masculinity. Miro was derisive about his fondness for the machine, accusing him once of perversity. Automobile necrophilia. Laughing his crazy laugh. But he could handle Miro; it was a matter of choosing the correct shade of jocular tolerance for the occasion.

At the first light he listened to the hiss of the carburators sucking air. The engine smoothed as it warmed, the exhausts rumbled upon the asphalt, and the car gathered to do his bidding. He swung north, accelerated to 4000 rpms, shifted, caught the next light and shifted again. Only when he was satisfied with the sounds of the car did he switch on the radio.

" . . . calamity. Company officials refused comment, pending the results of the inquest to be held Wednesday, but government sources confirmed this afternoon that unknown amounts of hydrogen sulphite had been accidentally released. Twenty-seven students have died, and six are in hospital. Their condition is described as fair."

King, Queen, Dundas, College, Wellesley. Gerry hit the lights perfectly. Toying with them, catching the oblique glimmer of amber which signalled the switch from red to green, timing so precisely the sweep of the machine through the intersection, sent a fluttering caress across his diaphragm. Synchronization! How beautiful that was! It had never ceased to fascinate him — on an athletic field, in a court, a boardroom, or here in this small game of chance against the lights. To perceive the moment, the instant, the splintering second when the time was right, and to give oneself utterly to it, to subordinate oneself and yet control, what a delight that had always been to him. It was that instant which he had courted all his life.

" ... trade deficit to be made up in the present fiscal year. The Minister of Trade and Development said in Montreal today that the time had come to remove the anti-inflationary restrictions imposed by the Government last year. Reflecting the new mood of optimism, the Toronto index gained 1.2 this afternoon, following a gain of 0.12 on Thursday."

Synchronization was style. A love affair with milliseconds. Style was letting your arms hang loose, watching the pinpoint of the ball come until it was almost too late, then taking it, driving, going over standing up with the tackler's fingers on your heels. It was spearing a shark's nose, alone, seeing him wind like a grey dowel. It was a handball court with the ball a half-inch beyond your opponent's glove. It was the instant of the impossible jib when the sail cracked, the boat shuddered and heeled wildly, and you were past the buoy and laughing. Style was the last run of the afternoon, when the slope lay treacherous with shadows and you were too tired. It was being alone and cold.

" ... children now born at a rate slightly higher than one per second. Speaking last night to a meeting of the Canadian Club in Ottawa, Dr. Martin said that the world birth rate had reached one birth every 0.8 seconds, and was accelerating. Noting the failure of all birth control programs co-ordinated by the World Health Organization in underdeveloped countries, Dr. Martin said that unless North America was prepared to commit what he termed 'nuclear and biological genocide', it could not resist invasion within this decade. He told the gathering of three hundred prominent citizens and government officials that we were destroying ourselves by what he called 'the illusion of affluence.' "

The light at Bloor stopped him. He thrust in the choke and let the wheel vibrate gently against his palms. Past him, in the rose haze of evening, people hurried through the intersection and down the grey canyons. All were going somewhere. Even the lovers, laughing with their arms about each other, strode decisively to destinations. The streets were no place to linger, unless one was beguiled by show-windows and the luxuries inside.

The green light. Gerry thrust the gear lever into first, swept around the curve of Davenport, caught the light on Avenue Road, and accelerated northwards towards the freeway and the promise of open roads beyond.

Once he would have picked up Janet. He would have said, slapping his hands, "Come on, let's celebrate. Let's just *go!*" And they would gather together a few clothes, lock the door, and find themselves together in the car, winding out Highway 5 to Stratford, her hair loose in the summer wind; or northward to Muskoka, dried leaves scuttling like crabs in the headlights, naked woods, cottage smoke, ice filigrees in the low sun of morning; or eastward, skis angling over the roof and the road to the Laurentians snow-blown but clear, to the top of the Autoroute, hot baths and drinks at the bottom of the day.

Once? Why, innumerable times, when he had loved her. But that was such years ago he remembered only isolate, limpid, bits of time. Once at Ste. Adêle they had laughed so hard that their faces froze in grins; once at Stratford they had lain with a bottle of wine, watching swans and uncertain canoes, and he had read to her:

He thought her flesh was touched with lightning,
Or magic impulses that guess how rivers meet.

In her hands he saw the golden key
To vistas of unending green, blinding
The enemies of his unity.

They had known then what the lines meant, and had not believed
the dour conclusion of the poem, which spoke of suffering and
of travelling alone.

He still did not believe in suffering, although his eyes had
grown heavy and full of facts. He had not suffered through the
loss of love. Love had evaporated like over-heated water, and
he was left with the dry container, believing it could be filled
again at any time. Often, indeed, he had been given moments,
mirages, when all seemed fresh and cool as ever, and he went
on believing that they proferred themselves eternally. They need
only be seized. He need only take the time.

He geared down on the freeway ramp, and then accelerated
onto the road. Traffic was sparse. He shifted to fourth, watched
the rpm's fall back and begin to climb again as he reached the
straightaway, chose his lane and let his foot bear down. At 3000
rpm's he flicked the overdrive and the engine settled like a runner
to its stride. The speedometer needle swept through sixty-five,
through seventy. He was heading east. Behind, the sun sank
into the city haze like a leaking red balloon.

" ... forecasts indicate a continued growth in the Gross
National Product of 5 to 7% per year. In a paper presented to
the Minister of Trade and Finance this afternoon, the Economic
Council warned that to allow the rate of growth to fall below
5% would start the country on a dangerous recessionary spiral."

Gerry flicked the light switch, and the headlights splashed
yellow pools into the dusk. He slipped to the left lane, overtaking
a string of transports bound for Montreal. Heavy with goods,
they glittered like decapitated Christmas trees with running lights
in orange, red, and green. He stayed in the left lane, gaining
speed. At seventy-five the car passed through the wheel shimmy
he had not yet been able to correct — troubling, like a pebble

in the shoe — but at eighty it had settled once again, gripping the road. He let the wheel rest lightly between his palms, sensing its trembling with a lover's touch. Again a feather brushed his belly.

How could you know that exultation, if you were not a man of action? How could Miro know it? Miro, raising his girlish questions, should we or shouldn't we, hesitant, vacillating, rummaging texts, a Hamlet with a microscope. How could he possibly know, with all that endless probing, what it was to act and to succeed? Or Franklin, patiently recording, turning the camera lens here, there, deluded into history? How could any of them, any of them who had drawn back from the struggle, know what it was to pit yourself against the purely unexpected, and to win? Paul? Well, Paul might; patiently building the power and prestige of his company, catching the instants in which contracts went soft, when the mood of the conference hovered, ready to settle. Yes, he might. But of course, this was something which should not be discussed. You knew it, you lived it, but you did not talk about it. *Omerta*, the Italians would have said: the rule of manly silence. *Pudeur*, the French would have said, casting a thread of shame across the modesty. But for Gerry Rattray the lure of business and the Law were part of motivation, simply that. And you did not talk about motives at any time, unless you were weak enough to end up on a psychiatrist's couch. Such talk was the pornography of business.

" . . . been referred to as the 'climatic flip'. Dr. Blakock, an advisor of the British Space Agency, noted that the cooling trend in the earth's atmosphere which he first observed and charted in 1969, was proceeding at a more rapid pace than he had predicted in that year. The cooling, said Dr. Blakock, is caused by the turbidity of particles in the atmosphere, and had been thought to be proportional to the square of the mass of particles. It is now clear, he said, that his earlier calculations, which predicted a cooling trend of 4 to 5 degrees per year, had been made invalid by the appearance of new and disturbing environmental factors."

The secondary roads. On them the car exulted. The hills, the bridges, the uncambered curves and erratic surfaces, all proved its versatility. In fourth, winding up to overdrive, his thumb already pressed on the toggle switch, he swept through a tunnel of maples, and the car's roar surged back at him from trunks and bare branches. Leaves scattered. He crested a low hill, flicking down the overdrive in the instant the car strove to be airborne, and accelerated. He picked up the tail lights of a car a mile ahead of him. Already he had calculated the distance and the speed at which he was overtaking. Already he was anticipating the moment when he would pass.

"This ends the world news," said the announcer. "Now for news closer to home."

He arrived home to find Janet's car gone. On the hall table, two notes awaited him.

> Come to Henry's when you get in. Paul called. Michael
> has been killed at school. 8:10.
>
> > J.

And underneath, on another of the tiny note slips she was fond of using:

> 6:30. Miro. Arrested. College Street Station. Wants
> you to represent him.
>
> > J.

Blinking, he held these notes together. He breathed air through his mouth, unable, for a moment, to get enough. There seemed a cleavage in his mind, as if two ham fists had pulled the halves of it apart. A bike. A boy. Your book, Mr. Rattray. Paul's grin, wave. Wait for me, you guys. No time. Miro's glasses. Illusions. Ways of spreading death through time, swallowed in tiny bits. But Mithridates, he died old! Law, ethics, rights, humanism, mere lobotomies. Your business is worms, Miro. Teach worms. Acquiesce in the soft and general ways of death ...

"Christ!" said Gerry Rattray. He turned in a circle, flicking the notes as if shaking out a match. And the glinting precisions which were life under control, the glimpses of reality which one caught as if through a winking camera's eye, gave place to a single, relentless exposure which laid grey light upon his spirit. "Silly little bastard!" Although he meant Miro, still breathing through his mouth as if he had jogged a block, dialling the station to learn the charge, he had not forgotten the kid whom he had liked (loved, perhaps, having had none of his own to know for certain) and who had carelessly, inconsiderately, gotten himself killed all at once.

chapter twenty-five

January 1, 1786. More than all else, the darkness of the country is an oppression upon my spirits. For two weeks we have not seen the sun, and the days have hung grey and cold, mere interludes in a swelling night. Were I not a man of reason, cognizant of the passage of time and aware that April will return again, my senses could founder amidst this ice and darkness. We have much fog. I have acquired the habit of walking out in it, against the advice of our hunters, who have warned me of the dangers of losing myself and perishing from cold. Indeed, it has happened twice that I have become confused in the forest, and have been drawn back safely only by my people firing a musket at intervals, and by Elborn's calling from the palisade. Nonetheless, I must be alone! The close conditions of the fort, the constant bickering and whining among the men, ill at ease from a surfeit of indolence, the intrigues of the women, and the cunning, constant presence of Elborn, are all more than I can bear for two days running.

Next week Elborn and I have planned to go *en déroaine* into the country to solicit the hunts of bands which have not yet come to us. Such a trip will alleviate the tedium to some degree, and allow me an opportunity to confront Elborn with my suspicions of him. This I mean to do directly, and to resolve at last the differences between us.

The trade has been less than anticipated, and declining for several weeks. Shongwashe insists that the season has scarcely begun, and that I must wait until Spring to reap the benefits of the credit I have extended on the Company's behalf. However, my people who are experienced in the ways of these Indians believe Shongwashe's band to be not large enough to supply our expectations in furs, and to judge from the hunts we have had from them to date I fear these misgivings are well founded. We can none of us understand the reluctance of other Indians to trade with us, the closest fort of our competitors being some fifty miles distant; however, we must now go out like flea-bitten *coureurs-de-bois* after our furs!

Shongwashe's people have by degrees moved themselves closer to our fort, and their lodges now stand for the most part on the flat ground between our buildings and the lake, although some few are scattered in the shelter of trees behind. We are thus effectively surrounded by them, and although there is little danger from them, yet they are a presence. Their bark lodges hunch like crustaceans in the snow. On occasion I am called to one or the other to visit the sick, and inside they are dark and thick with smoke. The sick lie on platforms raised off the ground. For the old, wracked by fevers and pains in the joints and a general superfluity of life, one can do little, although they hold great faith in the potency of our medicines. Similarly, little is to be done for those of any age in the extremes of consumption or venereal complaints, and I am not equipped to render surgery, beyond the setting and tying of broken bones, although I have resorted to desperate measures when a life hung in the balance.

Before Christmas I was summoned to attend a child, a girl seven or eight years of age, already far advanced in pneumonia and delerious with fever. Immediately I caused her to be warmly wrapped and carried to the fort and placed in my own quarters, where I laboured three days and nights to preserve her life, but without success. Throughout, Elborn admonished me frequently for these attentions, which he considered unwarranted, and for setting a precedent which we would be hard pressed to meet in future. At last, when the child had died, he affected indifference, casually lighting his pipe beside the small and still warm body as if her death were of no consequence; no, nor her life either. I flared at him, for I had worked desperately to save her and was overtired. He said, smiling, "but of what use is a mere savage child to the Company, MacKay? And a girl at that, who has no prospect of becoming a hunter!" I came near striking the man at this, and indeed hit the doorpost with such force as to injure my hand, whereupon I struck at it repeatedly, crying out in pain until my people came to calm me.

Indian men conceal all emotions except rage and lust, but the women give full vent to their feelings. So it was with the mother of this child, who first pulled out her hair by the handfull, then burnt her clothes, then cut her arms and legs in several places, so that she presented a shocking appearance, virtually naked and streaming with blood. She remained in the snow, wailing most distressingly for her child, and could not be induced to take shelter until she sank frozen and exhausted and was carried to her lodge.

On Christmas Day we sent gifts of rum, flints, and gorgets into their camp, and I instructed that our people be given extra rum. A debauch ensued. In its midst, Shongwashe appeared with some of his people and a young woman, perhaps fifteen or sixteen years of age who, he said, was his gift to me! He discoursed on the custom of gentlemen traders of taking a daughter of the country as a companion in order to pass the time more agreeably. He noted that most men in my command had followed this custom. It was in no way natural, he said, for a man in the prime of health and youth so to deprive himself of women as I had done. For these reasons, and because he was my friend, he asked me to accept the girl, who was his daughter.

As he spoke, I watched the woman closely but could detect no hint of her feelings at the transaction her father proposed. Her eyes would not rise to meet my own, and remained fixed on a point of ground mid-way between us. She carried herself well under the bulky winter garments, and her long black hair, caught loosely at the neck by a leather hoop, spread out across the robe on her back, sleek and glossy with bear grease in the Indian fashion. I confess that I had not been unaware of her movements about the camp during the autumn. I knew her for a passingly chaste and able girl, and I had no doubt that if I accepted her she would serve me well and faithfully for as long as I had need. I knew also that although I had procured the hunts of Shongwashe and his band for the Company, my acceptance of the girl would cement our agreements, and in no way damage the prestige of the chief for having placed a daughter among the whites.

And yet I could not take her, and told Shongwashe only that it was not now in my heart to take a woman but that I would perhaps do so in the spring; and although he was disappointed, yet he made a show of understanding. At this the woman looked at me, her face impassive, so that I could not tell if she was relieved or disappointed. But her look was deep and long, and I turned away from it on some pretext.

Antoninus has said that he who has not within him all that is needful for life, but craves the help of another, is a veritable pauper. But in truth, I will not risk the intimacy! It is a danger to all men and a peril well avoided. This lesson I have learned once so well that I have no need of a second teaching, for to abandon the bastion of mind and give oneself to the flesh is to venture unarmed and vulnerable into unknown country where enemies lie ready with knives and arrows. It is to admit oneself an animal, nothing more, and to do so not only for the moments of passion but for all of time! Following the Indian's proposition I foresaw my degradation as if it had occurred and I was by some magic permitted to review it. I saw how the woman would receive me passively at first, but then by increasing her demands and by the very constancy of her presence, begin to drain my strength and resolution until I was no longer an independent man but half a hybrid. I saw my ruin in her allure. Nor have I forgotten my rejection by Kathleen, after she had given me encouragements in my suit. I remember her laugh and mockery, the darkness.

I have little doubt that the way to avoid future injuries is to prove impervious to all female inducements!

January 6th. This day Elborn and I, together with three Canadians, one of them Marquette, a hunter, set forth into the country. We have appointed Mr. Henderson in charge of the fort, for he is an able person. The fort is adequately provisioned, and we left all in order. It is our intention to meet and parley with as many Indians as have not already committed their hunts to us, and to induce them singly and in bands to trade as soon as possible. Their reluctance I attribute to their fear of infection from smallpox or cholera, which diseases spread havoc among both them and our people three years ago. I have been told stories of that time which are singular in their horror — of dying savages bedaubing the fort walls with their offal, and of whole villages spreading the stench of death for miles upon the rivers, deserted of all living things but the ravens, which hopped like feathered imps among the bodies. I have little doubt that fear of disease to which they have no natural resistance keeps them from the fort and from contact with white men, and we must therefore allay these fears by a display of healthfulness.

Of one band especially I have high hopes. Reports of them are imprecise. They are I believe larger in number than Shongwashe's people and led by one Miskobenasa, or Red Bird. Our Indians regard them with both amusement and respect, saying that they cling to ancient ways and will not easily be induced to trade. It is such constant quarrels and defections which divide these people and prevent their achieving nationhood! Shongwashe himself has declined to speak of this rival band and has avoided my questions concerning them, and what I have learned has come from various of his hunters who have met them in the wilderness. In November I sent to them a gift of rum, cooking pots, and woollen goods, but this has gone unacknowledged.

We have passed today through murky and uncertain weather. It is not so bitter cold as it has been for some days past, and a fog has risen from the land to beset us, passing in its ghostly manner among the trees and obscuring our prospect on all sides. We have seen no living creature since morning, although we have heard both wolves and lynx not far distant. When the fog is close upon us it appears that we are marching without progress, with ever the same two yards of fresh snow ready to receive the imprint of our snowshoes, and the short track behind like the tail of our toboggan; it is as if we are captured like dull rodents on their treadmills, unaware and uncaring that they perform for the Sunday crowd in Vauxhall Gardens, but keeping on because they must, because they are pointed forward and have no option but to proceed or fall back, overturned by their own momentum. I find comfort in such abdication. I asked our hunter if he was aware where he was going, and he replied that he was following the river and would not be lost while he did so.

"Why, MacKay," said Elborn, overhearing my question, "we are continuing to go in, are we not? It is an expedition undertaken at your command. Do *you* not know where you are taking us?"

I replied that I did not, but that I went forward.

He laughed. "As for myself," he said, "I cannot tell in this uncertain day whether I go forward or back, for I swear that I am passing through country where I have passed before, and I would not be amazed to learn that we are walking in circles as lost men do, and shall come at last to the point from which we started."

I said, "You are mistaken. We go forward!" And I delivered this pronouncement with more vehemence than I intended, for I experienced a profound misgiving at his words, sufficient to make me doubt both Marquette and myself, and to drop fear like a distillate upon my senses. But I regained my presence at once. I know as well as he — better indeed! — the vastness and menace of this frozen land, and am better prepared to meet it. "Brush away all imagination," Antoninus has said, "restrain impulsiveness, dampen desire, and confirm the power of the mind!"

When we had made camp and built a great fire for warmth, Elborn came to where I squatted staring at the flames. We drank the broth which had been prepared. The others stamped and talked boisterously on the other side, glancing out at the fog, so that what we said was private to ourselves. The enchange is not long finished as I write, and I shall attempt to recall it in its entirety, since it will prove useful to my purpose, which is to rid myself of this man. I did not look at him, but at the fire.

"Elborn," I said, "I am pleased to speak frankly and clearly with you. I have made no attempt these many months to conceal my dislike for you. I regard you as a conniving and unprincipled man, and consider your influence pernicious."

Again he laughed, not at all amazed. "To whom are you talking, MacKay? Has this solitude and fear of the wilderness accomplished your derangement?"

"I am speaking to you," I replied. "I have endured your spite since our first meeting in Bristol, and I have borne with you throughout our voyage to Quebec, our journey to Frog Lake, and my stewardship as factor of the fort. I see clearly the depth of your envy, Elborn, and your eagerness to destroy my career and my usefulness to the Company. Chance brought us together, and has not seen fit to separate us. But you are intolerable to me, with your hints, your innuendos, your slights to my character, your questioning of my dedication to the Company! It is *you* who do not have the Company's best interest at heart! Now,

Elborn, let me serve clear warning to you: My patience with you has reached its limit, and either you will give your heart to our endeavours ..."

"Ah, MacKay," he interrupted, "what a fool you are! How you prattle! Heart? Heart? What do I know of that or care? Hm?" He smiled insidiously, and tossed the dregs of his cup into the fire. "I care less than *that* for your great words and your wounded pride and your beloved Company, and would readily commit them all to the flames could I do so without danger to myself. But I cannot, and so I am carried along by them and you, like flotsam on a current, circling the eddies. You amuse me, and I cannot forbear comment on your various absurdities. But do not ask me to be party to them, not with dedication, not with heart, for I do not know what you mean."

"And you will not stop your criticism of my decisions?"

"I cannot stop my laughter at being part of them."

"Then why do you not cease to be part? Why do you not get out?"

"Out?" he said with some surprise. "Out? How? Where? You ask me to get out of history? I am exactly as old as you, MacKay. I have had the same schooling, and there is no way out from that!" He nodded to the cold, endless, and silent forest lying behind the fog. "Even were I to join the savages, do you think I would not spread our foolishness like a pestilence among them, and so remain in the Company's service, whether or not I took its pay? Ah, no, MacKay, there is no way out but ..."

"Death?"

"So eager? Death, yes, and laughter."

"We are bound to be enemies," I observed, standing, "and shall continue so until one has destroyed the other!"

"Or," said Elborn, "until you join me in my laughter at your absurdities. Then, perhaps ..."

"I have too great a charge for levity."

"Or is it too great a fear? I assure you, MacKay, that the difference between your position and mine is that you are adrift in the midst of a solemn group, whereas I am alone. Your responsibility, such as it is, consists in refusing steadfastly to see that I am still afloat, that I am singing occasionally, and laughing at that pomposity which imagines our real positions to be different." He shook his head and adjusted himself so that he could gaze up at me reflectively, as he might upon a unique specimen.

"Oh MacKay, MacKay, I know men like you so well — men who believe that they must believe; you will always be successful, and your success will prove disastrous, and there is nothing to be done with you. You will always set your goal and strike to it, because you must believe you are in control. And you cannot stop. Each of you drives on the others, clutching at goals. Yes, I know you, and alas, I am part of you."

This interview left little doubt that Elborn must be removed. When all paddlers must stroke together for the progress of the craft, it is not tolerable to have one out of rhythm, or stroking feebly, or disrupting the others with convulsions of private amusement. To this matter I must give careful thought, for it is clear that I shall receive resistance from the Company in the question of his removal. As far as they are concerned he is as firmly placed at Frog Lake as I am myself.

January 8: All yesterday we followed the river course, travelling to the north-east, and at evening estimated our distance from the fort at twenty-four miles. The weather has grown cold and clear. The river has broadened into a series of inter-connected ponds, or small lakes, among which our guide leads us confidently. In general, my spirits lifted with the horizons, and I eagerly anticipated making contact with new Indians and with Miskobenasa's band in their winter camp.

Early this morning we encountered a lone hunter. Reluctantly, he halted at our call and waited sullenly for us to approach. He wore an outer garment of rabbit skins, which because of their whiteness allow the hunter to blend into the countryside and grow almost invisible. This man remained watchful and unresponsive to our questioning, shaking his head and answering in noncommital grunts and shrugs. Clearly he did not welcome our presence. Nor would he agree to trade or to guide us to Miskobenasa's band, although I believed that he himself was one of them. He left us to make our own way, and turned towards the riverbank with a perfunctory raising of the hand. Upon reaching the edge of the forest he vanished among the trunks of birch and poplar as swiftly as he had appeared, white on the white snow. I had no doubt, however, that he would hasten to tell his band of our approach, and that we should soon have contact with them.

So it was. Scarcely had we made our second camp and begun to heat our evening meal than we were visited by three Indians.

Their appearance at the edge of our camp was so silent and sudden as to startle my men, who cursed and took up their guns. But the savages for their part remained unmoving, except for the breath streaming from their nostrils at each exhalation. All wore cloaks of rabbit skin and deep hoods which gave them a stark and ghostly appearance, their faces being shrouded. The two outer figures held bows in their right hands, but the other carried no weapons of any kind. All three held themselves poised neither for flight nor attack, but with a kind of reserve and dignity I have not seen before in Indians, for I have found them ever ready to fawn upon the whites.

I advanced to greet these men, but had drawn no closer than ten paces to them when the central figure raised his hand so firmly with the palm extended towards me that although I recognized the gesture of greeting and peace, it had in this instance the effect of telling me I had approached close enough. I returned the greeting, whereupon he flung back his hood to reveal hair of a startling whiteness, drawn severely down the sides of his face and tied behind. His face was angular, not unlike those one sometimes sees in men who have spent their lives upon the seas, or in other extremities of endeavour. His cheekbones accentuated eyes of penetrating directness and intensity. I perceived that if we were to meet in trade, this Indian would drive a harder and shrewder bargain than my poor Shongwashe, who scrambled after what he could get.

"I am MacKay," I said, "factor of the Company's post at Lake Omuhkukke."

"I am Miskobenasa," said the Indian. For a moment he regarded me, and then at his gesture the attendant on his right drew forward a toboggan upon which I recognized the gifts I had sent to this chieftain in the autumn. "I am returning your belongings," said Miskobenasa, "which have come by accident into my camp."

"Not by accident," I replied, "but as tokens of regard and in hopes of friendship."

"Friendship is not purchased."

"It is not purchased, but neither does it spring from rock. It must have soil in which to root itself." And I gestured toward the toboggan.

But the Indian placed the flat of his snowshoe against the end cases and with a thrust sent the whole gliding toward me. "This soil I give you back again," he said. "It is not trees which grow in it but dead man's leather, *jebi e push kwa e gun. O tau pe num!* We want no more of it! You are not welcome among us should you come with your toboggans full of death for trading, with your canoes full of death. We know well your trade and friendship, and we have gone apart from it. Forever!''

Behind us the fire blazed high, feeding up into the tangle of logs piled upon it. It further lightened the face of the chief, which I saw was marked severely from the smallpox. Thus my conjecture was confirmed, I thought, for perhaps in the ravages of the disease his mind has been ravaged also, so that he fears contact with us. Perhaps, indeed, he suspects us of sending the pestilence among them, so that we may take their lands with ease.

"We have come to trade fairly," I said.

"There is no fair trade with you. There is only loss."

"We have come in peace, and with honourable intentions."

He grunted. "You do not know, you whites, what your intentions are. Even when they are evil you do not know it. So how can you know that you come in peace?"

I said, "This is no place for parley," and I gestured toward the fire, thinking that they might share its warmth and our meal. But Miskobenasa took no notice of my overture.

"You are right," he said, "and so we will take our leave. But hear me well, MacKay. You are a day's journey from my lodges, and my people hunt for many days' travel from that place in all directions. I cannot stop you walking upon the earth, for she receives all men; but you are not welcome to attempt trade with my people, or to send others to hunt for your Company's enrichment. You have heard me."

As silently as he had appeared, he faded into the night with his lieutenants. We opened the packs on the toboggan and found all gifts exactly as I had sent them, even to the rum, of which they had not tapped a single cask.

Liv sat with her knees drawn up, watching the parchments burn as Paul fed them one by one into the fire. The Indian's gesture had moved her deeply — so futile, she thought, and yet its seeming futility had been part of its magnificence. She knew about such gestures. A company wife, she had made dozens of them, unimportant, undramatic, meaningless in the game her husband played. And yet she made them, telling herself that if there were enough their cumulative effect eventually would change the scheme of things. She smiled now at her naivete, but she regretted none of them, for in the end she had been right. She had salvaged this, this last time they had together, this last time which was less than she had hoped for but infinitely better, infinitely more.

She watched the parchments curl around the butts of logs, crumbling to ash, bearing their lines of ink like welts, and she remembered the proudest of these gestures, and the last.

It had happened at the inquest. Throughout, she had sat by Paul's side, her face reposed but pale with grief, her eyes a deeper, darker brown, her mouth a steady line. She breathed shallowly. She had never in her life worn a hat, unless for warmth, and she had been the only mourning mother without one that afternoon. Her grey-brown hair hung straight and unadorned, tied simply at the base of her skull. When Paul had covered his face with his hands and said, ''We shouldn't have come. God knows there's no need for this!'' she had reached across and placed her hand on his knee, without ceasing to watch the coroner, for she knew that she should indeed have come, that this was exactly the place for her. She told him in her own way. On her left, Franklin Hook, whose wife was long gone — to the south, to Europe, to Australia? Who knew? It had been such years before, when they were both young and a child was the last thing any model wanted — Franklin sat with a hand across his mouth and his eyes full of such pain she could not bear to look at him. So she had stayed, a woman between two bowed men, listening to witnesses.

One after the other they answered their summonses.

The school officials: The boys had been released at four and were playing on the common. Their shouts could be heard in the room where the masters were taking tea. It was a low and gloomy day. All was in order until about 4:20, when the shouts diminished abruptly and the masters supervising the play cried out in alarm. In seconds, the boys on the far edge of the field could be seen crumpling where they stood, small piles of blue uniform. Some fell as they ran for the school, as if flicked by an enormous finger; and indeed, the trailing dollop of cloud which had touched them resembled exactly that. It was obvious immediately what had occurred. The windows were shut instantly and the exhaust fans turned on. Nothing else could have been done. Nothing.

The plant officials were called next, with Gerry Rattray representing them and avoiding her eyes: In the processing of essential gases such accidents are, regrettably, always possible. It should be noted, however, that the gas industry has had an enviable safety record, leading other manufacturers in the installing of emission control devices. The chances of such an accident were, perhaps, one in a million, for the simultaneous concurrence of all the factors was an almost impossible coincidence. However, it had happened. An unusually low and persistent localized temperature inversion, a new and careless employee misreading the instructions on a valve, a residue in a little-used repository, a cross-wind — the result had been the release of hydrogen sulphite in a small but lethal concentration. It had dispersed above the fields to the southeast of the school. There was also some question about the integrity of certain valves and cauldrons recently supplied by an American firm, and although they had fully met government standards . . .

The civil servants rose methodically to their own defence: All plant equipment had been inspected six weeks before the incident, and had been found to meet government regulations. However, it should be noted that training procedures for new personnel were apparently not fully observed in this case, and if such neglect could be shown to have resulted directly in emissions exceeding acceptable levels, then charges under the Air Standards Act of 1967 . . .

When they had all finished and the coroner was about to adjourn for the afternoon, completing a decorous proceeding, Liv Henry rose quietly, her hands on the chair in front of her. He said,

"Madame, I intended to call no further witnesses." But she stood saying nothing, for she knew that the coroner, who was clearly not an unkind man, was thinking all that would ultimately prove necessary: Here is a woman who has lost her son, and for whom formalities even in ordinary times mean little. Now she has lost her son, and she stands like an exclamation mark after our complicity. He said again, gently, "Madame ..." knowing she would not sit down, and at last he inclined his head, gave her her time with a parting of his hands, and waited.

She said, "I won't take long. I know time is important to you all. Time is money." She smiled, and her voice shook with the effort, but was firm and clear. "I know nothing of these tolerances you have spoken of. I don't know what the thing was that killed Michael, or if he died in pain, or if it was the same to him as falling asleep. I know he could have been killed on his bicycle, or that he might have drowned or died at any time by an accident or disease as gratuitous as this. But he didn't. He died of a poison gas." She turned to the side of the room where the Company officials sat, and where their attorney sat, looking at the floor. "Gerry," she said, and waited until he looked at her. "You say that these are essential gases. And I know that. I believe you, if you tell me that. And I know too that such accidents happen all the time, and that people are consumed this way by the things they have made essential. I know that it will not stop, that it will go on and on, that we shall make new horrors, thinking we can contain them, and our children shall be killed by them. May I ask you this, all you men who are a part of what has happened, and who do your jobs as well as you know how, and who never question, and who are proud of your profits and accomplishments, and who will train your living sons to play the same game and to beat each other if they can, yes, even to kill each other when they play the game of government later on? What has happened to us? What kind of animal have we become that in all our wisdom and culture we create and cherish the very forces that destroy us? What kind of animal would not give its young clean air, at any cost, and pure water, and healthy food? Are we so sick and aberrant that we cannot see what we are doing? Or do we work at it because we are hateful to ourselves and to life? Is depravity our element? And will we keep on until there is nothing left, and then say that we have a fine record, we have fumigated the world? Is that what we shall do?''

She faced the coroner, and the executives, and the teachers, and the government officials, aware that they were embarrassed, for her, because she had violated several important rules — the one that said women should not think, or at least should not show that they thought; and the one that said, ''Keep your questions small, so that they can be answered by specialists''; and the one, the most important one, that told her to take what she had been given, and be thankful. She saw that they thought her unhinged by grief, and made excuses for her, and sought to extricate themselves as gracefully as possible. But perhaps for an instant, too, they had glimpsed part of her perception before dismissing it hastily, knowing it to be inadmissable to any civilized system of logic. Even she herself, as the room emptied somberly and she was led by Paul into the diffused light and clamour of Bay Street, felt the perception fade easily, blend with the forms of grief. ''But, I was right ...'' she murmured, no longer sure, among all the ways of being right, exactly what she meant, but trying only to keep a little longer the thing she had seen — a perfect machine, a suspended sculpture, perhaps a sphere, immobile and alone on the sterile earth.

They had stood on the City Hall steps, the three of them. It was November, and cold. She said, ''Come for dinner, Franklin,'' and reached up to hold his arm. He was so big, so vulnerable, like a huge child himself. She knew he wanted a drink. But he shook his head and looked away from her. He had wanted his son to be a cinematographer. He had wanted him to flood with light and precision those areas he had never entered.

"Come on," Paul said. "We want you." And together they drew him to the car and he sat silently in the back seat close to the window, staring without recognition at the walls of concrete, the walls of truck tires, the walls of hurrying people in the streets.

After a while he said, "We all killed them, didn't we?"

"Yes," she said.

"With poison. With tolerance. With apathy."

She turned to face him. "We can change that," she said, not believing it. "We have to change that."

Slowly he shook his head. "You know, I haven't understood very much besides cameras and what makes good television. And I've always looked for both sides of every story. If there wasn't another side I made one. I was trained to be impartial, trained to find the facts that would strike a balance. But you know, I listened to those guys this afternoon, from the Company, and I saw how everything I've done has worked for them." He laughed. "Isn't that the horse's ass? All the time, all the goddam time *they've* paid my salary, *they've* controlled the Corporation, and everything I've done has been exactly as they wanted it. My issues were the ones they wanted aired, and everything I've done has won them time. That's it, isn't it? *They bought time!* And all we've done is to provide the illusion of concern, and the protests that are dead and forgotten six weeks after the program." He shook his head as if he had been struck, and his groan again became a laugh. "And you," he said, touching Paul's shoulder, "you and your goddam paper company, you're one of them, aren't you?"

"Yes."

"Sure. We're all part of the same bloody mess. We've all forgotten. And now we can't do a goddam thing about it."

"You can quit," Paul said. "You can resign."

"Then what do we do?" Franklin asked. "You tell me."

"We have to go back," Paul said. "Somehow."

And Liv had added, "And we must forget."

chapter twenty-six

Under the flourescents Miro's glasses were glimmering bars. He sat erect, palms on the grimy table, and he shook his head. "No bail," he said.

Gerry tossed his ballpoint on his notes. "Don't be a bloody fool."

"No bail."

"Miro, listen. It's now one thirty A.M. It will take all the persuasion I have to convince a J.P. that you should get out of here at all. I am very tired and am frankly not sympathetic to drama and heroics."

Miro spread his hands.

"So no postures. Please."

"No postures, but no bail either."

"Goddam it, Miro, you'll gain nothing! Believe me."

"Perhaps. Tell me, why are you here? I didn't call you."

"Somebody did."

"My Chairman, no doubt. I have a very worried Chairman."

"Okay, what difference?"

"The difference," Miro said, "is that I didn't ask."

"Look, if it's a slow news week the press will amuse themselves by chopping you into tiny cubes. Is that what you want? Jeez, you're such a bloody kid! It is very impolite to criticize other people's methods of self-destruction. Bad manners."

Miro smiled. "Do you know what is on trial here?"

"*You* are on trial."

"But not alone."

"What else?"

"Ethics. Good manners. Individual rights. Free enterprise. Humanism. The Law itself. All those lobotomies, those ways of inducing acquiescence, of keeping the illusion of choice." Miro laughed. The childhood edge of hysteria remained, but there was a control, now, that turned the laughter like a weapon. "Those ways of spreading death through time, to be gathered as we proceed. Those are on trial.''

"Shit. Run for office if you want to talk like that!"

Miro laughed again.

"Seriously. Of the two forms of theatre, which is the more entertaining, politics or what you're doing?''

"Entertainment is an obscenity. Effects are what matter. Effects. I can smell the effects of government even here.''

"But if you want power ... ''

"I want a clean land," Miro said. "It is a very small request.''

"Okay,'' Gerry shut his briefcase. "I'm getting out before you tell me that you're on the side of love and nature. Have a great night in this can. I'll be by to see you tomorrow. I suppose the others don't want bail either. No. How many are there?''

"Three.''

"Kids?''

"Students.''

"Jesus, I don't know why *I* should defend them. God knows there are enough guys who need the work.''

"Guys with ideals.''

"Exactly.''

"Ideals about ethics and good manners.''

"I've got an office full of them.''

"Follow your conscience, Gerry.'' Miro smiled. "But remember, my students didn't ask for you either.''

The next afternoon Gerry saw the boys.

Twenty years before they would have made a great backfield. All were larger, lither, than he was. All lounged with athletic indolence. Hair covered their ears. The youngest of the three wore his glasses like an affront, thrusting flourescent bars at Gerry Rattray. They smiled. Their brows wrinkled. They formed a single, antagonistic will.

"What?'' they asked, turning their heads in mock deafness. "What are you defending? Us? Oh, that's not true, Mr. Rattray. Not true at all. If you were defending us you would not be going into court.''

"Where else?''

They shrugged. "Ravines. Woodlots. Rivers. Any place away from men.''

"Sorry. I work in courts.''

"For men. For nothing else.''

"That's right.''

The eldest shook his head. "Ah, Mr. Rattray, you make a great mistake. Consider, for example, the beauty of the frog. Consider the ease and grace with which he moves in the stuff of life. Consider his gelatin eggs spreading among the reeds. Consider his strength, his perfection. Consider this saying of the Ojibwa: 'The frog does not drink up the pond in which he lives.' ''

"At the moment I'm considering other things. For example, the work waiting on my desk. Or the clients I would be meeting if Dr. Balch had not asked me to defend you. Or the police records you will all have if you continue your little games.''

Pitying laughter wrapped him. "*You*, Mr. Rattray, are playing the little games!''

Again the eldest leaned forward. "You refuse to understand. You know how little time remains, and *still* you refuse! Why should we talk to you at all?''

"Because,'' Gerry said evenly, "I can get you out of here.''

"On what condition?''

"On condition that you go back to your books. Forget the violence.''

"Shit!'' The youngest, trembling, pale and wide-eyed behind his glasses, said the word with such vehemence that a strand of spittle fell across his lip. "As if you don't live off violence!''

"Lost your cool,'' said his friend, looking at the table.

"Aw fuck, who cares! Look at him!'' His hand brushed out at Gerry. "Listen, you make me puke! You know that? As if what happens in this city *every minute* isn't violence. As if what happens in your board rooms, in your bedrooms, that isn't violence! And how about your factories, eh? Tell me that what they do isn't violence!''

The hatred in the young face struck like a dirk at Gerry's belly. His reason veered. When he stood up he was short of breath again, for the third time in a week. So even his body was no longer an ally. All right. That was okay too. He placed a palm on the table. "In Courtroom Five," he said, "at nine o'clock tomorrow morning, you will be college boys who made a mistake. You will have seen your error and be contrite. Your mistake is a mere excess of idealism. Is that clear?''

Two of them shrugged, grinning. The third, the youngest, started to speak.

"By *Christ*!'' Gerry said, gratified to see that his anger, at least, was still effective and that the young mouth pursed in surly resignation, "That had better be very, very clear!''

He felt exhausted, walking to his car. His legs hurt. This is how a weed must feel, he thought, when the gardener's probe severs its root. Still erect. Still green. Still moving in the breeze. But the earth has been cut away.

Late that night, fatigued and drunk past the point of caring, he lifted his empty glass to Janet and she obediently rose to fill it again. Her nightgown brushed the rug.

"In the clear," he said, as she returned with the drink. "And Paul would fade back with all the time he needed, faking towards left end. And then it would come. Fast and flat. Straight. And I'd ga-a-ather it in. Down past their tertiaries, feeling them close in on me and knowing I could beat them. I could *beat* them! You know?''

"Yes," Janet said. "I know.''

"I could. And I'd go. I'd go! I'd never look back. Never. I'd watch the safety man. I'd watch him commit himself. Oh, he'd be so *sure*! And then I'd pivot, give him a knee or a hip and take it back again. Slap his helmet sometimes. Remember?''

"Yes," said Janet. "I remember.''

"And then I'd be past the posts, laughing. And the fans'd

be on their feet. I'd heave the ball and let the ref chase it. And the cheers would go and go. Girls doing cartwheels ... Listen. Later I could have had any of those girls I wanted. Any of em. You know?''

"Yes, I know," Janet said.

"Guys pounding my back. Punching me. You'd always pat my shoulder. You'd say, 'good play, Gerry.' And, 'beautiful, Gerry!' Listen. How could things ever be better than that?"

"I don't know," she said, looking at her hands. "Maybe you make a lot of money. Maybe you have children."

"Nah! Oh, sure, you do those things. But you're still playing the game, you know. You play the game the rest of your life. Every case you take. Every deal you make. You're gauging the angles, sizing up the safety man, looking for a way past. Isn't that true?"

"I guess so, Gerry."

"Sure. Sure it is. You never get over that. And you never feel again the way you felt after a game, win or lose. Every muscle hurt. You stank, maybe. Maybe your jersey was ripped off your back. Maybe you bled. When you drank you held up the bottle and let it drain straight down your gullet. You won or you lost, but either way you knew what the rules were. Eh? It was simple. Straight. Like everything should be. Shit, why couldn't everything be like that?"

"I don't know, Gerry. It's not."

"Goddam right it's not. You keep trying, God knows. You do your best to make it like that, and sometimes maybe you really do. But then it changes. The whole game changes before you even realize it, rules and all. Christ, is that fair?"

"Should it be fair?"

"Christ! Half the time you don't even know who the opposition is. What kinda sport's that? You gotta have rules, eh? Well, don't you?"

"If you're playing a game," she said, "you need rules."

He contemplated her, and drank. "Listen. Do you know you're

getting old?''

"Sure I am, Gerry. Both of us.''

"Listen.'' He drank again. The lights of the room flickered and swarmed like insects, and the woman was the queen. The woman was the queen, apart from him, and mocking. "Listen, have you ever considered cosmetic surgery?''

"Oh. Well, yes I have, Gerry,'' and although he couldn't see them, her eyes were blurred with tears. "Sure I have. I've just been waiting for you to mention it. Just give me the blueprints, o.k? What do you want? And when you've got it, will you want it then? Well, name it, Gerry. Name it. That's what I'll be.''

"I want you to be eighteen.''

"Oh Gerry, you bastard.''

"And a virgin.''

"You poor bastard.''

"And I want to see you turn a cartwheel.''

"I know. With my little blue skirt flipping over my little blue-pantied ass. Right? And you want to hear me shouting yea, yea, Gerry Rattray. Hm? That right?''

He nodded.

"I know. I know. Come on, Gerry. Come on. My darling. You want me to dance with both arms around your neck, as we did then. Do you want to hold me? Hold me. You want me to say, Oh Gerry, oh my darling, let's go to the hotel.''

"Yes.''

"Gerry, I want you.''

"Yes.''

"There was a night clerk. A discreet night clerk.''

"Five dollars,'' said Gerry, grinning, "of discretion.''

"Come.''

"Were you scared?''

"No.''

"Not at all?''

"Only that I won't please you. Gerry. Only that I won't be

good enough. What should I do?''
   "Lie still.''
   "Oh Gerry my Gerry my Gerry.''
   "Shhh. Still. Lie still.''

chapter twenty-seven

Most of the day of his son's death, Franklin Hook spent in bed
with a script assistant. He didn't really know her. She had only
recently been assigned to his production unit; but they had spent
five frantic days together in the Alberta foothills, directing a
crew filming grizzlies. In and out of planes, trains, helicopters,
boats, and Land Rovers, this able girl anticipated his requirements,
relieved his worries; and a kind of intimacy had grown between
them. For both, the job came first. As they touched down at
the airport on their return, knowing that they had the footage
they required, he asked her to drinks and dinner. Sharing his
assumptions, smiling, she accepted. But at the studio they learned
the scheduling had been changed, and that the footage now in
the cans would have to be edited that night. They shrugged,
sent out for coffee and sandwiches, and went to work. Eight
hours later, exhausted but content that the job was properly
finished, they emerged into a bleak November morning and
walked to her apartment.
   He would never again use the word love, or wish to enter
its labyrinthine connotations. Comfort was sufficient. Desire,
warmth, tenderness, laughter, these were all sufficient and
measurable as light falling across a meter's cell, measurable as
a camera angle, or the length of a lens, or the duration of an
edited clip. It was sufficient to take this sane girl without ceremony
or nonsense, sufficient for them both, knowing that it might

last only a week, or a day, perhaps only for that afternoon;
it was more than sufficient — it was a gift he had no right
to expect.

He approached life fatalistically now. His big body accepted
unquestioningly what came to it. And he lived for his job, for
the hundreds of hours of patient work which built a program,
for the images which danced precisely through an hour of screen
time, flirting with the minds and phantasies of viewers who might
be either alert or comatose, and which then were gone forever.
An hour's programming, that was a lot of time. An hour in
bed with such a woman, that was a lot of time. But love? The
thing which one swore to protect for ever, as long as you both
lived, the thing that resulted in children and suburban bungalows
and two-car garages, the thing that rotted and stank in hothouse
domesticity, that was unimaginable anymore. He was past it.
It had failed him. And if all his actions, even his laughter, were
fraught with watchful sadness, why, that came from the loss
of innocence. That came from realism. That came from growing
up.

About six, he and the girl awoke. He lay sprawled beside
her, an arm across her breast, a leg between her legs. They
sent out for dinner, and while she showered he switched on
the television news, and so learned of the disaster. At first, the
significance did not register on him. He watched the editing
of the clip, watched the timing, assessed the tone of the announcer's voice, saw how the segment might be improved, and only
then, through a spread of technical considerations, did the name
of the school settle on his consciousness.

Cold with apprehension, he called the school but could not
get through. The line buzzed with staccato unconcern. Angrily,
he hung up and tried his own answering service. Yes, he was
told, the school had been trying to contact him for an hour.
No, there had been no message.

He dressed. The girl, her hair wet, drawing the bathrobe across
her breast, asked, "What is it? What's wrong?"

"My son," he said. "He's been hurt." He continued to watch the screen even as he pulled on his shirt, seeking solace in it, support, denial of the earlier report. But the news continued relentlessly.

" ... Dr. Miro Balch," the announcer was saying now, his articulation impeccable. "Dr. Balch was arrested with three students at the generating station this afternoon. Earlier, the protesters had attempted to block the evening shift of employees from entering the plant. Police were summoned and a melee ensued. Dr. Balch faces charges of trespassing, inciting to riot, and obstructing police."

There was footage — the turbulent, veering kind of film made in crowds, and Franklin imagined the photographer, bent under the weight of his camera on its curved shoulder brace, suddenly swept into the violence he had come to record dispassionately, suddenly pushed and cursed, cursing back in fear for his camera, holding it like a threatened lover. Taut faces swarmed, pale on tape, as if from infernal agony; young, shouting, joyless, tortured by hot ideals, they flowed, bobbed, churned. Clubs flashed. A broken placard said "STOP ... " and another, jiggling crazily before the lens, "NO TIME FOR TALK!"

Franklin zipped his trousers, fumbled with his shoes, watching.

A truck camera, perhaps half a mile away and safely behind the four o'clock freeway traffic, panned back and caught the scene in perspective. There was the raucous group which had so filled the screen, small now, dwarfed by the bulk of the plant behind them growing huger as the zoom lens contracted, until the humans were mere gesticulating insects at its base. Then the chimneys appeared, arrogant ranks of them. Along the bottom, roofs of cars passed endlessly. By the end of the clip it was impossible to see the protesting group at all. In one corner of the screen, a real estate agent's revolving sign proclaimed his affiliation. "I am unique," it said. "UNIQUE! I am unique ... UNIQUE! I am unique ... "

Franklin reached for his coat. He looked from the screen to

the girl, aware that she had spoken, perhaps moments before. "What?" he asked. "What?"

"I asked if I could help."

"No. I've got to go, that's all."

"Call me?"

"Sure," he said. "Yeah. Later."

It was an hour's drive. He wound out on pastoral roads past farms smug with harvest. Here and there in the twilight groups of hunters broke open their guns. Dead pheasants dangled among them. Their dogs frolicked. Franklin blew his horn as he approached, his fear and rage fusing with its monotone. Dear God, hadn't there been enough? Must they kill every small, free thing until nothing remained that was not as trapped as they? Must they kill every wild hope, every spontaneous flight or song, every impulse they failed to understand, until at last they had killed the possibilities for life itself?

Yet, he knew how they felt. He had hunted. He knew the frost under his boots, the dogs snuffling. He knew the instant of the point — the instant *before* the instant — when knowledge of the lurking covey brushed like a feather in the groin, and the gun was already coming up when the dog froze. He knew the thump of the 12-gauge in his shoulder and the gorgeous, ineffably sad tumbling of the bird. He had seen foxes tumble at a full run, a spurt of dust behind. He had dropped deer, and moose, and antelope, and mountain goats. And he remembered a grizzly rearing up in a spring meadow, raging at the thing which had come between her and her cub. He remembered his own calm. He had settled the sights of the 30-06 first on the fawn breast of the creature, coming at surprising speed, pausing, coming again, grunting like an engine; and he had remembered this about bears: that their adrenal glands are enormous; that they will sometimes batter themselves to a rage in order to perform massive feats of strength; that such a bear would be capable, with her heart shattering, of travelling yards and rending her tormentor. He had swung the sights up to the black snout and waited until he felt the ground tremble. Then he shot. The arms had gone up and out, like a furry man's, and a red haze shimmered behind the muzzle that an instant before had been coursing with blood and savagery. He remembered the great breast heaving and the great paws clenched in agony.

He knew how good it was to kill. He had done his share. He knew what it was like to come out of a cold evening and to drink with friends in the smells of sweat, and smoke, and greased leather, and gun oil, and wet dogs and drying blood. He knew how easy and good that was. You went along. It was sport. And you introduced your son to it with a .22 on his four-teenth birthday and a walk through greening fields where groundhogs took the sun.

But at last a day had come when he stopped. It had been a day like this, one of the last of autumn, and the animal had been a deer, stepping out upwind into a clearing. He had levelled the rifle and taken up the first pull of the trigger; and suddenly he knew precisely what would happen — felt the recoil, saw the impact which would lift the forefeet of the animal off the ground and toss it thrashing on its side. He saw the wild eye fix and glaze. He saw himself bend down and cut the jugular . . . Abruptly he had dropped the sights and sent a bullet thudding into the dirt a dozen yards ahead of the deer's fore feet. He never hunted again.

"We've been trying to reach you," said the headmaster, offer-ing a grey hand, his eyes smudged by grief and fatigue. "We tried . . . there was nothing . . . so fast, you understand . . ."

Franklin thought: And so you finish. After the decades of probity, caution, kindly veneers; you end by opening your hands in a dingy hall. He said, "My son is dead."

"Yes," said the headmaster.

"Where is he?"

"In the gym. But perhaps you should wait. The coroner has told us . . . the police . . . "

But Franklin was already past him, turning down the long

corridor where a distant constable, unsure of his duty, squat and grotesque in tricks of light and shock, first gnome, then monkey, then humpback jester, then, close at last, merely an aged local cop, his grey hair too long at the temples. "Now sir ... " he began, "I'm sorry, but my orders ... " He raised an uncertain arm.

Franklin pushed past. He found his son. The place was brightly lit and grease-pencilled names were thumbtacked to the butts of the benches. They had used army blankets to cover them. HOOK, said the sign. TERRY.

Absurd. There was no reason, no continuity. I would not give you again, he thought. Another time I would keep you and we would go together in simple ways and silences. I would show you what I had seen and look with wonder on your discoveries. I would accept fatherhood with a vengeance.

We shall rewind the tape. That is easily done. And when we come to the moment of our parting, each of us carefully not smiling, and the headmaster with his hand on your shoulder, then I will press a switch, and we will take it from there, the camera up to speed, the mikes ready, and I will say to him, "I'm sorry. I've changed my mind. I don't like your accumulations and attritions. I don't like your piecemeal deaths, which you call by other names." And I would take you out.

The headmaster's voice quavered at his elbow. Coffee. His office. Very proud.

"What?"

"He was very proud of you, Mr. Hook. Whenever your films were shown he would break rules and risk detentions to see them. He said you were the best cinematographer of wildlife in North America, and that someday people would turn to your films as they do now to history books, to see what those animals had been like."

"Cover him up."

"I must tell you this: Only a few days ago I overheard one of the other boys teasing him, saying you cared more about ducks and wildcats than you did about people. And he said that was true, that you didn't care much about aberrants, but that if you ever did decide to make a film about people, you would show them like lemmings, going to the sea. I thought that profound, for so young a boy."

"Please," said Franklin. "Cover him up."

chapter twenty-eight

Very few apartment buildings like the one where Kenneth Malcolmson lived remained in the heart of the city. They had courtyards with dry fountains where litter circled in the wind. Their windows were small, their vestibules cramped, their elevators jerkily outdated. Surrounded by towering complexes, they owed their lives to the whims of crotchety owners who could afford to preserve them. But, like their owners, they decayed. Some had not seen the sun for fifteen years. There lay on these a green-brown patina of mould, like that which creeps over stones in rotten rivers. Some offered geraniums to the amorphous days, to be raddled by bugs, but most had forsaken gentility and lay back blowsy with refuse and neglect.

All were the prey of vandals. At evening, carried softly down from their heights, young gangsters gathered and roamed in packs. They ferreted the concrete warrens. They taunted and terrorized. They smashed windows, forced doors, howled in the open streets. Their motorbikes roared defiance in the courtyards, malls, and shopping plazas. Behind their helmets and bug masks they were indistinguishable from each other, all their rattling laughter equally shrill, all their boots anonymous. Sometimes there were screams and splashes of blood among the garbage cans of the building where Kenneth Malcolmson lived.

They had smashed his bicycle. After that, like the other residents, he had had a heavy doorchain installed. His door was scuffed. Obscenities were scratched on its outside.

A muffled, rhythmic bumping had begun in the heart of the building. It was like the pulsing of a faulty valve, of which one is at first only faintly aware, or like a change in humidity, or an evocative scent stirring under the nostrils. It persisted, increased in force and tempo, and at last broke into a flurry of smaller sounds — squeals, stifled cries and scufflings, a scampering on ancient carpeted stairs — that drew Kenneth Malcolmson out of the notebook he cradled close to the insufficient light. "The door," he thought. "They have broken in the back door again!" He peered over the rims of his glasses, found a scrap of paper for a bookmark, and shuffled to the door, his own door with the bolt and chain safely in place, with the great lock prominent as a tumour on a bald forehead. He listened, holding to his chest the stained, tattered, chance collection of papers, and interposing himself between them and the indeterminate threat from outside which came now, as he bent closer, as a whispering, a sighing of nylon clothing, a surreptitious testing of the lock.

Enraged, the old man reared from the door with an inarticulate cry, and brought one slippered foot thumping against it. "Get out!" he shouted. "Do you hear me? Get back! Get back!" Again he kicked the door, and again, until the pain had increased his fury and he had tired himself. Panting, disheveled, outraged, he listened again, head bent, and heard laughter join him in that room with his cherished books, his manuscripts. He spun, snarling like an animal, but the laughter faltered and dissolved as he did so, and the hallway sounds passed on. "Vandals!" he shouted after them, bringing his mouth close to the door, consciously absurd and knowing how that word would amuse them. Comic-strip old man. But let us be accurate, he thought, for without precision I too become part of the swirling tribe in the swirling night. So he said again, "Vandals!" through the door into the dim hall, although he was certain he would not be heard.

January 10. I was impressed favourably by this Miskobenasa, for he appeared to possess character, firmness of resolve, and a forthright demeanour, qualities to which I was unaccustomed in Indians. He had made clear, however, that he would under no circumstances consent to dealings with the Company, and unless I devised a means of entering his confidence and persuading him over, we must lose his hunts. Throughout the night I gave this matter thought, and was fortunate in being troubled no further by Elborn, who slept with the rest. I remained alone at the fire, wrapped in my blanket and sitting upon the toboggan which Miskobenasa had returned.

At dawn I instructed my people to return to the fort, having decided to proceed alone. Elborn smiled at this announcement as if it were not unexpected, but the hunter Marquette protested that he should accompany me, for the country was strange and the Indian intentions unknown. I replied that I might be absent several days, and that the fort would require his skills; I stated also my belief that a single man might succeed in this enterprise where more would fail, and as for losing myself, I need only follow the river home.

In short, we soon took our leave of one another and proceeded in separate directions upon the frozen river. The night had been clear and still, the day was bright, and I had no difficulty in following the tracks left by Miskobenasa and his lieutenants the previous night. Only the creaking of my snowshoes broke the silence. Once a raven croaked, taking flight when I startled him, and once a tree snapped like a pistol shot in the keen air. The sun passed in a low arc. The shadows continued long throughout the day. At noon I warmed frozen pemmican in my mouth and chewed it down when it had softened.

At midafternoon I came upon the camp. It is considerably larger than I had anticipated, consisting of some fifty lodges. I therefore estimated the number of male Indians of hunting age to be in excess of seventy-five.

Children frolicked in a game upon the ice. Their cries reached me before I sighted the camp, and I paused at the unaccustomed sound, for they were laughing, and I had not heard until that moment the laughter of Indian children. On my approach their game ceased, and we regarded each other in a silence as profound as any through which I had passed that day. It is possible they had never seen a white man. It is possible that even so young, they looked upon me as an intruder against whom they must be on their guard. They stood like wary animals, and not until I smiled to show my good intentions, and began to spread my arms as if to embrace them, did the smaller ones cry out, rousing the dogs of the camp. These brought down both men and women, who filled the spaces among the children. I did not venture nearer until I saw that they had parted and that Miskobenasa himself had emerged in front of them. At this I raised my hand in greeting. He responded.

The Indian in his encampment is a gracious host, and I had believed that in the circumstances Miskobenasa could do no other than receive me. Yet he watched me with his chin raised, intently, as one might watch a strange-behaving dog, uncertain whether it is mad. "You did not hear me," he said, "when I told you we will have no trade."

I spread my arms to show I had brought nothing besides myself, neither goods nor weapons. "I have not come to trade," I said.

"For what, then?"

"For talk," I replied. "Between one man and another."

At this he smiled, but sadly, as at a poor joke. And yet I sensed he was not ill-disposed to me as a man, and that I had proceeded well in thus dissociating myself, for the time, from the Company. He had not replied before one of the children drew himself to my attention by raising his hand shyly, as if in greeting. I believed he mimicked his elders merely and that his gesture was without significance; but some quality in the child touched my memory. I looked again at him, and he spoke in a voice which pierced firmly through the hubbub of murmurs and growling dogs. "Ah-ray-ahd-nay," he said, and I recognized him for the child I had comforted with a tale at Grand Portage.

Miskobenasa inquired of the child if he knew this white man, whereupon he replied that I had once told him how monsters might be found and slain in dark places, and how the braves who killed them might find their way again into the sun. Miskobenasa observed that it appeared a heartening story for a winter's night, and the child answered that it was, and that he would tell it when it pleased the chief to hear, for he recalled it very well. It was, he said, a tale of the love of men and women. He spoke brightly, causing laughter among the women.

These women I noted specially, for like the men they differed from those of Shongwashe's band, being less humbled by drudgery, with countenances more open and pleasing. It is their habit to regard one directly and without shame and the slyness of the eyes which marked their licentious sisters at Grand Portage. Their posture is erect and their gait poised, except for the very old, even in their thick winter garments. They seemed, in short, to own themselves in a manner new to me among native women. Among them, one particularly drew my attention, for she was fair-haired and lighter-skinned than her companions, and presented a more striking appearance. I thought her gaze dwelt musingly upon me also. She is partially white, perhaps, or of Mandan ancestry.

Abruptly Miskobenasa gestured me towards his lodge, and I accompanied him there, together with his wife and daughter, his daughter's husband, and his mother, an ancient and wrinkled personage who peered at me in the smoke as if she would take the measure of my soul. Nowhere in or about the lodge was there evidence of trade with Europeans. Containers were wood or hide; all clothing was of hide, and the old woman in the shadows sewed with a bone needle. Their knives were flint, and their spoons and other utensils were horn or wood.

Miskobenasa showed me a place at his fire. He asked, "On what occasion were you kind to the child?"

I replied that I had found the child crying and sought to comfort it. I described the occasion, and added that it had been a small thing.

"It is a small thing," he agreed, "but it is much. It is enough."

The child's mother, he informed me, had been stabbed at Grand Portage, murdered by a Frenchman, and the child had been brought here by a member of the band passing that night over the Portage. This was no doubt the Indian I had seen with the child.

We ate in silence in the Indian manner. When we had finished, Miskobenasa addressed his family and certain others who had gathered deferentially in the lodge, evidently invited for this occasion. "Here is a man," he said, "to whom I have given warning that he must neither send his hunters nor seek to trade with our people. He has come to us alone because his spirits have told him that he must. He seeks a way to work us to his ends. He seeks to count us soon among his Company's slaves, to trade us his strong drink, his cloth, his cooking pots and muskets in exchange for the skins of our brothers. Already he has sent inducements and we have rejected them. Already he has begun a journey with his friends to beseech us, in the name of friendship, to work with him for our common good. We have turned him back, but now he has come on himself, alone."

The man regarded me steadily across the fire. Rising, the heat and smoke moved between us like a frosted glass in a winter's kitchen, where one might melt away a small space with a childish fist and see a blurred world, like the images recalled in waking dreams. The heat moved and distorted his face, making it appear now older, now younger than it was, as if time itself passed in sheets and curls between us tauntingly. Smallpox had deeply ravaged him, so that his face, framed by lengths of white hair, was the shade and texture of coarse sand, or of the brooding, small-pebbled beaches in the coves of Lake Superior. Yet its lines were angular, like outcroppings of stone. I could not tell in the uncertain light whether the line of his mouth turned downward in a scowl, or up in a smile both derisive and compassionate; or whether these expressions lay only in the shifts of light and shade upon his face, and in my own imagining.

He asked, "Are you a man, MacKay?"

I replied that I thought myself a man.

"Then you will fear death."

I said that I did.

"But I perceive," he continued, "that you have greater fears than that of death?"

"Dishonour," I replied. "And failure."

He continued to gaze at me through the heat of the fire, as did they all, and when he understood that I would speak no more, Miskobenasa said, "I cannot feel your fears, for you speak of death in other words. You speak of dishonour, which is the death of the soul, and the body of a man must follow where his soul leads. You speak of hunger, but if it is not satisfied, again the death of the body must follow close behind. And so I believe you have no fears greater than death.

"As for myself I fear death but little, for what is it but the return to the point where we began? Rather, I fear greatly that I shall pass by the proper time to die, as a man might miss his destination after a long journey, passing it in a fog or blizzard, and so go on in a state that is neither life nor death."

I told him that I did not know how such a thing could occur; that when the time for a man's death arrived, he died. But the Indian continued as if I had not spoken.

"And I fear what you have brought among us, MacKay. For although you are my guest I see that you are mad, and will strive to escape your death even for a little time, and that you will cause the death of others, and of the birds of the air and the creatures of the earth, and even of the earth itself, which you will lay waste to keep at bay your fear of death. You are all wabenos, you whites, maddened by fires. You flee the enemy within, and fleeing, burn the plains and woodlands. I fear you more than death itself. I fear for my land when you walk upon it, and for the creatures when you cast your eyes upon them." He resumed his original position, for he had leaned forward and gestured to me as he spoke. A silence broken by the howl of the blizzard and the snapping of the fire followed this speech. I made no reply.

On one side of the chief, in a place of honour, the old woman sat sewing; and on the other his daughter's husband worked with arrows. These were stone-pointed without exception, of flint laboriously chipped, shaped, and bound with sinew into a stalk of Juneberry bush ground smooth. Both Indians had listened attentively to the exchange, and the young man now spoke rapidly to Miskobenasa in a guttural undertone, glancing darkly towards me the while so that the import of his words was evident, although I did not hear them all. Miskobenasa attended gravely to him.

"My son asks," he said to me, "what are the limits of our hospitality. He is impatient with your presence, MacKay. He says that you stink of this death from which you flee, as if you carried it, like a rotting foot or belly."

I refused to take offence. "No doubt I smell of the Company and its goods," I began, but the young man interrupted, shouting out, "It is the same thing!"

" . . . as you smell of the hides of animals and of the smoke from many fires. But I do not come as a courier of the Company, but as a single man."

The youth scoffed at my reply. "When you are in the belly of a great fish you go where the fish swims!"

I made no reply to this, having no desire to jeopardize with foolish banter the welcome I had received. The young man also fell silent, somewhat abashed, I thought, at the vehemence of his reply and the prospect of insulting a guest in the lodge of his wife's father, which is a considerable offence among the Indians. He returned to the sullen binding of his arrows.

Miskobenasa selected an arrow in the ensuing silence and held it towards me upright, with the eagle feathers raised like small arms. He asked if I knew for what game this arrow was intended.

I replied that I did not, for although I was well acquainted with the variety and uses of musket shot I knew little of hunting arrows. He then explained in a subdued voice, as if he instructed a child in a matter of great importance, that such arrows were intended for deer, for they were fashioned to fall from the wound so that the animal might weaken itself by bleeding. At the chief's request the young man produced a second arrow, tipped with turtle claws and made to pierce small animals and birds. Others were meant for use on waterfowl, and these were long in the shaft so they would float should they miss the mark.

Miskobenasa observed me closely, seeing that I attended to his explanation. He then said, "Also, some arrows are made to go deep and to remain, such as this one from the Sioux." Here he opened the lacing of his jacket intending, I believed, to show me an arrowhead suspended from his neck like a charm or amulet. But his throat was bare of adornments. "Here," he said, and indicated one of several scars on his chest, more pronounced and angrier than the rest, surmounting a cartiliginous mound the size of a hen's egg. "An arrowhead," he said softly, looking from myself to his son-in-law, "does not understand the use for which it is intended. But when it has imbedded itself, then the body will absorb it if it must, and find the means to carry it."

After this, the young man mollified in his demeanour to me, and before we retired he asked my pardon for his remarks. I was of course not slow to give it.

January 12. This day and yesterday I have spent among the savages observing the temper of their lives, which is markedly different from those of Shongwashe's band. These enjoy an independence from the Company and its goods, to be sure, and yet their subsistence is so primitive that their conscious self-deprivation of even the most trivial amenities, such as metal utensils and woolens, must seem wilful even to an impartial observer. Surely a middle ground exists between the savage state to which they have reverted and adamantly maintain, and the abuses and excesses of civilization which they deplore. It is this which I must explore with Miskobenasa.

The women endure their deprivation without complaint, and indeed, I cannot but admire the apparent full-ness of their days and the pleasure they derive from ordinary tasks. I am informed by the chief that all adults in his band have previously undergone some experience with white traders, and I noted upon several the aftermaths of pox. Many of the children, however, are familiar with no other way of life than that which their real and adoptive parents have imposed upon them. All appeared indifferent to my descriptions of cities, ships, and palaces, as if I were a novice shaman unskilfully recounting dreams, and they returned as early as possible to their games and occupations. Men, women and children lack the sense of order provided by a belief in progress, for they share a naive and vague doctrine of repetition, linked to the regenerating earth; this prevents their acquiring a proper history, or forming more than the most simple expectations.

My time among them has been spent not disagreeably, for they are much given to openness and laughter when one has once entered into their midst, and my inquiries have been cheerfully answered. The young man who was antagonistic on the day of my arrival has asked me to accompany him on his hunt tomorrow, but I declined, saying I must return to my obligations. In truth, however, I am loath to think again of Elborn, of the dreary fort, and of the motley half-savages surrounding it.

At noon, I came to the lodge of the woman whom I had noted upon my arrival. It is near the edge of the encampment and somewhat removed from the rest. She knelt by her fire, but rose deliberately at my approach and regarded me through the heat-haze, as if amused. The day being mild, she had uncovered her head and the throat of her jacket to reveal fully the flaxen hair which had surprised me earlier. She is a woman above medium height, langorous in her movements.

She indicated that she wished me to join her in the meal which she was then preparing, and seeing that she was alone I accepted. In the instant, laughter like Elborn's rose from beyond the walls of her lodge and I started up at it; but she displayed concern at my alarm, laying her hand upon my wrist and pointing with the other to a group of children playing, their laughter thickened in the thawing air. It was the first occasion in twenty months that I had found reassurance in another. *It is no shame to accept assistance,* Antoninus has said, *for without it we are like maimed and solitary soldiers who cannot scale the battlements;* and in truth I took such solace in the woman's company and in the ease of her movements about the lodge and fire, that I stayed with her throughout the afternoon. At dusk, the chief's daughter came to fetch us to his lodge.

When we had entered there and again eaten at his fire, the old woman addressed me for the first time, inquiring if I would return among my people tomorrow, and if I would do so alone. I answered both questions in the affirmative, although I thought the second strange. Her voice was guttural, like wind among old boulders. She grunted at my reply. "Alone," she said. Her old hands twisted and worried the skin on which she worked. *"Eninne ne wawbo maw.* And yet there is the shadow of another, and I cannot tell the meaning of his smile, nor what it is he carries outstretched, like a gift ... Whiteman, it is not good that you should walk alone with this stranger, or that you should lie alone. It is good that you choose a woman from among us and enter her as you would enter the forest which holds the waters in the earth, and the earth which is life in death, and the rivers and waters where there is neither passing nor standing still. It is good that you look upon the face of a woman. It is good that you choose and rid yourself of shadows."

None were surprised at the candour — indeed the impertinence — of this advice, for the aged among them take and are allowed every liberty of expression.

"As you were chosen, my grandmother," said the girl, urging her to reminiscence.

"As I was chosen," she replied, nodding vigorously, "in that time when I was fair to look upon." A grunting came from her which I at first mistook for a fit of cough, and then for sobbing; nor was it until she raised her head and gave me a view of toothless gums that I saw she laughed at the memory. "Ah, as I was chosen by a stranger from among the rest. All day we fled the canoes of my suitor's kinsmen. All day we raced them on the waters and at the carrying places. At evening, in a marsh among great boulders, we overturned our canoe and lay beneath it with our faces above the water. So we heard them pass, calling that we had gone to the portage and that they would catch us there. Afterward, we went by another way to the lake where his vision had come to him, and I knew that we were safe. We warmed ourselves by the fire. He built our shelter from boughs of spruce and spread his beaver robe inside. So we wrapped ourselves there in that robe, our body one body and our joy one joy.''

The old woman had ceased her sewing.

"*Keet e kwa o,*" I said to him. "You are a man. You will be the father of a man. But at dawn when I awoke he was not beside me. The mists surrounded me. I heard the waterbirds like echoes of my fears, and when I called for him his call came from deep within the mists, thin as a bird's. With the sun he returned for me and took me to the place where he had gone. It was a great cliff, and there, under shelter of a ledge, he had mixed the red blood of rock with oil and drawn a new figure beside the medicine frog of his vision. And when I saw the man he had made to celebrate our joy, ah, then I laughed with him that morning, and our laughter raced with the mists upon the lake. For the man danced, and his manhood was alive," she said. "Alive!" And she thrust her needle obliquely upward to accentuate her meaning.

Again she laughed, so heartily in her wheezing manner that the others soon joined her. They were swifter than I to grasp her meaning and imagine the figure her young lover had painted upon the rocks those years ago. But when I understood then, I confess, the levelling contagion of their delight spread to me as well, and I heard my own laughter small and abrasive, like an instrument little used.

January 15. I have returned to my post and am embroiled again in duties and intrigues. Elborn watches me. The men grumble and stamp in the bleak sun along the palisade. Were they fed goose every meal they would not be pleased! Nor their women either; the fort life makes harridans of all!

In my last report to the Company I made no mention of Miskobenasa's people, nor of my failure to secure hunts from them. Why, I know not. Would the directors at Grand Portage and Montreal consult their copies of Antoninus as I do, they would be wise to act on the Stoic's advice concerning such stubborn Indians as this chief: "When you have come upon a true man living in harmony with Nature, kill him if you cannot endure him. For he will choose death rather than change the manner of his life."

chapter twenty-nine

Reports of flooding and destruction filled the news. For days the sun had blazed unnaturally at hillsides still deep in snow, and rivers had swollen above their banks, frothing into the fields. Topsoil vanished, swept into lakes already gasping under layers of silt and poison. It would be a bad year for crops, said the agriculturists, quoting statistics. It would be a bad year for the economy, said the men of commerce. And in the city, a mirage of safety in the beleaguered land, the lines of unemployed trailed around corners like tattered question marks.

Gerry Rattray switched off the car radio. He had been listening out of habit, as a sailor watches the wind indicator at his masthead. He trailed one hand out into the slipstream of the car. Maples, lining the country road, echoed back the whistle of the machine. They were just leafing out. The green hung in them like a haze, as it did as far as he could see across the sodden land. There was something obscene in such delicacy, in such a bland reassertion of Nature, surrounded by the devastation left by the floods. Random plantings had survived — the old hedgerows no one had thought worth rooting up; the occasional copses scattered on hillsides; the swamps where willowy shrubs opened buds like cavalier fingertips. All else, and especially the fields won with such labour from the forest, were translucent grey with mud, and cracking. From the air, he thought, it will look like an abandoned airport, with weeds poking through the crumbling asphalt.

Ten miles to the north the land rose into a vast plateau, and here April had gathered itself together. All was in order. The land was sodden but intact, and fecund. The farms squatted as snugly among their hills as they had done for generations, and behind them, to the west, he could see the woods where the river ran.

He slowed, turned at the frost-tilted, peeling sign, and approached the airport down its quarter mile of gravel road. He parked beside the hut that served as both clubhouse and office, leaving the key in the ignition. "Time Flies When You Do," said the faded crimson along the fence. "Low Rates."

Gerry unloaded his gear. The parachute he swung over his shoulder. The rest — boots and coveralls, helmet and reserve — he carried. We'll do this right, he thought. We'll do this like an ordinary jump, with everything clean. It may be that I'll want to pull it after all, he thought; so we'll leave the options open and let it come as it will. He crossed the grass and laid his equipment beside the plane. The sun was soft. Tom's wrench clinked inside the cowling.

"Gerry," he said, grinning. His baseball cap was twisted backwards, like a catcher's.

"How you doin, Tom." He began to dress. "What's the wind?"

"Just very nice, very nice. Seven, maybe eight, from the northwest. What do you want to go to?"

"Let's say 10,000. I'll get out over the triangle woods."

Together, when Tom had finished with the engine, they lifted off the door and slid the right seat out of its brackets. Gerry checked the interior. He would sit on the floor. He would watch the earth drop away under the wheel. And when he was ready, when they had reached the spot, he would swing his legs out and leave. And the action would be graceful. By God, the action would be graceful.

"Alone?" Tom adjusted his cap.

The lie came easily. "No one else was free," he said. In fact, he had called no one, for he wanted no distractions. Least of all he wanted another presence in the air, circling, circling above, watching for the puff of his canopy like a mushroom in the green bowl of earth. He wanted a free sky, empty of all but the Cessna and his own body, gliding home. "Here's your twenty."

"What? Pay me on the ground, for crissake."

He jiggled the bill and Tom shrugged, took it, stuffed it in his jacket pocket. "Suit yourself. Ready to go?"

"When you are." He hunched into the parachute harness,

bent forward to snap the chest buckle, and then straightened and wriggled his buttocks into the saddle. Behind him, Tom checked the ripcord pins, and the bungee straps that pulled the pack open like rubber fingers.

"You're okay," He slapped Gerry's shoulder.

The starter hummed. The engine ground briefly and coughed alive. Tom toyed with the mixture, revving it, listening attentively.

Gerry wound his stopwatch, set his altimeter, and pulled himself backwards into the aircraft, lifting his feet as the plane bumped out onto the runway. He drew on thin black gloves.

For fifteen or twenty seconds, facing west into the gentle breeze, the plane shuddered and strained against its brakes. Then Tom released it, opening the throttle, and it swept down the grass strip, past the hanger with its limp and faded sock, past the shack, past and over the orange pylons that marked the runway's end. It rose into the sun. They climbed steeply, spiralling clockwise in ever-widening circles. Gerry smiled. He would drop into a massive funnel, sunlight glinting on his helmet and silver buckles.

On such a day he had jumped first. His car had looked the same from a thousand feet, surrounded by other cars then, and by faces, pale fungus dots scattered on the green. When they had reached their altitude the jumpmaster swung his feet out the door, watching the alignment of the ground and the drift of the indicator, shouting his instructions back to the pilot, ten degrees left, then five right, then slapping Gerry's knee and swinging his own legs aside. Almost automatically he had taken the three steps into space, flinging his arms and legs wide, and at the instant when he felt the tug of the static line he heard Janet saying again, "Skydiving! *Sky*diving!" and he saw her face, at first incredulous, slowly smooth into a smile. "Oh, of course. Of course. It's a matter of *seconds*, isn't it, Gerry. Of course I see that you must do that."

He had hung in silence, turned the canopy and swung in a

parabola beneath it. He had sensed the breeze, noted his drift and the subtle changes in wind direction as he sank and when the ground surged up flexed his knees properly to meet it. He had rolled, stood up, and took off his helmet laughing. A hawk had circled him, crying its single, falling note. Bright orange and white the canopy had been, flowing like water in his arms.

He tapped his altimeter. Five thousand feet. It was cool now, although the sun was brilliant. The wind whipped at the back of his neck. Below, the fields of the plateau stretched in a wash of pale yellows, greens and greys; and beyond them, five or six miles from the airport, which lay almost at the center of the undevastated area, was the inert grey circle of flooded land. Farther out, lighter grey, and orange, and crimson toward the sun, lay the horizon. The country appeared as a vast target might to a colourblind man, with the airport and its adjacent rivers as the bullseye.

He was very calm. He felt as he imagined a drug addict must feel, suspended in a safe world of his own devising, a gorgeous place where all was sweet song and gentleness, and where love lay like light itself, trailing fingers from a riverbank.

Tom swung his arm wide and raised his index finger. One more circuit. It was now very cold. Gerry rubbed his gloved hands and hunched around the reserve clenched to his belly. Tendrils of wind snapped at his loins and down his flanks. He tapped the altimeter, jogging it the fraction of an inch to nine thousand feet. He wound the stop watch. Smaller landmarks were now indistinct, and even the airport was lost under a glaze of mist. But he knew its location from the two rivers that angled towards it from the north. Separately they meandered through the farms and joined a few hundred yards past the end of the runway, surging southward in a single current.

Layers of mist slid like celluloid filters beneath him.

He swung his feet out.

Half a mile to the northwest was the triangular woodlot, stuck on the landscape like a piece of stick paper left from a child's

game. Watching it, he jerked his thumb over his shoulder. "Five
left." The woods swung into line. "Steady," he called.
"Steady." The apex of the wood passed his toes. It seemed
a little far to the right, but if he tracked across the wind in
his descent, to the west, he could bring himself back on line
— straight down that south-flowing river. He held up his hand
and then, with the center of the woods under his boots, he called
back into the wind.
"Cut!"
He pulled his goggles down. He pushed the stopwatch. He
heard the engine feather, heard the wind whistle past the strut.
Then nothing more. All else was dream, slow and heavy and
silent. He swayed into the slipstream, forcing his heel back against
it to find the step, fell forward, free, turning, tumbling in the
turbulence of the plane's passing so that the earth spun around
and over him, as winding him in a grey cocoon of wind. He
arched his back and the horizon steadied. The air cradled him
like a buxom lover, and when he smiled its kisses licked his
lips back from his teeth.
Ten seconds. He had fallen almost a thousand feet. He angled
his arms back, dropped his right shoulder, and watched the land
slide away to the left. He pulled back his right arm and turned
in a slow barrel roll, so that for a moment he was on his back,
and when the land came swimming up under him again he
stretched out both arms to hold it there.
Fifteen seconds. Eight thousand feet. He laughed. What could
be better? Alone, that was the thing! You were born in alone-ness
and you lived it, and those who said otherwise were liars and
pretenders. You were alone in all the important instants of your
life, and most alone when you were most deeply with another,
when your bodies mingled and your cries mingled, then you
were utterly alone, and there was none of the meeting, or giving,
or one-ness that the philosophers talked about. Never. You were
just alone. And that was the epitome of all solitudes, lucid and
inviolable. It was solitude absolute. It was death.

228

Twenty-seven seconds. Six thousand feet.

He pulled up his knees, pushed down on the air cushion, and somersaulted backwards clasping his shins as he had learned to do as a boy off diving boards. Then he straightened as the horizon came down from the top of his helmet, and found the cushion again.

Fifty-one hundred feet, said the altimeter.

Again he barrel-rolled, to the right this time — earth, sky, earth, sky, — the rivers vivid now, and their juncture broad. The airport buildings stood out clearly, freed of the last wisps of haze.

Thirty-eight seconds. Four thousand feet.

With Janet he had learned that alone-ness well. Only on the surfaces of their lives were they together, and always something in him watched and remembered, something that never relaxed and would never be shared. An assessing core. Him. Watching with boyish eyes across a void.

Forty-three seconds. Three thousand feet.

Only once had he lost that core. There had been no alone-ness then. He and the woman had moved like a single body on the blanket spread in broom moss. High in red pines a squirrel rained bits of cone. Somewhere a heron cried, his voice stretched to breaking. Somewhere in the hot bay a fish sprang.

Fifteen hundred feet.

He should pull the ripcord now. He should elect for possibilities despite the languor which had claimed him. Not to choose form in hope that life might infuse it, that was the action of a fool. And a shrill and brittle voice which he disliked screamed *Pull it! Pull it!* as he might have done himself had he been watching.

But the jump was perfect. He was on target. The ambling rivers stretched past his shoulders like a silver mandrake's legs. And beyond their juncture the new torso swelled with life.

To hell with it, he thought. He made a slight adjustment of his arms.

To have been eighteen. To have been in love, complete. And

then to have let it go, let it go in fragments and become unsure
as any fat man aging at a stop light, that was inexcusable!

He intended to keep control till the last, and to see clearly
what was coming upon him, to the very last. Carefully, into
his teeth, he said, "Blind ... enemies ... "

The river juncture gaped hugely beneath him, shuddering with
the buffetting rush of wind against his goggles.

He said, " ... unity."

The land arched up for him.

He said, "Narah."

chapter thirty

"The Marshes," he said. Like spatulate hands they closed in
from the banks and blocked their passage.

"Is there a way through?"

"Right ... there," he answered, pointing with the canoe's
prow. "At least, it used to be there, but perhaps it's filled in
altogether and we'll have to carry over. It was always a problem,
this place. The Company ran a launch between the landing and
the river mill, and we'd have to deepen the passage every spring.
It was as if the land grew across under the ice."

She laughed. "I'm surprised that Bob Mansfield didn't blast
a passage."

"He did one year. He dynamited sixty feet across, but the
land came back."

She looked hard at the shore, and especially at the place among
the weeds where he was steering their canoe, but she could not
imagine a passage there. All the signs were lacking — reeds
bending in the current, a dip in the shrubbery where the channel
cut through. Not until they had actually entered among the stiff,

segmented weed stalks did she see where the shore was broken, and in the same instant she felt the canoe restrained, and the heat of the afternoon closed down on her. She thrust hard on her paddle, and drew it up clogged with mud. "Oh Paul!"

"Together," he said. "Shift your weight forward *now* ... now ..."

They moved, but sluggishly, as if they had been willed to mire and die in that place.

"No, it has to be together," Paul said, "or else it's no good. Ready? *Now* ... *now* ... And paddle!"

This time they slid toward land, and toward the narrow entrance to the gut which would have been their passage through. But there was no passage. The land had grown back, and there was only a shallow dent in the shore, full of mud and lush foliage. A tortured trail led across the isthmus, and she could see footprints sunk deep into the mud along it, for a few yards, until the path sank altogether and lost itself in marsh.

Paul shrugged. When he stepped out he sank to his hips in mud. "Funny," he said. "There must have been boats through here in the spring. There must have been."

"Maybe not," she said. "Perhaps the mill didn't open in the spring."

"Perhaps." He floundered ahead, slipping on hidden stones and roots, pushing the canoe as far up as possible. "Well, come on," he said. "This will take us both on every pack."

One by one they hauled the packs across. For a hundred yards they slid and crawled, laughing and cursing and swatting at the hordes of mosquitoes that rose and fell upon them. In places they waded above their waists in swamp like putrid soup. Their lungs ached and their arms throbbed from holding their burden as high as possible. And when they had reached the end they could not rest because of the insects, but had to start back immediately. It took the rest of their afternoon; by the time they had slid the canoe across and heaved themselves and the packs into it, darkness had crept upon them.

"Oh good lord! Can't we camp someplace? Can't we wash?" Her hair was caked with mud. Sweat trickled through the filth on her neck, and her face was spotted with blood and crushed insects. She swung her paddle outward, but there was no campsite, no rock or promontory where an evening breeze might have swept the bugs away — only the fecund, desolate swamps and mud banks.

"We can swim from the canoe," he said. "And eat and sleep there, in the center."

When they had paddled out and undressed, the light had almost gone. She swam away from the canoe towards the darkness, sinking with her arms and legs opened to the water, washing the mud away. "That's marvellous," she said.

He hooked his heels over the gunwales and lay back, the river black and cold on his body. The afterglow rose almost to the peak of the sky, but in the east the first stars shone. A feeding bat came low across the surface, bobbed over the canoe, and was lost in the night. "Stay close," he said.

There was no answer. He was alone.

"Liv?" His legs splashed down, and he seized the prow to raise himself and search the darkness for her. Then her head surfaced close by, and she laughed softly.

"Did you think I would leave without you?"

"I thought you didn't have a choice."

"Seized by a monster? A Missephesshu?"

"Get in," he said, looking at the dark shores. "I'll steady the canoe."

chapter thirty-one

Three mangy squirrels begged in a semi-circle around Kenneth

Malcolmson, but he had nothing to feed them. He drew his overcoat across his knees and tucked his bare hands between his thighs. He made sucking sounds at the squirrels. It was certainly colder than it had looked from his window. The wind cut. Of course, he should have brought his gloves along; his hands would be too stiff to write when he went home, even after half an hour's warming beside the tepid rad. But it was good to get out, even if the day equivocated with him, sending autumn clouds across the sun that had promised Spring. And in spite of the refuse in the scraggly grass, in spite of the asphalt walks that grew wider every year, in spite of motorbikes churning through what had once been flower beds, the park was still a good place to come to. Relatively good. Even if one only remembered other times, when the benches had been painted, and the trees had been lush, with little varnished signs identifying each, and students in sweaters had laughed with their books beside them on the grass, it was worth coming to. One could pretend, as long as there was life in memory. And the squirrels remained. He was sorry he had not thought to bring something for them.

From several directions sirens wailed close, converging on a point not far away, and a helicopter fluttered in from the northeast, adding its wash to the cold wind. It was so low that Malcolmson and the pilot looked at each other as it passed. The pilot was very, very young.

The sun emerged. Malcolmson raised his face to it as a man might who was coming up from underground. For a moment he sat smiling in the new warmth, and then he opened a paper bag on his knees and drew out a leatherbound manuscript. He had already read part way through it, and he now slid a stiff finger down the bookmark, opening the volume and hunching over it as he did so. The old ink glimmered with translucent shock, as if the sun would crumble it to powder.

> ... to our expectations. As soon as the lakes have thawed our people will transport these furs to Grand Portage, and I trust

the Company will not be displeased by the endeavours of my first season. My report makes clear the disadvantages under which I have laboured, and although it is in no way apologetic, nonetheless the fact that I have not enjoyed the co-operation of all the Indians has not been without effect.

Nor has the presence of Elborn. Again I alluded to the difficulties which attend this person, having as yet received no reply to my several complaints against him. Even my direct request that he be removed from my post and placed elsewhere when the waters were navigable has gone unanswered and, indeed, unacknowledged. I begin to believe that Elborn has prevented the delivery of my correspondence. Such an action would be typical of him, but why he should wish to remain, and to persecute me, I cannot imagine. I address him only of necessity, and then in the most perfunctory manner; in spite of my restraint we have in private several times come so close to blows that I have been deterred only by the indignity I would myself suffer at such a lapse. Yet, he appears to desire violence! Unless he is removed I fear he shall get his wish! And I have told the Company! I have told them in clear terms that his presence threatens the stability of this post, and their entire interest in this region. But they do not respond. What is this conspiracy against me? Have I not served them well? Have I not endeavoured to return good furs in respectable quantities, and been thwarted through no fault of my own? Nor have I requested special considerations — only that this man, this man whom I hate and fear like a malignant tumour, be removed from me before he destroys that on which he feeds!

They do not respond. Four times I have watched the messenger returning across the ice. I have rested my glass against the gate post and silently urged him on, seeing the parfleche of correspondence in which hope of my deliverance lies. Four times when the Company's sealed directives have been thawed from the pouch and passed to me, I have hastened to my quarters to hear Elborn's laughter as I read. Four times the instructions have concerned themselves with the trivial dispositions of supplies and of other men, with no word concerning Elborn. It has been as if I never wrote, or as if they sought to madden me!

Elborn is ever close. His voice mingles with the others, his laughter with theirs, mocking me. In the very privacy of my quarters I am prey to his whispered suggestions, as if they rose out of the logs. I have awakened shouting, "No, Elborn! I will not!" and crossed trembling on the cold floor to light the candle and read Antoninus until the dawn.

"The woman," he said when we were last together. "The woman in the band of Miskobenasa. What of her, MacKay? What of her eyes, her hair, her skin like burnished cedar? Is she a Mandan, do you think, captured in some southern raid and spared for her beauty?"

I replied that I did not know.

"Spared perhaps because she laughed so agreeably with the Chippewa braves. Hm?"

"Again you malign her, Elborn."

"Come, MacKay! A savage woman? But tell me, then: On what pretext will you return?"

"I require no pretexts. But I shall return, yes, because the man might yet be won to bring his hunts to us . . ."

"Miskobenasa?" Elborn's laughter rang out, and his eyes glittered like a predator's in the candle-light. "My poor MacKay, such a weary delusion! You might as soon solicit the beaver to offer their pelts! You might as soon contract them to bring their kits for skinning! Come now. Admit that you must have that woman, and she you!"

"I know nothing of her desires."

"But your own, man! Your own! Will you not at least say what is true about them? Will you not at least confess that this woman has claimed your thoughts, waking and sleeping?"

"No."

"That you dream of her laughter?"

"No."

"That already she has begun to envelop your judgment?"

"No! No."

"Why not, MacKay?" He spoke hard on the heels of my refusals, and my reply was given before I had considered it.

"Because it is weakness! Madness! I will have nothing more of it!"

"Ah, but you will. You will have more of it than you care to think about." And so saying, he reached across the table and grasped my wrist where it lay beside the lamp. I started back from him in horror, but he held fast, his face shimmering close to my own. "I promise you that, MacKay!"

Should a stranger have entered unannounced, he would have

believed he was witnessing the swearing of a pact between deep
friends, united in a single purpose, and would not have guessed
the depth of our enmity; for I believe that in that moment my
countenance mirrored Elborn's expression of intemperance and
passion.

May 13th: This morning, by the first canoe from Grand Portage,
I received the following instructions:

Grand Portage,
May 9th, 1786.

Mr. Drummond MacKay,
Frog Lake.

Dear Sir,
   We are in receipt of 16 packets, which we take to represent
your harvest.
   We are also in receipt of correspondence in which you
speak with vehemence of a Mr. Elborn.
   We wish to inquire into these matters at the earliest conveni-
ence, and would therefore be grateful for your coming down
in person by this same canoe.
   Mr. Henderson will take charge of the post, and has been
instructed accordingly.
   I am, sir,

Yours very sincerely,
Ezra Duff.

May 14: I read all night, and drew strength from Antoninus:
"Have you ever seen an amputated hand? A foot or a head stricken
off, lying apart from the trunk? That is the condition to which
a man reduces himself when he refuses to acquiesce to fate, cuts
himself off from other creatures, and acts without respect for
the world around him. You are cast aside, away from the natural
unity. Nature made you a part, and you have cut yourself off.
But there is a generous condition: You may unite yourself once
more . . ."
   At first light I arose and extinguished my candle. I gathered
into a parfleche my clothes and few belongings. From the storage
shed I took my canoe and set it quietly on the sloping rock at
the water's edge. Into it I placed my goods as well as a supply

of food, a rifle, and several tools. The post was silent, as was the Indian encampment; I woke no one. Some few dogs that knew me well watched with indifference my departure into the fog, but it had not enshrouded me before they returned to their sleeping, or to their desultory exploration of the shore.

By noon the sun had burnt off this coverlet in which I had been groping, and I saw the river's mouth open to receive me, its beach stretching on either side. I entered it paddling lustily, marvelling at the keeness of my anticipation, and at the joy which had filled me since my departure from the Post. I had laughed outright in the fog, startling some nearby herons into flight; and I did so again at the river's mouth.

The journey will not be without its obstacles, for the river is swollen and the portages flooded and mired.

May 17: In late dusk I came to the camp, where the children ran to my canoe and lifted it upon the shore. I met Miskobenasa in the doorway of his lodge. "I have come as a friend," I said. He replied that I was welcome as a friend, and yet he waited as if for me to speak further, as if I had uttered only the first part of a truth, or the first syllables of a password. "And I have come to the woman," I said.

Did she recognize my step? Had she watched my arrival from the edge of the encampment? She came forward on the path before I had called her. Her laughter was soft in the growing dark. Boldly, she took my face in her hands, and when I said, *"Keetekwao nemanenemin,* I love you," she placed her fingers upon my mouth and would not allow me to speak further. She brought me into her lodge and fastened the entrance. She inquired if I had eaten, and when I replied that I had not, she brought meat and rice sufficient to satisfy my hunger.

I had spread upon the furs the contents of my parfleche, among which I had included a strand of beads handsomely worked, as well as some two or three items of Irish linen. When I offered these to her, however, she paid them no more attention than the toys of children, and knelt beside me on the furs with her clothing loosened to reveal her breast. My desire overcame me with a turbulence I cannot describe. She drew me down upon her. For the rest, it returns to me like the phantasmagoria of a drunken man who cannot distinguish his realities from dreams; or like the blown leaves of madness. And indeed, I was demented by her, and by the long-pent urgings of my manhood, and I took her in a passion indistinguishable from agony. We lay together as in the grip of talons.

When I saw again, my eyes rested upon familiar things — my flint and steel, my powder horn, and the gleaming brass of my pistol. They lay scattered upon the fur, together with the trinkets I had brought. The woman held me, her hair spread over my face and shoulder. There stole upon me such a peace and languor as I have not known since childhood, on days of warm sun when I tended cattle, watching their hair spread out like weeds upon the river's current.

Were I no different then from a pimply clerk finding his tart at Vauxhall, or from the voyageurs roaring among their whores, I would still have come to her and lain with her on beaver furs worn soft from her body. I was a man, and there was nature in me as in the others also!

At length she moved, and I caught her to me, fearing she would leave me. "*Neebe,*" she said smiling. "Water. I want only to drink." Together, naked as children, we went through the darkness along a path at the side of her lodge to a *sabeainse,* a small stream, which ran exuberantly down to the river. Here, in a place closed in by alders, we drank and bathed; and here the demands of our bodies grew importunate once more, and again we coupled. But scarcely had we come together when I heard a laughter near at hand, low and taunting, more distinct than the distant noises of the camp. "Elborn!" I shouted, starting up, "Elborn, are you there?" And I would have drawn apart from her in my confusion, and from the hands which sought my face, and from her voice whispering, "*Kahkago.* It is nothing."

"We are not alone!" I said.

But she replied, "We are. We are alone," and she again drew me down upon her and brought my face to her lips. "Someone ..." I began, but she answered, no, no one; and in the ecstasy which came fast upon me I heard still a voice repeating her word no, no, mingling with our cries; my own voice, but far distant and woven helplessly with the laughter which had become her own and which wrapped us both together.

Later, I brought the robes from her lodge, and the night being warm we slept upon the bank of the stream. In the first light of dawn I awakened to a dense fabric of branches overhead, and to a whuskeejuk whimpering among them. Smoke from the encampment's cooking fires traced through the forest and found us where we lay.

She moved against me. I touched her face and cared no more for the Company and all of its affairs than a gliding fish cares for air.

All this day we have paddled together toward the east. We have removed most of our clothing, and have paused often while she has shown me some new evidence of the coming of summer to these lakes. She moves as if she were part of the canoe; she whispers excitedly; she points, looking to see if I have seen. The canoe slides in the heat, on waters so clear that it appears suspended in the air itself. For the first time I have observed living beaver. For the first time I have seen a bear swimming with her cubs. Twice deer have appeared at the water's edge, and once, as we passed down a winding stream where muskeg lay on either side, a moose lifted his head, drooling water and roots, so close we heard the action of his jaws.

At dusk we came to this large lake, and have camped on a promontory fringed with beach. I have constructed a shelter from boughs in the Indian manner, and we have covered ourselves well against the insects, of which there are now a great many. She prepares our meal as I write. Bats and night birds are active above the surface of the lake.

In the morning I shall examine more closely a small plateau at the base of this promontory, for I believe a man might look far and not find a more pleasant site on which to construct ...

Suddenly it was cold.

Clouds had covered the sun.

Kenneth Malcolmson, buttoning the throat of his cardigan, saw that he was no longer alone, but had been approached by three young men as he read. They were quite unremarkable. All wore discarded tag-ends of military clothing, all carried glittering motorcycle helmets, all grinned intently through portals cut in their hair. They were like interchangable parts. *How big they are,* he thought. All chemicals and desperate leisure. All strut and swagger. Boots. Were they born wearing them? And the flared animal nostrils — one would expect pinched mouths and noses to repel the city's stench; but instead, these generous apertures, as if they thrived on what had replaced the air.

He closed the book and began to fumble with the bag. The park was empty except for them and the whine of traffic.

"Hello, old man."

"What do you want?"

"Come here to read your porny novels, do yuh?"

"Dirty old bastard!"

"That where you find them big words, books like that? Words like, uh, *vandals*?"

"That's what you are," said Kenneth Malcolmson. Fear and anger pressed his lips tight. He squinted to see them. They were huge in the sun, leaning over him.

"Well now, that's a real useful word. Man could do a lot if he knew words like that."

"Could *improve* the *world*."

"Right on! Improve this fine, fine world."

"Leave me alone. I have nothing you want."

"Man knew the right names for things, he wouldn't need no knives, would he. Just use words instead."

"Words hurt, right?"

"Ignorance hurts," he said. "Not truth."

"Oh yeah. Yeah. And what you got in this here book ..."

"Manuscript."

"*Man*uscript, that's the truth, now, is it?"

"A truth," said Kenneth Malcolmson, holding the pages close. "One man's truth."

"Well now, ain't that something? One man's truth, all wrapped up nice and neat."

"Leave it alone! It's nothing!"

"The *truth,* you said."

"Only a fragment, a part of something else. You wouldn't ..."

"Don't tell *us,* old man. We know what we want, you understand?"

"Yeah."

"That!"

"No! No! Let go!"

Too gently, laughing, they forced his aching hands and wrenched the manuscript away. He was breathing heavily. Their laughter whined around him, pitched to the distant, passing traffic.

"Well for crissake! It's five hundred years old!"

"Truth doesn't last that long, old man."

"It dies! It *rots*!"

Helpless, he watched the journal's cover torn away and flung among the leaves. The first page followed it, then the second.

"Hah! Like I thought. A porny novel. Look!"

"Wha?"

"Here. The word *lay*. Is that truth, old man? Do you know what that *means*, old man? Remember? Huh?"

"Miserable old hypocrite! *Lay*, for fuck sake. And in a public park!"

In bunches that separated fast in the wind, they tore the pages loose. Nursing his hands, bowed to the wads of paper thrust at his nose and mouth, Kenneth Malcolmson saw the vellum leaves flutter like any refuse, scraps and shreds flattened on hacked bark, snagged on branches, caught and carried off on rusty bumpers speeding past.

When it was over, when they had tired of the game and left him, he sat holding the gutted cover and the paper bag. Then he stood slowly and cleared his throat. There was a crease of concern in the grizzled hair between his eyes. *I should have known better*, he thought. *I should simply not have come out, in spite of the sun*. He walked on the asphalt path, pulling the marbled cover more securely under his arm.

He thought, *I shall have sausages for supper*.

chapter thirty-two

"Get the rifles," Franklin Hook said to his cameraman. "Get the tear gas canisters." He almost added, "Get the faces," but he saw that there were no faces to be filmed, only plexiglass shields or gas masks that gave the police the huge-eyed skulls of ants. "Get the plaque," he said instead. "And the inscription."

Even with the zoom lens it was an optimistic direction, for the plaque was scarcely visible to the naked eye, merely a brass spot at the buildings' entrance, lit by random searchlights. But he watched the monitor as the lens stretched like an obscene proboscis, its aperture dilating, and saw written darkly but distinctly, 'Zoology Building. Dedicated to the Understanding of Life.'

"O.K." he said. "Now the windows again."

The camera swung up to the black oblongs. Intended never to be opened, the windows on the fourth floor had been smashed and now gaped like dead mouths. Spotlights played over them, but nothing moved inside.

"You guys better back up!" It was an order, not a suggestion. The officer approached scooping his arms as if herding geese. He was unidentifiable but very large. Gleaming boots picked their way among cables and debris.

"Get him," said Franklin. "Pan back. More. That's it."

"Gwan! Clear back! Get yourselves shot, stayin here!"

And at that instant, as if in confirmation, a pale form flickered at one of the shattered windows, hovered, spat a bright spark at the street, and vanished. The flasher on their truck popped, flinging red glass.

"See what I mean? Eh?" The officer straightened slowly, his curved mask reflecting the building like the Coliseum's ruin. "Now get back! Over there." The radio on his motorcycle squawked and he left them to answer it.

"Get the flasher," said Franklin, but the cameraman had already focussed on it. On the monitor it appeared as a dead

242

snarl of wires.

On the roofs of surrounding buildings helmets bobbed and vanished, silhouettes among the parapets. Here and there a rifle barrel jittered like a spear. Crouched figures moved through the gutters. Twice while the officer spoke numbers and fractured sounds into his mike, other figures appeared in other windows of the building and shot down into the street. But this time their fire was returned. The sound man swung his mike in slow parabolas, like a spray-painter, eyes glazed with concentration on the sounds which sprang through his earphones — glass, shots, radios, car doors slamming, a siren winding down. Behind them all, under them, the noises of the city continued like a cushion. Cars, motorbikes, buses slowed and accelerated in a cacophony of horns, squeals, throbbing exhausts.

Franklin laughed abruptly, unpleasantly. What a farce! How absurd that violence should so parody itself and become ludicrous at the moment of birth! How absurd and monstrous, this thing that men did to each other, as in an interminable bad movie, a Grade D matinee to be bought for a can of grease on a Sable Creek afternoon. Why, when he was twelve years old he could have directed this set! Next would come the burly, side-mouthing lieutenant in his Edmund O'Brien fedora, edging his megaphone over the carhood: "All right, Balch. You're surrounded! Come out peaceable with your hands in the air!" Then silence. "You hear me, Balch?" Then a shot, a near miss, and a snarl of defiance. "All right! Let's get em, men!" Then a wave to the masked, tear gas riflemen who would edge close, under covering fire, and pop smooth canisters through the windows. Then more silence while the first smoke emerged. Then coughs, weapons flung out, strangled cries of "All right! We give up! Don't shoot! We're coming out!" And then the bent and reeling figures in the doorway.

How could anyone take it seriously? Why would anyone get involved?

A whir of blades ruffled across the roofs. The sound man

caught it first, intent, swinging his mike in narrowing arcs until he had found the helicopter itself, a feathery, hovering insect. Franklin touched the cameraman's arm and pointed. Speakers were slung on the underbelly. The announcement through them was made in a good broadcaster's voice, clipped and anonymous. "Listen to reason, please. This building has been surrounded and its water supply cut off."

The voice settled thickly on the evening. Franklin imagined it welling through the doors, spreading into silent labs where rats ceased sniffing to hear, where rabbits, hamsters and guinea pigs froze listening in their cages. He imagined it wrapping the jars of hairless things, dishes of warm culture, bacteria swarming in tubes and beakers. "Further resistance . . . " He imagined it sinking through screens where insects hummed and whispered, spiralling into the burrows of worms, brushing the dens of nematodes. And he imagined it reaching too the weird and nameless things sunk in dark liquids — the produce of experiments incomplete, adaptations unsuspected. Soft aberrants, freaks, precursors of tenuous species grappling with the new raw stuff of life, lifting strange heads to listen. " . . . useless. Listen to reason, please." How could they fail to listen? Feathers, fur, slimy skins, chitinous scales and exoskeletons, it said to them, do you not know that you are obsolete?

"Listen to reason, please . . . "

He imagined it rising in the stairwells and elevator shafts, and seeping in at the upper windows where men crouched on broken glass under the sills.

"Come out now, please, and avoid bloodshed."

The beseigers listened, but there was no reply, no sound, only the fluttering rotor. Squinting, Franklin saw figures crouched like crabs, pressing along the wall toward the main doorway. "There," he said, pointing, and again the zoom lens brought to the monitor a closeup of light deflected off leather backs and rifle barrels. Soon they would bash lab doors, springing in with bared teeth, and things would die and die.

"Dr. Balch, can you hear me? The lower floors of the building have now been occupied . . . " It was a bland voice. A soothing voice for 11:30 radio. A new-breed policeman at home among extensions of himself, Franklin thought; we must interview him when it's over. At that instant he glimpsed, even as the sharp-shooters drew their beads on it, a swift apparition at one of the windows, spitting a single flame. He saw it prance weirdly, like a puppet in a palsied hand, caught by a fusilade from the street and rooftops. Then it vanished.

"Hurgeh!" said the loudspeaker, "Hurgeh! Hurgeh!" And the helicopter swept abruptly back and away, broadcasting the announcer's agony across the roofs.

"For God's sake, let go of the mike! Let go of the mike!" Franklin muttered, glancing at the sound man and gratified to see his own microphone pointed unerringly and following the helicopter on its lopsided, damaged flight back across the city. The cameraman too was alert. Without looking, panning back toward the window where dust still traced from pockmarks in the brick, he gave Franklin the thumb and finger circle of the left hand. O.K. He had got it all. In the can.

What a sequence! *That* was the kind of thing you got when you kept cool, didn't get involved. That was what you got when you were professional, and had a professional crew. "Don't think," he had told them when they had begun to film such violence, months before. "Just react. Just get the action." And he had told himself that, too; so often that he believed it now, again, after a little lapse. That was what you had to do if you stayed in the business. You didn't worry about causes. You didn't probe and ferret. You didn't rummage for significance. You recorded. Coolly, ironically, uncritically as if you were the lens itself, you recorded. And above all you kept apart, because when you got involved you made mistakes.

"Get the tear gas," he said, as the first fronds drooped from the windows.

They'll go up now, he thought, imagining the furtive scampering up through darkened conference rooms and offices. They would hasten past all the machines in their vinyl covers up to the roof, where they would squeal while the lead spat around them. And they would die there, looking up to where stars should be. Guerrillas? Hardly. He had seen good guerrillas operate, and they did not get themselves trapped with nowhere to go but up. No, these were just kids. Five or six maybe. And Miro.

Miro.

"Goddam!" he slapped his thigh, and seeing the sound man's blank eyes watching him he added, "There's where we should be! Up there where we can shoot the end of this thing!"

The sound man swung the mike in front of Franklin's lips so he could hear through the earphones and nodded, glancing at the surrounding roofs. But they had all been preempted by the police sharpshooters who slid their rifles out methodically and began to fire down onto the other roof.

It was over quickly.

For five minutes they filmed the shooting, the rooftops, the dollops of teargas bulging from the windows. And in the following silence, when the white helmets appeared on the roof of the Zoology Building, signalling for stretchers, they filmed those too.

Ambulances backed close to the entrance. Franklin detached the camera from its monitor cable and moved forward with his crew. They would have entered the building had they not been stopped by the police. Two officers held oblique rifles out from their chests, their curving masks impassive. And while Franklin groped for some ruse which might allow them in, away from the jostling of other journalists and photographers, the stretchers, three covered and two not, each borne by four attendants began to descend the steps.

"Back," Franklin said. "We'll get something when they load them." And so they worked down through the crowd, being careful of other people's cables, and took up positions beside a set of open doors. The flashers washed everything red.

246

Theirs was the fourth ambulance to be loaded, but the other three waited so that it might speed ahead, for its cargo was still alive. Miro's head was swathed in bandages which had done little to staunch the blood. His glasses were gone and his eyes were fixed and glazing. For a shocked moment Franklin thought that they had focussed on him, and that Miro was smiling in recognition. But then he saw that it could not be so. Already the jaw was slackening, and his throat had almost lost the pulse of life.

"Get that," Franklin said, his voice hoarser than it should have been. "Get the face." Then, as the stretcher was lifted at the foot and began to slide inward, he saw the lips moving in a manner not haphazard. He touched the sound man's arm and pointed. "Quick!" he said, loud enough for the man to hear him through the earphones. The microphone swung adeptly an inch above Miro's mouth, and followed it smoothly along and inside the ambulance, until the attendant flung it back with a curse, slamming the doors.

They got the siren pulling away. They got a perfect cop's voice saying, "Clear back, now! Clear back!"

And then it was over, except maybe for an interview or two.

They went back to the truck, lit cigarettes, and plugged into the monitor again. They rewound the tape and watched a few hundred feet of the early footage. And then at Franklin's request the soundman spun the tape ahead at double time, checking occasionally until he found Miro's face, magnified and bent by the small screen. Leaning close, Franklin heard shouts on the tape, shouts easily edited out. He heard his own voice saying "Quick!" and he heard the clatter of boots and metal fittings. Then he heard Miro's voice, drawn thin and childish by shock and the ebbing of life say, "m-master of *mon*sters . . ." There was something else as well, but the attendant's curse snarled like a scar across the soundtrack, and the doors banged.

"Well, let's get on with it," said the cameraman, butting his cigarette. "I don't wanna put in no goddam overtime tonight."

chapter thirty-three

The river began to narrow and to fold into bays and promontories. The main channel was still deep enough to allow the passage of large boats and barges, but the inexorable muskeg closed in from either side, with stark balsam trunks toppling across it. They would fall, and rot, and add their corpses as fodder for the new trees already springing up among their roots; and these in their turn would grow, die, and thicken the thin soil. So the muskeg would deepen, its tendrils reaching down until they found the mud bottom and clung to it. In time it would firm into land, and spruce would grow where cattails now lifted small explosions of cotton across the marshes. The river would shrink, become a creek; and ferns would grow beside it among the roots of pines.

Mists clung on the water. The canoe passed through them up the center of the channel, the paddles dipping in unison. Liv did not see the log before they struck it, but in the instant of impact she cried out, startled from her reverie by the lurking thing which had canted them to the left, she thrust her paddle against it. Fortunately it was rotten and had not torn the canvas. A brown cloud of punk spread around them. Gently they back-paddled and slid off. The log bumped free, bobbing just under the surface, but then approached them again, slowly, wilfully. Shuddering, she saw that it had been bored at the ends and carried iron hoops linking it to other logs. A boom! Broken free and drifting like a gigantic necklace down with the current, pressing them towards the shore. "Oh!" she said. "Can't we get over it? Can't we get out?"

But he was looking at the shore where grey buildings brooded above the mist, dark in the opened forest. Something had moved.

"What is it?"

"Hm? It's the river mill. Someone's there."

"Paul. Please. Don't go in."

But already the prow of the canoe was swinging towards shore.

He seemed morbidly drawn to the place as one is sometimes drawn to old brown daguerrotypes of bandits propped for their last portraits, or of dead Yankees in the mists at Bull Run.

They passed the dock with its rubber bumpers and went in at the beach. The canvas flank scraped softly. He slipped his paddle between the packs and the canoe side and stepped out, still watching the buildings and catching again a flicker of movement at the corner of the nearest, the office. It was scarcely more than the dropping of a lash across his eye, but it was real. "You'd better wait," he said.

"No."

"It might be someone crazed," he said, but she followed him.

Together they walked up, their moccasins soundless on the packed earth. He was surprised how ominously the buildings loomed on their rise; he remembered them full of light, beckoning far down the river through the launch's spray. He remembered the warm office, and two fingers of rye before the evening meal, and men in boots with heaped plates. He remembered smoking, looking out over the booms, watching the sun on the far bank
. . .

"That's close enough!"

"Who's that?"

"None of your goddam business who it is! Just back on down that path and get the hell out of here!"

"Bob."

"What? What? Who's that?" The shape moved fractionally out from the corner and its shadows, enough to reveal a large, compact body flowing up through the shoulders like the top-heavy, mad-Russian illustrations in a child's book, into the 30-30, the muzzle of which gleamed in a tiny O with the cross of the sight on top. "By God. It's Paul Henry. Liv too. Well for goddsake!"

"This the way you greet all your callers?"

"Hell no." He laughed hugely. "Sometimes I just shoot. Kick up a little water, you know. That generally keeps them off."

"You hold the place."

"Like a fort, like a fort. But by God, it's good to see *you*. Both of you. In spite of everything. Things have changed, eh? Fast. Who'd of thought it? Listen, you'll stay for supper, eh?"

"Liv?"

"All right," she said.

"Might as well stay the night, for that matter. Lots of room."

"You're here alone then."

"Yes. Sure. Who did you think would be here?" For a moment the face had hardened, but then he grinned again and flung an expansive arm around Paul's shoulders. "Waaal, I mean I'm here alone with enough food and oil to last the winter. *And* a few cases of Canadian Club. If you can call that alone. Listen. Let's pull that canoe up. You're not going anyplace tonight."

Later, they sat on the porch of the office. There was a high trailing of geese across the evening. "Hear that? I used to say it was the saddest sound in the world. The end of things. And who knew whether you'd be alive to hear them come back in the spring?" Carefully he refilled the glasses. "Sorry there's no ice. No mix."

"Water's fine."

He drank. "Do you know what you and I should do tomorrow? We should go up to the marshes and shoot a few. Eh? Have a little sport. What do you say?"

"We'll be moving on tomorrow, Bob."

"Sure. I know. You're going in. But you wouldn't go anyway, would you."

"And shoot them for sport? No."

Bob Mansfield laughed again, but more quietly. "I knew it. Same old Paul. You never did go along with the rest of us, did you."

"He went along with you long enough," Liv said.

"Oh sure, I know. And he did a good job, too. A real good job. But what I mean is, you were never *really* with us. Not all the way."

"All the way to the bank."

"Yeah. Yeah." He thrust his glass forward, emphasizing the words. "But there was always ... something ... in you ... that *laughed* at the rest of us!" Then he drank. "Isn't that true?"

"At myself, maybe," Paul said.

"*And* us. *And* us. What the hell, what does it matter now?"

"Yes," Liv said. "There was a place where he kept apart, and saw what was ridiculous. Of course there was!"

"And is, right?"

"What do you mean?"

"I mean you're still laughing."

"Bob, there's not much that's funny anymore."

"Well listen. No hard feelings. No disrespect intended. But I'll tell you something *I* think is funny: two people, one man, one woman, all alone, going back into the wilderness without enough food to last two months! And winter coming. Now I think that is goddam funny." He leaned forward with the bottle.

"No more for me, Bob."

"I mean, it's just a form of *sui*cide, for crissake."

"Perhaps," she said.

"Well, what else? What else? So if you don't mind my saying so, Paul, I don't think you have much right to criticize *me*. Because I'm gonna survive. I'm gonna come outta this!"

"For awhile."

"Thas right!"

"And when *your* supplies run out?"

"Aw listen. Listen. I gotta good warm place here, and I can hold it like a goddam fort. And I'll kill. Make no mistake about that. Basic law, for gossake, kill'r be killed. And one other little thing. Know what I got that *you* haven't?" Again he gestured with the glass. Rye sloshed on his knee. "Faith! Right. Faith in man. *I'll* see this mill come back. And I'll see a barge comin up that river, full of men. We'll come back. And next time we won't make the same mistakes, eh? Next time. We learn. We've learned our lesson. And we can adapt, can't we? *Can't* we?''

"It was the secret of our success,'' Paul said.

"Sure. And we'll keep doin it, s'long as we want to live. But you go this other way, givin up, not using the edge Nature gave us, *then* what hope is're? Why, feverybody thought that way . . .''

"If everybody thought that way,'' said Paul, "they'd manufacture disasters.''

Bob Mansfield finished his drink and placed the glass carefully in a puddle on the table. "But I'm gonna tell you something, too. Man to man. What's it matter now? Eh? So, o.k. I *envy* you the time you got. You and her. Thas all. Thas all I'm gonna say. 'Slike my old man, hm? Old Bob. When he was dying, know what he said? Said, 'Robert, it hasn't been worth a damn without your mother. None'v it. I'd give the last twenty years for a week with her. Back in.' So thas all. Thas all I'm gonna say. 'F you wanna laugh at me, laugh now.''

Formally, he said goodnight and staggered in the direction of his room. But after they had spread their sleeping bag, they heard him rummaging again among the bottles and glasses, talking to himself, and later they were wakened by his shout. It streamed out close by, a single cry of negation in the night — *no*, or *never* — followed immediately by a shot. Paul sat upright, his hand on the back of the woman's neck.

Silence.

"What's he . . .''

"Shh!''

Silence.

Then the erratic tread of boots.

"Bob?''

"Wha?''

"What is it? Why are you shooting?'' He left the bed and pulled his trousers on. Outside the stars hung in their millions like an inverted chandelier.

Still the geese were flying.

"Goddam," Bob Mansfield said. He stood with his feet apart and the weapon trailing. "Goddam her. Ever *night*!" And as Paul came close he saw that the man was crying. Absurd tears dropped down under the greying eyebrows, into the greying beard. "Ever night the same. Her out there. Didn't *you* hear her laugh? Didn't you hear her call?"

"The geese, Bob. The aspen leaves falling."

"No. Her. *Her*, I tell you! You think I don't know her voice? After all this time? You think I don't know? She says ..." and here he crouched and spread his left hand across imaginary hair, " ... she says, 'Bob? Bob? Come on, Bob. Come *on*.' You think I can't hear that? But I'm not goin! I'm not! Not ever. I'm staying, and that barge will come, full of men. And even then I'm not going with *her*. Not ever."

"You shoot at her?"

He shook his head.

"At what then?"

"The trees," he said. "Sometimes at the ground or sky. Then she stops."

"Why don't you shoot at her," Paul asked after a moment. "Why don't you stop her for good?"

Again the man crouched and his index finger came up slowly to point at Paul's breast, dead center. Sly, roguish, the lips parted in a smile made horrible by starlight and tears. "Ahhh," he said. "Ah, you're tryin to *trick* me, aren't you?"

"No."

"You are! Sure you are. You think I'm drunk. Think I don't remember what we talked about earlier. But I know what you're after. *I* know." Slowly, watching Paul's face as he did so, he drew the short rifle up to shoulder height and held it horizontal. The muzzle rested on two fingers, nestled against his temple, and the other hand drifted back along the barrel, over the breech and hammer, and wrapped the trigger guard. "Right?" he asked. "Right? Sure," he said, lowering the butt of the rifle to the ground. "I know what *you* want me to do!"

They left early, before Bob Mansfield woke. By sunrise they had paddled three or four miles into a deserted section of the river. It had narrowed into a single channel where the blonde reeds swayed in the current, and in the distance, to the east, they heard the stream which was the outfall from a beaverpond above.

"Hurry," she said. The pace of her paddling had quickened, so that he found difficulty in keeping up with her and steering the craft as well. Small whirlpools swept back at him from her strokes.

"We're not in a race."

"Yes," she said. "Yes we are. As long as we're on the river."

"Who's winning?"

"We are," she said. "And after the portage we will have won. Won't we?"

chapter thirty-four

"Chivas Regal! Ah, my boy, you nccd not havc done it! The prices! But I'm very glad you did, of course. Once again. But I know what you want to purchase with it. Oh yesyes, I know. The poems of the half-way man, hm? The poems and photographs which I have never found."

"No, nothing like that. I just came to say goodbye."

"I never shall find them now, you know. No, not ever. I've looked and looked, and I've given up. Not that they aren't here. Someplace. Well! Now we shall have a drink. Nepenthe to soothe the March night away. Ah yes, we have a good deal to forget, you and I ... your son. How long has it been since ..."

"Four months."

"How old ..."

"Eleven."

"Infanticide! Of course we shall kill the children, first! The children and the aged. There you are, my boy. To memories!"

"To life," Paul said.

"Life! Ah yes, you believe you have one still, you and your woman. Ever the optimist. You believe there is a core, yes? And that when you have peeled away and peeled away you shall find it there, finally reliable. But you are wrong, of course. You shall strip yourselves like onions, and in the end there will be nothing. Well, to life all the same! To the vital illusions! You're right, of course. I would run too if I were younger, if I knew where to go, if I could leave my books, if ... if ..." He waved his arms, scattering ash and glowing bits of tobacco among the papers. "Where *can* one go?"

"North," Paul said.

Kenneth Malcolmson came close and looked hard into Paul's face. His head swung slightly, like an old cobra's. "Half-way?"

"All the way."

The lights dimmed suddenly and stayed dim. In the cluttered room the old man seemed even frailer, and yellower, and more grotesque. "Superior?"

Paul nodded.

"And beyond?"

Paul nodded.

"Then you must take the journals!" He flew up one of his narrow paths and part way down another. "You must!"

"We have a lot to carry," Paul said.

"No, no, you must! What will happen to them here? They'll be destroyed! They'll be consumed! You know that very well." Rapidly he began to stack bits of manuscript on the corner of his table, seizing them at random from various piles and shelves.

"So will they be if I take them," Paul said.

"Yes yes, but that's correct. Don't you see the reason, the order in that consumption? No, you must take them. They must go back with you. You understand that, don't you?"

"We couldn't carry all of them," Paul said.

"These, at least." He thrust the bundle into Paul's arms. "You see? They aren't so heavy, are they? Take them. Find a place for them."

"All right."

Malcolmson came close. His bony hand gripped Paul's elbow, and his eyes burned in the gloom. "And do it!" he whispered, his voice hoarse. *"Go all the way!"*

chapter thirty-five

Even in twilight the portage was obvious, its beach a pale slit on the dark brown-green, like an opening eye. A trail wound away from it and was lost in the forest. A pair of grey jays fluttered off at the approach of the canoe, mewing like ghosts, and the band of aspens behind the beach scattered their golden leaves like the largesse of knights going impoverished into winter.

"We'll camp here," Paul said, "and go over in the morning."

Soon their fire blazed in front of the tent. When they had eaten, Liv stood at the water's edge and looked back down the river to the south. The water and sky were cold silver; along the far shore the low brush of the forest was perfectly reflected. Scattered white pines towered above the rest. A loose V of geese angled overhead, low enough for her to hear the whistling of their wings under their wild honking. She returned to the fire where Paul was sitting with the last pages of the manuscript, and she squatted opposite him. "I have a confession," she said. "I was wrong about something. I want to leave it behind."

He waited.

"Before we left I saw a doctor Janet told me about. She had gone to him. She wanted pills — something she could take when

the time came, and she knew he would give them to her because
he had done it for a lot of others. She said she guessed she
was a great coward, but she just wanted to go to sleep, and
to be absolutely sure. I got some too.'' She drew a tiny vial
from the pocket of her shirt.

"Burn them."

She nodded, but held the vial, turning it in the firelight. "It
was cowardly, wasn't it. I guess I thought that they would make
the choices easier, that's all."

"Too easy," Paul said. "Burn them."

She smiled, and dropped what she held into the fire. The
plastic cracked and gaped open like a black mouth. The capsules
melted. There was a puff of sulphurous yellow in the cedar smoke,
and then they were gone.

I have come with them to that region where their wild rice has
ripened throughout the summer. These are golden fields which
stretch over a mile in the shallow waters. The women, passing
in their canoes among the stalks, show only their heads. They
appear and disappear at intervals, and resemble insects gliding
and feeding. My own woman has gone among the rest, and I
have followed her progress through the fields by the sound of
her laughter only, for her hair is the colour of the rice itself
and in the sun I am unable to distinguish between them. She
has entered more robustly than I into the festivities of this harvest
season, of which there are a great many both of dancing and
song; for the rice is much of the diet of these people and a good
yield ensures a winter free of the threat of famine. This season's
harvest has been bounteous, and their pleasure has expressed itself
in an exuberant and festive atmosphere continuing through the
day and night. Yet they will do nothing to cultivate this plant
in shallows where there is a likelihood of its flourishing but where
Nature has not seen fit to propogate it; by such means they could
ensure a surplus of this staple, and their refusal to do so appears
a childish improvidence. To my questioning him on this point
Miskobenasa replied that one should be grateful for the voice
of the land wherever one heard it, and not seek to change it,
for it sang equally to all creatures, and all creatures made up

the singing. And so my inquiry, addressed towards the search for a middle way which I am convinced awaits discovery, a way between this savage life and the decadence of Europe, was met with yet another gnomic utterance. I replied by quoting Aurelius to the effect that if a man were sane his every action would be in accord both with Nature and with reason.

"If a man were sane," he retorted, "he would have no need to reconcile these two!"

A shout of merriment rose from the shore, where the chafing of the rice was in progress. The old man saw from my pallor how deeply his words had struck. He approached and placed a hand on my shoulder. He said: "MacKay, you have gone apart from your people and their dream of reason, but you have not yet come to us. You are a man journeying in fog. But we are here if you choose us; for a little time yet we shall be here. Let us speak no more of these things, for neither I nor she can show you what you will not see. Let us speak no more of these things, MacKay, for we have done so many times and you will not hear our voices. Stay if you will, for you are welcome. Or go. But let us not speak further of this path which does not exist."

I acceded to his request, in no way convinced of the truth of his position, but seeing little use in the reiteration of arguments familiar to both of us.

September 24. Yesterday we returned from the rice fields, and propose to stay at this place for the remainder of the warm weather. We have erected our lodge midway up the promontory among a grove of large pine. Both she and I find the place congenial, for it affords a pleasing prospect of the lake and the islands offshore, which resemble lush, anchored orbs of vegetation; the beaches, furthermore, are a source of pleasure, and we have spent much time upon them, swimming frequently.

It is from the beach that she calls to me now, even as I write. She is about to bathe and wishes me to join her. The setting sun deepens the contours of her body; her hair gleams like the sun itself upon her brown shoulders. I call to her: "One moment, I would finish what I write." And she waves toward me, laughing, and begins to walk slowly on the beach, her hands clasped upon her head.

She has been engaged since our return in foraging for certain nuts, berries and tubers of which there is an abundance at this season, and in which she has been well schooled. In a single day of leisured gathering she has added considerably to the preserved fruits of last month; and these stores, together with what hunts I might procure, as well as the fish of this lake which I find to be readily speared and trapped, would be sufficient to preserve us in this place throughout the winter. She is not averse to remaining, saying that we might move as we wish, whenever it is needful to do so. But I relish other endeavours ... (She calls again. She cups her hands to her mouth. Her feet are spread at the water's edge. Why do I write and write, she asks. What can be the wisdom in talking so solemnly to ones-self? It cannot be good company, she says. You will only tell lies to yourself that way, she says. "A moment!" I tell her.)

I have brought with me the tools from the fort. Were a man to build securely, for example on the plateau of rock at the base of this promontory, he might so devise means to conduct his life in a manner neither so perilous as the way of the Indian nor so smug and corrupt as that of white men and their women! He might demand only ... (Again her call! From the lake into which she has plunged. The water is warm. She waves me toward her. Her laughter encircles me like a thrown net.)

October 1, 1786: She did not come up at the first strokes of my axe, thinking perhaps that I was gathering firewood merely, as I did each morning; but after an interval, when the sound pine on which I had been labouring toppled with a roar, taking small trees with it and stilling for a moment the cries of birds, then she appeared, and found me dripping with sweat as I was, trimming off branches and pacing the trunk into the lengths of logs. At first she seemed incredulous, spreading her arms in silence as if to embrace the entire length of the fallen tree. Continuing to chop, I informed her that I had commenced our dwelling, and that it would require many trees and much labour before it was completed; indeed, I said, she could scarcely anticipate more than a single level, properly closed in and roofed, before this season's snows.

She answered as I had expected: That she anticipated nothing, besides the dwelling which was of the type which had served her well throughout her life, which was not a cage, which did not require the killing of great trees.

At this I laughed, of course, and instructed her to hold her opinion until she should see what I had made. I instructed her further to continue her gathering of food, for we would stay in this place the winter, and should store all we would require — and more, in case of spoilage or depredation by wolverine. I talked at some length as I worked, being eager to share my new excitement and my plans; but upon receiving no answer to some question, I looked up and saw that she had gone.

I continued my work without pause, and by twilight had constructed, with the assistance of levers and pulleys, the better part of a foundation; indeed, so utterly was I compelled by this project that I laboured until I could no longer see to make my cuts.

When I returned she was nowhere abut the camp, nor had the fire been set for the evening meal; but she returned soon afterwards, upon my building the fire and calling for her down the shore. She had spent the afternoon, she said, in compliance with my request to gather food. Beside the fire she placed the pannier which she had sewn for this purpose, and I saw it had been filled with toadstools. Their pale stalks, gills, and slimy caps were translucent white upon the bark and gleamed in the firelight like putrefying flesh. I was repelled and kicked the thing away, scattering some of its contents; but she gathered them in silence and placed the basket some distance off, but not so far that I was unaware of it while we ate. They are loathsome things, these fungi, and I believe she was not unaware of my aversion to them!

When we had eaten I again raised the matter of the building, more sharply than I had intended, and was again nettled by her indifference. As for myself, I foresaw the structure complete, properly joined and roofed, and am determined to see it rise to meet my expectations. This I told her, lighting my pipe and affecting casualness the while; and when she made no reply but continued to regard me as if both amused and saddened, as one might regard a troubled child, I added that I laboured for her benefit as well as for my own. At this she laughed and came to kneel beside me, taking my head upon her breast. "Ah no," she said. "No. It is not for my well-being that you would imprison me, and so imprison yourself. It is not for me that you must build such things to continue after you are gone, yet never live. It is very sad, that you must write in your books what you believe has happened to you. It is very sad that you cannot see the evidence on every side of what life is, and strength, and pride, but you

260

must invent your own ideas and exist by them and die. And it is sad that you cannot see what a woman is, but must use her as you would an implement, or an excuse for the evidence of your own disease. No, no. Do not say that you do this thing for me."

At this my patience reached an end. After Elborn, after Miskobenasa, to be brought to task by this woman who has seduced me away from the Company and led me here; to be brought to task by this woman whom I had sought to elevate in some degree above the savage state, that was insufferable! I rose up at her last words and caught hold of her by the head, entwining my fingers in her hair. And I was further angered by this state to which she has reduced me, that I should snarl like a cornered wolverine, or like a single savage ringed by enemies! "So!" I said. "I cannot see what a woman is, or what she requires! I am so brutish and unfeeling! I am such a stunted man beside the fine braves of the Chippewa, the fine greased braves all in a circle round you!" I shouted gibberish at her while dragging her to the shelter in such a manner as would not permit her to regain her balance, so that her pace was staggering whereas my own was direct and purposeful. I flung her inside and, even further maddened by seeing that she had perceived my intention and struggled to aid me by loosening her clothing, fell upon her.

She offered no resistance. Each savagery she matched with acquiescence and tenderness, indeed pressing me to her so that I might ravish her completely. When I rose above her, her hands entwined my beard and her eyes held my own. When I fell back upon her in a poor travesty of passion she held me as a mother might a child, soothing and speaking softly. Although I had longed to debase her and had striven to do so, yet I could not. Although I had longed to pour into her the turmoil I contained yet I could not do that either. Nor could I hate her, so strong was the recollection of the time we had shared, and so compelling was her body beneath my own.

By the morning she had gone. I doubted that my sleep had been so sound. Yet she had risen and gathered her belongings as if they had never been; I saw how little she had owned, for the camp lay unchanged from the previous night, even to the mushrooms lying damp with dew where she had left them.

But I knew I was alone.

I called for her, but my voice was lost in the mists above

the lake. My voice was mocked by the enormity of the sun. I called down the shores, cupping my hands to do so; but there came in answer only a flurry of morning ducks, and a raven's croak. I shivered in the chill of the morning.

November 15 (?): I am unsure of this date, for I have neglected my journal and the days pass with a sameness, fading into incidents in memory. Not even time is certain. One night, limp with fatigue after the day's exertions, I flung myself into my blankets without winding my watch as was my custom. By morning it had stopped. I have left it at the bottom of my parfleche, where it no doubt will register three o'clock eternally. It is no matter. The sun sets and rises. The wind sweeps curtains of rain across the lake, and then desists. To know the time of such things is of no importance.

I have laboured every day at the building, often until I was near collapse; in the dark I have lit fires to see. This night is my first within the walls. Much labour remains, but the thing is fashioned at least, and the roof packed securely with moss. Does it conform to my first plan? I think not, for I have adapted it according to the dictates of expediency. The winter hastens down upon me. Even as I write the forest glistens with frost; ice spreads from the flanks of the rocks and from the beaches.

I might have wished for a taller structure. Two stories, even three might not have been too much for which to hope. But I have built it close to the ground, and it must now suffice. I lacked proper implements and materials for a chimney; as a consequence the smoke rises as it will through a hole in the roof, and in this way the cabin resembles the lodge of any Indian. I have contrived a bench which I have drawn tonight close to the fire; the smoke hangs in a layer from insufficient draft. I slant my book to write.

I wait.

Loons gather for their flight away from the encroaching winter. A pack of thirty has roamed several days on the lake, their cries mingling together into thickets dense as the forest; but at night they separate, and then their cries wind singly upward, cold as icicles. The Indians say they are immortal and as old as the world. They laugh now like women crazed. What will replace them? The wolf? The raven? The moan of wind in endless pines at my back?

Why do I live?

In the mornings, waking from dreams of her so vivid I believed she had embraced me, or that her laughter had wrapped me like protecting arms, I have taken the canoe and followed the shore under the mist, calling her name. As often the forest walls close against me. As often the water resists my paddle. In all things I perceive indifference.

"All, all is ephemeral, the remembering and the remembered . . ."

I have burnt Aurelius! This night and last, page by page, I committed that book to separate fires. Reason and Nature! How glib was his prattle concerning them; how forced were his reconciliations! The parchment curled upon itself, burning with a blue flame. Even upon the ash I traced the mocking print, until I stirred all to atoms with my stick.

Why do I wait? Why should I not sleep? I believe hours have passed among my paragraphs. The loons fill the night; their cries are funnels wherein all else is gathered up.

I have built the fire. I am aware that I speak aloud. I am aware my beard has grown long. It mats and pulls between my fingers. My hands come away reluctantly and glimmer white and empty, like an ape's.

A cry among the loons?

Again, and clearly! My name!

November 16: Through the doorway, which filled with smoke upon my opening it, I saw his canoe suspended among reflections. The Indians believe such lights to be the souls of departed warriors dancing, and indeed the black shape of the canoe was now covered, now revealed as if by phantom dancers.

I came from the shadows. Even had he not called again I would have known him at once. He landed upon the beach and approached me empty-handed, laughing. "Why?" he asked. "Why have I come?" His smile was a hateful thing in the shifting light, and a mockery of my own. "Why, merely to visit you and to share the fruits of your solitude."

"The Company . . ." I said. My voice was gruff with loathing and with the unaccustomed usage.

"The Company? Oh no, I fear not, my poor MacKay. The Company cares as little for you as for any man who has forsaken it to go his own way. It is not an uncommon thing in the *pays d'en haut,* for a man to be lured by unchartered water, or by a woman, from what he has hitherto conceived to be his duty. The Company is well accustomed to vagaries of this sort, and has sent no more than a perfunctory inquiry concerning your whereabouts. And the post proceeds remarkably well without your ministrations. No, I fear that you are lost forever to the Company, and it to you."

"You have done this," I said.

"I? I? I have done no more than come to visit you at the place where you have chosen to settle. Come, will you not make me welcome? Will you not show me what you have elected instead of the Company's solace and protection?"

His moccasins made little sound on the packed earth. He paused when he first saw what I had built. "Ah MacKay," he said, shaking his head. "It is a little fort! It is a little trading post, and nothing else. I might have expected more from you, my poor fellow. But never mind. Let us at least proceed inside and make the most of what it has to offer, for the night is cold."

He settled himself on my single bench at the side of the fire, leaving me to squat like an attendant savage, peering and squinting at him in the thick atmosphere.

"Do not be deceived into thinking that this is the end," I said.

He filled his pipe with tobacco from my pouch, tipping it towards the fire to gather the few grains I had remaining, and his eyebrows arched in the light of the brand which he applied to it. He spoke between puffs on the pipe. "The end? Certainly not. Neither the end nor the beginning."

"I have plans ..."

"I am sure you do. Great plans. I have no doubt, for example, that you intend to exist here as long as possible, like an animal burrowed deep for the winter, in a state that is neither life nor death. I have no doubt that you intend to emerge dully, like an armoured animal, to hunt, to curse the snow which dampens the powder in your pan, and the trade knife which snaps against the bone, and the cold which closes on you like a vice, alone. I have no doubt that you are determined to see the coming of spring so that you may bare your poor body to the sun and the lake again. Alone. And I have no doubt that you will strive to squeeze a kind of comfort from this ... this little prison." He drew deeply and smilingly exhaled. "The woman was right to leave you, MacKay, for she saw what I have known all this time, that you are a poor, meek coward!''

"What? What do you know of her?''

"Afraid to choose. Afraid to die. Afraid to go into life even after you have seen what it might be. Even after she has shown you. You must plan, and think, and cherish your puny ideals until you end crouched by your miserable fire, alone.''

"You have done this!'' I shouted. "Had it not been for your mockery and your infernal laughter at my weakness ...''

"Yes? What then? Let me tell you: Then you would have forgotten your weakness, as you call it. Then you could have proceeded with equanimity to attending the Company's affairs. You could have dismissed misgiving, hardened all softness as your beloved Aurelius would have had you do, and seen only what it was expedient for you to see. You could have forgotten with impunity that you were an animal, with the passions of an animal.''

I shouted that I was not an animal. That I was a man. But he laughed lightly and continued as if I had not spoken.

"Like a tortoise you could subtly have thickened the layers of your shell, until even the osprey would blunt his talons on you. Ah yes, MacKay. You could have grown very old under accretions of dignity, had it not been for my reminders. It is easier — and more prudent — to take to one's bunk in a storm than to walk the decks where at any moment a wave might curl and engulf you, like a chip of flotsam. It is easier and safer to put forever behind you the joys of childhood when the world and all in it was fresh, and to forget the mother who walked you beside the rushes of the Tay, and whose voice was the current itself, bearing you down to the sea. And it is easier to forget the terror which came later upon you, to forget that you once entered a labyrinth of your own devising, and that the woman on whom you relied betrayed you and left you to claw your way in darkness. It is easier too, is it not, to pass a weeping child in the midst of revelry, and to return to the hall where all is meet and decorous. Oh yes, yes, I remember. It is easier in all ways to take refuge in the Company than to venture forth in dalliance with the elements in a frail canoe. Easier yes, and so would you have done had I not prevented you.''

"So it is true that you undermined my efforts.''

"It is true that you yourself undermined them.''

"With your connivance!''

"With my ... co-operation.''

I told him he was despicable, and again my voice faltered.

"Am I? Or are you, and what you would have worked for, and become?" He looked intently at me and slapped his knees. "But I have failed, alas. It is a pity you have no more tobacco; and I judge you are short of food also, from the looks of you. Yes, I thought as much. It might interest you that hunters from Miskobenasa's band felled a deer this very afternoon, and that there is meat enough for all."

"They are savages!" I said, and my anger overflowed in shuddering and brought me close to tears. I gathered my scraps of clothing about me. "They are filthy, wilful savages!"

"With nothing to teach *you*, I suppose, who at last commits his Marcus Aurelius to the flames?"

"With nothing to teach me! Nothing! For they lack all interest in their own betterment! They are devoid of shame and reason! Their women are no different from the rest, mere vessels of depravity and lust. I tell you, Elborn, they shall be destroyed!"

"All?"

"All. To the very last!"

"Very well." He leaned close to my face. "And tell me, MacKay, when that has been accomplished, as I have no doubt it will be, will the Company then be victorious? And will it proceed from triumph to triumph, trailing its blowsy Shongwashes down a Grand Portage which never ends, which winds forever through the forests and away from lakes and rivers? What precisely will the Company have conquered then, MacKay?"

I could not answer him. I saw it would go on as long as life. Yes. As long as life and men.

His gaze had grown insistent. "Well?" he asked.

"Enough," I said, and covered my face.

"Yes," he replied. His voice was scarcely stronger than the whisper of the fire. "Enough."

He sleeps now as I write. Building the fire has not disturbed him. He is a lumpish form in blankets, hardly recognizable as a man, except for his head. His head is distinct enough in the firelight.

All night the loons have cried like wolves.

I have drawn my parfleche close and seen to the priming of my pistol. It lies on the bench, its silver gleaming, waiting to make an end. The strongbox in which I have kept my journal yawns open, its hasp raised like an arm ready to strike.

Elborn, it is time. Now you will see that I can choose, free of memory, or thought, or the surfeit of measures you have laid upon me. Now, Elborn, Elborn, even as you laugh in your dream. *Now!*

Paul dropped the pages all together on the fire. It had burned down during his reading and the parchments almost smothered it. For a moment there was only smoke. Then he thrust a dry stick under the pile, and the flames licked out and began to burn.

At dawn he balanced the first pack on his knee while she bent backwards to grasp the tump-strap and then forward carefully to take the full weight on her back and down her spine. She turned, swaying a little, to smile at him; then climbed the curving grade and was gone among the trees.

He tied the paddles in the canoe. He preferred this method of carrying. Once or twice, years before, he had tried a yoke but had found it simply an encumbrance. He preferred the way of the paddles. He preferred the gleam of their varnish in the shadows under the canoe, and the creak of the blades against the thwart. He preferred the pain in his shoulders. Sometimes he tied a sweater around his neck and folded it into pads across his shoulder bones, so that when his arms were raised the paddles rode on smooth surfaces of muscle and wool; but usually he set the canoe on his shoulders just as they were, bare under the shirt or the moosehide jacket, and pushed the sweater between his skull and the inside bottom of the craft, searching with his head until he had positioned one of the flat ribs to ride in exactly the right place. Then he would tilt down the bow until the weight of the craft was taken by his neck muscles and straightening spine. The smell of his sweat would mingle with leather and shellac. His fingers would cradle the gunwales. And the snout of the canoe would swing like a sensing proboscis until it found the trail and began to draw him along it, toward the next water.

Beginning, looking for sound footholds on the grade, he thought
about portages. How had they come to be? Who had made them?
Oh, it would have been easy enough, belly-down in some lumber-
ing Catalina, focussing your cameras on a fresh grid, a fresh
patch of the earth's face, to see where the trails should run if
the multitude of lakes was to be linked overland. But actually
to be here, to risk, to drag your clutch of cells blindly up, bug-eyed
and gasping into the killing air, to endure, to persevere, somehow
to penetrate to the other shore which you do not know exists
or else to leave your oils and skin rotting softly among the ants
— that was a different thing! What had done it? Frogs, nymphs,
snakes and salamanders. And others followed them, creatures
of fur and hair, snouting along a faint scent, their pads flattening
miniscule green life, stiffening the earth into small sterilities.
And then others, heavier, padded and ungulate, leaving their
tracks, leaving their trace, until the path was made. Then the
first feet, the first splayed toes of this swaying creature man,
greased and watchful ...

He said, "We had no right." His voice, hoarse with panting,
taut with the pain in his shoulders and neck and head, filled
the canoe like a dark blossom. At the height of the rise he paused,
gasping, his mouth arid. He said, "Yes we did. We made the
right. We followed and are followed." The mosquitoes had found
his neck and the insides of his arms. Their excitement danced
like a haze. A fly joined them, circled for demented, rising seconds, and then dropped away.

He moved on, limping slightly ...

chapter thirty-six

Bad telephone service had broken and distorted Fred's voice, overlaying it with bits of other conversations.

"Fred? Are you there? I didn't hear you."

" . . . asked if your wife was going with you."

"Yes, of course."

There had been laughter on the line, but Paul was not sure whether it was Fred's or someone else's.

> " 'As unto the bow the cord is,
> So unto the man is woman;
> Though she bends him . . . . . .
> Useless each without the other.' "

Again the laughter echoed, as from a great distance. The other small voices pleaded, whined, threatened. "Learned it when I was fourteen," Fred Hale said. "Never forgotten it."

"We're getting packed, Fred. I don't think I can make it."

" . . . "

"Pardon?"

" . . . got to! You of all people . . . last time!"

"All right," Paul said.

"Look for you in an hour."

"I'll try. It might be longer."

It was raining. Beads of water on the panes broke and reflected in weird shapes the room's single bulb. "Be careful," she said as he got his coat. "Be careful in the streets."

Power shortages had closed the subway, although public transportation held a high priority — third after hospitals and theatres. In the dim station a few travellers stamped, and hunched, and peered hopefully down the track. After ten minutes Paul shrugged and began to walk. Around puddles and broken sections of pavement he moved from one streetlight to the next. Many were broken. Shards of glass crunched under his boots.

For the first half mile he encountered other pedestrians, muffled people who passed with heads down wishing to avoid all contact, even a meeting of the eyes. They moved at a scampering pace that was neither walk nor run, but which reminded Paul of the trotting of scavenger dogs, each with his private meat. No doubt each had treasures, concerns and memories vivid in the surrounding chaos; trysts, confirmations and responsibilities which gave desperate sense and meaning to this scurrying through the night. No doubt all, except for the young ones, bore secret distillations of fear. The younger ones, Paul thought, feeling their bright gazes on him, had passed beyond fear. Their worlds sprang like florid growths in the decay, and whatever else they may have been they were fearless worlds, free of concern, of shame, free of love, commitment, history, free of time itself.

Excuse me, sir. Do you have any spare change?

In the alleys, the doorways, circling the fringe of parking lot and playground, he watched them in their shadows, saw them either blindly drugged, sent spinning into inner spaces where they would roam achingly, swarmed upon by loves turned monstrous, by dropsical truths, by a flaccid lust for death; or black-clothed and bright-eyed, grinning behind masks and helmets which obscenely bulged their features. He saw them lurk, hesitate, fade like cats into each other, into shifting bands which moved like mercury touching, melding, breaking, shattering, through the channels and corridors of the labyrinth, touching and gathering around flashers and searching sirens, and coming back, always coming back.

All I want is a little bread, man. All I want is to go home.
Where's home?

Vancouver, last I heard. Thank you sir. Thank you very much.

He imagined himself as one of Franklin's cameras, recording implacably anything at which he was pointed; and yet his memory was neither a tape to be erased by re-exposure nor a storeroom packed with mere images — a receptacle, yes, but a living receptacle undulant with fresh fluids, altering membrances, infinitesimal osmoses. He was not afraid. What could be lost? How could one be afraid? Amused, he imagined the images shifting in the cool rooms where films lay, sliding from one can to the next and hopelessly, hilariously blending.

Something to make you warm. Six bucks a bag.

No.

Five.

No.

Four-fifty.

No.

Clocks were stopped on the outsides of office buildings, their wild hands pointing to all times. Paul smiled when he saw them. That's no way to make sales, he thought, and he remembered the Omegas on the backs of old National Geographics, their precise and expensive arms either lowered at twenty to four, or raised at ten to two. Cars passed at great speed, all tightly closed, and none offered him a ride. He kept walking, leaving the business sections behind and winding around curved residential streets. The drizzle trickled down behind the collar of his coat. His ankle had begun to trouble him.

Many houses were dark, but Fred Hale's was lit as brightly as possible. It made an orange pool in the darkness, a glow from which the streetlights seemed to have been flung off like embers. Gerry's car was parked in front, with Franklin's behind it. Paul climbed the steps between low masses of foreign evergreen.

"Ah. Now we can begin," Fred Hale said. His handshake was strenuous. Ropy muscles moved under the skin of his arms, browned by liverspots, and along his jaws. His brushcut was white. His eyes were pale and humorless, although his teeth showed. "We've talked about this a long time, haven't we? Getting some of you men together before you go separate ways. Not much time left, now." He hung Paul's coat in the closet and turned with his hands still raised so that they fell on either side of Paul's neck, shaking him. "So you're going back, eh? I . . . we are too. Perhaps we'll meet."

"Maybe, Fred."

"Perhaps you'll see us again in the wilderness," said Fred

Hale, watching him. "Narah and me."

"She's not ..."

"No, not tonight. She's out, out. She's changed a good deal, you know. Gotten old."

"Well, we all ..."

"Oh yes," said Fred Hale, patting his shoulder, leading him into the house, "we all helped. Of course we did."

In the livingroom a fire was blazing, and candelabra flared on the walls and tables, casting shadows everywhere. Already a slight pall hung beneath the ceiling. The room was very warm.

"We're doing this Fred's way," Franklin smiled, turning from the candles. "He's got ideas about the Beaver Club, and about old comrades who've endured hardships together."

"Fred's way," Miro echoed, laughing.

"That it, Fred?"

"Actually, Franklin my boy, it's just an excuse to do some drinking. That's all it is." He laughed carefully.

"Well then, for godsakes, let's get on with it. He wouldn't let us touch a drop until you came." Gerry clapped his hands. "Come on, Fred, where's the booze?"

"Here," Fred said. "All you can drink, I hope."

They gathered at the table, and he poured dark wine from a carafe. Paul stared at the plates of meat.

"Bear," said Miro. "Would you believe it? Venison. Even moose nose. Staples of the posts, he says."

Franklin shrugged. Shadows from the candles moved on his face. "He insisted. I called some hunting friends."

"And now, gentlemen," Fred had braced himself at the end of the table and raised his glass to the light. His eyes shone. "I give you ... the fur trade and all its branches!"

Grinning, they drank. Gerry winked behind Fred's shoulder. The wine glowed in Paul's mouth and throat.

The carafe went around.

"And absent friends!" Fred said.

Again they drank, again the carafe was passed.

"And finally, the Mother!"

Franklin hesitated. "Of all the saints," he said. "Wasn't that the old toast, the mother of all the saints?"

"What difference?" Gerry Rattray reached for the carafe. "Let's get serious, here!"

Rain rattled the panes, and the wind puffed at the chimney, swaying the candle flames and filling the room with a tang of wood smoke. The pall near the ceiling thickened. Paul's eyes burned. The wine raced to his head. Someone was handing him a heavy plate of meat and corn and hot rice. Someone else was filling his glass, although it was not yet empty.

"Fortitude!" Fred Hale shouted from near the fire. "That right, boys? Fortitude in distress. Stick together, eh? See it through!" He was not laughing. He had begun to sweat, and there were dark splotches across the front of his shirt. He spread his arms as if swimming towards them, and the fire bloated and distorted him. "We're all one here. All one."

"Right," Gerry said. "Here we share." He turned to Paul, offering a cut of wild meat between carving knife and fork. "No? Well then," he picked up his glass, "to you, my friend. And to your sad and lovely lady." He looked deep into the wine, his mouth brooding. "May you .... Ah," he said, "to hell with it!" And he drained the glass.

Miro's laughter fluttered mocking and alone from near the tray of crystal.

Paul drank. The voices began to warp for him as if played on a sluggish tape, and the muffled phrases thudded like slow drums, or like a chant, and he was moving from one to the next, feeling on his hand a pressure like an undercurrent, and seeing pale faces whose mouths opened and closed now under, now above him. He recalled Miro with his hands full of candles like bloodless growths, lighting them from those which had guttered down, and pressing them into hot wax which overflowed, spattering on the pine table. Translucent mounds formed like the caps of mushrooms, and began to grow. He recalled someone heaping dry wood on the fire. He remembered songs long forgotten, and was borne by old cadences like a dreamer to the swaying of Fred's arm. And when the glasses had been filled and emptied, filled and emptied so often that he had lost track of their drinking, and the room swam with shadows, and smoke, and liquid fire, he recalled them all at last sitting on the floor among scraps of things broken in the frolic. "Fred's w-way!" Miro was shouting, his voice high-pitched. "Gawdammit yeah," said Gerry. "He's gonna lose ush all again!" And they laughed at that until they were weak from laughing.

"Ready!" Fred was calling from behind. "Ready ... Str-r-r-oke!"

The rain had ceased and a new, pale light, not quite the light of morning, lit the windows. Somehow they had arranged themselves roughly in line, the legs of each stretched beside the one in front. Each held a stick, a cane, a fireplace implement, upraised like a ready paddle, and Fred himself had brought a real paddle from the basement, wiping its dust away. At his signal, frail as if from a great distance, they drew these paddles all together, once, twice, slowly at first and then again, again, driven faster by the rising chant at their backs, a chant which seemed itself driven relentlessly on and on, gathering vigour and urgency with every stroke.

At the peak of their endeavours, when the chant had soared past its crescendo into utter silence, the kitchen door had swung open across the bow of their phantom craft and a woman's face appeared, indistinct among the shadows. Even through the drink, the smoke, the sweat in their eyes, they could see that the face was not what it appeared to be — youthful and smooth, for the shoulders which carried it were bent and almost frail, and around the birthmark at the side of her throat were deep creases which could not be hidden. The chant stopped, the paddles faltered. She seemed not surprised to find them as they were, and while the silent moment stretched she smiled as if compassionately upon the games of children. Then she shook her head, and touched her fingers to her lips, and let the door close again so slowly they could not tell the precise instant of her vanishing, for it seemed that her face remained afterwards among the reflections on the polished door, cast by the dying candles and the last of the stars before the dawn.

chapter thirty-seven

At the top of the hill he stopped, gasping for breath. There was no place to rest the canoe. Its bow hung over treetops and a beguiling flash of water while he stood. Then he let it drop a little, beginning to follow the hill down among skinned roots and boulders, grateful for the changed pressure in his shoulders. At the bottom, the filament trail curved, brushed through a scramble of dense growth, and ended at the water.

She had waded in. A few feet from shore, she scooped water over her face and neck. She turned at his approach, laughing. The front of her shirt was drenched in a ragged V of mingled sweat and water, and her breasts rose against it with the nipples taut. She splashed him. Her laughter joined the jay calls and the squeaking of a sandpiper pacing like a bent old man along the beach.

He found a place where the bracken thickened, and he dropped the bow there until it almost touched the ground, lifted, ducked away, and swung the canoe smoothly from his shoulders, to his knees, and then gently into the bushes.

"Did it have a name," she called. "This lake?"

"Katherine," he said. He dipped water and washed the sweat from his face and arms. The bodies of crushed mosquitoes crumbled away.

"So many were named for women."

"Named and renamed. The women left behind, and dreamed about awhile, and then forgotten."

She leaned back, arms raised and hips canted forward. "Oh, what a relief to be rid of all of that! At last. We are free of it now, aren't we, Paul? Almost? Say we are."

"Almost," he said.

For many days no rain fell. The sun sprang like wildfire among the baring trees on the eastern shores, swung through an arc to the south, and sank enormously, leaving reflections like embers or like lava cooling. They entered a region where they searched for the portages, listening for the rivulets from other lakes. Sometimes they followed streams to beaverponds, or to lakes cupped like liquid turquoise among the hills. Sometimes they passed down tiny streams only to emerge on lakes so vast their edges caught the sky in puckered seams. On such a lake they might paddle for days, moving from one campsite to the next until they found a path beside some waterfall and followed where it led.

"If we had brought a map," he said once, to tease her, "we'd know where we are." He knew the uselessness of maps. Even as a child on tip-toe, peering into a display case at wrinkled old parchments, he had wondered what would happen if the traveller ever wandered off the route, up where vague lines ended like truncated nerves in the regions where monsters played. If he returned to the proper course, how would he know that he had done so?

"You mean we'd know where someone else thinks we are," she had said.

At last they entered a lake which stretched farther than they could see, laying its headlands one upon the other in gaping bays until the last blended with the grey of the sky.

It was cold. Paul's hands had stiffened in the wind.

All day they struggled against the crosswind from the north, and in the late afternoon they reached a small island, the first of a group. But it offered no prospect of a camp. Tangled and steep, the forest clutched the rocks at the water's edge and denied all solace to them. They skirted the lee shore, searching to the west, to the other islands. All puffed like funereal urns; but farther off, so dim as to be almost illusory, a low finger of land thrust out.

"A Missephesshu!" she called back; and the promontory, spiny with pines, undulating in the distance and darkness, became for a moment the water lynx, god and stealer of children.

He nodded, something stirring in his memory.

At the end of the island the wind caught them again, and although it was slackening it sent slices of spray across their packs and knees. He let it carry them down among the islands. One by one they passed the darkening lee shores until they emerged with the promontory very close on their right. A ridge of pine ran down it like a backbone, flanked on both sides by broad beaches. At the base of the point the forest thickened, and squinting through the dusk Paul thought he saw a rectangle of newer growth there, too lush, too geometric.

Soon they came into calmer waters, and the canoe touched the beach. She stepped out and steadied the gunwale for him, but he sat unmoving, the paddle across his knees. He stared up the length of sand and into the forest behind.

"What is it?" she asked. "What's wrong?"

The folds in his memory turned — a boy's face, stained with mud and tears and traces of cold egg; a pair of hammocks slung like cocoons; a ridiculous drenched hat, and a shrill voice, *Out! Out out!* spun like a filament around a deeper, denser drone. A fire. Dervish figures dancing down the rocks. And a low, woman's voice. *Would you have it opened up again, cased and catalogued?*

Paul smiled faintly. "Well, Rose," he said, "*somebody* dug."

"What? Tell me!" Liv half stood and glanced behind her at the forest, as if a monstrous thing came stalking down upon them.

"No," he said. "We won't stay here, that's all." He pushed the butt of his paddle into the sand and swung the canoe out. "Come on!"

Again the wind caught them and took them down into the open water.

"Cold?"

"Yes."

"There'll be other places," he said. "I promise."

"Why not there?"

He looked back. The point had grown smaller and the beach less distinct, only a pale reflection of the afterglow. "Because I think I recognized it. I don't want to know that I'm going back."

"There must be thousands of points like that."

"Oh yes," he said. "Yes. I could be wrong."

Days later they came to a vast marsh. Like a maze it closed behind them in swaying walls of grass and sedge, and only the gentlest of currents, scarcely enough to bend the silken strands beneath the surface, showed them their passage.

They emerged into a lake troubled by wind and trailing rain, so large that the sky shut off their view of its other shores. They left their canoe and walked down the beach which stretched on either side of the river's mouth. Their footprints mingled with the erratic tracks of birds and water creatures, but they saw no other life. Even the ravens were stilled. All was umber, and bleached ochre, and grey, shifting grey and black across the lake and among the clouds whipped ragged by the wind. It was very cold.

Once he raised his arm and waved down into the wind, into the obscured regions of the lake. Once they laughed. Once, before they reached the end of the beach they embraced, and their bodies became a single form joining their separate lines of tracks.

CHARLIE REDBIRD had waited all day on the rock slope which stretched down from the cluster of empty white buildings. He had been beset by phantoms, but one memory had lingered more tenaciously than the rest, and had faded only to recur. A small boy huddled among furs in the canoe's waist between a mother who laughed with him, whose body flowed with her paddling as if the water itself had claimed her, and a father whose strokes sent the canoe leaping so that the child's head bobbed. It was spring. The sun shone, and the water flashed with spirits, and the journey was a long breath for him after the closeness and threat of winter. Lucid, shimmering, the vision had filled Charlie Redbird's raddled mind with peace and he had lived in it, his eyes fixed to the place where water moved like tongues on rock.

At evening, stiffened by the wind, he rose to peer intently across the lake, for he had heard something different from the voices of the wind in the hollow buildings, different from the voices in the water which he had neglected too long and could not now understand. A call, a laugh, a knock of wood on wood . . . He searched the darkening water, searched the horizon where it had almost closed, sky and lake, along the far shore, seeking in the mists the canoes of his people. Soon they must come to take him home. They would receive him in great dignity and silence, and would wrap him in their best robes, as befits a chief. They would carry him home to the streams and the children playing, and he might make a last mockery of his age and splash with the children in the sun, in the pools of the streams.

But the lone canoe which he saw at last, moving close to the forest in tricks of light and shadow, was not approaching as it should. It was passing him, passing so far away that he would not be heard in the wind were he to shout, so far that he would not be seen as separate from rocks and buildings were he to wave. Frightened, breathless, his mind floundering like a broken insect among the shards of litany which might once have brought them in, had the chief been potent and his medicine secure, he watched it slowly draw abreast. Then, desperate, he seized from among the fragments of charm a name which he believed might once have been his own, although he could not be certain, so overgrown with whiteman's raillery had it become. He raised his arms in a gesture of both greeting and farewell, both command and supplication, and he spoke this name softly outward, letting the wind cradle it from his lips like a child and a promise.

"Miskobenasa!"

His arms reached out, giving the name all the urgency and power at his command. But there came no response. The canoe, proceeding, was lost to him by degrees, and into his palms fell the first aimless flakes of snow.